BEFORE YOU WAKE

DANIEL RIEDL

Before You Wake © 2024 Daniel Riedl

All Rights Reserved. No part of this book may be reproduced in any form or by any electronic or mechanical means including information storage and retrieval systems, without permission in writing from the author. The only exception is by a reviewer, who may quote short excerpts in a review.

This book is a work of fiction. Names, characters, places, and incidents either are products of the author's imagination or are used fictitiously. Any resemblance to actual persons, living or dead, events, or locales is entirely coincidental.

Printed in Australia

Cover and internal design by Shawline Publishing Group Pty Ltd

First printing: March 2024

Shawline Publishing Group Pty Ltd

www.shawlinepublishing.com.au

Paperback ISBN 978-1-9231-0135-7

eBook ISBN 978-1-9231-0136-4

Hardback ISBN 978-1-9231-0180-7

Distributed by Shawline Distribution and Lightning Source Global

A catalogue record for this work is available from the National Library of Australia

BEFORE YOU WAKE

DANIEL RIEDL

DEDICATIONS

Dedicated to Kathryn Riedl, who has always supported my writing, even though she hates that my first publication is a horror.

ACKNOWLEDGEMENTS

I am truly grateful to Matthew Smith and Rachal McKay, both of whom provided me with much input, feedback and support from my writing endeavours.

THE FIRST AWAKENING

The night was dark and still. The bare faces of the apartment buildings were illuminated only by the occasional streetlamps whose pale beams of light focused on the damp asphalt of the road. Empty, black windows lined the apartments, mimicking the void of darkness in the sky as thick clouds blotted out any shine of the moon or stars. Remnants of the recent downpour slipped down the glass of the windows like the sparkles of diamonds in a deep, dank cave. Though there was a considerable chill in the air, the residents of the apartments were tucked in their warm beds, deep in restful slumber at this late hour. Yet not everyone who lay cuddled up to their loved ones or nestled alone with their pillows were protected from the cold outside.

Despite his being cloaked within the reassuring confines of his blankets, one young man, a teenager, shivered in his bed. His small room was dark, shrouded in shadow. The large oak tree, which stood outside the apartment building, blocked out most of the white light from the streetlamp. Instead of clear, comforting light from the window, the rickety branches of the oak tree cast twisted and gnarled shadows across the boy's wardrobe door. In his younger years, the boy had often looked upon those shadows and his imagination gave life to them. He would cover his head in his blankets, hoping to hide from the ghosts and monsters he believed might spring from that shadowed wardrobe. Even now, at seventeen years old, he did not feel comfortable sliding the door open without the light of day, or at least his bedside lamp to guide his hand.

Across the floor, which was littered with wrinkled, worn clothes, sat the boy's desk. Where once the books and papers of his homework would have been neatly sorted, the desk had now been in disarray for some time. Scrunched balls of paper sat amongst the ruffled sheets of work. There were half-finished maths assignments, unopened history books, relatively talented anime-styled sketches – particularly of attractive girls – and a thoroughly examined book on demonology. Schoolwork had definitely taken a hit in recent weeks. First, it was the lack of concentration. The staring into space while the teachers' words jumbled into a monotonous garble. Then it was the distractions. The certainty that people were whispering, not only around him but about him. There were the constant excuses, leaving classes halfway through only never to come back until finally, he did not turn up to school at all. There were far more pressing matters on the boy's mind than schoolwork. The bedside table in the dark room was equally as messy as the desk but, instead of papers, books and pens, the little chest of drawers was covered in empty mugs, bottles, cans and packets of tablets. The stench of days old, unfinished coffee and sweet energy drinks lingered in the room like a heavy cloud that once breathed in, would provide the recipient with a dizzying high of caffeine and guarana. The vast majority of the shiny, foil pill packets were blistered open and their valuable contents consumed. The collection of boxes, brandishing multiple different brands of caffeine supplements were scattered about the messy tabletop with some having fallen to the floor.

Try though he evidently might to stay awake, the boy was lying back in his bed, his eyelids fluttering with troubled sleep. A limp hand rested on the open laptop beside him, the battery long since dead. When next it might be powered up, one would find the recent searches of demons and rituals, particularly that of exorcism, on the glowing screen. The boy had not wanted to sleep. He had successfully avoided it now for nearly five days. But the night had been cold. His body ached and his head swam with dizziness. He just wanted to sit down. To be comfortable in his blankets for a moment. But now he slept, light and troubled though his slumber might be. His name seemed to echo in his ears, repeating over and over in dry, hissing whispers.

Gary... Gary... Gaaaaaaary...

He twitched, eliciting a weak moan, instinctively trying to banish the sound away as he slept. *Gary... Gary... Gary...*

The whispers slowed down before finally vanishing into silence. The tormenting voice of his dreams was giving way, allowing him to sleep in peace.

GARY!!!

The whispering hiss had suddenly exploded, like waves of water that break through a poorly made dam. The scream was shrill and high with a guttural undercurrent. When the voice suddenly pierced the boy's ears as though it were right next to him, a loud bang simultaneously brought him to wakeful life. It sounded as though the palm of a hand had slammed with tremendous power upon the flat surface of a table. Gary immediately opened his eyes. The darkness pierced his lenses, causing them to ache. An unmistakable torrent of fear washed through Gary's body, enveloping him. He knew his heart was beating relentlessly in his chest. He knew he was panting, breathing hard and shallow, but was he? Gary realised with ever growing terror, he could not feel anything. He was frozen, stuck lying in his bed. Was he even in his bed? Gary had no way to tell. He couldn't feel a thing. He couldn't move. The fear was overwhelming him. He couldn't feel himself breathing. It was as though he were being forced underwater where he could not bring himself to take a breath. He was suffocating. Gary tried with all his might to move. To shoot up and gasp for air. To raise his head. Even just to move a finger. But Gary couldn't move. He couldn't feel anything but the burning sensation, somewhere inside, and he couldn't breathe.

Oh fuck! Not again, not again. Shit! I can breathe. Calm down, I can breathe. Gary attempted to control his frantic brain. He tried to calm his scattered, panic-stricken thoughts and focus on what he knew. He was still breathing. Knowing this could not quell the panic inside though. Gary felt as though he were going to die. That without taking a breath his very being would explode in a final moment of agony. He had experienced this before. Sleep paralysis. He researched it. Studied it. Learned how to deal with it. Or so he thought.

Oh God, no. Please, no, he thought. He couldn't control his fear this time. And he knew why. His gaze was focused on the wardrobe. His eyes were the only thing he could control in his paralysis and even then, only through great effort. He could glance this way and that, but his attention was drawn inexplicably to that wardrobe door. The twisted shadows of the oak tree's branches waved up and down as the tree creaked in the wind outside. Gary was in pain. Unable to cry out, unable to move. He feared his heart would burst. But with the pain, along with the fear that he could not breathe, something else caused his blood to run cold. The voice that had woken him. The bang. He had heard them before.

He watched, unsure if he was trembling or not, how the shadows of the tree branches looked like crooked fingers reaching out to him. As the shadows waved here and there, Gary noticed some did not move. A few of those shadowed twigs remained steady, crossing over the edge of the wardrobe door from within. Gary screamed with all his might. He heard the sound of his own feeble, almost silent moan of terror. It was all the sound he could muster though inside he screamed like a newborn child. The shadows that remained immobile… weren't shadows. They were long, pointy and gnarled fingers. Gary couldn't make them out any better than thin spines that were as black as the blackest ink which flows from a frightened squid.

Fuck, no. Not you. I can breathe. I can move. I CAN BREATHE! Gary's thoughts ran dizzyingly around his head. He needed to run. He needed to get away from that thing. But he couldn't move.

'Can you, Gary? Can you really… breeeeeathe?' a despicable voice, hissing and pitching like a pained howl echoed from the closed wardrobe. Gary had heard it before. He never wanted to hear it again. But it was back.

Fuck off! Please, just fuck off! Leave me alone, Gary pleaded in his head. There was a low, guttural sound in response. Laughter. The fingers tapped over the wardrobe door. It reminded Gary of the sound of cockroaches falling on the concrete after a rubbish bin was opened.

'Oh… I'm not leaving you… Gary. I'm never leaving… yoooooou, hehehe,' the voice mocked the teenager. Gary fought with all his might to do something. To do anything. The urge to flee was pounding in his head over and over until finally… Gary closed his eyes. He had struggled so much to leave the room and all he could do was close his eyes.

It's not real. It's not real. I can breathe. Just calm down, Gary started to repeat the mantra he learned a long time ago. All he needed to do was calm down. It was going to pass.

'HEY!!!' the voice barked like a crack of thunder in Gary's head. There was a loud clattering sound in the room as the voice screamed with hoarse rage.

'Don't think you can just ignore me, you little fuck! Look at ME!!'

Gary managed another stifled whimper. He didn't want to listen. He wanted the voice to just leave him alone. But he couldn't control himself. It was as though he was compelled to obey. He didn't want to look at those evil fingers again. But Gary opened his eyes. Another moaned scream escaped his barely parted lips, this time louder than before. The wardrobe door was open. Gary couldn't make out anything in the dark void within. Was that one of his shirts on its hanger or was it the thing that tormented him?

Rushing, heavy footfalls thumped onto the carpet of his room, getting closer and closer, though Gary saw nothing. He still couldn't move, but he could feel it. The cold, unrelenting terror told him that the thing was behind him. He couldn't look at it. Then, Gary finally felt something. The paralysis was finally passing. He felt pressure in his shoulder as he tried to move. It was as though the sudden feeling snapped him from his nightmare. Suddenly, he felt his shivering skin, the hairs tingling on the back of his neck. A wave of relief washed over him as the cold air rushed into his gasping lungs.

Oh, thank Christ! Jesus, God, thank you. Oh, God. Gary wasn't overly religious but he couldn't resist thanking whoever, whatever, might have saved him from his torments. He could feel the cold sweat on his forehead as he instinctively began to pull himself to sit up. He couldn't do it. But he wasn't paralysed anymore. His toes grazed the blanket that covered them. He could bend his fingers. His left shoulder was holding him back somehow. A fresh wave of fear coursed through Gary as he slowly turned his head. His eyes were bulging in their sockets.

The long, shadowy fingers were clasped over his shoulder.

Gary's heart jumped into his throat. He couldn't make a sound. Slowly, he managed to look up, following the dark length of his assailant's arm. He looked to a dark, shadowed thing. Was it human? He couldn't tell. The body was shrouded in a darkness that it seemed to produce itself. But Gary saw the eyes. Bright, luminous eyes that glowed like two small beads of fire. It was as though Hell itself burned within them and those eyes pierced into Gary's soul with sheer hatred and malevolence. Suddenly, what looked to be thin, dark lips peeled back into the featureless face. The lips exposed long, sharp teeth, like needled fangs twisted and wound together like melted prison bars. The teeth bared into a smile that could never be seen as anything other than horrific.

'Let's be together always, Gary,' the voice sneered with evil delight. Gary's voice finally broke free and his scream echoed through the entire apartment building.

*

Aiden Wood woke with a start. He blinked his eyes, trying to recall the frightening image in his brain that had woken him so suddenly. The memory was fading fast. He had been in some bedroom he didn't recognise. A messy one, like one that belonged to a kid, maybe. He could barely even picture it now. His dreams were always quick to vaporise into thin air after he woke up. But Aiden felt uneasy. He remembered darkness. Shadows. And something in them. Something sinister.

At that moment, as the faded memory of a sharp-toothed grin in the darkness crossed his mind, Aiden realised he wasn't breathing. He tried to take a deep breath but found his body didn't obey him. It felt as though something heavy, like a large dog, was sitting on his chest. As he struggled to work out if he was breathing or not, Aiden instinctively sat up. Or at least he tried to. He couldn't bring himself to move. He could feel the warmth of his blankets about him. He felt snug in the comfortable, memory foam mattress and soft pillows. But a feeling of panic grew in Aiden's chest. He felt as though he were going to suffocate and, try though he might, he couldn't even move his fingers.

Jesus, okay. Okay, calm down. Just relax. This isn't a bad one. It's going to pass... Aiden composed and reassured himself. He couldn't remember how long it had been since he last had an episode of sleep paralysis but he damn well hated how it could get the jump on him like this. He lay there, focusing on the knowledge that he was breathing no matter what his body tried to tell him, and stared blankly at the ceiling. The dim light of the morning was beaming in through the half-open curtains. The warm, yellow glow was comforting to Aiden but even it couldn't keep his nerves completely under control. If he lost his focus, he knew that he could very quickly devolve into a frightened mess. Sleep paralysis was strange that way. No matter how much he might have gotten used to it in the past, every experience was a test of his will. He wondered what time it was. Could Rebecca still be in bed with him? Aiden knew it was likely. If his alarm hadn't gone off, neither had hers.

'Hey, Bec? Bec!' he said, hoping to get his wife's attention. But as he said it, Aiden heard his own voice. It was little more than the faintest squeak emitted from his frozen lips.

Goddamn it! he thought with growing frustration. The emotions began to overtake his sense of reason and, as he still felt like he was struggling to even breathe, the fear began to set in.

'Bec! Bec! REBECCA!' Aiden began to scream, to beg for his wife to notice him. His squeak turned to dull moans and then to stifled groans. The need for help was becoming overwhelming.

'Aiden...'

Aiden paused in his cries. Did he just hear someone whisper his name? It seemed to come from the bathroom that joined their bedroom.

'Whaaaaat, Aiden?' the disgruntled moan of Rebecca asked from beside the paralysed man. In the corner of his eye, Aiden could see Bec's arm stretch upward as she reached up to undoubtedly rub her eyes. He cried out, screaming loudly, though he heard little more than another moan. At least he seemed to have finally gotten his wife's attention. She appeared to pause and Aiden could feel her looking at him.

'Aiden? What's wrong? Honey?' Her voice was groggy with sleep but there was a sense of concern in her tone now. Aiden felt her hand on his shoulder as she tapped and shook him in an effort to rouse him. It was as though the touch of his wife had broken some fairy tale curse. Suddenly, Aiden gasped in great mouthfuls of air and he shot upright.

'Holy crap, Aiden, are you alright?' Bec asked, evidently worried now. She sat in close to her husband, holding his hand with one of her own while her other arm reached around his shoulders.

'Ugh, God... yeah, yeah, I'm fine. Don't worry.' Aiden finally managed to speak clearly while he rested his forehead in his hand with relief.

'What the hell was that? You sounded like you were having a stroke or something?' Bec asked. She watched him keenly for a sign of anything amiss. Aiden looked to his wife and couldn't resist a smile as he saw the love and worry in her glistening brown eyes.

'Really, I'm okay, babe. It was just that... sleep paralysis thing, I think,' he explained in a manner far more casual than he felt. Truly, it had been quite a long time since he had experienced anything like what he had just woken up to and it understandably shook him up a bit.

'God, is that what it's like? It sounded horrible,' Bec said after heaving a sigh of relief that her husband wasn't apparently dying anytime soon.

'But you haven't had that since –'

'Since I was like sixteen, yeah.' Aiden finished Bec's sentence for her.

'Weird. What do you think brought it on?' Bec asked, evidently in thought as she absently stroked Aiden's hand.

'I dunno, a bad night's sleep? Seriously, don't worry, hon,' Aiden replied, feeling better and better by the minute. As though to reassure her, he leaned in and lovingly kissed Rebecca's lips.

'Ugh, morning breath,' he whined, backing away from his wife and waving his hand.

'Oh, piss off! It's nowhere near as bad as yours,' Bec retorted with a chuckle.

'Yeah, yeah,' Aiden responded as he got out of bed and walked towards the ensuite.

'Are you sure you are alright? I suppose it will give you something to talk about with Lauren tomorrow, huh?' Bec asked again. Aiden could hear her pulling away the sheets as she started to get up as well. Though she spoke with a lighter tone, jokingly mentioning his long-time therapist, Aiden could still pick up a hint of concern in her voice.

'Yeah, finally. We never have anything to talk about,' he replied, trying to mimic his wife's humour of the situation. 'Really though, I'm fine,' he added as he reached forward and set his hand on the doorknob before pausing for a moment. A chill ran down his spine before he quickly opened the door. He half expected to find someone hiding in there. He was sure that first whisper came from the bathroom. But it was empty. He must have been wrong.

*

'Only two days until the weekend,' Bec said as she stepped into the kitchen while putting the second of her small, stud earrings in.

'Heh, for you maybe,' Aiden replied as he turned and handed his wife a mug of fresh coffee.

'Cheers.' Bec smiled. She didn't even blow on the coffee before taking a sip.

Aiden knew how to make a good coffee like it was the back of his hand, especially for his wife. Their espresso machine was mid-range, maybe even more on the cheaper side of things, but as a barista for the last nine years, Aiden could make some decent coffee with what he had. He was usually the first in the house to be ready to leave in the morning. As such, it had become something of a second nature to him to give their Labrador, Leena, her breakfast in the backyard and prepare a coffee for Rebecca while he made his own.

'Hey, at least you don't have to work the Sunday shift this week. Family day,' Bec said with a sly smile. She turned to the loaf of bread Aiden had left on the bench, predictably to make herself some toast.

'Good point. I mean, are Sunday shifts even worth it after the government axed the penalty rates? And speaking of family – Hannah! You better hurry if you want to get some breakfast in before school!' Aiden called for his daughter as he set his empty plate in the dishwasher.

'Coming!' the teenager's voice echoed down the hallway. The bedrooms were located down the hall which ran the length of the house before joining to the kitchen and living room.

'Thank God she actually likes school. I don't know what we would do if she was anything like Anne's kids,' Bec said, referring to her sister's family.

'Did I tell you she's taken to turning a spray bottle on Billy when he refuses to get out of bed?'

'Shit, really? If Hannah were that bad, I'd want us to just send out for a new kid.' Aiden laughed and Bec smiled.

'Ugh, please. You guys love me too much to get rid of me,' a familiar girl's voice said. Aiden and Rebecca looked to the entry of the kitchen to find their fifteen-year-old daughter dropping her backpack against the wall.

'Yeah, but just because you're so good to us,' Aiden retorted with a cheeky grin.

'Honey, she has you wrapped around her little finger and you know it,' Bec pointed out before taking a bite of her jam toast.

'Yeah, Dad,' Hannah agreed matter-of-factly. She opened the pantry and fetched out a box of cereal. Aiden shrugged.

'I just like to look after my bug,' he said with a nod. He sipped his coffee and absently watched as Hannah set about making herself some breakfast. Her long, dark hair was tied back into a ponytail and her thinly rimmed glasses were neatly perched on her nose.

How is she so old already? Aiden thought, wondering where the time had gone. Hannah looked so much like her mother it was almost scary. Save for the glasses. Rebecca was the only one in the family who wasn't petrified of contact lenses. Aiden felt lucky to have such a good family and yet, sometimes he couldn't help but imagine what might have been...

'Whatch'ya thinking?' Bec asked, snapping Aiden out of his silent thoughts. He fixed his glasses after feeling them slide slightly down his lean nose.

'Oh, nothing really. Just where does the time go?' he said, averting his eyes. He always felt so guilty when he let his mind wander, as though Bec could sense the resentments he kept suppressed deep inside.

'Who knows? All I know is I'm going to be married to a thirty-four-year-old pretty soon,' Bec said with apparent dismay. Aiden thought about his upcoming birthday next month before chuckling.

'Hey, if I'm going to be thirty-four that's gonna make you...' he started before Bec shot him a warning glare.

'Don't go there,' she said slowly. Aiden stepped forward and reached down, lightly patting his wife's backside while she stood facing the bench.

'I wouldn't dare! You're still as pretty as ever, though,' he said softly.

'Um, eww,' Hannah scoffed and she pretended to gag while Bec laughed.

'Sorry, Hannah, too mushy?' Aiden joked and his daughter snorted before returning to her cereal.

'You two always are,' Hannah said dismissively. Bec looked at her watch.

'Come on, enough now. Time we all got moving. You get to school. You get to work,' she said with a sudden authority that only a wife and mother could possess.

'Jawohl, mein Mrs!' Aiden said, clicking his heels and downing the last dregs of his coffee.

'Yeah, you better do as you're told,' Bec said. She slid her hand behind Aiden's head and pulled him in for a kiss.

'Have a good day, honey. Love you,' she said with a smile. Aiden adored her smile so much. No matter what pitiful things he thought, he knew Bec and Hannah were worth it.

'You too. Love you, babe,' he said before turning to take his set of keys from the hook on the wall.

'Have a good day at school, bug. *Love you*,' he said, pointing to Hannah as he opened the front door. He saw that the emphasis he put on his final words had the desired affect when his daughter sucked her cheek with a half-hidden grin.

'Love you too, Dad,' Aiden heard his daughter say as he stepped outside to start a new day.

THE GLEN MARSH GRIND

AIDEN

Having lived in Glen Marsh his entire life, Aiden thought it was a decent place to be. The city was situated in the far reaches of the south-eastern suburbs of Melbourne. There was, in Aiden's opinion, the perfect balance between the hubbub of a busy, suburban town and the rural serenity that so many people strived to enjoy. The locals of Glen Marsh were spoiled for choice when they became weary of their responsibilities and needed some time off. They could catch a show or enjoy the night life in central Melbourne, disappear into the beautiful mountain forests of the Yarra Ranges to the north or head south to simply enjoy a day at the beach along the southernmost coast of Australia – unless one included Tasmania, of course.

Aiden certainly couldn't complain about his hometown, even though he was risking being late to work as the morning traffic began to peak. Thankfully, he neither lived nor worked in the central city, where driving some five kilometres could take more than twice as long as normal during the busy times. The Wood family lived on the southern side of Glen Marsh and, while the neighbours were abundant and the nearest shopping centre was only two streets away, if one drove a mere ten minutes further south, they would find themselves in apparent rural country. It was just one of the things that Aiden loved about the place. He enjoyed taking Leena walking through the nearby wetlands on good, sunny mornings when he was able. There were wetlands all around the place, hence the city's namesake, which attracted all kinds of native birds and wildlife. Sometimes Rebecca and Hannah would tag along and every now and then they might even enjoy a barbeque while they were out.

Work comes first, fun comes second, I suppose, Aiden thought as he fantasised about just such an outing while he waited amongst the traffic for the lights at the next intersection to change. When he could begin to drive forward again, Aiden's mind drifted back to when he had woken that morning.

I mean, what the hell was that? It really has been... shit, it's been almost eighteen years since that last happened, he thought with astonishment. He knew that, statistically speaking, he still had more time left on the clock than had already ticked by, but sometimes he felt his life was moving faster with every year. Aiden wasn't so concerned with how old he was already feeling this morning, however. Instead, he thought about the paralysis. The feeling of helplessness as he lay there, unable to move, unable to speak. The very memory of it sent a shiver up his spine and he shook his head.

'It's just in my head. Stupid, bloody stress, that's all. What have I got to be stressed about? I dunno, just what everybody stresses about. Needing money, having to work, not being able to use said money for things we actually want,' Aiden muttered away as he drove on. He often spoke to himself when he was alone. It was his way of working through things. Coping with them. Hell, even his therapist recommended it as a coping mechanism when his depression was at its worst.

Thank God for the meds. Maybe I should see if something else could help with this, he thought. Aiden certainly didn't feel depressed these days but he continued to see his councillor every now and then, just to check in really. He never wanted to be back where he was a good ten years ago. He couldn't do that to Rebecca and Hannah. Not again.

Aiden found himself shrugging uncomfortable thoughts from his mind for the second time in as many minutes.

'Jeez, come on, man. It was a once-off. No need to go turning yourself into a drug addict straight away,' he scolded himself as he flicked the indicator and pulled into an empty parking space. The familiar row of shops that ran along the street stood before him. Wedged between a chemist and a grocer, The Glen Marsh Grind café was already open for business.

*

'Sorry, I'm late, Wendy,' Aiden said, almost on autopilot as he walked through the door. The sign marked 'OPEN' smacked against the glass as the door tapped shut behind him. There was a warm, welcoming theme to the room. Dark, hardwood walls and tables with black crockery. The few pieces of art that adorned the walls were suitably colourful with soft shades of green, blue and yellow so as not to clash with the overall tone. Likewise, there were some pot plants here and there, each sporting native plants which, even in bloom would not become overpowering. A fridge of cold drinks for sale was behind the bench and the lights were kept to a minimum, just like the glass cabinet which housed all manner of homemade cakes, slices and sandwiches. A couple of inviting, black leather couches and a low coffee table sat in the corner opposite the bench of the café.

This spot was Wendy's pride and joy. She and her husband, Marcus Eskdale were the proprietors of the Glen Marsh Grind and, while Marcus managed the kitchenette and the finances, Wendy had the final say on the way the place was presented. She wanted their customers to feel welcome, safe and snug in the café. Their patrons were free to grab a quick takeaway coffee or stop by for some lunch, but Wendy aimed for return customers who really loved the place. People who would come in and lounge, bringing a good book or working on their laptops. All the while continuously buying products, of course. Wendy herself was in the process of taking the last of the black chairs down from the tabletops.

'Hmmph, you should be sorry. I've had to do this all myself,' she snapped. Aiden knew she was just messing with him. He didn't officially start until 8am and it was still only five to. Aiden would typically get to work about quarter to, just to help set up everything.

'Yeah, I can see that. Marcus not around to help?' he said as he managed to help Wendy by setting the last chair down.

'Hah, how long have you worked here? You know he wouldn't take the time of day to help,' Wendy retorted, setting her hands on her wide hips. She was a stout, middle aged woman. The tell-tale signs of the stress of owning a small, independent business could clearly be seen on her face. The constant creases in her forehead, the dark, sunken rings around the eyes that could only be partially hidden by makeup. Aiden didn't doubt that Wendy's hair would be sporting a decent amount of grey now if she didn't always have it dyed jet black. Yet there was a certain shimmer in her brown eyes that Aiden always found endearing. There seemed to be a sense of self-confidence, maybe even pride. It was perhaps the only fleeting glimpse of any resemblance he could see between Wendy and Rebecca. He was not surprised, however. Cousins could very rarely be distinguished as relations at the best of times.

'Look at this, not eight in the morning and she's already going off me today,' a voice called from the small kitchenette towards the back of the café. Aiden could already smell the beginnings of whatever the day's lunch specials would be.

Thursday, lasagne, vegetarian korma and sweet chilli chicken, Aiden thought. He had the daily specials pretty well memorised by now. They didn't change often, not that the regular clientele complained. They had plenty to choose from, especially after you consider all the focaccias, wraps, paninis and sandwiches Wendy made. And that was only the savouries.

'Morning, Marcus,' Aiden said as he walked behind the bar, through the kitchen and to the small staff area out back. Marcus had his back turned to him, focusing on the stove top and merely held up his hand in a casual wave. Aiden signed in, the Eskdales continued to use a simple logbook which he appreciated was not very common in this day and age, took a fresh black apron from the hook and returned to the out the front. While he started setting up the espresso machine and all of the necessities to serve their first customers, Wendy organised the till.

'Speaking of being late, this will be the whole week running for that girl,' she said with a touch of spite in her voice. She didn't look up from the card terminal she was starting and Aiden continued to get out the milk jugs and utensils he would need.

'How long has she been here now, five months?' he asked casually in reference to their youngest staff member. Along with himself and the Eskdales, three other people worked at The Glen Marsh Grind. Eric was one of Marcus and Wendy's two children. He was set to inherit the café one day and managed the place on the weekends as well as chipping in most other days. Then there was James, Marcus' go-to guy in the kitchen. He was basically a second cook and didn't deal with the customers much, unless things were tight, of course. He didn't start work until ten o'clock before the lunch rush kicked in. The newest addition to the team was Samantha. She was an allrounder, serving customers, cleaning tables and helping with the coffees. Although she seemed to have her problems, Aiden thought she was a good egg. He wasn't certain how Wendy felt about her recently. Sam had started turning up late to work all too regularly in recent weeks.

'Six. It's been six months,' Wendy said curtly.

'Well, it hasn't been that long. Give her a bit more of a chance. I think she's just been going through some stuff,' Aiden said. Wendy nodded slowly.

'We'll see.'

Aiden knew that, although she put on a stern face, Wendy was truly soft on the inside. She was a caring person, a mother of two adult children, Eric, the heir to the café, and Claire. She had moved away from the family business and was studying law in Melbourne and Wendy supported her all the way. Aiden suspected that Wendy possessed that mothering instinct for her entire life. She certainly had taken him under her wing all those years ago. When he was having his troubles, Rebecca did all she could to get him the help he needed. She let him have space but refused to allow him to be alone with his thoughts for too long. She took on more shifts at work and, thankfully, her parents could step in every now and then to help look after Hannah during the bad days. It had taken a long time. A lot of therapy, a lot of trialling different meds, but eventually Aiden started to be more in control of himself. He was terrified about returning to work. He had been a salesman at a big brand electronics and hi-fi company. He was good at it too. When the trouble started, his managers were understanding. They let him have some time. They didn't want to lose a valuable team member like Aiden. He made them a decent profit after all. But a year, give or take, is a long time to not be able to work and in the end, they had to let him go. Aiden despised himself for losing the job he had dominated so well for three years. He was making good money and the work had come so easily to him. At least it had back then. Rebecca knew he couldn't go straight back to something like that. He needed a job with less pressure. Responsibility sure, but he needed to be somewhere that he could be better taken care of, at least for a while. Bec called in a little help from her family and Wendy was the solution. She offered to take Aiden in, train him up and see how he went. The Glen Marsh Grind was very small back then but soon it thrived, and Aiden along with it. He became passionate about making the best coffees and through dedicated practise and study it eventually became almost second nature to him. Wendy was impressed. Marcus too. They had taken a gamble bringing Aiden into their small business but it had paid off. Now, he couldn't imagine working anywhere else.

'Anyway, how are you today, Wendy?' he asked, turning the topic away from Sam's lack of punctuality.

'Nothing new, as usual. Watched the latest match 'em up show last night,' Wendy said, turning to speak to Aiden now.

'Utter rubbish. You know those things are all scripted right?' Marcus called from over the hissing sound of the frying oil. Wendy rolled her eyes.

'They might be scripted but I still enjoy them!' she shouted back to her husband. Aiden chuckled.

'You two can never see eye to eye about TV. Though, I've got to admit, I'm with Marcus on this one. How can you stand all that fake drama crap?' he said.

'That's what I'm saying!' Marcus called again, clearly eavesdropping on their conversation while he cooked.

'Hmph. That's just because you're both men. You have no sense of empathy at all,' Wendy scoffed. Aiden gasped, acting taken aback.

'Wendy, I'm shocked! You know I can empathise with anyone about anything. I just exclude the backstabbing of plastic fame hunters who are clearly, if not told exactly what to say, then at least pushed in a direction of action by their producers,' he said.

'Preach!' Marcus called and, in the corner of his eye, Aiden saw him raise a fist into the air. Even Wendy was fighting back some laughter.

'Well, I think it's good,' she said with an exaggerated sulkiness. She knew they were only teasing her.

'Fair enough. So, that's it? A new show?' Aiden asked, intent on giving up his reality TV show rant.

'Pretty much. Chores, dinner and bed make up the rest of the evening,' she responded with a nod.

'If you know what she means,' Marcus said, turning away from the stove to look to them as he spoke. He had a cheeky smile on his face and winked to his wife.

'Hah! He wishes,' Wendy said with her arms crossed. Aiden snorted.

'Nice to know all's still well in paradise,' he said jokingly. Marcus raised his eyebrows and chuckled suggestively as he resumed cooking. Wendy took up one of the neatly folded tea towels from the bench and snapped it at Aiden.

'Ugh, don't encourage him,' she scolded like an embarrassed mother.

'Woah, truce,' Aiden raised his hands in surrender.

'Anyway, how was your night?' Wendy asked, turning the attention back on Aiden.

'Same old, same old,' he said with a shrug. The previous night ran through his mind. After he had finished work, he did some grocery shopping and he still beat Rebecca home which wasn't out of the ordinary. Hannah had been chilling out on the couch, watching TV and playing around on her phone. No surprises there. When Bec got home, they had dinner together, watched some TV and went to bed. Pretty boring and ordinary really. Then, Aiden felt a subtle tremble run up his spine. There was the slightest tingling sensation on the back of his neck and he gave a small shudder. He couldn't help thinking about the paralysis that morning.

'Looks to me like something out of the ordinary happened. Aiden?' Wendy was leaning forward, tilting her head to look to his face. The thoughts had blinked across Aiden's mind in an instant but, apparently, he was staring into blank space longer than he thought.

'Oh, uh, yeah, I guess. Just something this morning. Have you ever heard of sleep paralysis?' he said, shaking his head to clear his thoughts. Wendy raised her eyebrows.

'Can't say that I have. Sounds serious, though. What is it?' she asked.

A shadow crossed Aiden's peripheral vision and he looked up. A man was walking down the street, passing the wide window of the café. He passed the door by. Looks like the first customer of the day wasn't arriving just yet. It was barely ten minutes into the day so Aiden wasn't surprised. He set his hand on the bench and leaned back, settling in to speak more with Wendy. Marcus was humming to himself as he cooked. He didn't mind being alone in the kitchen.

'Well, it's something I've had before. When I was a lot younger though,' Aiden began. 'Basically, it's like having your brain wake up before the rest of your body is ready. You can maybe open your eyes, have a look around the room, but that's about it. Otherwise, it's just like being paralysed. You can't feel anything, can't move your body. You can't even feel yourself breathing,'

'Jeez, that sounds terrifying. So, you had that last night? What causes it?'

'Yeah, I woke up with it this morning. Thankfully, it only lasts a few minutes, though it still freaked me out. I tried to wake Bec up but you can hardly make a sound.'

Wendy shook her head and shuddered. 'Well, I guess feeling like you can't breathe will do that,' she said with a light chuckle. Aiden laughed too. He liked that Wendy was making light of the topic.

'At least it was only a small one. Sometimes it used to make me hear things. Thumping and banging and stuff. I didn't have that this time. I've heard that sometimes it makes you see things, but I've never had that before,' Aiden explained. Wendy's eyes grew wide.

'Bloody hell, it sounds more like a scary movie than something real!' she exclaimed. Aiden shrugged.

'Nah, it's just some weird thing. I don't think they really know what causes it. Stress, I suppose.' At this, Wendy squinted her eyes and looked to Aiden with suspicion.

'And what exactly do you have to be stressed about?' she asked with her arms crossed. Aiden couldn't blame her for being concerned. It might have been a long time ago, but she knew what had been going on with him when she took him on at the café.

'I dunno, nothing really. Don't worry. I think it was just a random thing,' he said innocently. Wendy continued to watch him with uncertainty.

'Well, alright. But you know you can talk to me about anything, yeah?' she said slowly after a moment's silence.

'I know, Wendy. Really, I appreciate it.' Aiden smiled with sincerity. Wendy reached up and patted his shoulder.

'Just looking out for my café,' she said with a grin.

'Your café? It's mine too, you know!' Marcus called and Aiden laughed. Wendy clicked her tongue and rolled her eyes. At that moment, the door to the café opened, attracting their attention. A young woman with bleach-blonde hair strode into the building. She was short and thin with very pale skin. She wore black leggings under her black skirt with a nutbrown polo shirt just like the one Aiden wore.

'Morning, Sam,' Aiden greeted.

'Morning. I know, I know, sorry I'm late,' Sam responded. Though she shot Aiden a quick smile, she cast her eyes down to avoid Wendy's gaze as she walked behind the counter and towards the kitchen.

'That's alright. How are you today, dear?' Wendy said with a smile. Aiden bit his tongue and tried to hide his smirk. He knew she wouldn't be hard on Sam. At least not yet.

'Yeah, I'm alright. How have you guys been?' the girl asked while she took an apron from the hook. She seemed, somehow, flustered to Aiden. Wendy glanced to him and he wondered if she could see it too.

'All good, thanks,' he responded, turning back to face the kitchen while Wendy went to check on Marcus. In the corner of his eye, Aiden could see the glass front of the fridge filled with all manner of bottles and cans for the customers to buy. In the reflection of the glass, he saw the dark shape of someone standing just inside the café by the front door. He gasped, taken by surprise. He hadn't heard the door open.

'Looks like we have our first customer,' he said before turning to the first patron of the day.

'Really? Where?' Sam asked as she quickly stepped out of the kitchen, still tying the straps of her apron behind her back. Aiden froze. There was nobody there. Sam looked at him curiously, watching as Aiden's mouth slowly opened and closed silently like a fish for a moment.

'Uh, I dunno. I just, thought I saw someone I guess,' he said softly. He turned his head, looking back to the fridge. There was nothing there.

Then, his blood ran cold. He saw the figure again. Not only was it outside the café, but now it was across the street. He couldn't make it out very well, just the generic shape of a person who seemed covered in shadow. Was it a man or a woman? Did they even have any hair? What were they wearing? Aiden couldn't tell. He was frozen to the spot, helplessly looking on with the unnerving feeling that the stranger was watching him. Almost as if confirming his fears, he saw it raise an arm, ever so slightly waving its hand.

Aiden... Aiden...

'Hey, Aiden!' Sam shouted and smacked the back of her hand against Aiden's arm. He gasped and looked to her.

'What's going on, man? You alright?' she asked. There was, perhaps, the slightest hint of concern mingled with the amusement in her pale face. Aiden glanced back to the fridge. The reflection was completely free of any figures again.

'Uh, yeah. Yeah, I'm fine,' he said before shaking his head to snap out of his thoughts.

'Just didn't sleep well, I guess,' he added, noticing that Wendy was watching him.

'Heh, no shit. Me either. Anyway…' Sam's voice died away as Aiden pictured the figure in his mind again. He probably hadn't seen anything at all. Just imagining things.

'Sometimes it makes you see things,' he recalled his own words.

A DAY AT THE CLINIC
REBECCA

Bec ran her thumb up the screen of her phone, browsing the internet. She often wondered, *What did people ever do before smartphones? Before the internet?* She seemed to have forgotten that all through her childhood she had managed just fine without both. Well, at least in the nineties the internet was restricted to the sluggish dial-up system. At that time, Bec was too young to care anyway. She would much rather have gone out riding her bike or seeing a movie with her friends than sitting in front of a computer screen. Yet here she was in the present day, carrying something with the power of at least a hundred of those old computers in her pocket all the time. She had the wealth of knowledge at her fingertips, just like everyone she knew.

Bec was sitting outside, enjoying the feeling of the warm sunshine while she had her lunch. A homemade salad of spinach leaves, chickpeas, tomatoes, egg, pepper and parmesan cheese. It was one of Bec's staples. A healthy lunch to give her the energy she needed for the day. She had been absent-mindedly scrolling through social media before closing the app in frustration. Bec had long been struggling to break free of her addiction to the social media sites. Sure, there was no harm in sharing her life with people and checking in on those she cared about. But how often had she caught herself reading some ludicrous comment that either made no sense or made her mad, only to find out it was by someone she neither knew nor cared about? She probably couldn't calculate the total of wasted hours she had spent lost in some vortex of celebrities, memes and virtual gossip.

Bec had managed to break free of that very vortex, sliding her phone back into her pocket before she thought of Aiden. That morning had to be one of the weirdest ways she had ever woken up. Instead of the shrill cry of her alarm, she woke up to the sound of something just as annoying, but far more unsettling. The groans were long and strained, like someone who was too weak to get enough air in. She had been sluggish, lost in that fleeting moment between sleep and wakefulness when the groans came clearer. When she had wiped the sleep from her eyes, she could finally see her husband clearly. He was lying on his back, his body limp and relaxed. She would have thought him simply to be asleep if she hadn't seen his eyes. Though his eyelids fluttered, they were very obviously open. His eyes were watery and something about them, a particular shine within them, expressed a certain sense of terror. Bec likened it to the look people showed in horror films before the serial killer drove a knife into them. Aiden was focused on the bathroom. His lips were parted only a little and from them, he was expressing the low, morbid moans. It was like he had been turned into a zombie. Bec didn't know what to think, other than Aiden was having a nightmare and she shook him awake. To be honest, Bec hadn't really given the morning much thought after that. She showered and got ready for work, had breakfast, said goodbye to Aiden and Hannah and started with the labours of her day. Working at the Greenfield Medical Centre was very occupying. As a medical receptionist, if Bec wasn't admitting patients, she was chasing up account details, filing sensitive patient information, cleaning, stocking, ordering supplies and in her down time, fixing that goddamned printer that jammed every second day. She hadn't had much of a chance to ponder the morning's events.

But now, as she ate her lunch and discarded the latest updates of an old high school friend she never saw anymore, Bec's mind wandered back to that very morning. Almost instinctively, she pulled her phone back out of her pocket and loaded up the search engine. She soon found herself awash in sites with explanations and testaments of sleep paralysis. They ranged from the scientific to the absurd. Was it a miscommunication between the brain and the body during the last stages of REM sleep? Or was it a small, goblin-witch that was sitting on the victim's chest? Bec was inclined to think it was the former of the two. Even so, sleep paralysis seemed far more common than she would have thought. She would never have even heard of it if Aiden hadn't mentioned suffering from it in his youth. Yet after a brief look through the internet, it appeared as much as fifty per cent of people could suffer from some form or another of sleep paralysis in their lifetime. The symptoms were abundant. Some were so quick and subtle that most people wouldn't even know they had them. Others were so bizarre, like the feeling of an evil presence in the room or the sensation of being swept out of bed, that some researchers believed many claims of alien abduction were simply the result of bad episodes of the paralysis.

Damnit, babe. This better not get any worse, Bec thought. She knew it wasn't Aiden's fault. Just like it wasn't his fault when he suffered from his depression. She couldn't blame him for not being able to keep the chemicals in his brain under control. That didn't mean that dealing with someone suffering such things wasn't fucking awful though. It looked like the most, if not only, effective treatment for sleep paralysis Bec could find was improving your sleeping habits.

Great. Now I'll have two kids to make sure are in bed on time, she thought sarcastically. Bec couldn't help but smile at the amusing idea, though she really did hope Aiden didn't have any more problems. She glanced up from the medical article she was reading to the clock on her phone. Her breaktime was just about up. Bec pocketed her phone again and scooped up the remains of her salad before she headed back inside.

*

The Greenfield clinic was a rather small doctor's office in comparison to the standard centres these days. From the open reception and waiting room, a hallway continued eastward, leading to a bathroom and three exam rooms. That was it. If the patients needed any medical testing or prescriptions filled, which they often did, then they would have to cross the road to the nearest chemist and collection centre. Thankfully the two businesses were nearby.

'How was lunch?' Liz asked when Bec returned behind the desk. Elizabeth Freemont was Bec's only subordinate at the clinic. They were both medical receptionists but, as Bec had been there longer and worked more hours, there was an unofficial rule that she was higher up the ladder. Liz worked part-time to help out. It was always good to have someone available to take calls when there were patients already being tended to, not to mention Bec could use all the help she could get keeping on top of all the records, data entry and accounts. Thanks to Liz, Bec could also go to lunch guilt-free. The doctors would never have been impressed if they had to do the reception duties themselves. Bec and Liz were good friends. They had been working together now for six years after Bec's previous co-worker, Margaret, retired. There was no love lost there. Margaret was, in Bec's own words, *'a stubborn old cow'*. She had a certain way of doing things and didn't tolerate any change or disruptions.

Thankfully, Bec didn't have to deal with such petty disagreements anymore. The doctors were content with the way Bec ran things and, so long as the patients were adequately taken care of, they didn't care what methods Bec and Liz had.

'Yeah, lunch was good. Want to go for your break now?' Bec responded to Liz's question as she sat down beside her at the desk. Liz thought for a moment before shaking her head.

'No, I should really sort out the Miller account first. Maybe another half an hour, if that's okay?' she said while she resumed inspecting the files on her computer screen.

'Alright. I mean, it's really up to you.' Bec smiled. She appreciated Liz's commitment to the work. They made a good team, always helping each other out.

'Yeah, I'm all good. I'm not feeling all that hungry yet, anyway,' Liz responded.

'Cool. So, what have we got going on right now?' Bec knew she had plenty of paperwork to catch up on but it was always a good idea to keep on top of the appointments and who was in the building.

'Uh, pretty quiet at the moment. Mrs Cole is just waiting for her 12.45 with Dr Pannu,' Liz said with a slight nod to the row of chairs in the waiting room where a lone young woman was seated. She was evidently pregnant by the small but undoubtedly growing bump in her belly. The sight reminded Bec of her own pregnancy with Hannah all those years ago. She had been so young. Certainly not ready for everything she was about to go through. Even so, if she were given the chance, she wouldn't change anything in the past if it meant she couldn't have her daughter.

'Dr Pannu is currently seeing Mrs Greyson and her son while Mr Meadows is with Dr Winstead,' Liz continued to update Bec, drawing her mind back to the present.

'Right. Not a lot going on, as you say.' Bec nodded her understanding. It was a curiously quiet point in the day. Usually there were at least three of four patients waiting. Bec was content to utilise the lull to finally check off the stores order that was due to be sent off tomorrow.

'Did I tell you that I found out Tom has been at it again?' Liz said after a few minutes of silent work where the only sound came from the wall mounted TV in the waiting room. The usual midday television show was playing. A man and woman were sitting on a couch in a very brightly coloured studio, undoubtedly talking about the latest celebrity hypes. Bec didn't understand the appeal of daytime television. She could only see the fake wide smiles of bleached teeth, perfect skin and flowing blonde hair in shows like that. Thank God the TV was always so quiet it might as well be muted.

'Oh no, what has he been up to this time?' Bec asked as she looked away from the TV and back to her computer monitor.

'Oh, not a lot. He just spent $120 on lotto tickets this week,' Liz replied, the sarcasm evident in her voice. Bec looked slack jawed to her companion.

'Jesus! What the hell is he thinking?' she said incredulously. Liz shrugged and scoffed at her husband's antics.

'It's all on the same game too. The jackpot for tonight. Three million dollars. If he wins, maybe we can pay back some of his debt for a change,' she said. It was Bec's turn to scoff. She had nothing against placing a bet every now and then, just for fun really. And who knows if you might get lucky one day? That said, she had no doubt that one had more chances of being struck by lightning or, at the very least being hit by a car, rather than winning the jackpot. A little fun was one thing, but people struggling to recover from serious gambling addictions was another. Bec didn't know the exact details, but Liz had previously told her thanks to Tom's troubles they were thousands in debt.

Maybe even tens of thousands by now, Bec thought as she remembered it had been some time since Liz had last shared such information.

'I thought he was doing so well. Wasn't he seeing someone about it?' Bec asked. At that moment, a small boy, maybe five years old came charging down the hallway from the exam rooms. He was crying with tears streaming down his red cheeks as he ran. He clearly hadn't enjoyed his visit to the doctor.

'Nathan! Nathan, get back here right now! Sorry,' a woman's voice called from the hall before Mrs Greyson, the boy's frustrated mother, quickly paced after her son.

'It's alright. Nobody likes injections,' Dr Adya Pannu said as she followed at a more leisurely pace. Mrs Greyson managed to catch up to her frantic child and was now squatting before him, gently holding and consoling him. She was speaking softly and quietly to soothe the boy but Bec only made out the word *'ice-cream'* in there somewhere. While he wasn't completely happy, Nathan was at least coming around as he rubbed his eye and snuffled. Bec remembered using such bribery to get Hannah to do what she wanted back in the day too. Hell, it still worked on a teenager sometimes. Just instead of ice-cream the bribe was seeing a movie or buying something she wanted.

'Mrs Cole?' Dr Pannu asked, turning to the seated pregnant woman in the waiting room. Bec could see her eyes were fixed on the distressed child, her face waxen and pale.

Yep. That's what you're in for, sorry, Bec thought. Liz was evidently thinking something similar as she looked to Bec and they shared a subtle grin. Mrs Cole stood up and joined the doctor who politely directed her to the exam room. Dr Pannu was Bec's favourite of the two attending GPs. While they weren't exactly close friends outside of work, they usually attended each other's birthday celebrations and occasionally had dinner or the like. Noting how the day was currently not too busy, Bec suddenly considered asking the doctor for any advice she might have on sleep paralysis for Aiden. She had to bring some paperwork to the doctor soon anyway so it would be the perfect opportunity while there were no patients. As Dr Pannu and Mrs Cole disappeared from view down the hallway, Mrs Greyson and a relatively calm Nathan stepped up to reception.

'I'm so sorry about that,' the mother said with an exasperated sigh. She leaned on the counter with her purse in one hand, debit card in the other. Bec just gave her an empathetic smile as Liz tended to the woman's payment.

'Don't worry, we've both been through it before. And seen much worse,' Liz encouraged a grateful-looking Mrs Cole.

Bec focused back on her work while the women beside her engaged in some light banter. She wanted to make sure she had the notes ready and printed to give to Dr Pannu when she was free. Just as she clicked the print button, some more people came wandering down the hallway. From where they were seated, Bec and Liz could see anyone approach from the hall, at least in their peripheral vision. The other attending

GP, Dr Winstead, was closely guiding the way for his patients. Dr Winstead was in his sixties with a receding line of silver hair. He was a well-to-do gentleman who had made quite a successful career in neurology. He used to work at one of the high-end private hospitals in Melbourne before retiring to settle down in a smaller position at Glen Marsh. In his own words, Dr Winstead had said, *'I wanted to settle into something a little quainter, and Glen Marsh is perfect, no?'*

Bec could never forget the way Dr Winstead had spoken about her hometown when she first met him. He always had an air of superiority about him, as though anyone and everyone he spoke to was beneath his grand stature. Bec just thought he was a pompous arse. Even so, he was pleasant enough to work with for the most part. Usually, he just didn't speak with the staff unless it was of utmost importance to him. Beside the good doctor walked a large woman, perhaps in her forties. Her long, curly hair was dark, matching her brown eyes. Bec recognised her immediately. Belinda Meadows. The woman was quite a regular to the clinic, not so much for her own sake, but as the primary carer of her father, Jonathan. As Bec predicted, Belinda was gently holding her father's arm, leading him towards the bench. Jonathan was roughly the same age as Dr Winstead, but he could pass for quite older. He was bedraggled with a thin, lanky frame. His short hair was completely grey and he had a constant expression of exhaustion which was not helped by the dark shadows around his sunken eyes. This was hardly surprising as he had long been suffering with a particularly terrible ailment. He needed a great deal of help walking, often becoming limp in the arms of those who aided him. Speaking was sometimes difficult with his articulate words devolving into incomprehensible slurs and babbles. His hands often shook. Sometimes he could not help holding his thin arms tightly tucked to his chest and other times they might spring out beyond his control. Naturally, due to patient confidentiality, Bec didn't know exactly what disease poor Mr Meadows suffered from, but she had a good idea. His involuntary convulsions and twitches reminded her of her late uncle on her father's side. He had developed

MS and, though she would be ashamed to admit it, Bec was frightened of her uncle when she was younger. Something about the unnatural jerking, the unpredictability of it maybe, made her feel anxious. Whenever Bec saw Mr Meadows, it was as though she were looking at her uncle through a window into the past. Maybe it was in a subconscious effort to make up for her own discomfort as a child that she was always extra nice to Mr Meadows. Liz was still finalising Mrs Cole's payment; the damned card machine was acting up again apparently. As such, the new patients headed towards Bec herself.

'Good afternoon, Mr Meadows. Ms Meadows. How have you been?' she greeted them cheerfully. She made sure to look the old man in the eye, almost to prove to herself she had nothing to be uncomfortable about. One would have thought after seeing Mr Meadows as a regular patient for so long she would be used to it by now.

'Well, well, thank you,' Mr Meadows responded with a smile. His eye twitched slightly.

'And how many tuh-times must I tell you? C-call me, Jonathan,' he added. He stuttered a little as he spoke and Bec could see a flash of frustration cross his face, if only for a second. Before Bec could reply, Dr Winstead began to speak.

'Alrighty then, you are all set. I'll see you the same time next month but of course, any problems before then, don't hesitate to come in sooner,' he said while gently shaking Mr Meadow's hand. Mr Meadows smiled and politely nodded, evidently finding words too difficult at that precise moment.

'Thank you, Doctor,' Belinda spoke on her father's behalf. She said so little and yet, as Bec could see it, so much. The twinkle in her eyes, the light pitch to her voice. Belinda admired Dr Winstead. Bec wondered how much.

'A pleasure. So, 12.20, Thursday the ninth of May,' Dr Winstead said. This time, he spoke directly to Bec, tapping his finger onto the desk as if to enunciate every word.

'Certainly, Dr Winstead,' Bec said. *Patronising bastard,* she thought as the doctor turned on his heel and wandered back towards his office.

'I'm glad to hear your doing well, Mr Mead ... sorry, Jonathan,' Bec spoke kindly to the old man standing before her as she booked in his next appointment. She noticed a tremor run up Mr Meadows' arm, causing his elbow to quiver while he stood with his palms set atop the reception desk.

'Certainly, I am-am well! S-seeing you two pretty ladies is-s-s the highlight of my m-month,' Mr Meadows said with his lips curling into a grin. Bec gave a coquettish laugh and bit her cheek. Mr Meadows was always just very kind or a hopeless flirt.

'Dad!' Belinda scowled at her father as she opened her purse to pay for their visit. Apparently, she didn't like her father potentially flirting with people. Bec didn't really see the harm in some kind words here and there which was all that ever happened with Mr Meadows.

'W-what?' Mr Meadows asked, looking shocked and innocent to his daughter's protestations.

'It's alright, Ms Meadows. We're always just glad to see your father doing so well. Okay and insert your caaaard, now,' Bec said while she worked.

'S-see? She gets... it,' Mr Meadows joked with another big grin directed at Bec. Belinda just pursed her lips and looked unhappy with her father.

'Hmmm. Thank you,' she said, only paying half her attention to paying the bill.

'How is the f-family?' Mr Meadows asked pleasantly while his daughter started to focus more on the payments and rebates.

'Oh, you know, we're all good. Hannah's keeping on top of her schoolwork. Aiden's had some trouble sleeping, but that's about it,' Bec explained briefly. She never liked to go too deep into the details of her life with patients at work but it never hurt to be open sometimes and, as Mr Meadows had been a regular for as long as she had worked there, Bec had no problems updating him on their lives. Mr Meadows nodded in a stop-start sort of manner.

'Oh, good. Th-they're lucky to have y-you,' he said and Bec's cheeks warmed up as she blushed a little.

'Well, that's very kind of you to say, Mr – ugh, Jonathan! Don't worry, I'll get it one day,' she said before resuming business as usual with Belinda. After the next appointment had been confirmed and the payments all processed, Belinda took her father's arm once more to lead him outside.

'I-I'll see you next m-month, then?' Mr Meadows asked with a hopeful twinkle in his eye.

'We'll be here,' Bec said with a smile.

Mr Meadows nodded and gave a small wave while his daughter began to guide him to the sliding door at the front of the clinic. After some minutes of silence, the door opened and another man strode in. Liz was now standing back from the desk and checking the sheets on the printer so Bec invited the newcomer over.

'Hullo, uh, Dennis Somers for a one o'clock with Dr Winstead,' he said as he stepped up the bench.

Just as Bec directed him to sit down, Mrs Cole wandered down the hallway towards them with Dr Pannu by her side. Liz was still at the printer, stapling files together. Bec gave a stifled sigh as she minimised the stores order she was working on once more.

'Hello, Mrs Cole. Will you be after a new appointment?' she asked as the pregnant woman approached.

'Oh! Dr Pannu!' Liz called from behind Bec's shoulder. Adya, who, after noticing her next patient wasn't in the waiting room and had begun to return to her office, turned back.

'Yes?' she asked, stepping closer. While Bec was helping to set a new appointment for Mrs Cole, she could see Liz reach over the desk beside her.

'I think these ones are for you. Bec printed them off, I think?' Liz said as she passed the paperwork to the doctor. Bec glanced to her colleagues and gave a quick nod and smile before returning to attention to Mrs Cole. She would have to come up with another excuse to pop into Adya's office now.

'Alright, that's all booked. So, that's sixty-five dollars for today, thank you,' Bec said, as she indicated the card machine. Mrs Cole thanked her before inserting her card and beginning the payment process.

Bec felt a shiver run down her spine. It was one of those curious tingles that caused your whole body to shudder. The temperature of the clinic was well monitored for the comfort of the patients and there were no draughts. Bec would have passed it off as a simple twitch of the nerves if she didn't feel something else. The hairs on the back of her neck stood on end and her skin became sensitive to the very air around her. Bec had the peculiar feeling that she was being watched.

Instinctively, she glanced at the entryway of the clinic. Her breath caught in her throat. Mr Meadows was still standing inside the building, just within the doorway. His lanky frame was very still with his long arms hanging down his sides, almost like a statue. With his head slightly bowed forward, the old man seemed to be looking right at her. Bec opened her mouth to say something, but no words came. She was inexplicably paralysed under Mr Meadow's gaze. His eyes were fixed upon her, unblinking and darker than usual. The daylight seemed to reflect off of his shining black pupils. Along with that piercing, intense stare, Mr Meadows was smiling at Bec. It was not a kind smile. His lips strained back into a wide grin, baring his teeth in a manner that seemed as though it would be painful to endure. Bec was frozen, looking back as the statue of a man stared at her with such intensity that she felt an undeniable urge to hide under the bench. She caught sight of the smallest droplet, a trickle of something red run down between Mr Meadow's bottom teeth. Was that blood?

A computerised beep roared in Bec's ears. She quickly swivelled around to look to the source and found that Mrs Cole's payment had been accepted. Liz was still working beside Bec and Mrs Cole was ready and waiting for the rebate to be put through. Bec glanced back to the front door. Mr Meadows wasn't there. The door opened and another patient entered the clinic. Bec shook her head. *What the hell? That was just weird*, she thought to herself, rationalising that her imagination had just gotten the better of her.

Bec continued with the next step in Mrs Cole's rebate as the new patient spoke to Liz, confirming their upcoming appointment with Dr Pannu. It appeared Bec would have to find another time to speak with Adya about her husband's sleeping troubles.

WAITING FOR THE BELL
HANNAH

'Paul, pay attention, will you?!' Mr Novak's gravelly voice echoed through the science classroom. The low murmuring and chattering quickly died down as the cantankerous teacher leered over the students seated before him.

Mr Novak was tall, at least six foot and his heavy-set frame only exacerbated his dominant nature. He held a blue marker in his hand, though he was currently turned away from the whiteboard on which his notes had been scrawled. Mr Novak held that marker as though he were ready to throw it at the student who had been causing disturbances all through his lesson. The sudden tension in the air held everyone present in a trance. Hannah, seated in roughly the middle of the class, risked a quick glance over her shoulder. She saw Paul Hubbard, leaning upon his forearms on his desk, his face bright red with embarrassment at being called out. His two mates, Eddie and Tyler, sat either side of him, stifling their snickers at their friend's predicament.

Ugh, idiots, Hannah thought as she turned away from the class clowns. She looked to her best friend, Abbi, who rolled her blue eyes before looking back to her notes.

Hannah had known Abigail Young since they were little kids. They had attended the same kindergarten, the same primary school and now, they were pushing through their second year at the Ibis Secondary College of Glen Marsh. Though they got along better than some sisters, Hannah and Abbi were physically stark contrasts to one another. Where Hannah was a medium-length brunette, Abbi had always worn her golden hair down past her shoulders. Hannah's soft, puppy brown eyes (inherited from her mother) were always protected behind her sleek, black-limbed glasses. Abbi's blue eyes always seemed to sparkle even if the day was completely overcast. And, while Hannah did not suffer as much as some of her classmates, she often sported a few spots of acne since she was ten years old. Abbi, on the other hand, either never had a problem with pimples or she was very clever at hiding them. Instead of any hormonally charged blotches, she had a cute line of freckles across the bridge of her nose. Was Hannah jealous of her friend's looks? Hell, yes! But, having grown up with her for most of their lives, she had become used to the idea that Abbi was the pretty one. Hannah contented herself that she had her brains. Of course, she didn't think Abbi was slow. Far from it. But Hannah felt that what Abbi enjoyed in looks, she herself could enjoy in intellect. As such, Hannah quickly took back to scribbling down the notes that Mr Novak had been scribing on the whiteboard before them.

'Last warning, Paul. That goes for you two, as well. Any more from you three and it's detention!' Mr Novak scolded the troublemakers for their jokes and disrespect. He stared the boys down a moment longer to emphasise his point before turning back to the whiteboard. 'Now, as I was saying, the circulatory system consists of three separate systems that work in unison. The systemic system relates to the blood vessels including the veins and arteries. The pulmonary system relates specifically to the lungs and the cardiovascular system, to the heart.'

Mr Novak was rereading his own work, seemingly in an effort to allow his students a chance to catch up. Hannah didn't doubt he was also trying to find his train of thought again. She had already copied everything down and was waiting for him to progress. Now, aside from the teacher's dictations, the classroom was almost silent. The warm sunlight of the afternoon was beaming in through the high windows of the science room and Hannah squinted from the bright reflection of one of the sinks along the wall. Although she was interested in the work, she glanced over her fellows with the time she had free.

Most of her classmates wore dreary, bored expressions on their faces, including Abbi. It was the sixth period and everyone was just waiting for that final bell to ring so that they could escape the school for the rest of the day. Hannah shot a glance at the boy who sat next to her. He looked like he was deep in concentration. His eyes were focused on his workbook as he wrote down Mr Novak's dictations. Brian Zhang. Hannah had known him since she first came to Ibis Secondary College. They might not have been best friends, as Hannah and Abbi were, but they were still pretty close for teenagers. They often studied together, attended the same classes and were part of the same group of friends who would get together at recess and lunch. Hannah watched for a moment, enjoying the sight of Brian's soulful, dark eyes as he concentrated on his work. Hannah and Abbi practically knew everything about each other. But Abbi didn't know that Hannah liked Brian more than the average boy. Hell, Hannah wasn't sure she knew if she liked him or not either. All she knew was that she couldn't resist sneaking discreet peeks when Brian, nor anyone else might notice and every time she did, Hannah felt a flutter in her chest.

Brian apparently caught up with Mr Novak as he set his pen down and stretched his lean fingers. He glanced back in Hannah's direction and she quickly turned away, looking blankly at her own work. *Crap, he didn't notice me, did he?* she thought. Her heart pounded in her chest. The exhilaration of admiring Brian and almost being caught raged her body.

'Now, tonight you are all to read chapter three in your textbooks.'

Hannah tried to focus her attention back on Mr Novak who clipped the lid shut on his marker as he spoke. A unison of hollow sighs and groans filled the air at this revelation.

'I know, I know, I'm breaking your hearts. But there is also... ah, damn it.' Mr Novak picked up some papers and quietly counted them for a moment. 'There is also a worksheet you are to complete but it looks like I need to print off a few more,' he said, half to himself. More groans echoed in the room.

'Yeah, yeah. Uh, Kelly? Take these and pass them on. One for each of you until they run out. I'll be back in five minutes with the rest,' The teacher explained. He took one of the worksheets to photocopy and handed the rest of the papers to Kelly who sat closest to him. There seemed to be an awkward moment of silence and Hannah noticed students staring, some whispering together as Mr Novak looked down to Kelly who took the papers. A moment later, the teacher was striding to the classroom door. He opened it before turning back to look at the students.

'Behave yourselves. I won't be long,' he said and, after giving a final warning look to the troublemakers at the back, he was gone. There was an instant sense of relief in the room which even Hannah couldn't deny. The sighs and almost instant chattering seemed to soothe everyone in the room.

'God, can today just be over already?' Abbi moaned, falling forward to rest her forehead on her desk. Hannah nodded. She was one of those oddballs who enjoyed school but even she couldn't wait to finish up by the last period of the day.

'Right? I can't wait to get home,' she said in agreement. The worksheets were very slowly making their way along the rows of the class but Hannah couldn't tell if they would make it to her or not.

'He was totally looking at me!' A girl's voice rang above the others. Most people looked in the direction of the voice. Kelly was sitting in her spot, looking flustered. Her friends were leaning in to talk with her.

'God, he is disgusting. Such a perv, everyone knows it,' one of the girls, Hannah knew was named Simone, hissed.

'I know! He was totally looking down my top!' Kelly responded. She didn't sound as distressed as her words would have indicated. Rather, she seemed to Hannah to be enjoying all the attention.

'You should totally complain to Principal Tibbins about him. Maybe you could even sue him,' another of the girls said, though Hannah couldn't make out who.

'Ugh, are they on this again? I mean, get a life, Jesus. Nobody cares about your A cups,' Abbi said with annoyance. Hannah giggled.

'You just think you're top shit because you're bigger than her,' she teased. Hannah didn't swear often but the need to fit in with school life brought it out of her sometimes.

'Well, you're bigger than Kelly too,' Abbi retorted after poking her tongue out. Hannah felt her cheeks blushing. Like Abbi, she was a B cup but, unlike Abbi, her bras still felt a little loose.

'Shut up,' she said meekly to Abbi before glancing in Brian's direction. To her horror, she realised he was looking at her. He quickly averted his gaze when she caught him.

Oh God! Did he hear us? Hannah wanted to just lower herself back into her chair and disappear out of sight.

'Anyway, you don't think they're true, do you?' Abbi's voice brought Hannah back to their conversation. She tried to shrug off the fact that Brian had potentially been listening to the allusion to her breasts.

'I dunno, I mean, Mr Novak is pretty strict but that doesn't really make him a perv, does it? They aren't even related,' Hannah thought aloud to Abbi's question. Of course, she had heard the stories about Mr Novak. Apparently, he was often looking at the girl students, leering at them, making them uncomfortable. Hannah had never noticed him doing it, neither to her nor anyone else.

'I mean, I've never seen him be weird with anyone, really. I dunno, I think maybe the rumours are what make people uncomfortable with him? Like, they expect him to be creepy so they imagine him being creepy when he isn't, you know?' She spoke her mind and, even though she couldn't find the right words for it, it appeared through her nodding that Abbi understood what she meant.

'Yeah, I get that. It's just weird, like, if it were true, which *everyone* thinks it is, wouldn't you think he'd get fired or arrested or something? It must be all crap,' Abbi said, trying to rationalise out the rumours.

Hannah just nodded. Abbi did make a good point. Surely all the other teachers and parents wouldn't just turn a blind eye to some sort of predator working at the school? Unless Mr Novak was just weird and looked here and there but never touched? Hannah shuddered. She didn't like to think about it. It wasn't that long ago that she first understood what sex was, let alone learned all the good stuff and bad stuff that came with it. She already missed being a real kid. When romance was simply kissing your handsome prince and then you were married and happy. All this sex stuff just confused things. Now guys supposedly thought all kinds of filthy things about the girls they liked. Hell, some of the girls were just as bad, weren't they? Hannah read all the books. She searched all the topics online. She knew puberty was confusing. But simply saying how confusing it was didn't do shit to help her get through it. She just had to plod along with all the other teenagers and deal with the weird urges she didn't wholly understand. Yet, with that said, somehow Hannah felt Brian was different to all the other guys. He was quiet and shy and came across like a sensitive sort of person. Much like Hannah herself. Maybe that was why she liked him?

'Why are you reading that, Brian?' A boy's voice rose behind them. Hannah looked over to see Brian was reading his science textbook, already starting on chapter three – the circulatory system. Paul was stretching over his desk, peering over Brian's shoulder with his mates.

'I just wanted to get a head start. It's interesting,' Brian responded without really turning back to look at Paul.

'Pff, yeah right. You're just pretending so you can take a peek at the naked chick pics in chapter six when no one's looking,' Tyler teased and his friends laughed. Brian just shook his head and ignored them.

'Hey, maybe he doesn't wanna look at the chick. Maybe he wants to see the dude?' Eddie added, nudging Paul's elbow. The boys pretended to look shocked.

'Oh my god, Brian, is that true? Are you just trying to get a good look at all the dicks?' Paul hollered. He and his friends were speaking loudly, making a scene. It was one of the ways bullies like them seemed to work. Attract all the attention, make the other kid feel small while they felt big.

'Ugh, you guys suck. Why don't you just leave him alone?' Hannah found herself snapping at them before she could stop herself. For a moment, the three boys looked genuinely taken aback. They had been gleefully picking on Brian and didn't expect anyone else to protest.

'What's it to you, Hannah? Do you like him or something?' Tyler retorted. Hannah felt her cheeks blush. She noticed Brian looking at her.

'Hey, Hannah, it's okay...' he said softly but something in his eyes told her he appreciated her standing up for him.

'No... no, that's not it at all. I just think you guys are being stupid and mean,' Hannah said. It took her a moment to gather her words again after Tyler's accusation and her heart was pounding in her chest with anger and embarrassment. She was scared that the boys might have seen through her hesitation.

'Oh my god. Hannah likes Brian! Hannah likes Brian!' Paul started to say in a patronising sing-song voice.

'Shut up!' Hannah growled through gritted teeth. She couldn't bring herself to look at Brian. She had no idea what he was doing or thinking as she disappeared within a bubble of self-consciousness.

'Hey, Paul, even if that were true, you're just jealous because no girls like you,' Abbi sneered.

'Ooooooh,' Eddie and Tyler said amongst the laughter of the surrounding students. The debate had grabbed a decent amount of attention from those around them.

'He's not worth it, guys. Just ignore him,' Brian said. He didn't go back to reading his textbook though and shuffled a little closer to

Hannah, as though there was some sort of protection if they were nearer each other.

'Hey, you just go back to your dick pics, Brian! And Abbi, I got nothing to be jealous about. I know how much you'd love to blow me out by the bike shed,' Paul said. Hannah gasped with shock and Abbi just looked grossed out.

'Yeah, in your dreams, arsehole,' she said as she showed him her middle finger.

'Come on, Hannah. Brian's right. Just ignore them,' she added before turning back to face the front of the classroom. Hannah followed suit and tried to ignore the boys' taunts and jeers. After some more attempts without success to grab their attention, the boys lost interest in picking on the little group before them and began joking amongst themselves. Hannah felt like there was suddenly a brick wall standing between her and Brian. She couldn't bring herself to look at him. She was terrified of what he thought about her now. Did he suspect she really did like him? How would it affect their friendship if he did? Never in her wildest dreams did Hannah think he would like her back. She wanted to say something. Anything to just break the tension.

'Thanks,' Brian said ever so softly. He didn't look to Hannah as he spoke and she still couldn't bring herself to look at him, although she felt her cheeks blushing once more.

'That's okay,' she replied quietly. A flush of appreciation for Brian flowed through her. If he did in fact feel as awkward as she did, he wasn't going to let it stop him from speaking to her.

'No, that's okay. I'm just the one who gave them the finger,' Abbi said with a fake tone of annoyance. Her comment seemed to brush the tension away from her friends and they both found themselves giving weak laughs.

'Heh, yeah, sorry. Thanks, Abbi,' Brian said a little louder.

'*Thanks, Abbi,*' one of the boys mocked behind them. Hannah fought down the growing anger and desire to snap at them. Thankfully, at that moment, the classroom door slid open once more and Mr Novak stepped back inside.

'I could hear you lot from two doors down! Could you really not last five minutes?' he snapped as he approached the nearest student.

'Thank God, Kelly is at the other end,' Abbi mumbled, eliciting a stifled giggle from Hannah. Mr Novak passed the new copies of the worksheets to one of the boys at the front of the class and instructed him to pass them down. There were only five minutes left until the bell for the end of day and the anticipation of everyone in the room was building with each tick of the clock.

'Now, I want you all to make sure you have read through chapter three, at least over the weekend,' Mr Novak called as he returned to stand behind his desk. He had the attention of most of the class now and he continued to speak as though he couldn't care less for those who weren't focusing solely on him.

'Because on Monday, we will be performing a dissection of the heart.' There were sudden gasps and whispers of intrigue as everyone perked their ears. Hannah couldn't deny she was curious.

'A human heart?' A boy lost in the crowd of students called out. There was an eruption of laughter. Mr Novak rolled his eyes and clicked his tongue.

'No, not a human heart. A cow's heart. They're similar enough to ours,' he said.

'*Stupid boy.*'

Hannah was certain she heard Mr Novak mutter the last words but it could have simply been her reading into the subtle movement of his lips.

'Now, for those of you who are squeamish, there will only be one heart and I will make the incisions. You will only observe. It isn't like the old days when we could trust fifteen-year-old kids with a scalpel,' Mr Novak explained. There were some disappointed faces in the class but most remained interested. A hand shot up into the air. Hannah recognised the girl it belonged to. Kimberly Fletcher. Hannah sometimes hung out with Kimberley and her friends and she was always nice, if not a little opinionated.

'Um, Mr Novak, should we really do a dissection? I didn't think they really did them in school anymore. I mean, we have models and computer images and –' Mr Novak cut Kimberly off with a dismissive wave of the hand.

'Yes, yes, you're right. We have many different methods these days and most teachers don't feel dissection is necessary anymore. But personally, I feel nothing compares to the real thing,' he said. Kimberly looked pale. Though she might not have known her as a close friend would, Hannah knew Kimberley was a vegan.

'Now, I've already spoken to my peers about this and there are no problems with my performing a dissection for you provided I say this. Any of you who do not wish to participate may take the period in the library,' Mr Novak explained. Kimberly breathed a sigh of relief but she still didn't seem satisfied to Hannah.

She probably won't be completely happy unless the whole thing got cancelled, she thought before mentally scolding herself for generalising someone based on their dietary preferences alone. Even though she personally was not a vegan, or even a vegetarian for that matter, she didn't approve of killing animals for any reason other than food, defence or to put them out of their misery. She was confident Mr Novak would probably just get the cow's heart from the butcher, in which case, she rationalised the cow was already dead. If part of it went to teach students, who was she to complain? At that moment, the bell rang. The movement of almost every student in the room was instantaneous. The ringing sound declared their freedom for the rest of the afternoon and they were keen to enjoy it. 'Remember, chapter three and finish that worksheet!' Mr Novak called over the bustling hubbub as the students took up their belongings and marched out of the classroom. Brian stopped and stepped aside, letting Hannah and Abbi walk out before him. Hannah shot him an appreciative smile.

'Huh, dissection. I didn't think they even did that at school anymore,' Abbi said once she, Brian and Hannah were free from the confined masses of the class.

'It sounds like Mr Novak might be the only teacher who still does it here,' Brian suggested. Hannah nodded in agreement.

'Yeah, but I mean, aren't you curious?' she asked a little sheepishly as she realised her friends might not feel the same way she did about the dissection.

'Nah, it just sounds gross,' Abbi said while making an unpleasant face. Hannah wasn't surprised. Abbi was never the sort of girl who enjoyed getting her hands dirty, let alone the sight of real blood and gore.

'I think it could be interesting,' Brian said.

Hannah looked at him. He just looked ahead and seemed thoughtful. Hannah already knew that Brian was at least somewhat interested in the medical sciences, much like herself.

'Apparently they used to do it at primary school. Like, every student just took a cow's heart from the butcher, a chopping board and a knife and did it. I never did that, though. Did you guys?' Brian asked as they walked along, heading to their locker bay.

'Nope, must have been before my time,' Hannah replied. Abbi just looked put off.

'Ew, no,' she said simply. They continued on, joining the masses of students from all over the school. The locker bays were distributed throughout the school, and everyone was walking this way and that to try and leave as soon as they could. Thankfully, the individual year levels were always pretty close to each other so Hannah didn't need to separate from the others right away. Brian took the bus home but Hannah and Abbi both lived about half an hour's walking distance so if the weather was good, which it was, they walked home. It wasn't long before they were all collecting their backpacks, filled with the laptops, books and sheets they needed for homework from their lockers.

'Alright, well, I'll see you tomorrow? Thanks again for, you know,' Brian said, checking the time on his phone as they each stood by the entry of the locker bay with the straps of their backpacks over their shoulders.

'Yeah, of course. Don't worry about it,' Hannah said a little sheepishly. She glowered at Abbi when she saw how she was wearing a smug smile.

'Yeah, have a good night, Brian. We'll see you tomorrow,' Abbi said after she continued to look at Hannah for a moment before turning to her smartphone to check the latest social media. Hannah locked eyes with Brian for a single moment. Both of them shared a small smile.

'Well, see ya,' Brian said.

'Yeah, bye.' She didn't know what was wrong with her. She and Brian could usually speak so easily together. Even just at lunch they were joking around like normal. But now, after the awkward encounter with Paul and the others, it was like there was a weight in her chest that prevented her from speaking like a normal person. She watched as Brian turned and began to follow a group of students who were heading to the front of the school for the buses.

'Hey, you ready to go or what?' Abbi asked as she nudged her elbow. Hannah shook her head, the curious weight upon her clearing almost as soon as Brian had walked off.

'Yeah, I'm good. Let's go,' she said after finally finding the renewed ability to speak. There weren't too many students left wandering about now as most had rushed to catch the bus or meet their parents. A few stragglers were walking here and there, some even just standing around and chatting. Hannah and Abbi began to walk towards the back of the school. From there, a small gate led to back streets where small packs of kids would wander home for the next hour.

'Hang on, I have to pee,' Hannah said. They were just passing one of the school bathrooms outside the locker bay when she felt the urge, almost as though the sight of the place reminded her body.

'Meh, me too,' Abbi said with an acknowledging tilt of the head.

They walked into the bathroom and Hannah closed the door of one of the four cubicles and heard Abbi do the same next door. Hannah didn't really need to take too long but as she sat there, she tried to work out what to do about Brian.

Seriously, do I just pretend like nothing happened? Should I talk to him about it? As she thought, she pulled out her smartphone and opened the text thread to Brian. The last thing they had messaged about was to potentially organise a time to see a new movie next week. It was so innocent then. Abbi was invited too. It was just going to be a catch up with friends. But now, as she looked at their messages, Hannah was worried how awkward it looked. She didn't know how to jump from 'how about the five o'clock session? – sure, sounds good!' to 'hey, I think I like you' or 'so, do you know I like you now?'. Hannah leaned back and gave an exasperated sigh just as the toilet next door flushed.

'Hey, you okay in there?' she heard Abbi call from outside the cubicle. She was moving through the bathroom and Hannah could hear her washing her hands.

'Yeah, I'll be out in a minute.'

'Alright, I'll just be outside,' Abbi said before the sound of her footsteps receded out of the bathroom.

Ugh, I'm just being stupid. It's all going to be fine, Hannah thought after she spent a few more moments contemplating whether or not to message Brian. She put her phone away and finished up in the cubicle. She took to the sink and began to wash her hands, content with her decision.

'Yeah, I'll just wait and see how we go tomorrow. It's all good,' she said in a half whisper to herself.

A curious sound echoed in the small bathroom. It was a low, short bellow, like something one might expect from an animal. Hannah looked up and saw her own face in the mirror. In the corner of her eye, she saw a shadow shift slightly behind the door of the farthest cubicle in the mirror. The door wasn't locked and she hadn't noticed anyone else in the bathroom since Abbi had left. *Weird*, she thought dismissively as she switched off the tap and grabbed some paper towel. Just as she dropped the scrunched paper in the bin, there was another hoarse bellow. It was louder this time and Hannah unmistakably recognised it as that sort of snort a horse or cow would make. She froze, looking to the door of the cubicle. *Man, someone really isn't feeling well…* she thought. She wondered if whoever was there was actually alright or if they needed some help.

'Hello? Are you okay?' she asked, taking a tentative step forward. She knew that if she were ill, she wouldn't want some random walking in on her. At the same time, if it were really serious, some help would surely be the best thing. There was nothing but silence from the cubicle, so much so that she wondered if she had just imagined it all. Or maybe the sound was coming from somewhere outside the bathroom?

'Seriously, if there is someone there, do you need help?' Her own voice seemed to motivate her to step closer. She reached for the door to push it open. The bellowing sound came back, this time loud and guttural. There was something desperate in the cry, like whatever made it was in pain. At the same time, the door of the cubicle battered and trembled against its frame and Hannah jumped with fright.

'What the hell?!' she cried out. She was too scared to move any closer. In fact, Hannah took a step back with her eyes glued on the door. There was a low, ear-piercing creak as the door slowly began to swing open. Hannah stared, wide-eyed and suddenly petrified. The door slowly opened, the hinges squeaking like old, rusty metalwork that hadn't been used in years. Hannah's breath caught in her throat. In the widening gap left in the door's wake, she saw the pale green floor was stained with red. The red splatters were shiny and slick, the sight bringing a hollow chill deep down into her stomach. Then, something else caught her gaze. A dark, thick lump that was matted with blood-stained fur extended from behind the door. A hoof? A hand clamped over Hannah's shoulder from behind.

'Hey, Hannah! What the hell is going on? What's wrong?' Abbi was almost shouting at her as she pulled her around to face her. Although she had just been to the toilet, she wouldn't be surprised if she had actually wet herself. She looked blankly at Abbi's face, seeing the concern in her friend's expression.

'Hello? Hannah? Seriously, you're freaking me out. Do I need to get help or what?' Abbi persisted after her friend hadn't responded. Hannah opened and closed her mouth a few times before she finally found her voice.

'I, uh... uh,' she hesitated before glancing back to the cubicle with splattered blood. The door was completely ajar, just like those around it. There was nothing there but a relatively clean toilet and a half-used roll of toilet paper on the wall. No blood. No... hooves. Hannah didn't know what to think.

'Uh, I... yeah, no, um, I'm okay. I just... saw something... weird,' she said uneasily, struggling to comprehend what happened. Did she just have a seizure? Maybe blacked out? Surely it couldn't have just been her imagination. It seemed far too real.

'Um, okaaay. What did you see?' Abbi asked, inspecting Hannah as though looking for some hidden bump on her head.

'Uh, nothing. Don't worry. I guess it... was nothing.'

With each second that passed, the freaky vision became more distant and unclear. Hannah suddenly felt stupid. She couldn't possibly have seen anything. She must have just zoned out for a minute. Probably daydreaming, fuelled by some scary movie she saw once. Not that she watched such things very often.

'Right. So, you're okay then?' Abbi asked, the concern still evident in her voice, though she stood upright and looked more bewildered than worried now. Hannah swallowed hard and shook her head. She felt completely fine.

'Uh. Yeah. Sorry, don't know what happened,' she said with a lot more confidence than before. Abbi seemed mostly convinced.

'I mean, if you're sure? Like, if you pass out on the way home, I'm not lugging you the rest of the way.' Her grin was contagious and Hannah felt even better than before.

'Ha, yeah. I wouldn't expect you to risk straining anything for me. Just call triple zero and leave me to the birds.'

'So long as you know.' Abbi shrugged.

'Shall we get out of here?'

'Yeah, God. Let's go. I need to get out of here. Sorry for freaking you out,' Hannah said and together, the two girls quickly exited the bathroom.

ANALYSIS AND EMERGENCE

AIDEN

'It happened this morning too. But somehow... worse.' Aiden played absently with his fingers in his lap.

He was seated in a comfortable black leather chair. The small room around him was a typical office, albeit quite a welcoming one. The walls were a generic cream colour and the afternoon daylight shone in through the wide window in the wall to Aiden's right. A couch of matching black leather to his own chair sat along the opposite wall next to a pine bookshelf laden with books. Potted flowers and ferns were scattered here and there and the calming bubbling of a small water feature on the coffee table resonated in the room. Across the coffee table, sitting with her legs crossed, was Aiden's counsellor, Lauren Cunningham. She was in her mid-forties, with short auburn hair and intelligent-looking hazel eyes. She didn't adopt the stereotypical, Hollywood attitude of a therapist. There were never any predictable questions about Aiden's parents or how certain things made him feel.

Lauren had a smart casual fashion about her and didn't wear expensive suits or dresses. While there was a file lying open on the coffee table for any important reminders from meeting to meeting, Lauren didn't have a notepad at the ready with a pen in hand, just waiting to jot down every little thing her visitors said. Aiden had been seeing Lauren for many years now, but he had felt comfortable speaking with her from almost the very beginning. She just seemed to be a good and honest person to share your problems with. Aiden thought it was a much better approach to some of the more clinical counsellors he had seen in his youth.

'How was it worse?' Lauren leaned forward as she spoke, showing a genuine interest in what Aiden had to say. He had already explained the events of waking up on Thursday morning to her. Even just recalling that short period of paralysis made him feel uneasy. Now, thinking of last night, his chest grew tight and sore. He knew it was irrational and he took a deep breath, burying the tension down until he couldn't feel it anymore.

'Well, it didn't just happen when I woke up like the first time. This time it actually *woke* me up, I think. It was about three a.m. when I could finally check the time afterwards,' Aiden explained. Lauren nodded, evidently hanging on every word. She didn't say anything and just let her patient speak in his own time.

'Anyway, aside from that it was pretty much the same, for the most part. I woke up, basically freaking out. I couldn't move. It felt like I was suffocating. I could barely see anything because it was so dark. I tried to say something, to get Bec's attention right away. But I couldn't make a sound. Then, my chest started burning again. I had that feeling. That feeling like I was going to die.' Aiden shifted uneasily in his seat as he spoke. Recalling the experience so vividly was having an effect on him, no matter how much he tried to hide it.

'It's alright, Aiden. Take your time,' Lauren said supportively. She didn't make a fuss or check to make sure he was okay. They had spoken together for so long now that she knew his cues. During the worst years of his depression, Lauren learned to read his body language, his expressions. She had seen Aiden in some of his most anxious moments and she knew that this particular case just needed a minute's recovery. Aiden reached forward and took a sip of the glass of water which sat before him on the coffee table.

'Thanks. I'm all good. Anyway, I was trying to get a hold of myself. I'd forgotten how hard it was. I mean, if I weren't already seeing you today to talk about it, I think I would have booked myself in to see a doctor in case I actually was dying.' He managed a small chuckle. He knew now that he wasn't dying. The paralysis episodes weren't signs of some horrible disease. At least, he didn't think so. It was all psychological as far as he knew. But try telling that to someone while they're actually going through one of those episodes. *You don't think so straight when you think your literally suffocating to death*, he thought.

'Well, I think we can safely say you're not dying. But I know you already know that.' Lauren smiled. Most of the time, she didn't even seem like a therapist at all. More like a long-time friend who he caught up with once a month or so. Aiden laughed again.

'Yeah, I know. Uh, where was I? Um, so, yeah, struggling to breathe and all. Well, just as I started to think I was getting over it and maybe I could finally make some noise to wake Bec up, something else happened.'

'What was it?' Lauren appeared very curious but Aiden wondered if she didn't have an inkling in the back of her mind already.

'It was, kind of, just a feeling. I just got… really scared,' he said before heaving a swallow. Lauren raised her eyebrows.

'It sounds to me like you had enough reason to feel scared already?' she suggested while leaning her chin on her fist.

'Ha, yeah, right? But I dunno, this was different. I wasn't scared of the suffocation stuff. Or that I couldn't move or make a sound. It felt like… a terror. Sheer terror. The sort of thing you only see in movies or imagine people in real danger feeling. You know, soldiers being shot at or something.' Aiden's heart started racing as he remembered the previous night, but he pushed through.

'I felt… cold. It's weird, I know. Because you can't really feel anything, but I swear I did. But that wasn't all. It felt like… like someone was watching me. Or something. Something just, kind of standing out of my view. No matter how much I wanted to look, to just show myself there was nothing there, I couldn't move. And… and it just felt like… it was staring, you know? Really staring.' A shiver run down his spine as he spoke. The memory was vivid enough for him. It almost felt as though, just speaking about it was summoning back whatever thing it was. He could almost feel it. Feel it standing behind him, looking at it him. Instinctively, he snapped his head around and looked back. There was nothing there except Lauren's desk and empty office chair. The computer hummed quietly and the sheets of files and pens lay undisturbed.

'Well, that definitely sounds freaky. I know I wouldn't like to go through that,' Lauren said. Her eyes were wide and she looked, at least faintly perturbed by Aiden's descriptions. He just nodded.

'Yeah, it was pretty fucking awful.' He knew Lauren didn't care if he swore. Hell, she did herself half the time. It was just a part of her technique that he liked so much. 'I mean, I had no idea what it was. But it really felt like some… evil, fucking thing was looking at me. Just watching and waiting. But I could just tell. It wanted to hurt me. To *really* hurt me.'

Lauren continued to nod as she listened, though this time she moved slower, more entranced.

'Anyway, I have no idea how long this went on for but it felt way too goddamned long. I must have been screaming my lungs out, or at least trying to. But eventually, the light came on and Bec was shaking me like crazy, pretty much shouting at me to wake up. And, well, I basically stayed up reading for the next hour because I couldn't bring myself to try and sleep again.'

'And did anything else happen when you finally did get back to sleep?' Lauren asked. He shook his head.

'Nothing at all. I woke up to my alarm like normal. I was pretty groggy from lack of sleep but that's about it.' He shrugged.

'Hmm, I see,' Lauren said as she contemplated her visitor's story. Aiden thought she almost looked disappointed that he had nothing else to add. But that would be ridiculous, surely. She wasn't listening to his experiences for her own entertainment.

'So, we know you've had some sleep paralysis before. When you were younger,' Lauren began thoughtfully after a few moments' silence. Aiden nodded.

'Yeah, just a few times when I was like, fifteen or sixteen. It just, sort of randomly happened every few months. I never really thought to talk to anyone about it. Mum and Dad never knew. I just thought I was overtired and couldn't wake up properly. It would always happen around exam time. Nothing like this though.'

Somehow, speaking about the near forgotten, milder experiences of his youth made Aiden feel a bit better. It encouraged him that it was just a weird mental phenomenon and that his fears were unfounded.

'That does make sense. I'm sure you've looked into this sort of thing at some point?'

'I kind of never bothered to be honest. Not until yesterday. Just a quick internet search really, so I don't know too much,' Aiden admitted.

'Well, I can't say I'm an expert, but I have dealt with a few similar cases before,' Lauren said.

'From what I know, the paralysis is basically a scenario when your brain essentially wakes up before your body does. You become aware of yourself and your surroundings just like you would normally. But because your body is still in a powered-down state, there seems to be a disconnect between it and the brain. Does that make sense?' She looked questioningly to Aiden but he was confident she knew what she was talking about. Lauren was simply inviting him into the conversation, to verify he understood and avoid their meeting turning into a one-sided lecture. Aiden liked that.

'Yeah, I get it. That's basically all I got online, too. That's why it feels like I can't breathe even though I am. Why I can't seem to make a sound. My body just hasn't worked out I'm awake yet so I don't feel anything.' Talking about the clinical side of things helped to put his experiences into perspective. If he detached from the emotional side of things, the rational side could help him feel better.

'That's right,' Lauren agreed.

'Apparently the paralysis can feel like it's taking ages when most cases only last for about a minute or two. But, did you know research has shown the brain is still processing as though you are dreaming sometimes? It makes sense, doesn't it, that if the limbic system, the part of the brain responsible for all of our emotions, is overactive, you might have some very lucid experiences?' Though she spoke casually enough, Aiden could sense such topics of the mind fascinated her. He didn't mind them himself but certainly wasn't as intrigued as the counsellor.

'So, you're basically saying I would be imagining things?' he asked. He wasn't upset with the idea. Far from it, considering the alternatives were either some serious illness or there actually was some supernatural presence involved.

Yeah, somehow I don't think that's it, he thought. He never took easily to superstitious rubbish.

'Yes, basically. But, because you are dreaming, it can feel extremely real. So, if having a nightmare when you're asleep is scary, I can only imagine what it must be like to think it's actually happening in reality,' Lauren said.

'I guess that means I've just been dreaming about ghosts or something?' That cold tingle was back now that Aiden thought about that thing watching him again. He certainly hoped it was just a dream.

'I suppose so. I think I read somewhere that visions of intruders or spirits are fairly common when people have the paralysis. It might even help explain why so many people believe in alien abductions or religious experiences. I certainly don't envy you. I wouldn't be surprised if I imagined creepy crawlies and spiders everywhere if I went through it, blech!' Lauren said with a shudder.

'What makes you say that?' Aiden asked. There was a very different feel to this conversation than during their other appointments. Somehow, despite the topic being wholly unsettling, the light-hearted manner in which they spoke helped Aiden to feel content.

'Well, if the theory that you experience your fears and nightmares while only being half asleep is true, surely it makes sense that different people might have different experiences? I, myself am scared of spiders and bugs where someone else might be scared of ghosts,' Lauren explained. Aiden saw her point. Lots of fears were shared by lots of people, but everybody was different.

'Yeah, I get it. I'm not a fan of spiders either. But maybe I've just had something else on my mind lately,' he agreed.

'Hmm, and what have you been thinking of lately? The paralysis is thought to come about mostly through stress. That must be why you had it during exams back at school.'

'Ah, now we're getting to it. If it is just a mental thing, how do I get rid of it? Probably drugs and lifestyle changes?' Aiden said with an air of sarcasm. He had been through a lot of mental trials in the past. He had tried so many different types of antidepressants and techniques during his battles with depression that he knew the routine. Lauren laughed lightly.

'Pretty much, yeah. I don't actually think there is much we can do medically. Some supplements to help you relax and sleep, but apart from that, I think it's all about destressing. So, what's been going on?'

'I honestly don't know. Everything has been fine lately,' Aiden replied with a shrug. Lauren looked unconvinced.

'Come on, Aiden. You know stress can just be all the little things rolled into one. Finances, personal space, work, lack of sleep. It all builds up,' she said, clearly encouraging him to consider everything he could. Aiden took his glasses off and used the hem of his shirt to clean the lenses while he thought.

'I dunno. Bec's doing fine. Hannah's excelling at school,' he said slowly. Lauren lightly shook her head.

'What about you?' she persisted. Aiden felt on the spot, but he knew that was exactly what Lauren intended.

'Hmmm. I mean, we could always do with more money. It would be nice if I could provide more for us all. Working at a café doesn't exactly bring in a lot,' he thought aloud.

'Mhmm, and how is work going? You're still enjoying it?'

'Yeah, I think so.'

'You don't sound so sure?'

'No, I mean, I do like it. But... I dunno, I thought I might have been doing something a bit more... substantial by now. I mean, Jesus, I'm nearly thirty-four and I'm stuck making coffees.' Aiden grimaced.

Lauren found the sweet spot apparently. She sat back, gazing at him, watching his reaction. Neither Aiden nor Lauren were very surprised by his sudden revelation. He had done pretty well in high school. His grades were good, no matter how stressed he might have gotten about those bloody exams. He was interested in studying law at university. He could have been a lawyer; perhaps even pursued a position as a judge one day. But as often happens, life got in the way. Aiden and Bec met when he was sixteen in year ten. There were definitely sparks and it wasn't long before they were going out. Bec was set on becoming a doctor. She wasn't sure what speciality she would have chosen, but she knew she wanted to work in medicine. Aiden could see their lives before them. They would study, settle down in their careers, get married, have kids, grow old. But sometimes things don't happen the way you want them. Aiden and Bec weren't stupid. They gave in to their teenage desires but they were safe. Cautious even.

Sometimes cautious just isn't enough, Aiden thought as his youth flashed before his mind.

A year later, Hannah was born, Aiden had dropped out of high school after completing year eleven to get a job. His parents told him what he was in for. They weren't going to pay away his troubles and he had to support his partner and daughter now. Bec's parents were less strict but neither Aiden nor Bec wanted to rely on their good will. Aiden worked a fast-food place first, but that barely covered the nappies. He got a job at a service station too. He didn't mind at the time. He would do anything for Bec and Hannah then just as he would now. But his dreams of studying went out the window the moment Bec told him she was pregnant.

'Aiden? Do you think you might still have a little bit of resentment tucked away in there somewhere?' Lauren asked. She was leaning forward, her eyes fixed on his in an attempt to get his attention. Aiden snapped out of his thoughts. He got the impression it wasn't the first time she had asked the question.

'Shit, I want to say no...' he said slowly. A wave of guilt came over him. How could he possibly still be harbouring any frustration at that? It was ancient history now. He loved his family more than anything in the world.

'It's okay to think about the life that might have been and get upset sometimes. Hell, do you think I wanted to spend my life in this little office talking people out of their vicious cycles of depression and anxiety?' Lauren smiled. Aiden couldn't resist chuckling with her.

'What, you mean you don't like telling me how lucky I am and how grateful I should be?' he joked with her.

'Well, when you put it that way.' Lauren looked thoughtful before laughing softly. 'Anyway, you know it's okay, don't you? To wonder if the grass on the other side is really that green or if it's just a fake lawn sometimes?'

'Yeah, yeah. Still feels like shit to realise when you do though,' Aiden said with a nod.

'Hey, I know you. You love Bec and Hannah so much. I don't think you need to worry about this. And now that Hannah is growing up, who's to say you can't look into studying again soon anyway?' Lauren added. She spoke positively and Aiden smiled, but he didn't really share her enthusiasm. To be honest, he didn't even know what he would want to study anymore, even if he had the time and could afford it.

'Yeah. It's not real. Just... wondering, like you say,' he said quietly.

*

'So, Lauren didn't mention anything about me having to trade you in for a new husband, did she?' Bec called out.

She was sitting in bed, leaning back on her pillows with a book in her hands. Aiden heard her voice, but her words were slightly muffled under the sound of him brushing his teeth. The door to the bathroom was open and Aiden could see his wife in the corner of his eye. Her dark hair draped freely about her creamy neck and shoulders while she continued looking down at her book as she spoke.

Multitasking. How does she do it? Aiden thought with a smile. He could never focus on two things at once. He had to mute the TV if someone were talking to him and he would have to read the same sentence over and over if their roles were reversed right now. He finished brushing, bent down and spit the toothpaste into the sink.

'Oh yeah, I'm a total dud, babe. You really need an upgrade. Maybe they'll be offering new husbands with the next phone,' he said.

Bec chuckled, though she kept reading. Aiden cleaned himself up before switching off the light and heading to the bed.

'Seriously though, what did she say?' Bec must have been genuinely interested as she set her book down on her lap and looked at her husband. Aiden slipped under the sheets beside her.

'Meh, not great, not terrible. Looks like it's all down to stress and I just have to take it easy until it passes.' Bec snorted.

'What have *you* got to be stressed about? You've got a family that loves you, a steady job... a dog.' She grinned. Aiden laughed.

'That's what I said but Lauren wasn't convinced. I need lots of bedrest, I get first pick of what we watch aaaand, oh yeah, lots more sex.'

'Excuse me? Now I know you don't tell her anything! She doesn't know what I have to go through for you once a month,' Bec said before biting her tongue in a playful manner.

'No, no, I told her about that. She said you have to try harder. Twice a month at least,' Aiden replied. He lay on his side and reached over, gently stroking Bec's side. She giggled at his touch and his jokes.

'Twice a month? Screw that, you can do that yourself.'

'Yeah, yeah, come here.' He leaned in, reaching around Bec and pulling her close. She laughed as she fell beside him and they shared a loving kiss.

'So, just stress, huh?' Bec asked quietly after their lips parted and they lay beside one another. Aiden nodded.

'Uh-huh. Ironically, the best way to fight sleep paralysis is to adopt "good sleep hygiene",' he said, quoting the term Lauren had used. 'Basically, just take some valerian, drink some milk, try and get a good night's sleep so I'm all rested when it's time to wake up again.'

'Pfft, that sounds pretty boring. Couldn't we just… wear you out?' As she spoke, Bec slid her hand under the sheets and cupped Aiden's crotch through his shorts. He looked at her with a glint in his eye.

'Oooh, you willing to take, hmmmm, three minutes out of your reading time?' he asked. Bec looked troubled.

'Hmm, a whole three minutes? I dunno…' she said, looking doubtful. Aiden looked down at her. With her hand still cupping his crotch, he felt his desires grow. Even in the simple, grey t-shirt Bec wore to bed, Aiden could make out the soft, inviting curves of her breasts.

'Maybe I could try for ten minutes? I need to really wear myself out,' he said slyly. He felt Bec's hand massage his groin, arousing him further.

'Oh, I bet you do. And I mean, it's all to help you… destress, isn't it?' She rolled onto her back, raising her arm above her head and lying rather invitingly. Aiden ran his hand gently up Bec's side, sliding under her shirt. The feeling of her warm skin drove him wild and when she gave a small, pleasured moan when his hand softly cupped her bare breast, he knew the night was about to get a lot better.

*

Aiden opened his eyes. He found himself in darkness but slowly, very slowly, he could start to make out the chest of drawers beside the bed. He was lying on his side, facing outward and staring at the darkened wall. His first instinct was to roll over, change position and drift back off to sleep. But he couldn't move.

Oh, fuck, again? Really? he thought. He realised that numb sensation had enveloped him again, giving him an impression of floating in nothingness. An unrelenting sense of panic washed over him as the suffocation began to take hold. *Okay, just calm the hell down. You know this is nothing. You're fine. You're breathing,* he thought, willing himself to try and relax. It was exactly what Lauren had advised him to do. The panic, the sense of doom, they were just emotional responses as his brain tried to cope with the disconnect to his body. He just needed to think it out rationally. It had happened before and he had been fine. If he truly weren't breathing, it wouldn't be too long before he blacked out. That had never happened and Aiden convinced himself that wasn't going to happen this time either. *Everything is fine. Just need to wait it out, you idiot.*

While the pressure that he couldn't breathe was still there, Aiden felt himself calming down, if only a little. If he kept this up, it could be at least a little more bearable before he could force out a moan to wake Bec up. But then, the thing that had troubled Aiden in the back of his mind, even as he lay down to sleep after the sexual bliss he had shared with his wife, emerged. As he lay on his side, he knew Bec was behind him, sleeping peacefully. He couldn't feel her, but her knew she was there. But he felt something else. *It's nothing. It's nothing. It's just your imagination,* he repeated, though his thoughts were less cohesive than before. It was watching him. He could feel it's stare in the nook of his neck, as though it were merely inches behind him. Whatever it was, it was leering intently at him like a cat watches an injured bird. *It's nothing. It's not real. It's… God fucking damn it!*

Aiden lost track of his mantra as that feeling of being watched broke him. The panic set back in. His lungs were on fire. Without thinking, Aiden screamed. At least he tried to. Did he even make any bloody sound at all? He couldn't tell. A loud bang, like the slamming of a door rang in Aiden's ears. It came from behind, from where the bedroom door would have been. Was it Bec? Maybe she had been up in the kitchen and he hadn't noticed her missing? Had Hannah woken up and barged in? Why would she do that? Aiden wanted to call out. To ask who it was. But he couldn't. Yet somehow, he felt like whoever it was, wasn't friendly. Aiden couldn't do anything but lie there, waiting for... he didn't know what. He felt those eyes still on him but he tried to focus again.

Calm down. Just calm down. It's just your imagination, but his thoughts froze in their tracks. Did he just hear a footstep? It sounded slow, heavy and deliberate. Aiden waited, surely panting fearfully for breath even though he couldn't feel it. There was another footstep. Closer. Then another. It moved slowly. Torturously slowly. Aiden tried screaming again. He needed to wake Bec so she could help him. Or did he need to wake her so she could protect herself? He didn't know what was real anymore. Was he imagining it or was there really a fucking intruder in their bedroom? *Jesus, please, Bec, wake up. Please!* Aiden fought with all his might to move. To scream. To beg.

'Hello, Aiden.' The sudden voice froze Aiden's heart. His eyes went wide. He couldn't see anything but the dark silhouettes of the chest of drawers and the pictures hanging on the wall. The voice sounded so close, as though whoever had spoken was leaning over his head. The voice was hoarse. Somehow hollow. It was like a hissed whisper from someone who had smoked two packs a day for forty years. Aiden tried in vain to glance up to see the owner of the voice. *What the fuck? This can't be real. There's nothing there,* he thought but then, there was a dry, taunting cackle right next to him.

'Oh, believe me, Aiden. I'm... reeeeal,' the voice croaked. It lingered like the last note in a song. Aiden didn't know what to think. Could he really be imagining this? It felt so real.

'Don't worry, Aiden. I'll take care of you...' the voice continued. It was as though whoever was speaking was perched on the bed behind Aiden's back, wedged between him and Bec. The intruder must have been leaning over him, just behind his peripheral vision.

What are you? Aiden found himself thinking. He couldn't help it. It was too convincing. Something was there. The voice laughed again.

'I'm… a friend, Aiden. Here to take care of you during this… difficult time.' The words might have been nice on paper, but the hoarse voice carried an undoubtedly sinister tone. It spoke slowly. Hissing and grinding. Sheer terror gripped Aiden's heart as it spoke.

You're not a friend. You're not really there. You can't be. He tried to trust his own logic. There couldn't be anyone there. How could they hear his thoughts? Suddenly, the voice barked like an aggressive dog.

'I've said it already, Aiden! I'm real. You know I'm… real. I had to say… hello.' Somehow the voice seemed nearer if that were possible.

Aiden could hear himself groaning, moaning like a stroke victim as he internally screamed with unrelenting fear. He saw it. A shadow. A shadow of someone, something. A head hovering over him. *Fuck! Fuck! Oh God, fucking shit! What are you? What do you want?!* Aiden was thinking with incomprehensible panic. There was another, sickening chuckle. As though whatever it was, was enjoying watching Aiden's horror. Enjoying the feeling of it.

'I'm… Gary,' the voice introduced itself in a strangely casual way despite its vileness. It was a common enough name, but Aiden didn't know anyone named Gary. Even so, it seemed eerily familiar to him.

'You and I are going to be… veeeery close from now on… Aiden. I can't wait to… meet the family.' The voice laughed and somehow, it sounded worse than ever. Aiden was suddenly not only afraid for himself here and now. He was afraid for Bec. For Hannah.

No. No! You leave them the fuck alone. Whatever you are. Fuck you! He was screaming in his head. If he could speak the words aloud, they probably would have been little more than weak, defiant sobs due to the immense dread he was immersed in.

'Oh no, Aiden. I'm not leaving you… or them alone. You and I are together now, Aiden. Forever. And they… they will do… nicely.' Again, the voice lingered on its last word, devolving into a threatening hiss which grew closer and closer. No matter how Aiden tried to look away, he could still see the shadow over him. He managed to tightly close his eyes.

Jesus. This isn't real. It isn't real. It's just me. My imagination. Calm down. Just calm the fuck down. With his eyes closed, Aiden started his mantra again. The voice laughed but this time, it seemed to drift further away. Sort of like a thought that slowly dissipates into nothing as one might struggle to remember it. The staring was still biting into the back of Aiden's head but slowly, slowly it became less intense. There were no more sounds. No more threats or evil voices. Aiden felt like he could almost breathe again. Slowly, he opened his eyes.

'AM I STILL NOT REAL, YOU MEAT FUCK?!' the voice screamed in Aiden's face, roaring like the sudden onset of a gale at sea. The shadow was right before Aiden's face. Sheer darkness blotted his view. He could see nothing but two, blood red eyes that burned like wildfire. Just looking at them seemed to burn Aiden's own eyes as though he had just been staring into the sun. Beneath the eyes, amongst the mass of darkness, was a wide, gaping maw. A vile, clumpy black goop was running down the razor-sharp teeth which were jagged and menacing. The sudden smell was revolting and Aiden felt as though he might vomit from the foul odour alone. He shot upright, screaming wildly like a man insane. An instant later, the bedroom lamp flicked on.

'Aiden?! Baby! Honey, honey, calm down. Please calm down.' Bec was pleading with Aiden. She was trying to control him, holding his shoulder and rubbing his back but Aiden could barely feel her touch.

'What the hell? Is everything okay? Mum? Dad?' Aiden could just make out Hannah's voice when the bedroom door opened. Bec was talking to her, but Aiden couldn't hear her.

'Oh God. Shit. Oh Jesus, shit… shit… fucking hell,' he finally panted, speaking in jittering whispers. He snapped his head back and forth, looking all over the room. There was no sign of… Gary anywhere.

VISITING THE PARENTS
REBECCA

Bec took a sip of her freshly made coffee. It wasn't bad for an instant brand, but she had become pretty spoilt with good coffee since Aiden had perfected his skill at the café. Even so, she appreciated the bitter-sweetness of the grind, softened with a little milk. Bec hadn't lost too much sleep the previous night, maybe an hour at most. She felt as though her heart had leapt out of her chest when she woke in the middle of the night to Aiden thrashing and screaming. When she had managed to settle him down enough to speak, he had said it was just a nightmare.

'Some bloody nightmare,' she had said. Aiden admitted he had another bout of that sleep paralysis but he wouldn't go into the specifics. Bec couldn't imagine what he must have dreamed or just how bad that paralysis could be to have made him so frightened. She didn't know what to do, other than to comfort him. She held Aiden for a long while afterwards, listening to his ragged breathing and feeling him shuffle with unease. Eventually, they had fallen asleep but Bec wasn't sure which of them had done so first. Yet when Aiden's alarm went off the next morning, he sluggishly got up and ready for work as he always did. Bec had asked him if he was alright.

'Maybe you should take the day off?'

But Aiden just shook his head. He told her again how it had just been a bad night and there was no need to skip work over a bit of a poor night's sleep. He seemed so collected, so back to normal that Bec trusted his judgement. Being Saturday, she lay back down for a sleep in and when she properly woke maybe an hour later, Aiden was gone. The morning had then progressed as a typical Saturday for Bec and Hannah. They had a simple breakfast before Hannah took Leena for a walk while Bec showered and put on a load of washing. Bec had previously planned to visit her parents that morning and Hannah agreed to join her. Now, she was sitting with her parents around the coffee table in their living room. Hannah was very comfortable in her grandparents' house and she was currently in the kitchen, fetching some biscuits for them all.

'So, when were you planning on going to Queensland?' Bec's mother, Pamela Hudson, asked. At fifty-eight years old, Pamela was doing well. Like her husband, Thomas, she was a little overweight but it seemed to work for her. She had always worn her dark hair at a length shorter than her shoulders and, though there was no trace of grey amongst the brunette yet, Bec knew that was due to dye.

'September. We're yet to really set the dates but I'm pretty sure that's when the weather is at its best up there,' she replied as she set her coffee mug down on the table.

'Still have to get through the winter months first then,' Pamela responded. It was a rather nothing statement. The sort of light banter Bec knew so well of her mum.

'I figure it will give us something to look forward to,' Bec said and her mother nodded to her logic.

'What about you, Hannah? Looking forward to it?' Thomas called into the kitchen while his granddaughter put the old biscuit tin away. It was one of those blue, round tins that used to house some old Danish butter cookies. Bec was certain those things were accepted as wages by the older generations because everyone older than fifty seemed to have one.

'Yeah, it's gonna be awesome. I haven't been to the Gold Coast yet,' Hannah said, her face lighting up. She walked back into the living room with the plateful of biscuits. If Bec were hosting, she would have seen nothing wrong with just bringing down the tin and letting people dig in. But her mum had a different way of doing things. There was the right way and the wrong way to serve houseguests and both Bec and Hannah knew it.

'Well, you will be beating us at any rate, Hanny. We've been to Brisbane, Cairns, the Sunshine Coast, but we've never been to the Gold Coast.' Thomas chuckled while looking to his wife. Pamela just waved a hand dismissively.

'Oh, what would we do at a place like that? Full of party people, tourists and theme parks. Give me a beach to settle down on and I'm set,' she said.

'You do know they have beaches there, right, Grandma? I mean, it's the Gold *Coast*,' Hannah said and Bec smiled at her daughter's wit.

'She's got you there, hon.' Thomas laughed as he leaned over and playfully tapped Pamela's arm.

'Well, that may be, but I'm sure it would be a very busy beach too,' she said defiantly. 'Exactly, it's going to be great! Tell them what you're looking forward to at the beach, Hannah,' Bec joined in. Her daughter looked at her with apparent uncertainty. Bec just grinned. She knew how her parents would react.

'We're going to ride jet skis,' Hannah said finally. Thomas put his hand up to his mouth to stifle a laugh while he glanced at his wife. Pamela's eyes went wide. She looked to Bec, then to Hannah, then back to Bec before throwing her arms in the air.

'You're going to let her go on one of those death traps? Really? And don't you know how loud they are?' she said.

'The louder they are, the faster they are, right, Hannah?' Bec retorted with a smile. Hannah grinned and nodded.

'Yep. I can't wait,' she said. The excitement was evident in her voice.

'Ugh, on your own heads be it. But don't complain to me when she breaks something and can't go back to school for weeks,' Pamela said after clicking her tongue and shaking her head.

'Bah, what's wrong if the girl has some fun? Good on you, Hanny,' Thomas said. Bec appreciated her father's positivity. She liked to tease her mother like that sometimes because she could honestly be quite a prude, but her dad usually backed her up.

'So, wasn't Auntie Anne supposed to be coming today?' Hannah asked while she took up one of the sugar-coated biscuits.

'Hmm, we'll see. Apparently, she's got a lot on today. The kids have been giving her grief all week and she's fallen behind,' Pamela replied. Bec could see the disappointment, no matter how quick and subtle it was, in her mother's face.

'Those two do sound a handful lately, don't they?' she said in defence of her sister. Bec had just spoken to Anne earlier that week. It seemed every morning was a battle to get her boys ready for school. Billy in particular had taken to refusing to get out of bed no matter what she did.

'Well, you know what I think about that, but apparently it's damn near illegal to smack your kids these days,' Thomas said with a disgruntled sigh.

'Dad!' Bec scoffed and Hannah laughed.

'Oh, we never smacked our girls, Tom!' Pamela snapped to him and Thomas shrugged.

'Well, we never had to! Mind you, if you acted the way those boys do with their mother, Bec,' he said while pointing his finger at his daughter. Bec looked shocked and innocent.

'Oh, like I would have ever deserved a smack! I mean, Anne, maybe,' she said and Thomas dropped his dominant pretence right away. His lips curled into a smile and he took up his cup of coffee.

'Rebecca! Your sister wouldn't have done anything to warrant a smack either,' Pamela said. If there was one thing Bec knew about her mother, it was that she couldn't tolerate any form of discontent in the family. At least not when it was displayed so obviously, even only in jest. 'Anyway, Michael and Billy are what, ten and twelve? If you tried to hit them, they would just hit you back, grandad,' Hannah pointed out. It was Thomas' turn to scoff.

'Hah, I'd like to see them try,' he said.

'Maybe let's not find out, hey, Dad?' Bec suggested and her mother gave a curt nod of approval.

'Indeed. Anne and Dennis will just have to work those boys out themselves,' she said with a note of finality in her voice. Thomas raised his eyebrows and glanced to Bec and Hannah as though non-verbally advising they drop the subject, lest they poked the bear too much. Bec bit her tongue and Hannah pulled out her phone while making sure not to let her grandma see her smile.

'So, how is Aiden doing? It's a shame he couldn't make it today,' Pamela continued, apparently having decided to change the subject.

'It is, but he was needed at the café. Not that we mind. More money to save for the holiday,' Bec said as her mind wandered to her husband. 'Anyway, he hasn't been bad. Well, that is aside from his sleeping.'

'Oh? What's wrong? He can't get to sleep?' Pamela asked, her ears perked for gossip.

Typical mum. Always on the lookout for something amiss to talk about, Bec thought.

'Sort of. He hasn't had so much trouble dropping off as he has staying asleep. He's been waking up in the middle of the night,' she explained. She looked over to Hannah who might have been listening but her eyes were glued to the screen of her smartphone.

'He should get that checked out. Might be sleep apnoea. I should be keeping an eye on that myself, apparently,' Thomas said.

'Oh, don't you worry. The doctor said you could stop breathing. I'll let you know if you ever stop snoring,' Pamela said and Thomas shrugged.

'Just think of it as a nice reminder that I *am* still breathing.' He grinned.

'Thanks, Dad, but it isn't sleep apnoea,' Bec said.

'Oh? So, what's going on?' Pamela persisted. She was looking to Bec with keen interest now.

'It's nothing really. Just stress-related. Something called sleep paralysis.' Both her mum and dad looked curious, clearly unfamiliar with the condition. Hannah lowered her phone into her lap and looked at her mother.

'Paralysis? Dad's alright, isn't he?' she asked with evident concern. No doubt the word brought all sorts of ideas to her head of wheelchairs and crippling diseases.

'Yes, your dad is fine, Hannah. It's not as bad as it sounds, certainly not an illness. It's more like … night terrors. More psychological than anything,' Bec explained with a soft smile. Her words seemed to put her dad at ease too, but her mum's eyes narrowed. Hannah looked less concerned now though. She grew up into a family whose members often needed therapy and antidepressants so a new mental issue wasn't so dramatic in her mind. Pamela obviously felt differently.

'Psychological? He *is* still seeing that counsellor, isn't he?' she asked flatly. Bec sighed while her dad averted his gaze. He was more of the mind that such concerns were private. But try telling that to her mother.

'Yes, he's still seeing Lauren, Mum. Really, there is nothing to worry about,' Bec said, speaking with more confidence than she truly felt. She was actually quite worried about Aiden, not only because his experiences were clearly very upsetting for him but also because she had no idea what had triggered such stress in him. She thought everything had been going so well lately. But, while Bec was worried about her husband, she couldn't deny she had been feeling on edge for the last couple of days, herself. She felt as though she always had to look over her shoulder. Like she was being watched, even though she never saw anyone. Save for that weird experience on Thursday. Bec felt uneasy about it, but she wasn't sure why. It was something to do with Mr Meadows, wasn't it? For some reason, the more she tried to think about it, the more of a blank space formed in her mind. Whatever it had been, it had surely just been her imagination.

'Well, if you say so. I just remember you saying something very similar last time,' Pamela said while paying more than a necessary amount of attention to her cup of tea. Bec swallowed down her personal concerns and looked sternly to her mother.

'Mum, that was years ago. Aiden hasn't gone through anything even close to that for a long time.' She hated that her mother had always seemed to have a chip on her shoulder about Aiden's depression. While the conversation hadn't turned sour, there was something in her mother's tone that just irritated her. An unmissable note of disapproval. Bec wondered if her mother would ever forgive Aiden for causing his family such strife, even in his time of personal turmoil.

'Alright, say no more. I'm sure you know what you're talking about,' Pamela said dismissively. Bec sighed and glanced to her daughter. Hannah quickly looked up to her mother, discreetly rolled her eyes, and returned her attention to her phone. Hannah was not unfamiliar with her grandmother's attitudes and Bec admired the way she could just let the subtle digs slide off of her shoulders.

'Yes, we're fine, Mum. Trust me. Aiden just needs to destress a bit,' she said with a little bite in her voice. Pamela pursed her lips and took a sip of her tea.

'See, it's all under control, honey. Let it be,' Thomas finally said. He spoke casually, as though he couldn't feel the growing tension in the room between his daughter and her mother. Bec knew it was his way of trying to defuse the situation.

'I know. I know,' Pamela said huffily. At that moment, the chime of the doorbell rang through the house.

'Ah, I'll get it.' She set her cup down and quickly rose to her feet.

'Looks like Anne might have made it after all,' Thomas said while his wife squeezed past him before wandering out of the room to answer the door.

'You know she just worries about you, don't you?' he asked softly while he leaned forward and looked to his daughter with a sparkle in his eyes. Bec shrugged.

'Yeah, I know. She can just be difficult sometimes,' she said bluntly. As she spoke, she could hear the muffled voice of her mother speaking down the hallway.

'Ha! You talk as though I didn't know that myself. Don't listen to your grandma, Hanny. If your mum says your dad is fine, he's just fine.' Thomas turned his attention to his granddaughter. Hannah locked the screen on her phone and set it down beside her.

'I know, Grandad,' she said simply. Hannah always got along better with her grandad than her grandma. Actually, if she had to choose, Bec would have to say she got along better with her dad too.

'Thomas, Pastor Richard is here,' Pamela announced as she stepped back into the living room, followed closely behind by a lean, mature gentleman.

'Not Anne then?' Thomas asked, looking up to his wife and their new guest before he shot up out of his chair.

'Just joking, Rich. A pleasure to have you here, of course,' he added while offering his hand which the pastor politely shook. Bec looked up to the pastor and gave him a smile and nod of greeting. She didn't know the man very well, only having attended her parents' church once or twice on special occasions, after all.

'Sorry to barge in on a family get together,' Pastor Richard said while running his fingers through his thinning, peppered hair. 'I just came to return a book Pamela had lent me and couldn't say no to the offer of a cup of coffee.'

'Oh, no need to apologise, Richard. The more the merrier! Of course, you know our daughter, Rebecca? I don't recall if you've actually met Hannah yet?' Pamela said with a renewed sense of levity.

'Yes, yes. How are you doing, Rebecca?'

'Not bad, thank you. We just thought we would pop in to see what sort of mischief these two have been getting up to lately,' Bec replied. Thomas grinned broadly at his daughter's jesting. Pamela did not.

'Ah, good, good. And I'm sorry, Hannah, was it? I don't believe we've met.' Pastor Richard didn't appear bothered by Bec's joking as her mother was.

'Hi, yes, I'm Hannah. Nice to meet you,' Hannah said politely. Bec could tell that her daughter was more or less feigning the pleasantries. She likely didn't feel a great desire to socialise with a peer of her grandparents.

Hell, what teenager would? Bec thought. Pamela invited the pastor to sit on the couch and Thomas disappeared into the kitchen to prepare their new guest's coffee.

'So, everything has been well, I trust?' Pastor Richard asked Bec's mother.

'It has been, yes, thank you. Although...' Pamela glanced to her daughter, their eyes meeting for an instant.

Don't you dare, Mum! Bec thought, but her mother spoke before she could suitably protest.

'Rebecca has just been telling us about some hard times her husband, Aiden, is going through.'

Bec gritted her teeth. The bloody woman had done it. She had brought up a topic that was not hers to discuss. And practically to a stranger at that. Pamela looked questioningly to Bec, undoubtedly trying to non-verbally push her into speaking. The pastor also turned to her with curiosity, though his expression was kinder than Pamela's.

'Oh? I do hope he isn't in too much strife?' Again, someone spoke up before Bec had the chance.

'He's fine,' Hannah said abruptly. Her voice was flat and her arms were crossed. She didn't look to anyone in the room but stared blankly to the coffee table before her.

'Rebecca? Perhaps Pastor Richard might be able to offer some advice?' Pamela pressed further. Hannah glanced to her mother, clearly uncomfortable. Bec couldn't honestly say she was feeling much better. She didn't want to share her husband's problems with a random man she didn't know, no matter what his profession.

'It's nothing really. He's just been having some sleeping problems. Well, Hannah, we'd best get that shopping done, hadn't we?' She tapped her knees, prompting her daughter to stand. Hannah quickly obliged, evidently eager to leave.

'Oh, don't be so silly, Rebecca,' Pamela said dismissively before turning to the pastor.

'You see, Richard, Aiden has a long history of depression. He's apparently been having terrible episodes at night lately. Night terrors, Rebecca said.'

'Mum! I told you it was nothing!' Bec snapped. Hannah had stepped past her and was now standing impatiently at the entrance to the hallway.

'That might be, Rebecca, but I think the thoughts of a man such as Pastor Richard's standing might be helpful,' Pamela responded haughtily. The pastor looked somewhat uncomfortable sitting between the disputing mother and daughter and he cleared his throat.

'I certainly don't mean to overstep any boundaries. I have no doubt that your mother only wishes to help you and your family in any way she is able. With that said, allow me to say only that you are all quite welcome to attend our Sunday services with Thomas and Pamela. If you have any questions, or if I can provide any assistance of a spiritual nature for your husband, you have only to ask. I shall pray for the wellbeing of you all,' the pastor spoke kindly. His manner was gentle and calm and Bec didn't doubt his sincerity. She honestly had no issue with the man. No, it was her mother who had taken it upon herself to fix her poor little daughter's broken family that upset her.

'Well, thank you. I'll mention it to Aiden. Sorry to have to run off like this but we've still a lot to do today, don't we, Hannah?' Bec said while wearing one of her best work smiles.

'Yep,' Hannah agreed curtly, now looking at her smartphone again. The short silence was broken when Thomas stepped into the living room once more from the kitchen, holding a freshly made cup of coffee. He stood there, frozen in the doorway, looking at Pamela, Pastor Richard, Hannah and Rebecca.

'Sooooo... what did I miss?' he asked lightly.

'Sorry, Dad. Hannah and I have to head off.' Bec walked forward and put her arm around her father before giving him a light peck on the cheek.

'I'll speak to you soon, alright?' she said while her dad shrugged and moved onward to pass the mug to Pastor Richard.

'Oh, alright then. So much to do, so little time, hey?' There was a note of disappointment in his voice though he acted unbothered by his daughter's sudden departure.

'Yeah, exactly. Okay, see you later, Mum. Nice seeing you again, Richard,' Bec said as she began to turn out of the room. The pastor gave a small wave and called an overly cheerful 'cheerio' before Pamela spoke up.

'Well, you know where to find us. And if Aiden does need some guidance of faith, I'm sure Pastor Richard can help!' Bec didn't turn back but gave a quick wave of her hand as she followed Hannah into the hallway and away from the awkward tension of the living room.

*

'Why does she have to do that?' Hannah asked sulkily. She and her mother were in the car, driving along the Old Centre Road towards their nearest shopping centre, East Meadow. Bec's parents lived on the same, southern side of Glen Marsh as she and her family did, so the commute was never long. Thankfully, that also meant that their local shopping hub was only ten to fifteen minutes away. Hannah was looking absently out of the passenger window and Bec could tell she was upset with her grandmother's behaviour.

'She only does it to help.' She sighed. Even though she knew it were true, she couldn't justify her mother's callous nature. Pamela always had to have the right answer and if you disagreed with her, well, she would just keep on the same track until you changed your mind.

'I know but, ugh, I dunno,' Hannah said. Bec glanced to her daughter but continued to focus on the traffic ahead of her.

'What's up?' she asked, hoping to prompt her daughter to share her thoughts. Hannah sighed, possibly wondering if she should say something or not.

'It's just... I know what Grandma and Grandad believe and I'm totally cool with that. But... why does she always bring it up? I mean,

Grandad never does, but Grandma will always mention something. This time she even brought a pastor into it,' Hannah spoke quickly, unloading her thoughts in an abrupt heap. Bec needed a moment to realise where her daughter was coming from.

'You mean, their faith? I didn't know you had a problem with that?' she asked. Bec, herself, wasn't an overly religious woman. Her parents were devout Lutherans but she had never been so involved. She did believe in God, but after some soul searching, she believed that whatever God was, it was a much more personal thing than any of the organised religions professed. Bec believed God was something unique to each individual and she didn't buy into the mythos of heaven and hell, sin and righteousness. To her, God was better described as the universe as anything else. She believed it to be whatever force had figuratively clicked its fingers and began everything that existed. Bec could tolerate her parents' strong faith because she felt it was simply their way of relating to their idea of God. But maybe Hannah wasn't so accepting?

'No, I don't have a problem with what they believe,' Hannah said. 'Well, I mean, I kind of do. I mean, talking snakes? Every living thing drowned save for a family and a couple of every animal on a boat? I mean, how do they really think *every* type of animal fit on a boat? And how did the kangaroos get there? And the penguins? Not to mention all the innocent babies and animals dying and –'

'Anyway, back to the point.' Bec interrupted her daughter's ranting. She was honestly amused by Hannah's passion, if not proud. Clearly, Hannah had no problems thinking critically if she came up with all these problems by herself.

'Oh, yeah. Sorry. I just… ugh, it makes no sense. Anyway, I just get annoyed when Grandma brings it up. You know, she'll quote something here or act all high and mighty there. And… it just really upsets me how she talks about Dad sometimes. Like there's something wrong with him and she knows the answer is in her book.'

Bec didn't know what to say. She was surprised to learn her daughter was so against the religious mindset of her grandparents. But she couldn't deny she could relate with her point. Even when Hannah was a little girl and Aiden was suffering with his depression, Bec's mother had said the best thing he could do was to find Jesus. There was no doubt that Pamela cared and wanted what was best for both Aiden and Bec, but she believed therapy and drugs could only get someone so far. After all, 'if the soul is broken, there is only one cure'. At least those were the words Bec remembered her mum using all those years ago.

'I know. She can be difficult sometimes, Hannah,' she began slowly. 'Mum just… tries to help by doing what she thinks is right. But, trust me, I know how you feel. She can really drive you crazy sometimes, huh?'

Hannah gave a weak laugh.

'Yeah. I know. It's just, I dunno, frustrating sometimes,' she said while she fiddled with the air vent in the dashboard.

'Anyway, you promise Dad is okay?' she asked after a moment's silence.

A cold shudder ran down Bec's spine though she didn't know why. It was as though Hannah mentioning her dad brought some unwanted eyes on them. She clicked the indicator on before veering into the turning lane and waiting at the light for their turn to pull into the East Meadow centre's carpark.

'I promise, Hannah. Your dad's just not sleeping well but that's all. He's fine,' she said, and though she smiled and spoke with certainty, Bec wasn't sure if she felt certain at all.

BOARDS AND BIOLOGY

HANNAH

The sunlight glittered upon the light green water of the ocean's surface. Small, fluffy clouds drifted here and there across the clear blue sky. The sound of the waves crashing upon the sandy beach and the rocky bluffs echoed throughout the bay. Despite April nearing its end and the approaching winter, today was undoubtedly a good day to spend at the beach.

Hannah's long wet hair clung to her neck and shoulders while she paddled further away from the shore on her bodyboard. She loved gliding over the light, oncoming swells and feeling the saltwater spray on her face. Ever since she was a little girl, Hannah always loved going to the beach, though the photos of her two-year-old self screaming with bright red cheeks suggested otherwise. At least Hannah enjoyed the water for as long as she could remember at any rate. There was nothing better to her than spending a hot summer's day chilling out in the water. She didn't mind swimming pools but was more enamoured by the ocean. The saltwater felt more real to her. Something about the grit and sand that was far more natural than a chlorinated, glorified bathtub. Also, there was so much more to do in the sea.

Hannah was a good swimmer and one of her favourite memories was during a holiday the family had taken to New South Wales when she was eleven. They had joined a touring group that took them a few kilometres out from the shore by boat to snorkel among the reefs. Hannah saw all kinds of fish and even glimpsed a turtle that day. She was mesmerised by the craggy reef formations, the coral, the sea sponges, the anemone. She had discovered the mysterious and alluring world within the ocean and she loved it, even though it intimidated her. Who wouldn't be at least somewhat daunted with the knowledge that, looking down into the murky depths, you would see little but darkness beyond your flippers?

The coral reefs, beautiful though they appeared, also housed thousands of creatures in hidden holes and crevices and many of those animals could bite and sting. Naturally, sharks were always a common fear among people who chose to explore the ocean's wonders but Hannah also didn't forget such things as jellyfish and stonefish. But, even if one was careful not to cross any of the hungry and poisonous residents of the oceans, there was still the water itself. Strong currents and riptides could be especially deadly and it was perhaps this very danger that Hannah's father had been considering when she heard him call from just behind her.

'Alright, I think we're out far enough, Hannah!' he shouted over the constant rushing sound of the waves on the beach.

Hannah paddled her board around, turning back to look at the yellow sands of the beach, flanked by the rocky red and brown cliffs. She and her father must have been at least forty metres out from the shore. Most of the other people in the water were closer to land, though Hannah had seen several others – surfers, she suspected – had gone out even further.

'Yeah, I think you're right, Dad. Hope we get a big one soon,' she said as she used her hands and feet to steady her board so that the nose was parallel to the beach. She saw her father doing the same, sitting on his board with his pale legs dangling in the water. While she rarely noticed it day to day, the faint tan line of her dad's arms from his shirts was so much more evident when they were at the beach. Not only because he was topless, but because the combination of the sparkling water on his skin and the bright sun caused his pale body to almost shine with light. Hannah chuckled as the image of her dad reminded her of some cringey teenage romance movies. Her father paid no notice, unashamedly flaunting his dad-bod while he paid close attention to the oncoming waves, ready to take advantage of the best one he saw.

Having not seen anything decent approaching them just yet either, Hannah glanced back to the beach. Her eyesight wasn't terrible, but without her glasses on she could only just make out the shapes of the people on the sand. She was fairly sure she could see her mum, standing knee-deep in the water and throwing a ball for Leena to fetch. The dog was undoubtedly having a wonderful time as she bounded through the shallow water. Hannah loved days like today. Every month, the family would try to spend at least one Sunday together, even if it just meant lounging on the couch for a movie marathon on a cold, rainy day. But Hannah much preferred this and she was grateful the weather was so good. While her legs and arms were cool within the water, her back was beginning to toast in the sun. Hannah was about to roll off her board and dip her body into the water for a moment before her dad spoke again.

'Ooooh, this could be a good one! What do you think, bug?'

She looked back and followed his pointing hand. The second of the two oncoming waves was quickly gaining momentum, the white foam beginning to spray and hiss as it approached.

'Let's go for it!' She steadied herself on her board and slowly began to direct it forward. The first swell passed under them, the board heaving fluidly over the water. Her dad directed his board too while she watched the wave get closer, becoming more boisterous every second.

'Okay... wait... aaaaand... go!' she cried excitedly. Her dad enjoyed bodyboarding, her mum too, but Hannah was the expert in the family. Aiden followed his daughter's direction and began to ride the wave. Having aimed back towards the beach, Hannah felt the power of the wave begin to propel her forward. Water sprayed in her face and her hair whipped in the wind. She whooped and hollered just as she heard her father doing the same with the exhilaration of riding the wave. As the water crashed onward, Hannah felt herself picking up speed and she tightly gripped her board to avoid losing it under her. Her dad was not so lucky and she laughed when he tipped forward with a yelp before he became lost to the mass of white, roaring foam. The beach was much closer now and Hannah could easily make out her mum, who was indeed standing in the water.

Leena was proudly returning to her owner with her ball in her mouth while her mum was standing with her hand holding down her blue, wide-brimmed hat as she watched her daughter approach. She cheered and waved as Hannah continued to ride the wave, feeling as though she were on top of the world. The wave had grown in size and would soon crash in a crescendo upon the shore. But, as the water became more chaotic, her board trembled. There was a sudden jerk in the wrong direction and she was toppled from the board and engulfed by the water. She managed to hold her breath just in time as heavy, rushing water enveloped her. She let herself become limp, rolling with the water and praying she didn't run into any rocks hidden in the sand. It had never happened to her but she knew it was always possible. Finally, as the wave began to subside, Hannah felt herself more in control and she rose to the surface and gasped for air. At that moment, a sharp pain burst in her face, just below her eye.

'Ow, shit!' she cried out as she clamped her hand to her face. Though she didn't normally swear, her parents didn't mind *some* words if the situation called for it. Hannah felt being smacked in the face by her own board was probably worth it.

'Ugh, that was stupid,' she spluttered, coughing up some water as she took hold of her board. The strap on her wrist had secured the line of the board so she wouldn't lose it but as she emerged, the wave had pelted her own board at her. Hannah could hear the familiar sound of her father's laughter as she blinked the salty water from her eyes.

'Hahaha! You alright, bug? That was hilarious,' he said as he waded his way closer to where Hannah stood. He was wiping his face with one hand while trailing his own board behind him with the other.

'Oh, ha-ha, it's not like you went down ages before I did!' Hannah retorted after making sure there was no blood on her fingers from her cheek.

'Hey, your dad knows his limits, that's all.' Her dad shrugged. She looked to him, unconvinced.

'Nah, you just lost it. You were leaning too much again, weren't you?' she teased. Her dad did tend to push too far forward and let the wave push him over from underneath.

'Nu-uh!' he snapped back, splashing water at Hannah for good measure.

'Yeah, real mature, *Dad*.' She laughed with her father. She truly enjoyed daughter/dad times like this.

'You sure you're alright? Good for another one before I tag your mother in?'

With Leena running rampant on the beach, it was necessary for at least one member of the family to attempt to keep her under control while the other rode the waves and they each took turns. Hannah's cheek was throbbing but the initial pain and shock had certainly subsided.

'Yeah, one more. But then let's go see if mum wants to eat, maybe? I dunno what time it is but I'm starving,' she said as her stomach grumbled.

'Good idea. Come on, let's get out there. I'll show you how to really crash and burn.' Her dad grinned.

Hannah followed his lead and began to wade back out to sea. It wasn't long before they were both lying on their boards and paddling out once more. This time though, despite the enjoyment of the day, Hannah felt troubled. Something about the way her father had asked if she was alright just made her think about his own wellbeing. She hadn't actually spoken to him at all about his problems, having only just learned about them from her mother the day before. She wondered about his night terrors. What was actually going on? If he was having trouble sleeping and was stressed, he definitely wasn't showing it at the moment. Hannah thought to ask her dad about it.

To ask what he was going through. If there was anything she could do to help.

'Hey, Dad?' she started while they paddled alongside one another. He glanced to her before looking forward again.

'What's up, bug?'

But Hannah bit her tongue. *What if bringing it up will just upset him? He's having fun. Why should I ruin his day?* she thought. Her dad looked at her inquisitively.

'Just wanted to check you're still having fun?' she ended up asking meekly. Her dad smiled at her, but there was something in his face, something which made her wonder if he wasn't hiding something.

Damn it, I did upset him.

'Yeah, of course! Today is awesome, isn't it? The sun, the water, my family – what more could a guy ask for?' he exclaimed, perhaps a little too enthusiastically though Hannah couldn't tell if she was just looking for things to pick at now.

'Hmm, fish and chips?' she asked, hoping that she could help her dad to forget his problems once again. Her father groaned like a hungry animal.

'Mmmm, yes. And potato cakes! After this wave, I'm totally grabbing our lunch.' He certainly seemed to be his usual, old self.

A few minutes later and they were once again floating in the water, waiting for a good wave to ride back to the shore. Looking back to the beach, Hannah could see dark patches of seaweed collecting in the water. It was good this was going to be their last ride for a while. Hannah hated getting caught in the seaweed. She looked back out to the ocean, reading the oncoming swells.

'Ready to go, Dad? This could be a good one,' she said when the tell-tale signs of foam began to form. Aiden shook his head to whip the water from his hair.

'Let's do it,' he replied, putting on a bad American accent in some ridiculous attempt to sound like some action movie hero.

Hannah laughed and shook her head at her father's antics. The wave came closer and they readied their boards. The seconds passed torturously slowly but then, the moment came. The wave's unrelenting power continued onward and forced their bodyboards along with it. Daughter and father glided over the wave, utilising its sheer force to propel themselves forward. To Hannah's dismay, her dad overtook her, his board rushing through the water before her.

'Oh, come on!' she shouted as she heard his boastful laughter faintly among the roaring waves. An instant later, he plummeted into the wave and Hannah cheered.

'Ha, I knew I'd last longer!' she cried, knowing full well that while he was being rolled under the water, her dad wouldn't be able to hear her. Her smile dropped when she saw an ominously dark patch of seaweed directly ahead of her.

Oh crap! she thought while her fingers instinctively gripped tighter to the board. The wave urged her onward and the board skittered over the surface of the water. Hannah could feel the tendrils of seaweed tickling her feet and tangling in her toes. But she was going to make it. She was still in control of the board and she would pass over the patch in a second.

The slimy strips of seaweed wildly twisted and curled around her ankle. It felt so restrictive she couldn't help but give a yelp of shock and uncertainty. As the water powered on, Hannah's board trembled. She was still in control, she was still riding the wave but then, suddenly, the seaweed around her ankle became taut.

A hoarse cry was jerked out from deep in her chest as she was instantly sliding back, her board still raging forward with the wave. The violent water cascaded over her and she was instantly submerged in the sheer chaos of the wave. The saltwater burned her nostrils and throat. She hadn't had a chance to hold her breath. She desperately needed to leap out of the water to breathe but she had to wait out the wave. As the rolling began to subside, she dragged herself upward. But then, the glimmering daylight of the surface disappeared. Hannah was suddenly enshrouded in darkness.

SEAWEED! she screamed in her head. She could make out the floating tendrils in the darkness, blotting her vision of the surface. She felt the soft, gripping texture of the plant life as it wrapped around her body. The bare skin of her arms and calves was coated in it and Hannah felt it all over her wetsuit. Her lungs were near bursting for air and she frantically whipped her hands through the dense clusters of seaweed. She caught a glimpse of the light above and instantly made for it, swatting through the seaweed to get to it. The water wasn't even that deep this close to the beach; why was it so difficult to get out? A dark clump of seaweed hovered above and, as Hannah looked at it, she paused in the water.

The ebony weeds had formed into what looked to be a strange face. It was misshapen, twisted and malformed by the weeds but Hannah could definitely see a face. It wasn't a face one would see on a person though. The corners of the mouth seemed torn and ripped wide. Strange tentacles of some deep-sea flora sprouted from the mass like eyes that, instead of seeing, were reaching out in an attempt to feel her. The mouth was opening wider as the weeds drew apart and vile teeth seemed to emerge from them made from twisted and jagged bones of fish and sea creatures. Hannah made to scream. Bubbles of what little air was in her lungs rose before her. Then, she felt something tightly gripping her neck. Her hair, the collar of her wetsuit, her very skin was caught in a vice-like grip. The next thing Hannah knew, she was out of the water coughing and panting for breath.

'Jesus, Hannah, are you okay? I lost you in all this damn seaweed. Hannah?' Her dad was speaking, his voice broken with agitation. Hannah coughed more and saltwater spewed from her lips and ran from her nostrils. She looked to the water with stinging eyes. The seaweed had broken up and there was no sign of a face anywhere at all.

'I – urk – I… I'm fine,' she finally managed to groan. Her father put his arm around her and slowly began to lead her to trudge back to the beach.

'She's alright! Don't worry,' he called, waving a hand to Rebecca. Hannah's mum wasn't far and she was watching them with concern on her face. Leena was just standing next to her with her tail wagging and the ball floating before her.

'Jeez, you scared me there, bug. You sure you're okay?' Hannah's head was spinning, her chest was burning and her heart pounding as she forcefully trudged through the water. She didn't know what to think.

I was probably just seeing things. Being trapped like that... she thought, attempting to rationalise the face in the water. The more she thought about it, the more ridiculous the whole thing became. The less real it had seemed.

'Yeah. Yeah, I'm okay, Dad. I think... that's enough for today though, huh?'

*

Hannah leaned her crossed arms upon the classroom benchtop, watching with keen interest. She was surrounded by her classmates, though at least three had opted out of this particular science class and were spending the period in the library. Mr Novak was hunched over the bench, his large hands encased in blue, latex gloves, the fingertips of which were now coated in gore. The scalpel in his hand was tainted with strings of raw muscle and smears of blood. The cow's heart on the tray had been expertly dissected and now lay splayed open like a meaty flower in bloom. After each action he took, Mr Novak had paused and explained what the students around him could see. Before making any incisions, he had introduced the class to the outer appearance of the heart, pointing out the aortic arch, the pulmonary trunk, the left and right atriums and ventricles. Hannah recognised at least some of the main points from her textbooks but there was something different about seeing an actual specimen. She found it, somehow, more absorbing. After offering the box of gloves to anyone who might be interested, Mr Novak even let the students feel around the heart, especially to probe their fingers into the superior and inferior vena cava and pulmonary arteries. Hannah was game to try, as was Brian but Abbi had been wearing an expression of distaste during the entire procedure and refused any gloves.

Mr Novak had proceeded to slice and open the heart for the next twenty minutes, revealing the internal structures of the organ and pointing out the many different valves and chambers.

'Finally, here in the ventricles, you can see the chordae tendineae. The heart strings, so to speak,' Mr Novak said as he waved his finger along the thick tissue. Hannah could make out the curious looking webs of fibres and she looked at them with interest. Yet even she recoiled a little when Mr Novak slipped the blade of his scalpel beneath them and lightly pulled upwards, stretching the sinews like taut strings.

'So, this is what it's like to play the heart strings then,' Mr Novak said with a rather disconcerting smile as he ran a gloved fingertip down the tendons. 'Anyone else care to try? Hannah, perhaps?'

Hannah jumped a little to the sound of her name. Her eyes had been fixed on the heart on the table and she was shocked to find Mr Novak looking to her intently with his dark eyes. How long had he been looking at her like that? Something about his gaze made her feel uncomfortable.

Is this what all those girls meant? she thought as the rumours of Mr Novak crept into the back of her head.

'Um, okay,' she said when her mind caught up with what the teacher had actually asked her. She slowly reached forward and aimed a finger towards the heart's webbing.

'Be careful not to get too close to the scalpel,' Mr Novak muttered as Hannah grazed over the strings. They felt a curious mixture of soft but extremely tough. Hannah watched as the walls of the left ventricle tugged inward with her interactions.

'Ah, see here, how the tendineae sprout from the papillary muscles. And here, they join with the atrioventricular valves. Can anyone tell me why?' Mr Novak addressed the class and Hannah stepped back, fighting the urge to wipe her hand on her top. Her skin was clean, but the tip of her glove was cold and gave her finger a false feeling of being wet. No one attempted to answer Mr Novak and he shrugged with a brief sigh.

'The chordae tendineae are essential in holding the tricuspid and bicuspid valves in place while the heart pumps blood,' he explained while pointing to the relevant parts of the organ. There were a few half-hearted nods and murmurs of acknowledgement amongst the class but Hannah guessed all the medical terminology had flown over the heads of most of her peers. She couldn't really judge though. She barely understood any of it herself, save for the basic concepts. Suddenly, the bell loudly rang to signal the end of the period. Most of the class began moving, seemingly without a mind of their own. It was as though the bell was simply activating something in their brains to grab their belongings and meander like zombies to their next class.

'Right, well, that is the dissection finished, I suppose. I hope you have all been paying attention because there will be a test on the workings of the heart tomorrow,' Mr Novak announced to some groans. Hannah was taking off her gloves to dump in the biohazard bin by the bench with Brian and some of the other students while Abbi had been one of the first to abandon her post to collect her things.

'I thought it was pretty interesting. How about you?' Brian asked softly, though his eyes were focused on his hands while he attempted to remove his gloves with minimal contact.

'Yeah. Yeah, I think it's pretty amazing. Just so much detail that goes into making our bodies and stuff, you know? Even if it makes the place smell like a butcher's,' Hannah replied with a weak laugh. What was it about Brian lately that she struggled to speak like a normal person around him? Brian nodded but, before he could speak, another voice spoke up.

'Well, I don't think you need to worry about the test tomorrow, Hannah. You have a knack for this stuff, I can tell,' Mr Novak said.

Hannah turned to find the teacher was much closer behind them than she had expected. He looked down his sharp nose to her while he sealed the biohazard bag now containing the ravaged heart and tossed it into the bin. Hannah felt small beneath the towering man and something about his gaze made it worse.

'Oh, uh, thanks, Mr Novak,' she said with a small, awkward smile. Mr Novak just returned her smile. His eyes darted over her once more before he gave a curt nod, turned and walked back to the bench to resume cleaning before his next class of students arrived.

'He's right. You seem to really get this stuff,' Brian said, stroking his now ungloved fingers through his short, jet-black hair, evidently to soothe an itch that had been bothering him for some time. He was clearly oblivious to the weirdness Hannah felt in Mr Novak's presence today. She couldn't help blushing from his compliment though and glanced down.

'Heh, thanks. I mean, I really don't get it that much. It's just...'

'Interesting?' Brian helped Hannah to finish her thought after she had trailed off. She looked up to see him smiling at her and she grinned back.

'Yeah. Interesting.'

'Come on, Hannah! We have to go all the way to the G rooms for History,' Abbi said as they slowly approached.

'Yeah, Yeah, I know.' She took up her books and belongings while Brain did the same.

'Aw, I've got English now. I guess I'll see you guys at lunch?' he said and he let his head fall back with disappointment. Hannah couldn't deny there was a hollow feeling in her chest too. She pushed it down though.

Get a grip. It's one class, for God's sake! she thought. This crush was getting out of hand if she felt upset that she wouldn't see Brian for fifty minutes.

'Yeah, alright. See you then,' she said, feigning a casual attitude that in no way reflected the whirlwind of emotions inside. A few minutes later, Hannah and Abbi were walking amongst the bustling students outside.

'Well, thank God that's over with anyway. How do you like that stuff, Hannah?' Abbi asked while dodging an oncoming student. Hannah didn't reply.

'Ugh! Not just knowing about it but... touching it? Blech!' Abbi continued in lieu of her friend's silence. Hannah continued to look blankly forward, lost in thought.

'Hannah? Hannah! Yo, airhead!' Abbi punched Hannah's shoulder to grab her attention.

'Hey! What the hell?' Hannah finally responded with a distracted chuckle as her friend's physical touch brought her back to reality. Abbi just shrugged.

'You weren't listening to me, so I hit you. I thought you knew to how this whole friendship worked by now?' she joked. They stepped out from the cover of the tin roof that ran along the rooms to cross one of the school courtyards. The sky overhead was dark and grey, the rolling clouds threatening to release their torrents of rain soon. The beautiful, sunny sky of the previous day at the beach was just a fleeting moment. A reminder of the good weather that would soon be left behind as winter took hold. Hannah shuddered and was grateful to be wearing the forest green jumper of her school uniform, relatively thin though it was.

'Sorry. I was just thinking...' she said slowly. Abbi looked to her friend and cocked an eyebrow.

'Going to actually explain that or...?' she asked, the sarcasm dripping from her lips. Hannah inhaled deeply.

'Well, I dunno, I mean... do you think Mr Novak was, well, looking at me weird?' she asked finally. She shuddered again, but this time she knew it wasn't from the cold air. In her mind, she could see Mr Novak's brown eyes, staring at her. The way he glanced down her body before she left. Was he really perving at her?

'Oh, Jesus, not you too?' Abbi asked with an exasperated sigh. 'I thought you agreed with me those were just rumours spouted by those vain idiots who think they're God's gift to the world or something?'

Even though Hannah knew Abbi was right, she couldn't help but instinctively feel defensive against her ridicule.

'Yeah, I know I just, I dunno. He made me feel weird, okay?' she snapped.

Abbi took a step back. 'Woah! Take it easy, Miss Irritable, I didn't know you were really bothered by him,' she said lightly. Though Abbi acted as though nothing was wrong, Hannah knew she was genuinely apologetic about making light of her concerns.

'Sorry, I know. But I mean… you didn't notice anything?'

'Oh yeah, totally. Like, the way he played favourites getting you to grope that heart? If it were his own, I bet he would have given it to you whole.'

'Abbi!' Hannah growled.

'Okay, okay, sorry, jeez! Um, I mean, I guess he looked at you a bit? But seriously, Hannah, don't you think it might just be in your head? Like, hearing all those rumours has just got you thinking about it?' Abbi had lowered her voice now so that, even if the hustle and bustle of students about them wasn't overbearing, no one might hear them speaking. Hannah could see some of their classmates were already hanging around outside the room for History, joking and talking amongst themselves. She pondered about what Abbi said.

Maybe I am just imagining it? Like… the other stuff. The face in the seaweed had sprung to her mind and the vague image of something bloody in the school bathroom though she honestly couldn't remember much of that particular experience at all now. She wondered if maybe she was stressed out or something.

'Yeah, I dunno. Maybe you're right,' she said quietly while she tried to figure out what was wrong with her lately.

'Of course, I'm right. Like I said, I thought you knew how this friendship worked? I speak, you listen, everything works out fine.' Abbi grinned before she playfully nudged Hannah's elbow with her own. Her smile was infectious and Hannah quickly reciprocated. At least she had her best friend to help her feel better.

TO GET SOME SLEEP

AIDEN

Aiden blinked his aching eyes and shook his head. He had just finished making a takeaway flat white and needed to consciously think about what to do next. Usually, when there were no customers to tend to, the generic tidying and maintaining of the café came naturally to him. He would simply go on autopilot and clean out the espresso machine filters and wipe down the benches. But today, he had to pause for a moment and think about where to go next. He could hear the light chatter of the few customers who were dining in, mixed with the spitting and sizzling of the cooking in the kitchenette. Marcus and James were both working at the stoves while Wendy was transferring the pans of freshly made food into the bain-marie in preparation for the lunchtime rush. Aiden's brain finally caught up with him and he detached the last portafilter he had been using to make the last coffee from the espresso machine and knocked the used coffee grounds into the nearby bin.

'So, what's been up with you this week?' a voice piped up from behind.

Aiden jumped; his nerves frayed from his lack of sleep. Not to mention the bizarre things he had experienced over the past few days. He hadn't heard any more from 'Gary' as that terrifying thing had called itself, but he had suffered from bouts of paralysis every night since it had appeared that Friday. It was Wednesday now. Aiden knew it had all been in his head, but simply rationalising to himself that it wasn't real didn't help to break his insomnia or his nervous state of mind. The best he had felt in recent days was when he had gone to the beach with his family on Sunday. Riding the waves with Hannah, enjoying a fish and chip lunch, even spending the evening in with a movie had all seemed so blissfully normal to him. He had barely even thought of Gary that day. At least, not until the time came to actually lie down in bed and try to sleep. That's when the dark shadow and horrid smell of Gary came seeping back into his mind.

Aiden almost dropped the portafilter when the voice had startled him and he turned to find Samantha behind him. She was wiping down the benchtop with a wet cloth. It was all for appearance of course, while there was a lull between customers. The bench was already clean and, even if it were dirty, the pathetic motions Sam made with the tea towel would barely wipe away a puddle of water. She had made her way over to him from the register, clearly bored out of her mind and wanting to strike up some conversation.

'Uh, not a lot. Just another week really,' Aiden said after his slow mind finally acknowledged what Sam had actually asked him. She looked him in the eye and shook her head.

'Nuh-uh. I don't mean what you've been up to. I mean, what's with you? You've been all twitchy and shit these past few days. Have you been sick or something?' Aiden wasn't surprised by her forthright manner. Sam was the sort of girl who was brutally honest and didn't waste any time in getting straight to the point. In truth, while some people found her attitude as sharp as her pale features, Aiden actually liked that about her. He looked back down to the portafilter in his hands and gave a shallow shrug.

'Nah, I'm alright. Just haven't been sleeping so well lately,' he said. Sam huffed.

'Oh, well that's boring then.' She smirked.

Aiden chuckled dryly. 'So sorry my life isn't more entertaining for you.'

'Good,' Sam replied flatly, though her subtle smile betrayed her light-heartedness.

'So, what's the deal then? Just can't sleep? Been binge-watching some new series or something?'

In the corner of his eye, Aiden saw Wendy look over to them. She rolled her eyes before wandering back into the kitchen to collect the next tray of food. She certainly hadn't been a big fan of Sam's. Aiden wasn't rightly sure why she hired her.

'Just can't sleep. Lie awake thinking too much, you know?' he said while he focused back on his work.

Aiden didn't mention his paralysis, the night terrors or anything else about the sense of fear that seemed to grow each day. He felt as though mentioning it would bring some calamity upon him, though he didn't know what. It made him think of those old wives' tales that teenagers used to play. Look into the mirror and say 'Bloody Mary' three times in a row and sure enough, the ghost of some murdered girl would jump out at you. At least, that was the party game he heard tell of anyway.

He glanced up from the espresso machine to find Sam just looking at him with an unconvinced expression on her face. She had crossed her arms and was just leaning back against the counter. It was any wonder Wendy wasn't impressed with her. It wasn't the greatest impression she could give their few patrons yet somehow Aiden didn't think they cared very much.

'Right. Well, I know what that's like at least. Sometimes you just can't shut your brain off when you really want to, huh?' Sam said finally. Perhaps she didn't believe Aiden's generic explanations but she didn't seem troubled enough to push him further.

'Yeah, exactly.' He nodded. Sam looked back over her shoulder, watching the open entryway into the kitchen. Wendy was still in there with Marcus and James. She leaned in closer to Aiden, her arms still crossed.

'If you want, I could always give you something to help?' she said softly. Her hazel eyes seemed to gleam as she spoke and her mouth grew into a sly smile.

'What?' Aiden asked dumbly. He heard himself toning down his own voice to match Sam's though he didn't think of doing so. It was simply an instinctive response, as though he were engaging in some clandestine conversation to bring down some higher oppressors.

'I've got some pretty good stuff in my bag today, actually. Valium. I'll give you some if you like.'

Aiden silently opened and closed his mouth like a guppy fish. 'Valium? You need a script for that stuff, don't you? Why would you give me any?' He couldn't deny the idea of a solid night's sleep with the help of some strong drugs was quite tempting.

'Pfftt, I've got plenty. I've been taking it for years. And what's wrong with me just wanting to help out a friend? We've been working together for six months now you know.' Sam waved her hand dismissively.

'Also, as far as I see it, if you get more sleep maybe you'll relax and stop being so on edge at work. It weirds me out,' she added with a grin.

Aiden thought for a moment. He and Sam had gotten along well enough since she started working at the café. From their varied conversations, he knew that Sam was a bit of a party animal, even for a twenty-four-year-old. A seed of doubt grew in the back of his mind as he wondered about her offer. Sure, lots of people had prescriptions to take things like Valium, but how many of those people kept some in their bag at work? Surely the drugs would be hidden away in a bedside drawer or something. But Sam hadn't mentioned anything about money and, though he didn't have any experience in such things, she didn't seem much like a drug dealer to him.

'Alright. Say I do take you up on your offer. What do you get out of it? Aside from a happier co-worker?' he asked, looking at Sam suspiciously. He didn't think she intended anything sinister, but he wasn't dumb enough to think he would get anything for free. Sam's eyes grew wide and she audibly gasped.

'Aiden! I'm shocked. Shocked! You really think I would just do something for you so that you'll do something for me?' Her protestations may have been legitimate but the way she spoke, Aiden knew she was playing around.

'Sam...' he said sternly, playing the role of a dad who wants to know why their teenage kid *really* wants to borrow the car. The young woman laughed.

'Uh, alright. There's a concert I want to go to next weekend. It's up near Bendigo and, I mean, who wants to drive all the way there and back again in one day?'

Figures as much. She wants me to cover a shift. Aiden knew how often Sam tried to skip work for some concert or party and having a co-worker offer to cover her would always look better than calling in sick the day before.

'So, what you mean is, you're going to be hungover?' he said smugly, crossing his arms and acting more like the disapproving father.

'Yes,' she said unashamedly.

'So, you get a few good nights' sleep. I get a few good nights... not sleeping, it's a win-win! What do you think?'

Aiden acted thoughtful for a moment, though if he were honest, he had already made his mind up.

'I mean, next weekend is my Saturday off but who am I to turn down some extra money? And God knows I need the sleep.'

'Awesome! So, if you could just let Wendy know and I'll fetch the tablets, okay?' Sam beamed.

*

For the first time in almost a week, Aiden was actually looking forward to going to bed. First, he had to deal with the sleep paralysis attacks and then, as a result, he had been struggling to actually get to sleep at all. He'd lately only been functioning on a good three or four hours' sleep a night with some intermittent dozing in between. By now, he was feeling drained. His head was heavy, his eyes sore and it was like there was a fly constantly buzzing around just close enough that he could hear it in the background. Finally, a good night's sleep would fix it all.

He was currently rinsing off in the shower, letting the warm water soothe his muscles while he stood with his eyes closed and let himself relax before bed. Sam had actually given him an entire packet of Valium, a full thirty tablets! He didn't even care that there was no sticker for the prescription on the box. What did it matter to him if Sam knew someone who could get her some things on the side? The box itself and the foil-enclosed contents within all appeared perfectly legitimate. Sam had just saved him a trip to the doctor and pleading his case for drug assistance after which he would probably only have received something half as good. Not to mention, the money he had saved.

'Well, I still don't like it, but I mean, it's up to you, babe,' Bec said, her words stifled a little as she brushed her teeth. Aiden sighed. He was always honest with his wife and had told her about his little deal with Sam when they retired to the bedroom.

'I know, it's not really the right way to go about it but, come on, honey? You really think I should have said no?' he asked while enjoying a final rinse under the shower. He could only hear Bec brushing her teeth in response. Her silence reassured him that she disagreed with his decision. Aiden said nothing more as he turned off the water, stepped out of the shower and grabbed a towel. Bec spit her toothpaste into the sink.

'I just don't like how, I don't know, underhanded it was? I feel like you should have been making the swap in an alley with taped-up plastic bags or something,' she said before rinsing her mouth.

'Come on, baby, it's not like it's anything illegal.'

'Exactly! Valium isn't illegal when you have a script for it. So why make it more complicated than it needs to be?' Bec pointed her toothbrush to Aiden in accusation.

'I dunno, it just made sense?' he said with a dry laugh. Bec just rolled her eyes and looked back to the mirror. She leaned forward and used her fingers to open her eye wider. Aiden winced as he saw his wife reach up and retrieve one of her contact lenses with her index finger.

'God, I'll never understand how you do that,' he said with an exaggerated tone of disgust. Bec just smiled as she continued to focus on what she was doing in the mirror.

'Maybe I'm just not as big a pansy as you are,' she joked. Aiden acted as though he had been stabbed in the heart, clutching at his chest like a dying man.

'Ouch! Don't hold back or anything, will you?' He laughed before slipping his glasses on. He stepped past Rebecca and into the bedroom to put his boxer shorts on.

Knowing Bec wasn't far behind him, he got ready for bed and turned to the bedside table. He always had some water on hand for through the night and the packet of Valium sat next to the glass he had already prepared. He reached down and opened the packet when he suddenly heard a distinct whimper from the bathroom. Aiden snapped his head upright and turned to the open door of the ensuite. From where he stood on his side of the bed, he could only see the toilet and part of the shower's frame. He couldn't see where Bec would have been standing before the sink.

'Babe?' he called out. There was no response.

Instinctively, Aiden moved closer to the bathroom. His heart was pounding in his throat. What had happened to her? Had she simply poked herself in the eye? Had she fallen over? For some reason though, Aiden felt afraid. He wanted to just run to check on his wife, but something stopped him from moving very fast at all. A chill ran down his spine and goosepimples tingled on his skin.

'Bec, are you okay?' he asked again. This time, his voice sounded less sure. More distressed. Again, there was no reply. Aiden stepped closer, the sudden idea that some horrid thing would jump out at him played on his mind. He shook his head.

Grow up, moron! he scolded himself in his head. Bec wasn't responding. He needed to help her.

A scraping sound echoed from the bathroom. Something like metal scratching over glass or ceramic. Aiden couldn't help but freeze at the sound. There was something about it. Something… sinister.

'Bec, come on, talk to me!' he snapped, as he finally managed to push through his fear. There was nothing evil. No monsters. His stupid nightmares had gotten the best of him for the last time. Aiden found he could properly control his own body again.

He immediately dashed forward, expecting to find his wife lying on the tiled floor, struggling to move as she tried to call for his help. But, as he moved into the doorway, he saw that Bec was standing just fine. She was still at the sink, facing the mirror, though now she was leaning forward intently as though to get a better look at her reflection. Her posture was accentuated by her light blue nightie, the fabric hanging seductively short over her cute behind. Suspecting it had simply been a slip of the finger while removing her lens, Aiden almost smiled at the sight of his wife's alluring body. But then he was reminded that something was wrong by a grotesque squelching sound. Looking further than his wife's waist, Aiden froze in place, his mouth gaping. Drops and tracks of bright red had tainted the white sink.

At the sound of another squelch, more drops plummeted into the growing, ruby pool. Aiden tried to speak, to simply say his wife's name but his voice defied him. He watched as Bec continued to hold her hands to her face, evidently in an effort to get that damned contact lens out of her eye. Aiden looked in the mirror and saw his wife's face. Her features were obscured not only by her hands but also by a curious fuzziness in the glass. The more Aiden tried to focus on her, the blurrier her image in the mirror became.

'Do it, Aiden,' she said, her voice flat and monotone. Aiden couldn't reply. He couldn't move. He just watched, frozen in terror as Bec lowered an arm. Setting her hand down on the bench, Aiden saw her fingers were coated in shiny, red blood. There was a distinct clatter when her hand fell too and Aiden lost his breath. A nail file with a sharp, hooked tip was in her hand. The shining metal was tarnished with thick blood.

'B-Bec?' Aiden managed to utter in little more than a petrified whisper. Bec lowered her head and the blurred glass of the mirror dimmed to become darker than her brunette hair.

'Do it...' she repeated. This time, there was a hiss in her voice. A hiss that was frighteningly familiar. Aiden just wanted to run. To turn away and flee from his own wife. But he still couldn't move. What the hell was she saying?

'Do... what?' Aiden croaked, his dry throat clenching painfully as his spoke.

'Do it. And you'll see...' Bec said, the hiss now overcoming her own voice. She turned as she spoke. Aiden was paralysed.

Bec looked at him. Streaks of blood were running down her nightie and splattered over her breasts. The blood flowed down her cheeks, running from ... her eyes. Where her beautiful, glistening eyes should have been were gaping, dark holes. The eyelids were tattered and shredded, evidently crudely carved up by the nail file in Bec's bloody right hand. But it was her left hand which she held outstretched and presented to Aiden. In her open palm, in pools of blood, sat two sliced and mutilated eyeballs. They stared blindly forward but they pierced Aiden's soul. Aiden whimpered, tears and drool running down his own face as, in a gargantuan effort, he managed to step back and feebly lean against the doorway. Bec took a step closer, stumbling like some undead monster.

'Take them! Take them! Take them and you can see!' she screamed in high, shrill cries. A deformed smile twisted upon her bloody lips and Aiden saw the mirror behind her move too. Two, burning red eyes shined from within the glass as though it were merely a window. The eyes were soon followed by a smiling web of tangled, shining teeth.

'Do it, Aiden. And you will see.' Gary's foul, hissing laughter echoed in Aiden's head.

*

'Aiden? Aiden! What the hell? Snap out of it!' Bec said while vigorously shaking her husband. Aiden blinked and suddenly took a deep inhalation of breath. He was standing beside the bed, the box of Valium in his hand.

'What? What the fuck?' he asked weakly.

Bec looked to him with concern. 'I was just about to ask you the same thing. I finished up in the bathroom and came in here to find you just standing there,' she said.

Aiden violently shook his head. The horrible images he had seen were imprinted on his mind. He was sure it had been real. But it couldn't have been. Bec was standing there before him. She was wearing the same blue nightie. Minus the blood. She looked to him with worried, shining brown eyes. They were definitely there.

'I-I don't know, honey. I... I blacked out?' Aiden said with uncertainty. Bec took his arm and gently led him to sit on the bed.

'Shit, babe. I know you've been having some issues sleeping with that damn paralysis stuff but I didn't think it was this bad?' Aiden shrugged.

'I dunno. I guess I just... really haven't been sleeping great at all.' Bec stood upright and looked at him for a moment. She turned and took up the box of Valium and examined it carefully.

'Right. Well, maybe it is good you got this then. Looks like you need it. I'll message Wendy and let her know you need the day off. I think I'll even see if I can start late tomorrow. Just to make sure you are alright in the morning.' Bec had made up her mind and was taking control. Aiden knew better than to question her.

'Thanks, honey,' he said softly while Bec punched a couple of the tablets from the foil and passed them to him.

SHOWERS AND SHOP TALK

REBECCA

Bec set her bowl of cereal on the dining table and slumped into her chair. Outside, the morning sky was grey and gloomy, apparently mimicking Bec's emotions. She closed her weary eyes and listened to the light rainfall pattering on the windows of the dining room and kitchen. She hadn't gotten much more than a few hours' sleep last night. Thankfully, the Valium Aiden had taken had worked quickly and he was fast asleep within an hour of going to bed. Bec was happy that her husband had managed to get some rest but she couldn't help but lie awake and worry about him. The memories of his period of depression plagued her thoughts.

Back then, Aiden's mental state had gotten so bad that he could barely bring himself to get out of bed. He ended up losing his job and, while Bec had already managed to get a part-time position at a department store, they wouldn't have been able to get by without her parents' help. After all, even though he couldn't work, Aiden couldn't take care of Hannah either. Bec's mum and dad had already done so much for them by that stage. They had taken Aiden in so that he could be the partner and dad he promised he would be. They paid for a decent chunk of Bec and Aiden's wedding, humble though it was, and even provided the down payment for the house they now lived in.

When Aiden was at his worst, Pamela and Thomas often looked after Hannah while Bec worked. The timing really wasn't great. Bec had enrolled in her medical receptionist course before Aiden's problems. She had to defer for nearly two years while they focused on her husband's troubles.

When Aiden was able to get back on his feet, he thankfully excelled in his trial week for Wendy. He'd been working at the Glen Marsh Grind ever since. Bec was finally able to take up her studies and eventually got her job at the Greenfield clinic. Thinking back on the trials of their lives, Bec realised that her mother had successfully managed to sow the seeds of doubt in her mind.

What if it happens again? We can't go through it again, Bec thought over and over in the darkness of the night. Their budget was tight enough as it was and, if Aiden lost his job at the café, they would barely be able to cover the bills and cost of living, let alone the mortgage.

'Mum? Are you there?' Hannah asked, waving her hand slowly in-front of her mother's glazed, vacant eyes.

'Huh? What?' Bec shook her head, returning to the present of the dining room, her cereal slowly becoming soft with the milk.

'Um, I just said good morning?' Hannah said with a raised eyebrow. She sat at the end of the table and took a bite of her jam toast.

'Oh, right. Morning, honey. Sorry, I just didn't sleep very well last night.' Brought back to reality, Bec began to slowly eat her own breakfast.

'Hmm. First Dad, now you. Don't tell me I'm gonna start being up all night soon?' There was a light tone to her voice but Bec could tell when her daughter was really joking and when she was acting the part to hide her genuine concern. She knew this was the latter.

'Don't worry. Your dad's just having a hard time and I'm worried about him, that's all,' she said reassuringly.

'So, is that why I heard him still snoring in bed? Is it all because of this sleep paralysis thing?' Hannah asked. She continued to eat her breakfast and speak nonchalantly but her curiosity was obvious.

'It is. It's... difficult to manage and he's just having trouble getting through it. But we'll get there. We've been through tougher things before.' Though she wasn't lying, Bec was encouraging herself as much as her daughter.

'You mean like when Dad just, I dunno, stopped doing anything for a year or something?' There was a touch of spite in Hannah's voice. Bec's chest fell. Of all the things she remembered of Aiden's problems, it was the fact that Hannah had to deal with the consequences when she was only six years old that broke her heart the most. Hannah hadn't just lost quality time with her father; she had basically lost him entirely for some nine months. Sure, she knew he was still around, but he had become something like a ghost. An entity in the house to just be left at peace. Bec hated that Hannah had to go through that.

'Well, yes,' Bec said slowly in response to her daughter. 'But hey, I remember when you were a baby. I wouldn't say you got sick a lot, but when you did, jeez it was tough. If we could make it through that, we can make it through anything.' She spoke light-heartedly, almost in jest.

'Oh, so I'm just too much to handle, am I?' Hannah asked with a sly grin.

'When you have a kid of your own, crying and spitting up, not giving you enough time to go to the bathroom, let alone catch up on some sleep, then you can tell me how tough being a parent can be.' Bec laughed.

'Noooo way. I'm not having kids for a looong time,' Hannah said with a sweeping gesture of her arm.

'Good. Don't do what your father and I did. Finish school first.' She pointed her spoon at her daughter to playfully emphasise her point.

'Crap, I'm going to be late for school! Mum! You had to sit here, all easy to talk to, didn't you?' Hannah cried as she rose to her feet. She threw the last crust of toast in her mouth before brushing the crumbs from her uniform.

'Wow, how is it eight-thirty already? Good thing I told Liz I'd be in late today. Why don't I drive you to school?' Bec suggested after she checked the time on her phone. There was a perfectly good analogue clock hanging on the wall in the kitchen behind her but phones just seemed to be the way of the world these days.

'Awesome, thanks, Mum! Just let me make sure I've got everything,' Hannah said before downing the last of her orange juice and turning to check her backpack on the bench.

*

The steam from the hot water of the shower rolled throughout the bathroom despite the ventilation fan whirring away. It was a cold morning and the simple tracksuit pants and cardigan ensemble that Bec threw together to drop Hannah off at school wasn't enough to keep her warm. She didn't mind that she hadn't dressed up a bit better as she never intended to leave the car and, thankfully, the need never arose. From their conversation on the way, Bec was happy to find Hannah was still pretty content at school. She wasn't too keen on maths but was at least passing. It was science, however, in which Hannah seemed to be the most interested.

Bec wasn't surprised, of course. Her daughter had always been curious. Always looking for answers, learning how things worked, why they were the way they were. As she thought about it, Bec suspected Hannah's interest in science was inevitable. She smiled, thinking about her daughter's curricular accomplishments while she enjoyed the soothing, hot water of the shower on her skin. When she had gotten home, everything was how Bec had left it. Leena was curled up in her dog bed under the shelter at the backdoor and Aiden was still fast asleep in bed.

Those Valium are damn strong, she thought when she had checked on her dozing husband. At least he was still sleeping peacefully.

There was no sign of paralysis, night terrors or any other kind of distress. Maybe that was one of the reasons Bec was enjoying her shower so much. The hot water felt so nice after being out in the cold. Hannah seemed to be doing well on all fronts and now Aiden might be doing better, even if he needed a bit of medicinal help. It must have been past nine o'clock by now but Bec decided to make the most of her morning. She allowed herself to lounge in the shower. She had lathered herself thoroughly, shaved her legs and shampooed her hair. Just as she was adding her conditioner, she heard a soft groan from the bedroom. She and Aiden were in the habit of leaving the ensuite door ajar while they were in the bathroom and she was pleased to hear that Aiden was probably waking up.

Just then, Bec paused and looked through the opening of the door. She couldn't see much but the dark shapes of the furniture in the bedroom, but she wasn't really looking for anything.

He'd better not be having another attack, Bec thought as her concern for her husband grew. She didn't hear anything else and, after a moment in which nothing but the running shower and the low hum of the fan could be heard, Bec focused back on herself. She stood back, feeling the streams of water running over her breasts, belly and hips as she ran the conditioner through her hair. There was another small moan from the bedroom joined by quick cough. Bec sighed.

'Baby, are you okay?' she called, only half turning to the door this time. Aiden didn't reply, just as she expected. But had he not responded because he hadn't heard her or because he couldn't no matter how much he tried?

He's probably just still asleep. Surely I can just have a few more minutes? Bec closed her eyes once more and let the water soothe her body once again. She swayed in the shower, letting the conditioner do its work on her hair for a moment before she would rinse.

'Mummy?'

Bec froze and her eyes snapped open. Had she really just heard that? The voice was so timid. So childlike. It sounded like the pathetic moan of a sick little girl. Bec stood still, her body instantly tense. Her ears were perked, listening for anything else.

'Muuuummy,' the voice moaned again.

Bec choked on her breath. It was so clear. It sounded almost exactly like Hannah when she was little. Little and unwell. Slowly, she managed to turn. She peeked over her shoulder, looking at the mirror first. There was nothing there but her own, foggy reflection. She looked back at the bathroom door. There was nothing there. Nothing but the silhouettes of the furniture again in the dark bedroom beyond. The bed. The bedside table. But was something else there? Bec squinted, trying to look from the illuminated bathroom into the darkness. Something in those shadows moved, eliciting a sharp gasp from her lips. She must have imagined it. Maybe it was Aiden? She couldn't make it out. But then, what she thought was the bedside table, moved. It slowly came closer and the nearer it approached, the more it appeared hunched and living.

'Oh, God...' Bec groaned from deep in her chest.

Her eyes were fixed on the moving shape in the bedroom. As she stood under the flow of the shower, the water ran through her hair and drips of conditioner started to sting her eyes. She squinted before giving in and blinking. Bec raised her hands, vigorously rubbing her eyes before looking forward again. After waiting a moment for the floating black spots in her eyes to dissipate, Bec saw nothing in the bedroom that shouldn't be. No moving figures, no eerie silhouettes. Her heart was pounding hard and she was breathing fast, but Bec exhaled in relief. It was just her imagination after all. Even so, she took a minute to compose herself before she turned back into the shower. She couldn't help feeling that something was wrong. That something was there.

She shot a glance back. Nothing. Bec finally dropped her head under the water and ran her fingers through her hair, rinsing out the conditioner. She had to close her eyes as the water and chemicals ran down her face.

Just my stupid imagination. That's all, Bec mentally reassured herself as she cleaned.

With her eyes closed, she couldn't help but feel instinctively afraid. No matter what she tried, her heart rate rapidly rose again. She was terrified that she would open her eyes and something would be standing there, looking at her. Bec took a deep breath and finally opened her eyes. Nothing was there. She looked from the wet tiles to the shower screen. She turned and looked to the bathroom door which was just as it should have been. She opened the screen door.

'Mummy!!' the voice of a sickly child screamed loud enough to be in the bathroom with her. Bec screamed to the loud surprise and, beyond the glass door which now stood ajar, stood a small, black figure. It looked like a girl, no more than four years old. Her hair was long, black and very messy. It covered most of her face and seemed almost to meld with her dark, ragged and dirty dress. But, through the mess of hair, Bec could just make out the lower half over the girl's face. Her skin was red and blotchy with some sort of rash and revolting, yellowed chunks of creamy vomit ran down her chin.

Bec fell back in sheer shock and terror and she cried out in pain when her lower back jammed into one of the shower's taps. The hot water began spraying in torrents, sending waves of steam into the air. Bec shrieked and pulled instinctively away from the scalding hot water. As she did so, the girl behind the glass seemed to fall backwards, as though in a state of fear herself. As Bec tried to turn off the water, she couldn't believe her eyes. The girl scurried off, running on her hands and feet with her back to the floor. She looked like some, despicable crab scuttling into the darkness.

Gasping for breath through her fear and pain, Bec finally managed to turn off the shower and was left alone in the steamy bathroom with nothing but the repetitive dripping for company. She leaned back against the wet, tiled wall and stared with wide eyes towards the bathroom door. There was no sign of the girl at all. No one was moving around in the bedroom and Bec couldn't hear anything at all. The seconds passed torturously slow as she just stared at the bathroom door, the adrenaline still pumping through her veins.

'Baby?' the sound of Aiden's groggy voice woke Bec from her trance. She blinked and rose to her feet, her hands slipping along the wet tiles as she went. She wanted to speak, to call for Aiden but her throat was achingly dry. She let out a small whimper of shock when she saw something move once again outside the bathroom door. Relief instantly washed over her when Aiden emerged from the darkness of the bedroom. He was dressed only in his boxer shorts and, though his face was stricken with panic, Bec began to laugh uncontrollably at the sight. She didn't feel particularly humorous, but while Aiden stood half naked in the middle of the bathroom, looking to his wife with a confused expression on his face, Bec felt her fear melting away with her laughter.

'Honey, are you okay? Were you screaming in here? Did you slip?' Aiden asked hurriedly. He had evidently been roused quickly from his deep sleep as he spoke hoarsely and was panting as though he had just run a marathon. Unable to form any words just yet, Bec waved a dismissive hand, trying to encourage her husband that she was alright. She didn't feel as though the girl she had seen was any less real than when she stood right before her eyes, but somehow, the very idea of her existence seemed ludicrous now.

'I-I... I'm okay...' she finally managed to say as her laughter gave way so she could finally catch a breath. Aiden looked uncertain as he reached forward and gently took Bec's arm to help her step out of the shower. She winced and twisted to see a bruise was beginning to form in her lower back where she had hit the tap.

'Jeez, honey, look at that! You did fall over, didn't you?' Aiden said, seeming at least a little more at ease with the situation. He looked at the bruise for a moment before draping a towel around his wife. While Bec felt comforted in her husband's presence, she shot a glance to the doorway of the bathroom and a fresh shiver ran through her body that might just as easily have been due to the cold morning air on her cold skin than her deep fears.

'Yeah, I uh, thought I saw something. That's all,' she said dismissively, though she couldn't meet her husband's gaze as she spoke and rather focused on the water-splattered floor tiles.

'You're a ditz! What did you see?' Aiden asked with a half-hearted chuckle. Bec could tell he was still concerned for her, after all, who wouldn't be worried if their partner fell in the shower? But there was something else in his tone that she didn't recognise. Something more... nervous.

'Oh, really, it's nothing. Hannah and I were talking about when she was a baby. When she was sick all the time, you know?' Bec expressed her own rationalisations of what might have happened aloud. 'Anyway, I guess I just had that sort of thing on my mind. I thought, well, I thought I saw a sick girl.'

She expected Aiden to laugh. To playfully tease her, comfort her and write off whatever happened as her imagination. She wished he would. But Aiden just froze and the colour quickly drained from his face. Bec found his reaction almost as unsettling as when she had first heard something in the shower.

'Honey, really, it was nothing,' she said, trying to reassure herself as much as her husband. Aiden licked his lips and said nothing. He jerked his head, as though he were banishing some mental picture from his mind.

'Um, yeah. That's ridiculous. Are you sure you haven't hurt yourself?' he asked distractedly. 'I'm fine. Are you?' Bec scoffed in response.

'Oh, yeah. I'm all good. Just… still waking up from those drugs,' Aiden said with an encouraging smile. Bec didn't find it at all convincing.

*

'It sounds to me like your concern for Aiden is making you stressed, yourself,' Dr Adya Pannu said softly. She sat with her back to her desk and held her chin in her fingers while leaning on the armrest of her office chair. Bec decided to take her time getting ready for work after the events of the morning and had only just gotten in at eleven thirty. She needed to talk about what had been happening at home. With Aiden. With herself. Who better than with a friend who was also a trained medical professional?

Bec fully intended to wait until the end of her shift to talk privately with Dr Pannu about her experiences but, as luck would have it, she had to take some paperwork into the doctor's office during a lull in the appointments. She suggested speaking to Adya at the end of the day, but the doctor would hear nothing of it and instead insisted they spoke then and there. Thankfully, as there were no appointments scheduled for the next twenty minutes, Liz would be able to handle any walk-ins that might turn up. Taking up Adya's offer to speak right away, Bec had explained Aiden's current situation with the sleep paralysis and, though she felt extremely self-conscious about it, she also spoke of the incident in the shower.

'So, you think it's just stress? Really? I mean, it seems so stupid now, but… but I swear, she seemed so real,' Bec said. She was encouraged that Adya didn't think anything serious was going on, but could such a thing really just be attributed to stress?

'Bec, you know as well as anyone what stress can do to a person. You know how complicated the brain is. Hallucinations, auditory or visual aren't solely experienced by those with advanced mental conditions. I'm sure Dr Winstead would be happy to fill you in on everything he knows,' Adya explained. Her lips widened into her pretty, bright smile when she mentioned Dr Winstead. She knew what an old gas bag that man was. The only thing that made him happier than hearing his own voice was hearing his own voice when he spoke about subjects in which he could claim superiority, which was a frustratingly long list. Bec laughed at Adya's quip.

'Okay, so you don't think there is anything to worry about. Really?'

Adya tilted her head in thought. 'Well, I don't know. Stress is a very difficult thing to handle. I hope Aiden is still seeing someone about his condition?' Having been their doctor and friend for some time now, Adya was familiar with the medical history of the Woods family.

'Yeah, he's still seeing his therapist. I hope, I mean, I think it's helping. At least a little. And he's gotten some, uh…' Bec hesitated. She didn't want to mention the Valium in case Adya asked how he had gotten them. She was their GP after all. 'Exercises to help him sleep. You know, focus on his breathing, warm milk, meditation, that sort of thing.'

Adya didn't appear any the wiser from Bec's faltering sentence, but then, she wasn't the sort of woman to pry into personal details uninvited.

'Well, that's good at least. Perhaps it wouldn't hurt for you to make an appointment yourself? You know that just talking about things sometimes makes a world of difference,' she suggested.

Bec nodded. 'Yeah, maybe. To be honest, I think even just talking about it now has really helped. Maybe we're overdue for a holiday. That could help.'

'Ah, the best treatment! Just be sure and give us plenty of notice, won't you? Liz is reliable but I think we'll need some prep time if you're going to be gone for a while,' Adya said, her compliment accentuated by her contagious smile.

'Ha! Well, who knows? Maybe we could make it work, but who has the time for holidays when the bills need to be paid? Anyway, thanks, Adya. I guess I should get back before Liz starts to wonder where I've got to,' Bec said while she rose to her feet. Her heart felt lighter, it was true and she was in no way traumatised by the morning's events. With Adya's help, she was convinced the experience in the shower was nothing more than a mental manifestation of her own stress and worry. But somewhere, deep inside, Bec still felt a cold foreboding as she imagined that sick girl staring at her with dark, cruelly judging eyes.

FRIENDS, FAMILY AND FOLLOWERS

HANNAH

'I still think it isn't right that Mr Novak dissected a real heart. It's just barbaric!' Kimberly said haughtily.

'Are you still going on about that? Jeez, wasn't that on Monday? Isn't a week enough for you to get over it?' a boy named Jason retorted.

Hannah just lay on the grass with Abbi and Brian on either side of her to enjoy what little sunshine there was to the day. The westerly breeze had a wintery chill to it, but Hannah found that, if you remained low to the ground and stationary in the sunlight, the warmth was pleasant enough. She still wore her school jumper though. She and her friends had chatted about nothing and everything while they ate their lunch but had since fallen into a quiet peacefulness as the break period went on. In the corner of her half-closed eye, Hannah could see Abbi was scrolling intently through one of her vast collection of social media apps on her phone. Brian seemed to almost have fallen asleep, his dreamy dark eyes closed gently in relaxation. They had been listening to the constant chatter of the students, the thumps of footballs being kicked and the hollers of those who played makeshift games on the oval. Sometimes Hannah and the others would join in some game or another, whether it was four square, footy or even just tossing a ball to one another. But more often than not, they found themselves chilling out and chatting as they had done today. Even so, Hannah felt a great sense of comfort in their ability to be together without feeling the need to say anything. Though she and her best friends were content to be silent, the rest of the small group of students were more inclined to keep chatting while they played with their smartphones. Hannah just listened with a sort of bored interest.

'No, it's not, Jason! I mean, there are so many different ways teachers can show us that sort of thing now. He didn't need to use a piece of a real cow who had to die for it.' Kimberly's stubborn voice floated in the breeze.

'You weren't even there. You got to go hang out in the library, didn't you? What does it matter?' Jason responded with an incredulous laugh.

'The cow still died, didn't it?' Hannah heard the other of the girls, Sarah, say. She was part of the group and a vegetarian to boot so it made sense that she would join in the fray. Even though she didn't actually attend Mr Novak's science lessons.

'Well, yeah, but what can you do? The heart was there, it might as well have been used, right?' Jason said.

'Yeah, it's not like the cow died just for the heart. I mean, you know the rest of it ended up in the supermarket or something?' another boy spoke. It could have been Andrew or Will but Hannah wasn't really fussed either way. She just felt a curious sense of amusement in listening into an apparent battle of the sexes.

'Anyway, I gotta ask. I'm all for the whole "ethical treatment of animals" stuff,' Jason started up again.

A sense of tension creep up Hannah's neck and scalp, her facial muscles tightening. Surely, he knew better than to poke the metaphorical bear and start one of those long, awkward arguments? They always seemed to become too personal too quickly in her experience.

'Like, I hate how bad the meat industry can be, too. But let's say people only get their meat from places where they know the animals have had good long lives before the sudden, painless death. Would that really be so bad?'

Hannah didn't need to look to know that the girls where staring at Jason with daggers in their eyes now. She heard some stifled chuckling from the group.

'Why don't we stick you in a cage, feed you up until you're all bloated and fat and hit you in the head with a hammer? Do you think you would be happy with that?' Kimberly snapped, her voice trembling with anger.

'And that's a best-case scenario!' Sarah added smugly. There was more laughter from their peers.

'No, that's not what I mean, I –' Jason was frustratedly muttering amongst the laughter.

'Leave it alone, Jase. They won't let up if you keep going,' one of the other boys said. Hannah was sure it was Andrew's voice this time while Will just kept guffawing away like an idiot.

'Yeah, quit while you're ahead. But it would be better if you quit meat too,' Sarah added.

'Ugh, screw you. What about you guys? What do you think?' Jason asked and it took a moment for Hannah to realise his question was directed at her and the others who were lounging in the grass.

'Nope. I'm not getting dragged into this,' she said, finally tilting her head to look at the group sitting beside her. 'You like meat. You don't like meat. Leave it at that,' she added, pointing to both Jason and Kimberly in turn before looking away to disengage.

'Exactly. Shut up already,' Abbi added without even looking away from her phone screen.

'Pffft, so basically you guys are happy to just sit back and let it keep happening?' Kimberly asked. She was obviously goading them into the debate but Hannah bit her tongue and ignored her. She didn't want to spend her limited break time arguing about anything, no matter the topic.

'Okay, but you know what does annoy me?' another voice spoke up. Hannah let out an exasperated sigh.

'Brian, really?' she moaned, consumed with annoyance that he had taken the bait to keep the conversation going. She was tempted to get up and walk away for some peace and quiet.

'Uh oh, you annoyed *another* stupid meat eater, Kim,' Sarah said mockingly. Brian sat upright with surprising alertness.

Guess he wasn't napping after all, Hannah thought.

'Well, that sort of thing annoys me for one. I hate when people assume, just because someone doesn't agree with them, that they must be stupid,' Brian spoke coolly and he didn't seem angry, just sort of bothered. 'Anyway, what I was going to say was that yeah, animals dying to be eaten sucks. If not stopping completely, could people do better? Sure. But think about it. Everyone lives in houses, right? Well, how many trees and animals had to die for everything that's ever been built? I mean, we don't say, "Sorry, bird, can we borrow your tree?" We just cut it down. And bulldoze land for the space.'

Everyone was silent while Brian spoke. Hannah wondered if any of them were thinking he had lost it.

'And what about cars? It's not even like, one car per house. *Everyone* has a car. You all probably want one too? How good are those going to be for the environment? The way pollution is going, you might as well pick some randoms and give them cancer yourself. Jeez, and clothes? You are always talking about some new outfit you want and isn't it so cheap at the store? Do you know why they are so cheap? Thousands, millions of kids in slave labour. Millions of people living in poverty so that people like us can get those cool shoes for only eight dollars! Anyway, my point is, I get annoyed when people – just as an example, a vegan – go on and on about what the right thing to do is while they drink their soy latte. Oh, but do they care or know where the coffee comes from? Then they drive their car to the shop, buy some pretty clothes some kid somewhere starved to death making, before going to the movies so they can give their hard-earned money to some celebrity who earns over a hundred million dollars a year. Then, someone next to them eats buttered popcorn and they'll get angry because some cow on a farm somewhere had to provide the milk. Does any of that actually make sense?' Brian never raised his voice, but he spoke quickly and he was panting at the end of his rant as he tried to take in all his lost breath. Everyone was just looking at him incredulously.

'Woah, you're just a killjoy, aren't you, Brian?' Sarah said with a sarcastic smile on her face.

Brian huffed. A silence pervaded the air as though everyone was worried that saying anything might cause Brian to launch another verbal assault.

'So, what you're saying,' Will said slowly. Everyone looked at him. It was the first thing he had said during the whole conversation. Hannah had almost forgotten he was even there at all. 'Is that technically the perfect vegan is a dead vegan?' Will finished his thought.

Everyone just looked at him in shock. Hannah suddenly remembered why he didn't say very much. Jason and Andrew laughed. Kimberly and Sarah looked offended.

'Really?' Abbi asked with an expression of disbelief. Will had gotten her to look away from her phone at least.

'Well, I mean, all that stuff Brian said. Think about it. If a someone is dead, they can't harm any other living thing. They're body decomposes so they're actually giving nutrients to the plants and worms and shit. Isn't that a good thing?' Will explained.

'What's wrong with you?' Kimberly asked while most of the others just laughed away Will's random comments.

'Ugh, no that's not the point.' Hannah found herself speaking before she could stop herself. She cursed herself for getting involved as she drew everyone's attention. 'I mean, I think what Brian means is, it's good to do what you can to help but you can't just focus on a single issue. Right?' Hannah looked at Brian with uncertainty. The anxiety of being singled out amongst her peers was creeping into her mind. To her relief, Brian nodded with a smile.

'Yeah. I just mean, there's good and bad in just about everything. People just have to try and balance it out, that's all,' he explained. Hannah looked away to hide the blush she felt growing in her cheeks. She liked that she could understand Brian's logic. It was even better that his line of reasoning was always similar to her own.

'Yeah, and just stop being dicks to each other too,' Abbi added, her comment eliciting another laugh, this time from almost everyone in the whole group. The tension of the debate had thankfully been nullified.

'Ugh, lunch will be over in a minute. Want to get our stuff ready?' Abbi asked, her question directed at Hannah. She had looked back to her phone and had evidently seen the time.

'Yeah, okay.' Hannah nodded before rising to her feet along with Abbi.

'Pfff, you never want to get to class early, Abbi. Who's the guy you're hoping to meet?' Jason asked to the mild amusement of his companions.

'No one, I'm just bored out of my skull listening to all of you,' Abbi sniped back.

Hannah turned and looked at Brian while the rest of the group pretended to be hurt by Abbi's comment.

'Are you coming?' The question was innocent enough but for some reason, Hannah was paranoid that anything she said to Brian might be indicative of a romantic interest by those around them. Or worse still, by the boy himself. Luckily, Brian just sat up and scratched his head with a small smile to Hannah.

'Yeah, coming,' he said as he got up.

Hannah couldn't help smiling herself and as she turned to begin walking back to the school buildings, she noticed Abbi looking straight at her with a knowing expression on her face.

*

'No! Why would he let her go?!' Hannah cried in dismay.

Her favourite contestant in the latest, trendy dating show had just been rejected by her potential partner. Hannah looked at her mother's shocked face, knowing that the hanging jaw was simply a mirror of her own.

'I don't know! Jess was so perfect for him,' Bec said with a disgruntled shrug. The suspenseful music of the show had given way to a barrage of adverts which, thankfully, Hannah's dad had quickly muted. It was a rare thing to suffer through the several minute slog of ads these days but, while Hannah usually found them torturously annoying, she didn't mind so much on nights like this. The short interval gave her and her parents the freedom to talk about what had been happening on the show without fear of missing another detail and being forced to skip back a few lines. Naturally, the streaming networks were great, but Hannah was amused by the nostalgia of her childhood with the ads of free-to-air TV sometimes.

'You know these shows are completely scripted, right?' Aiden softly laughed while he continued to stare into the glowing screen of the laptop on his lap.

'Dad!' Hannah cried.

'Just let us have our fun!' Bec also retorted as she picked up one of the cushions on the couch to smack her husband's side with. Aiden grinned cheekily.

'Alright, alright! I just hope you know we've missed a perfectly good opportunity for a good movie to watch this crap,' he said lightly.

'Oh, yeah, you look so upset, honey,' Bec mocked. Hannah, who was lying along the couch with her feet up by her father gave him a quick kick in the side.

'Yeah, Dad! Get back to your gaming,' she said before poking her tongue out.

'Oh, we're kicking, now? Maybe I should just...' Aiden began to slide the laptop aside to stand before Hannah curled up and squealed. She knew when things became physical there would be a torrent of wrestle and tickle wars and she couldn't deal with that sort of thing with the latest shock of the show still settling in. The ads would stop soon, anyway. Thankfully, seeing that his threat of retaliation had caused his daughter to comically cower away, Aiden sat back down.

'Right then. You watch your ridiculous stuff and I'll… go back to my games,' he said with an apparently sudden realisation of what he was doing. His usual quirkiness elicited some giggles from his wife and daughter, though Hannah felt a niggle of doubt in her mind.

Her dad seemed content enough, but she couldn't actually see what he was doing on his laptop and he usually wore headphones when he played games. Hannah just hoped for the best and that her dad was having as good a time as she and her mum were. It was honestly the best night she had had for a while. Her mum and dad were acting pretty much normal tonight and their relaxed state had in turn, helped her to rest after a stressful week. The smell of the leftover pizza on the coffee table lingered delightfully in the air. The regular place they got their pizza from was pretty awesome. While Leena ate her dinner and slept outside, for now the loving Labrador was curled up and snoozing on her floor bed by the couch. Hannah was tired, but she was also full of good food and entertained with her parents by her side. Hopefully, the good night was a sign that her dad's sleeping troubles were finally over with and there would be at least one thing less for them all to stress about. Even so, there was always homework.

*

Hannah adjusted the bedsheets around her waist. She was sitting cross-legged in bed, her laptop open on the mattress before her. The show had ended on a cliff-hanger as usual, though that didn't bother her so much as when Jess was sent off. It was still reasonably early when the show finished and, as she still had school tomorrow, Hannah decided to head to her room to make sure her most pressing load of homework was done. She had said goodnight to her parents, showered and changed into her pyjamas and got to work. She had only looked at her assignments for five to ten minutes before Abbi got in touch online. Now, that oh so important homework sat in the background of the screen while the webcam of Abbi took up the fore. Hannah could see the messy pile of clothes in the corner of her friend's room while Abbi herself had her face clad in a clay mask. The light, creamy colour that coated her skin and ran clear circles around Abbi's eyes made her face look eerily like a skull. Hannah was pretty used to this weird appearance of her friend, however. After all, she and Abbi had been friends for most of their young lives and had more than their share of sleepovers and after-hours video chats in the past.

'I mean, now that Jess is gone, they might as well just give up on the whole thing,' Abbi said with a disappointed shake of her head.

'I know, right? She was clearly the best one there. I guess, the next best is Chloe but –' Hannah agreed, relieving herself of the show's frustrations with further venting before Abbi interrupted her.

'Oh, please, Chloe's such a bitch! Mind you, after letting Jess go, Max and Chloe would be perfect for each other.'

'Yeah. I can't believe I thought he was a good guy. I mean, maybe he still is, but he isn't smart.' Hannah laughed with Abbi joining in.

'Okay, so, Hannah,' Abbi said after her laughter had died down. She was contently brushing her long, golden hair but she looked more serious now. A heavy weight dropped in Hannah's chest. It was as though a sudden rock of anxiety plummeted inside her.

'Oh no, what?'

She had no idea what Abbi might be intending on saying, but for some reason, she felt scared to find out. She could see her own face in the corner of the screen that showed the view of her own camera and made an effort to look unfazed. Abbi looked down and stopped brushing her hair. She appeared to be thinking of the right way to broach her intended topic. The delay just made Hannah feel worse and she shifted in an attempt to relieve the knot of stress in her stomach.

'So, what's going on with you and Brian?' Abbi asked finally, looking her friend directly in the eye and wearing a sly smile. Relief flooded through Hannah's tense brain, even though she was still hesitant to talk about such a sensitive subject.

'God, Abbi. I thought something was wrong,' she said with a long breath and a giggle. Abbi laughed too.

'Uh, no, sorry. Everything's good here. But come on, what's the deal?' she persisted, leaning forward and resting her arms on her desk to focus all her attention on Hannah in the camera.

'Um, I dunno, nothing,' Hannah replied, though she felt her cheeks flushing to give away the truth and she couldn't look her best friend in the eye. She couldn't help evading the question and she didn't even know why.

'Uh-huh. Sooooo, you like him?' Abbi asked, her playful expression making Hannah think of how a cat must feel when they are playing with a mouse.

'Well, yeah, it's Brian. You like him too. We're friends.'

Abbi just shook her head. 'No, you like him, like him, don't you? Come on, Hannah, you know you can tell me,' she pushed further.

Hannah closed her eyes tight and grimaced as the truth forced its way to the surface. 'Alright, alright. Maybe… maybe I *like* him,' she said finally. The simple act of speaking the words seemed to lift a weight she didn't even know she had from her shoulders. It felt good to openly say it. But Hannah couldn't revel in the feeling for long as her computer erupted in an ear-piercing squeal. She quickly turned the volume down as she watched Abbi practically screaming with excitement.

'God, shut up, Abbi! My parents will think I'm being murdered or something.' She laughed.

'Oh my god, oh my god, oh my god, this is so awesome! You two will be so cute together! I've seen it happening for so long,' Abbi rambled.

'Wait, what? Really?' Hannah asked with honest surprise. She thought that liking Brian was a big enough revelation to herself, let alone anyone else.

'Well, yeah. I mean, you know. You two like the same stuff, you're really smart, you just click, you know?'

Hannah could see her reasoning, but she was still impressed Abbi had seen it before even she had felt anything. Her mind wandered as she listened to her friend explaining how well she and Brian would work together. Abbi's words encouraged her and she allowed herself to fantasise on the notion of 'what if it actually works out?' A warm, comforting feeling swelled in her belly and as Hannah thought about how sweet Brian was, she began to feel a tingle between her legs that had become all too familiar since puberty had taken hold. She quickly shook her head of her thoughts and focused back on Abbi before she might embarrass herself.

'So? What about Brian? Have you guys talked about it yet? Oh my god, are you together already?' Abbi continued, apparently without having noticed her friend's vacant expression as she imagined Brian in her mind's eye. Hannah cleared her throat, the short-lived elation of her confession giving way to sheepish awkwardness.

'Um, no, we're not together. I, uh, I don't know what he thinks,' she admitted, shifting with unease. Again, she couldn't look Abbi in the eye. She had no idea why she felt so embarrassed, so anxious. But it was the first time she had talked to anyone about liking someone for real, after all.

'So, he doesn't know yet?' Abbi asked slowly. Hannah just gave a short nod and a nervous chuckle in response. Abbi was silent for a moment and looked thoughtful.

'I mean, I like him. But... if I say anything, what if I ruin our friendship?' Hannah expressed her thoughts aloud. God, it felt good to finally talk to someone about the things she had bottled up for what seemed like forever.

Abbi remained quiet for another moment before a smile crept upon her lips. 'Well, maybe you don't have to risk it? Maybe I could, I dunno, test the waters?' she suggested.

Hannah cautiously raised an eyebrow. 'What do you mean?' she asked slowly.

'Don't worry, I'm not trying to steal your man or anything! I was just thinking I'll... discreetly see how he feels about you,' Abbi explained as casually as though she were talking about the weather.

That nervous energy was boiling in Hannah's chest again. 'Uh, how discreetly? You're not going to tell him, are you?' she asked without thinking.

Abbi's jaw dropped into a gasp. 'Like I would do that! Come on, Hannah, you know you can trust me.' She pouted.

'Yeah, I know. Sorry. The whole thing just has me on edge,' Hannah quickly responded, hoping to make amends.

Abbi just laughed. 'Sounds to me like someone's keen to see if somebody likes her,' she said in a sing-song voice.

Hannah blushed and gritted her teeth. She hated how right Abbi was. 'Shut up!' she said with a grin she couldn't hold back.

Abbi laughed again before clapping her hands and letting out another small squeal of delight. 'Sorry, I'm just so excited for you guys! Don't you worry about a thing. I promise I won't let anything slip tomorrow. I'll just see what I can get out of him.'

'Tomorrow? You want to talk to him tomorrow?'

'Uh, yeah, obviously. Don't you want to be his girlfriend as soon as you can?'

Hannah gasped, her heart pounding with nervous excitement. She didn't really know how long she had dreamed of being Brian's girlfriend, but hearing the term spoken aloud sent a shiver down her spine. 'Hmmm, okay,' was all that she could say in response. She was daydreaming about Brian actually liking her again. This time, Abbi noticed.

'Oh, you are going to have some sweet dreams tonight, huh?' She laughed wickedly. Hannah pushed her tongue into her cheek and said nothing as she glared back at her friend.

'Well, I need to get some beauty sleep, myself. If you and Brian start going out, I need to find myself a guy so we can double-date! Need to look my best.'

Hannah clicked her tongue. 'Hey, you always look amazing.' Hannah was just being honest. She appreciated Abbi was the prettier of the two of them. It used to bother her when she was younger but she got used to it over time.

'Suck up. But thanks, anyway. I'm really happy for you, Hannah. Sleep well. Love ya.' Abbi waved into the camera.

'Love ya, too! See you tomorrow.'

Abbi blew her a kiss before reaching down and the image of her looking off screen paused for a moment before the camera disconnected.

Hannah's head was running wild with all sorts of ideas of how Abbi might try to get some information out of Brian tomorrow. She couldn't focus on the remnants of her homework assignments and instead set about closing the files before she would lie down and drift into a pleasant fantasy. As she closed the last window, she was surprised to find another randomly popped open.

Ugh, stupid thing, she thought, unfazed at the random behaviour of her laptop. Computers always seemed to lag and glitch from time to time and she just assumed one of the minimised windows had popped up again. But, as she quickly cast her eyes of the new program, Hannah froze. Her sharp inhalation of cold breath hissed in the bedroom and she her entire body went numb with the sudden unease. Hannah found herself looking into a view of a webcam again. She recognised who was on the other side, but it wasn't Abbi. It was herself.

She could see her own startled expression, her mouth slightly agape with disbelief as she recognised her own bedroom wall behind her.

'Ummmm, okay....' she mumbled disconcertedly. Hannah shifted on her bed and watched her mirrored self, doing the same. She didn't know what she was expecting. It was definitely her on the screen. She directed the cursor and closed the window with a shudder.

'Well, that was just weird.' It felt as though hearing her own voice would somehow reassure her. Just as she reached up to close the laptop, the window opened again. Hannah's breath caught in her throat. She didn't know what was going on. Had she been hacked? Was someone else messing with her computer? A chill of discomfort fell over her like an icy sheet as she wondered if someone else was watching her right now.

'Screw this!' she said in a more confident voice than she felt. If someone was watching, was listening, she didn't want to give them the satisfaction of seeing they had gotten to her.

Again, Hannah reached to the top of the laptop and was about to slam it shut when something in the mirror image caught her eye. Since she had shuffled on the bed, the angle of the camera had changed. She could see the left side of her bedroom window in the corner of the image. She always closed the curtains at night. They were only made of a thin, pale cream fabric, though at least they kept the light out. But, as Hannah looked at the curtain in the camera image of her room, her blood run cold.

The silhouette of a figure was standing behind the curtain, appearing as though someone were looking into her room. Try though she might, Hannah couldn't bring even a groan of fear to escape her gaping lips. She instinctively whipped her head around to look at the window and, to her great relief, there was nothing there. It must just be a shadow, a trick of the light or just some bizarre addition to the already unusual activity on her computer. Hannah turned to the laptop. This time, she let out a frightened yelp from deep inside her body. In the camera, the figure was still there, silhouetted in darkness. But now, it was standing inside the bedroom. The hairs on the back of Hannah's neck pricked up and she felt the unmistakable sense that someone was watching her. Quivering, she slowly turned back to look into her room. She saw nothing. Hannah didn't know what to think. She was chilled to the bone and trembled in her pyjamas.

'D-dad?' she struggled to call out, her quaking voice barely rising above the volume of her normal speech. Hannah couldn't bring herself to turn back to the screen. She was terrified that if she did, she would see the figure was even closer. Instead, she kept watching the empty space of her room before the window and reached back, trying to close the laptop. She was sure she knew where the edge of the computer was but for some reason, her hand couldn't find it.

'Dad? Mum?' she called again, trying her best to control her constricting vocal cords.

Unable to find the top of the laptop to slam shut, Hannah reluctantly began to turn back to find it. She could see the white plastic of the keyboard and she was determined not to look any higher. But then, Hannah heard a curious tapping sound. The room was so deathly silent that the small tapping might as well have been the booming of a drum.

The abrupt noise drew her attention and she couldn't control her skittish fight or flight response to see what was making the sound. Her eyes were drawn to the source of the tapping. Drawn to the computer screen. The camera had become almost a complete mass of darkness but a great row of long, disfigured teeth was stretching into an impossibly wide smile. Hannah was paralysed with fear, watching with blank terror as the shadow in the camera of her room moved. Amongst the darkness, she could just make out the shape of a thin hand with long, crooked fingers outstretched towards her. The hand drew closer and closer to the screen, as though whatever was in there, was trying to reach out of the computer. Hannah couldn't breathe. She couldn't believe what she was seeing but she was certain that the sharp ends of those dark fingers began to actually protrude from the computer. At that moment, a chilling grip took hold of her shoulder from behind. The room, indeed, the whole house echoed with the cascade of screams that Hannah realised were coming from her own mouth. A moment later, the door burst open as her father barged into the room with her mother close behind.

'Hannah?! Hannah! What is it? Hannah? It's okay. You're okay!' her dad was saying as, after making a quick and frantic scan of the empty room, he knelt down and clutched his daughter's shoulders. Her mum looked pale with fear for her daughter and she almost shoved Aiden onto the floor before she desperately wrapped her arms around her.

'Hannah? What is it? You're alright. Everything is alright,' she was saying and though her voice trembled, she spoke in a much more soothing manner than Hannah's panicked father.

She just sobbed uncontrollably into her mother's shoulder while she tightly held her back. Even as she did so, with the fear still coursing through her, she already felt the cause of her terror begin to fade from her mind. She managed to reach up and point feebly to the laptop on the bed.

'The… laptop. Something… someone was…' Her voice trailed off as she struggled to even imagine what she had just seen. What had just been so real to her that it caused her to hyperventilate. Aiden turned the laptop and examined it. After some moments he shook his head.

'There's nothing here, Hannah. What were you looking at? Nothing's open at all,' he said with clear uncertainty in his voice. Bec looked up to him and mouthed something but Hannah couldn't pay enough attention to know what her parents were trying to communicate to each other. In the corner of her eye, she could see Leena poking her head around the corner of the door. The dog's brown eyes were wide and staring, seemingly at nothing. She was baring her teeth and her hackles were standing on end. She took a tentative step into the bedroom, undoubtedly in an effort to protect her human family but the dog froze in her tracks. She growled and held her body in a tense stance.

'Leena?' Hannah managed to ask meekly while the dog continued to growl at thin air.

'Leena, stop it!' Aiden snapped but the dog took no notice of him. She continued to stare and growl until all three of the family were looking back at her. A moment later, Leena yelped and bolted down the hallway.

'What the hell? Leena!' Aiden called. He stepped to the door before turning back to his wife and daughter.

'Honey, do you have her okay?' he asked, the concern for his daughter's wellbeing evident on his face.

'Yeah, yeah, we're alright,' Bec reassured Hannah's dad.

Aiden gave a short nod before turning and moving out of the room to see if something was wrong with the dog. Hannah felt soothed in the warm embrace of her mother, something she hadn't really noticed since she was a little girl. But even then, a foreboding chill seemed to hang in the air about her. Finally, after some minutes of reassurance from her mother, Hannah managed to draw back and look her in the face. She could see the concern her mother felt for her in her worried expression.

'Hannah, are you okay? What happened?' Bec asked softly, her eyes imploring her daughter to explain.

Hannah opened her mouth to speak but the words stuck in her throat. She tried in vain to articulate what she had experienced. Why was it so hard to remember? Whatever it was, it had been so vivid just five minutes ago. 'I … I don't know,' she said finally.

Bec gave her daughter a comforting smile. 'It's alright. Maybe you fell asleep. Had a nightmare?'

Hannah nodded and meekly smiled back before she glanced over to the laptop. It was closed now, but Hannah still didn't like it. She looked back to her mum. 'Can I sleep in your room tonight?'

LOSING CONTROL

AIDEN

Aiden reluctantly stared into the darkness of the bedroom. He examined the dark shape of the ceiling fan as it hung stationary above him. He didn't think he had been awake for long but something about the dark around him seemed to slow time down.

He had no idea what time it was. He couldn't reach for his phone to check. He couldn't turn his head to see if the dim light of the early dawn was peeking through the upper edge of the blackout curtains or not. All Aiden could do was lie there, frozen in dread like a child who is scared of the dark. He focused all of his energy on simply trying to relax. Assuring himself that no matter how immobile his limbs were, how little he felt aside from his burning lungs, that he was truly breathing and functioning as well as ever.

Aiden longed to move. He struggled with all his might to just lift his hand. He knew that if he could do that, the spell of paralysis would break and he could feel the air rush back into his lungs. Bec was calmly breathing beside him, deep in sleep. As bad as Aiden felt, having disturbed his wife's sleep so many times in recent days, he still wished he could scream out her name. Even if she begrudgingly lifted an arm and smacked his chest, it would be enough. But, as was becoming an all too regular occurrence, he couldn't bring a sound to pass his lips.

The longer he lay there, frozen and helpless, the more the fear began to take hold of his mind.

The off-white plaster of the ceiling was a fuzzy grey to his eyes and from it, the walls crept lower and lower into an abyss of sheer blackness. Aiden knew that somewhere down there, down beside the bed on Bec's side, Hannah was also lying asleep on the floor. The memory of her sleeping in the bed with her parents when she was small brought a warmth back to Aiden's heart. He remembered how beautiful his daughter was when she was a little girl. Of course, he still thought her beautiful, but it was altogether different now. He remembered how cute and playful Hannah was when she was little. How he used to be able to have her cuddle up in his arms when they sat on the couch and watched kid's movies together. He thought about how Hannah's light, little girl's laugh used to radiate through the house. He regretted how much of Hannah's youngest years he had missed while he was lost in the stupors of depression and he never wanted to miss out on any more of her life.

He didn't rightly know what had been going on lately, but he knew he wouldn't let it beat him. If he needed to get back onto the antidepressants, to change the routines of his lifestyle, to force himself to do what was necessary, he would do so. Nothing would keep him from living his life with his family anymore. Aiden felt a strength coming from deep within as he motivated himself to take back control. He was determined to get the better of his current disorder and he thought more of the many happy moments he had shared with his family. Not only did the pleasant memories distract him, but he felt they encouraged him, urged him to push out of his paralysis.

'Aiden...'

The image of the golden sunlight shining down on the smiling faces of Bec and Hannah as they played with Leena in the park vanished from Aiden's mental eye in a puff of smoke. He was suddenly enveloped back in the darkness of the bedroom, the fire in his lungs bringing pain but no light. The whisper was hoarse and distant. He wasn't even sure where in the room it had come from. But the warm feelings brought on by his memories were frozen the moment the voice broke through the air. Worst of all, the voice was familiar.

You're not real. You're not even a you. It's not real, he started to think, attempting to regain control of his panicked mind. He tried to ignore the sound of the blood pumping through his ears so he could listen for anything else. There was no sound aside from the soft flow of breathing from Bec and Hannah. But then, Aiden noticed something. It wasn't a sound. It was a smell. The unmistakable metallic smell of blood aggravated his nostrils. Though he couldn't feel it, he was sure his body shuddered with revulsion.

What the hell? What's going on now? Suddenly, he heard a low, hissing laugh from the foot of the bed.

'Didn't I already tell you? I am real. I am here.' Gary's voice pierced the silent bedroom like a knife through flesh. Aiden couldn't look to the source of the voice. It came from the void below his line of sight. But he could feel it. Gary was standing there. Watching him.

No, no, no! You aren't here. You're just in my head, he thought defiantly. A long silence followed before another short chuckle broke out.

'You're a bad liar, Aiden. You know you're wrong. But I have something… very important to show you,' Gary hissed.

Aiden didn't know what to expect, but he was terrified to find out what might come next. He managed to close his eyes, determined not to see anything that this presence could conjure up in his mind. *No. I don't want anything to do with you. Go away. Just fucking go away.* Try though he might, he couldn't bring himself to move and was forced to lie back at the mercy of the thing that he just prayed was his own imagination. He heard no more of Gary's foul voice but somehow, he knew it was still there.

The foot of the bed dipped as though a weight had been set upon it. Aiden was convinced he had taken a sharp intake of breath in his fear but he couldn't be sure. The sound of muffled, raspy breathing came from his feet and he doubted he could have moved even if he weren't suffering an episode of paralysis. Slowly, the weight on the bed was shifting, climbing up Aiden's legs. He couldn't help himself and half opened his eyes with a great effort. Glancing down, he saw a growing hump under the doona. It looked like there was something, someone, underneath the bed covers. Whatever it was, it was climbing on top of him, the ragged sound of its breath echoing under the sheets. Aiden helplessly watched on, his dread growing with each uneasy movement the lump under the blankets made. His body wasn't responding as it should, but he could definitely feel the pressure of the weight on his body.

It pressed firmly down on his pelvis and stomach. As it climbed higher, weight crushed his ribs. The mass in the doona moved so close that the sheets were lifted back and Aiden found himself staring into the black abyss under the blanket. The raspy breathing was slow and heavy and the smell had become unbearable. The scent of blood and decay burned his nose and eyes.

God, please. Please make it stop. Please. Aiden found himself begging in his mind.

The breathing before him came to a stop. The mass under the doona was still there, the weight still pressing on his chest, threatening to suffocate him more than his paralysis. But the room was silent. The doona lifted higher and Aiden's terror reached its peak. He was certain if he had the ability, he would have been screaming at the top of his lungs. He could even hear his own struggling gargles to scream as his fear forced its way past his paralysis. Dark, sunken eyes were staring directly at him. They glared from a hollow, pale face. The thin skin stretched over the skull as though it was moments away from peeling from the bone. Dry and crusty blotches of blood and gore were splattered over the forehead and cheeks while dark stains tainted the ragged, long blonde hair. At first, he saw nothing but evil in the decaying face. But then, as it exposed its crooked teeth in a hideously twisted smile, Aiden realised he recognised the face beneath the deformed features.

Sam? He couldn't believe his eyes but the young woman's face which stared at him from under his own bedcovers was undoubtedly that of his colleague.

'Saaaaam...' the girl said in a guttural hiss. A dark substance oozed from her torn lips as she breathed out her own name. Aiden's heart couldn't have been pounding any faster. He couldn't move. He couldn't breathe. And he couldn't comprehend that this foul apparition that lay over him was really there.

'How did... the Valium... help, Aiden?' Sam tilted her head to the side as she spoke and Aiden heard the sound of her bones twisting and splintering like twigs. He felt he would vomit if he could as she lay her rotted face on his chest and the black ooze from her mouth pooled on his skin.

This is impossible. What the hell is wrong with me? Aiden thought frantically. Sam laughed, coughing thick clumps of gunk and gore from her throat as she grinned.

'I just wanted... to help, Aiden. See how... Gary... repaid my trouble,' she said with an unnerving twitch of her head. Her grin was impossibly wide, her lips stretching so far across her face it looked as though her cheeks had torn open just to expand her smile.

No. This is insane. Gary isn't real. Sam is fine. The girl's smile dropped into a scowl, evidently as she heard Aiden's thoughts.

'You don't... appreciate what I did for you? I helped you, Aiden. I let Gary kill me to help you,' she sneered. Her dark eyes seemed to boil with hatred now.

It isn't real. This is just my fucked-up brain messing around with me. Aiden refused to take the undead Sam seriously. Again, the girl smiled a hideous smile.

'Oh, I know how you always dreamed about me messing around with you.' She grinned deviously. Aiden saw something shift under the doona beside Sam's face before her bony, decayed hand sprang out from under the covers. She lifted her hand, the bones in her wrist splintering out of the paper-thin flesh as she coquettishly pushed a finger to her teeth. At least, she would have done if said finger was anything more than a broken, bony stub.

What the fuck? That's not true! Even as he thought it, Aiden knew in the back of his mind that ever since he had met her, he had found Sam attractive. But, Jesus, that didn't mean he wanted to sleep with her or abandon his family. There had just been some fantasies, that was all. What was wrong with that? Sam narrowed her black eyes.

'Well, let's just see how you feel...' she said as her hand disappeared back beneath the blankets. Aiden could sense the hand was creeping down, sliding over his body like some slithering invader.

No! Stop! Shit, please stop it! Sam's smile just widened, her skin beginning to actually tear at the corners of her mouth.

'Gary knows you so well,' she hissed. Sam gave what might normally be seen as a suggestive wink, but in her current form, in this current moment, Aiden could feel nothing but disgust and terror from her expression.

Sam's disfigured hand tightly grasped over his crotch. Her thin fingers gripped around him and squeezed tight like a vice. Even Aiden's paralysis couldn't keep down his wail of pain as what felt like a metallic set of pliers gripped his genitals. Among his own screams, he heard laughter. Laughter that sounded drowned with fluid. Laughter he recognised both as Sam... and Gary. Light flooded the room and Aiden saw Bec hovering over him. A moment later, he felt her hands on his shoulders as she shook him out of his immobility.

'Aiden? Come on! What the hell is going on?' She was crying out with distress. She wore her worry on her face but Aiden could see something else in her eyes. Frustration. He groaned as the pain between his legs lingered despite now being able to sit up.

'God, Dad! What is going on with you?' Hannah groaned in an annoyed, sleepy voice. Aiden saw her head rise up from behind Bec's side of the bed. She was rubbing her eye and yawning.

'Talk to me, Aiden. What was it this time?' Bec asked as she sat beside her husband and rested her heavy head in her hand.

'I... I don't know. It was... just, you know. The paralysis,' he said slowly. He couldn't bring himself to talk about any of his actual experiences. Bec wouldn't believe him about Gary. And, though he had done nothing wrong, Aiden felt an overwhelming sense of guilt when he thought about Sam.

'No, come on, honey. These things have been getting worse every time. What's going on? You can't breathe, you feel like you're dying, but that's all happened before. What's changed?' Bec's eyes were half closed with the weight of her own exhaustion and though she likely asked after Aiden because she cared for him, her concern was mingled with her draining patience.

'It... it's complicated. It... I feel like something bad is here when I'm paralysed. Like, something wants to hurt me.' He hid a wince of discomfort from his crotch. He was scared something had actually hurt him this time.

'Uh, that's messed up. Please tell me it's just a bad dream?' Hannah asked.

Aiden looked at his daughter and nodded, though he felt none of the confidence he attempted to express to her.

'Yeah, sorry to wake you, bug. I've just been having... bad dreams a lot lately.' He smiled weakly. Hannah seemed convinced there was nothing to worry about at least. It was as though she had completely forgotten why she had insisted on sleeping in her parents' room in the first place.

'Poor Dad. It's all good,' she said sluggishly as she fell back into her sleeping bag on the floor. She was evidently only half awake as it was. Aiden looked at Bec. His wife was resting the side of her head on her fist and she was looking to him with heavy eyes. She pulled a face and lightly shook her head.

'Are you really okay, honey? This is getting ridiculous. Is there anything else we can do?' she asked in a hushed voice so as not to disturb their daughter.

Aiden shrugged. 'I don't know, Bec. I'm trying.' He was trying to appear calm for his family. Behind his eyes, his head was racing. The horrifying image of Sam's grotesque face glaring at him from inside the bed was burned into his mind. What did it mean? What was Gary trying to do?

'Well, I just hope you're alright. Do you need anything?' Bec asked after acknowledging her husband's response. Aiden shook his head.

'No, thanks, honey. I just need to pee then I'll come back to bed. Try and get back to sleep. I'm sorry.' He didn't care that Bec actually let an expression of relief slip over her face when he refused her help. She nodded wearily before slumping back into bed and rolling away from him to nestle in her pillow.

'Okay. Goodnight, honey. I hope you get to sleep soon,' Bec mumbled as she reached up and switched off her lamp but Aiden wasn't really listening. The pain in his groin had become little more than a throbbing inconvenience, but he instinctively felt the need to check if he could see something was wrong.

He slipped out of bed and stepped into the ensuite. After quietly shutting the door, he switched on the light. Aiden slipped down his shorts and examined himself. He had no way to explain it. His skin was marred by red marks that were undoubtedly the first appearances of bruises. If Sam, or even Gary, weren't really there, then Aiden had no idea how his body had received some actual physical damage. Maybe he had trapped his groin between his legs, pinching himself somehow? In his paralysis, Aiden couldn't move an inch. He could barely take a relieving breath of air as he could only come to one conclusion. Something, he didn't know what, had really been there.

*

Aiden hadn't gone back to sleep when he got back to bed. He couldn't switch off his brain, nor could he convince himself that Gary wouldn't return if he ended up dozing off. Checking his phone after coming back from the bathroom, he found it was just past three a.m. He lay awake for the next three and a half hours just trying to make sense of what was happening to him.

Until now, he had been convinced everything he felt and saw had just been in his head. Sleep paralysis was a perfectly natural phenomenon, after all. He had dealt with it before and he was sure he could deal with it again. He knew that hallucinations were a potential symptom. But hallucinations can't physically harm someone. Either Gary was really visiting him during his paralysis or Aiden was truly losing his mind. The mental hurdle of considering the possibility of the supernatural had taken him a long time to overcome. He had been in denial of Gary ever since he first turned up. But what if he was wrong? If Gary was real, what could he do about it? He found himself thinking of the sort of tropes one sees in horror movies. Would he have to go on a worldwide hunt for some expert who would know everything he was going through? Did he have to turn to the Catholic Church and allow himself to be essentially tortured in the name of the Lord in some exorcism ritual? Aiden couldn't help but scoff at the thought. He didn't believe in any of that rubbish. But then again, he didn't believe anything of the supernatural. Until tonight.

Who could he turn to when it came to dealing with some sort of ghost? He thought about the ghost hunter people throughout history that he had heard about. He had never been overly interested in the subject but he had seen a few documentaries and read a few books in the past. But, despite all their showmanship, every one of those kinds of witnesses to the surreal had turned out to be frauds or just delusional. As the hours slowly pushed on, Aiden began to doubt what he even considered reality. If spirits and hauntings were real then surely, in the history of the world, there would be more evidence of such things than simple word of mouth and ghost stories. How could he really be sure that he was even awake at that moment? Couldn't he still have just been living out some lucid dream? As he questioned his very own sanity, a sudden thought occurred to him. *Why Sam?*

Aiden didn't know Sam all that well. Sure, they got along well enough in the six months she had been working at the Glen Marsh Grind but he had never spoken to or even seen her outside of work. From their workplace banter, he knew that Sam still enjoyed going to parties relatively frequently. She watched a lot of the latest trending shows and was studying to hopefully end up working in the hotel industry. But that was about all Aiden really knew about her. He had no idea where she lived, who she lived with or even her phone number. So, why, of all the people he knew, did Gary choose Sam to haunt him with? Despite potentially giving in to the belief of the supernatural, Aiden was convinced that Sam hadn't *really* been under the covers with him that night. After all, how could she be? Not only did she have nowhere to run or hide when the light came on, she also couldn't possibly have been alive in the state she was in. She looked like an animated corpse, not an actual person. No, it was his imagination, or Gary, that made him see Sam.

Aiden racked his brains, trying to work out why. In his drowsy state, he caught himself thinking the same line over and over again and trying to make a comprehensive thought was difficult. He admitted that he found her attractive, but was that really enough to bring her horrific visage into his bed? Then, he suddenly remembered. He thought back to only a few nights before. But was it a few nights before? Surely, it couldn't actually have happened. He thought about Bec in the bathroom. He remembered how his wife had carved out her own eyes with her nail file. She had said it. Gary had said it. *Do it. Do it and you will see.*

Did Gary *warn* him? After he had that terrible vision of Bec in the bathroom, Aiden took the Valium. The Valium that Sam had given him. That was why Sam appeared to him now. He had taken the drugs she had given him. As the light of dawn crept into the bedroom, Aiden became determined to go to work. He couldn't explain why, but while the knot of fear had never dissipated from his chest, it had somehow changed. He wasn't scared Gary was going to turn up again at any moment now. He was scared for Sam. *Do it, Aiden. And you will see.*

*

Ten o'clock and Sam still hadn't come in. She was due to start at nine. Aiden had burnt the milk of his fourth coffee this morning as he kept his eye on the front door, just hoping to see her walk in. She was usually a little late, there was nothing odd about that. But an hour late? Even Sam wasn't usually that bad.

'Sorry about that. This one should be better.' He handed his latest customer a complimentary coffee to make up for their complaint.

The man took a sip, stood there for a moment and finally gave a quick nod of approval. 'Much better. Thanks,' he said before turning and heading for the door.

Aiden lifted his glasses and rubbed his aching eyes with his palm. 'Hey, Wendy?' he asked as he turned toward the kitchen.

'Aiden. Are you feeling alright? It's like you've been somewhere else all morning,' Wendy responded as she approached. She had evidently been keen to speak with him herself.

'Uh, yeah, sorry. Still not sleeping well,' he mumbled.

Wendy clicked her tongue and shook her head with pity. 'Think it might be a good idea to get it checked out? How long has it been now?' Her face gave away her mothering nature almost as much as her voice.

'Yeah, yeah, I think I might do that. It's been almost two weeks. Hey, anyway, Sam is definitely rostered on today, right?' He hoped there would be a logical explanation why Sam hadn't shown up.

Wendy just sighed with evident frustration. 'Yes, she was due to start over an hour ago,' she said as she busied herself making sure the counter was tidy.

'So, she didn't call in sick or anything?'

Wendy just shook her head. 'Nope, I've not heard a word from her. In fact, I should see if I can reach her right now,' she said with annoyance. She seemed to become more upset the more they talked about Sam. Aiden couldn't blame her. He had never been in a managerial role but, even if it had been offered to him, he wouldn't have been interested anyway. Who would want to deal with the stress of handling staff who miss their shifts or being the last point of contact for a complaining customer? Even so, Aiden wasn't really worried about how stressed Wendy was. All he wanted to know was that Sam was safe.

'Yeah, I wonder where she is?' he said with feigned disinterest while Wendy stepped out the back to use the phone. Aiden waited impatiently. He shuffled from foot to foot.

Come on, it's Sam! She's probably just hung over and hasn't even woken up yet or something. She's always randomly not turning up for work. But the niggling doubt in the back of his head wouldn't relent. He knew he was stretching the truth to try and make himself feel better. *Well, she's always late anyway,* he corrected himself. He jumped when Wendy suddenly announced her presence with a disgruntled huff.

'So, Sam had too much fun last night and won't be in today again?' he said with a forced laugh.

Wendy just shrugged. 'I wouldn't know. I tried her mobile twice with no answer. She better damn well ring back when she gets my message. She ought to know how pissed I am when she hears it.'

A rock dropped in Aiden's stomach. Sam wasn't even answering her phone. That wasn't a good sign but Aiden just continued to reassure himself that she was fine. Yet by the end of the day, when nobody had been able to reach her, he couldn't help but feel like something had happened to her.

YOU NEED HELP

REBECCA

The Saturday morning drizzle was icy cold as Bec walked along the path that ran by the wetlands in the neighbourhood. Usually when she went out for a run, she could keep going for the entire stretch. But today, she felt tired. Her sleep had been disturbed by Aiden's episodes of paralysis for the past week and she was beginning to feel the effects of the deprivation. Thankfully, Leena was content to amble along at the steadier pace.

She was a good dog and while Bec held the curled-up leash in her hand, she didn't really need to use it. Leena would happily look up to her as they walked, just enjoying the fact that she was free of the yard for a while. Bec's mind had been running non-stop since she got home from work yesterday. Aiden just wasn't himself when she got home. He just sat in the living room, staring at his phone. But it wasn't as though he was bored and just surfing social media. He was transfixed, intently focused on whatever he was looking at. Bec had asked what he was so interested in only to receive no reply. She leaned over Aiden's shoulder, joking that he should stop whatever porn he was watching right now if he valued their marriage. Of course, she made certain Hannah wasn't in ear shot before making such a crass joke. She knew her teenage daughter would be just mortified if she heard anything that related at all to her parents' sexual inclinations. Bec couldn't blame her. She would still be horrified to hear anything of her own parents' sex lives after all. But even as she delivered the joke, Aiden didn't seem to notice her. Looking to the bright screen, Bec wasn't surprised that she didn't see any naked skin. Naturally, she knew Aiden watched porn every now and then. Sometimes she even joined him. But he knew better than to do so in the middle of the living room after work. Instead, Aiden was looking at an article. She couldn't read much of the tiny text from behind the sofa chair but she did make out a few words. *Sleep. Nightmares. Trouble waking.*

When she asked Aiden if he was alright, he simply responded, 'Yeah, I'm fine. Just looking something up.'

Bec was encouraged. He seemed focused, but otherwise fine. A peck on the cheek and she was off to get changed out of her work clothes. But Aiden didn't move for hours. No matter how Bec and Hannah tried to get his attention, to lure him away from his phone, Aiden just repeated he wouldn't be long. When dinner was ready, Bec finally managed to get him off of his arse, but she had to basically shout at him to get him moving. Even while they ate, Aiden kept looking at his phone rather than engaging with his family like usual. In the end, no matter how pissed Bec got, she grew tired of trying to get through to him and just let him be. She went to bed alone and briefly woke up to Aiden joining her at about two in the morning.

When she woke up, she decided to leave Aiden to get some rest. With whatever sleeping problems he was having, he surely needed it and Bec wanted to get some fresh air so she took Leena for a walk. Now, she was on her way back home, listening to the magpies warbling amongst the chittering insects in the wetlands. The cold air had not only soothed Bec's tired eyes, but it had also helped to clear her head. She had gotten upset with Aiden last night. Who wouldn't be upset when their spouse basically ignores their family all evening? But, given some time to think, Bec knew that Aiden was just struggling. In fact, she was growing all the more worried about him. She couldn't help but fear that this sleeping problem of his might devolve further and further until Aiden stopped getting up for work. Until he stopped getting up at all and just sat around the house like he did in the past. Bec decided that she wouldn't take no for an answer when she got home. Aiden needed to talk to her, to share his feelings and what he was going through, whether he liked it or not. It might be difficult, but it was worth it to help him.

*

Leena ran excitedly through the house as Bec closed the door. The sweet dog made a beeline through the living room and by the time Bec caught up with her in the kitchen, she was jumping up and trying to lick Hannah's face as the girl sat eating breakfast at the table. Unlike her father the night before, Hannah set her phone down to be forgotten on the table as she lovingly scratched behind Leena's ears.

'Morning, sweetie. How are you doing?' Bec greeted her daughter with a smile as she walked to the fridge to grab some orange juice.

'Did you have a good walk with Mum? Did you? Alright, come on. Off now.' Hannah was speaking playfully with Leena before gently encouraging the dog to wander about as she pleased. 'Yeah, not bad. How are you? Dad's still in bed?' She looked back to her mum now as she resumed her breakfast.

Bec gave a curt nod as she took a sip of her freshly poured glass of juice. 'Yes. He's still been struggling but we'll get there. Anyway, I can't remember, were you meeting up with Abbi today or tomorrow?' she asked after smacking her lips and leaning on the benchtop.

'Nah, that's tomorrow. I dunno, I think I'll just veg today. It's pretty cold out. Maybe wanna watch a movie later?' Hannah responded.

Bec nodded. 'Yeah, sounds good. I'm just going to go see how your dad is going, alright? Narrow down the choices for me?'

'Yep. No rush, Mum. We have all day.' Hannah grinned.

'Got to love the weekend,' Bec said before draining her glass and heading down the hallway.

She was happy that her daughter could have some time to relax. She noticed how, since starting high school, the homework just kept on coming. Had they really had so much when Bec, herself, was a teenager? She couldn't comprehend how much Hannah had to do and was always impressed to learn that she was usually on top of it all. She was so grateful her daughter was a studious learner.

As she walked down the hall, her mind wandered from Hannah to her husband and the conversation they might be about to share. She felt apprehensive as she pushed the bedroom door open, though she didn't know why. Bec and Aiden had a good relationship. They communicated well. Usually. But there was something about Aiden lately. Something about his paralysis, his sleep deprivation that seemed to change him. Bec pushed through her hesitation and stepped inside the bedroom. She knew she had to talk to Aiden. To help him. To her surprise, she found he was awake. He sat upright in bed with his back propped against the wall with his upturned pillow. The blue glow of his mobile shone upon his unshaven face and reflected white glare in the lenses of his glasses. The lights were still out and with the black-out curtains drawn, the screen of Aiden's phone seemed to be the only source of light. Bec thought there was something eerie about the light on her husband's face but she shook her fears away.

'Morning, honey. How are you feeling today?' she greeted lightly as she closed the bedroom door.

She didn't expect a reply. Aiden appeared to be in the same catatonic state of last night. His eyes were transfixed on his phone and his lack of movement caused Bec to wonder if he even noticed if she was in the room. She wandered over to the window and pulled open the curtains, letting in the light of the overcast morning. It might have been dark and cloudy outside, but the daylight shone in the room as though the sun was unobscured. Expecting no response, Bec actually jumped a little when she heard her husband's voice.

'Hey. I – I need to talk to you about something.' He mumbled his words and he didn't take his eyes off of his phone but at least it was something.

'Finally talking, are we? What's up?' Bec spoke lightly, casually, as though nothing was wrong. She sat down on the bed next to her husband and watched him closely, wearing a gentle smile.

Behind her pleasant behaviour, Bec's heart was in her throat. She didn't know why, but she felt as though something serious was coming and she knew she wouldn't like it. Aiden kept looking at his phone, his eyes darting back and forth as he read something.

'Hey, come on, babe. Put that down and look at me. What's going on?' Bec prompted after a few moments. She reached forward and set her hand over Aiden's phone.

Aiden jolted, instinctively tugging his phone away from his wife's hand as though she were trying to steal it. He looked up and Bec finally caught his gaze. His eyes were bloodshot and watery. But when he looked at his wife, Aiden's hard gaze seemed to soften. It was as though looking at her face had brought some sense of self back into his mind. Bec was relieved to hear her husband heave a deep sigh. He seemed to relax and, though he looked back down, his phone flopped down on its back, even though he still held it in his fingers.

'So, what's going on, honey? Are you alright?'

Aiden opened his mouth several times to speak but couldn't seem to find his voice again. Bec ran her fingers up and down Aiden's arm in an attempt to physically soothe him and he heaved a deep breath. She opened her mouth to prompt him further when Aiden's head snapped around and he looked right at her again. This time, his eyes were wide. Wild.

'I just... you're going to think I'm being crazy,' he said with a tremble in his voice.

Bec shook her head. 'Come on, how long have you known me, honey? Of course, I think you're crazy,' she said with a smile. She knew something was off, that Aiden needed to be serious. But Bec wanted to remind him that she was there for him. She was the safe place he could turn to in his time of need.

She hoped she was helping to lighten the mood though she wasn't surprised when Aiden didn't laugh, or even crack a smile. He just huffed a breath and looked down blankly to his hands. Bec waited. She tried to hide how much she was losing patience. Finally, Aiden looked at her again.

'I – I think I'm being haunted,' he said weakly.

Bec stifled a scoff. She didn't know what to say. Surely Aiden couldn't be serious? But as she looked at him, she knew her husband was being deadly serious. 'I... honey, what do you mean?'

While he was still not himself, Aiden seemed a little encouraged that his wife hadn't just laughed in his face. He sat up, finally taking an interest in another human being.

'Uh, well, I've been looking into things. You know, with the paralysis. I mean, I know it sounds crazy, but I don't think it's just in my head.'

Bec noticed how he nervously wrung his hands together as he spoke. He was looking more pale than normal. She really hoped he could be free of his paralysis symptoms soon.

'Okay. So, why do you think something else is going on? What's been happening?' Bec inquired further and Aiden nodded with more enthusiasm.

'I mean, you know what happens. When I can't move. Can't speak. But... but when that happens, something else happens too. I... see things. Hear things.'

Bec nodded slowly as her husband spoke in crazed jitters 'I think I know what you mean. I've looked into it too. We've talked about it before, remember? It's pretty common to hallucinate. I don't know, to see shadows and hear voices. Like you're dreaming while you're awake,' she said. Bec was almost reciting the article she read verbatim as she recalled what she had learned. All in all, the whole sleep paralysis phenomenon sounded terrifying to her.

This time, Aiden shook his head dismissively. 'No, I know. I know what they say it is. All just some psychological thing. But you don't know, Bec. It's so real,' he said shakily. 'What do you think I've been doing all this time? I've been looking into everything I can find on it. Look here.'

As Aiden spoke, he took up his phone again. Unlocking the screen, he held it up for Bec to see. She could barely read it as Aiden's hand shook but she could distinctly make out the image of an old, renaissance-style painting. Bec saw a woman lying back on an ornately decorated bed. Her white face was twisted with fear as she stared at some ghastly looking black creature that sat on her chest.

'See, this sort of thing has been going on forever! The more I've read, the more I wonder if people didn't have it right ages ago! Okay, maybe it's not witches or goblins. I mean, that shit's crazy, right?' Aiden laughed weakly at his own inane babbling as he looked back to his phone. 'But there are lots of stories about it. Lots of people think it might be something else. I don't know, ghosts or something. Demons.'

Bec was lost for words. She had never known her husband to honestly believe in anything of the supernatural before. How much sleep had he lost recently? Yet, even though she couldn't quite put her finger on it, Bec did feel a sense of unease at the idea of something supernatural. Try though she might, she couldn't say why the idea bothered her so. It was as if her memories were hidden in a thick haze. She shook the uncertainty from her head and focused back on her husband.

'So, you really think it could be a ghost or something? Honey, you know what stress can do to a person's head. And if you haven't been sleeping ...' Bec said but her words trailed off as Aiden shook his head more vigorously. He rubbed his eyes, his glasses bouncing over his knuckles before falling back to his nose.

'I know! It sounds crazy. I knew you would think I'm nuts. But please believe me, Bec! I've hallucinated before. This isn't like that. Gary is real!' Aiden ranted.

Bec gently took her husband's shoulders as he became more erratic. 'Okay, babe, calm down. Calm down. It's okay,' she soothed.

Aiden slowly sat back against the wall again. Bec made sure he was looking her in the eye.

'Please listen to me, honey. Just breathe. I can't say I know what's going on with you. But I'm here, alright? We can get through this together. I know it seems real. But this Gary? He isn't there. It's all in your head. We just need to help you get some decent rest again, okay? Have you been taking any more of that Valium you've got?' She spoke softly and calmly. She was glad to see Aiden was breathing deeper and calming down. Until she mentioned the Valium. As soon as she mentioned the tablets, Aiden's eyes grew wide and frantically shook his head.

'No! No, I shouldn't take that. Sam hurts me if I do,' he said in a hoarse whisper.

Bec raised her eyebrows in surprise. 'Uh, what? Who's Sam? I thought it was Gary? Do you mean Sam from work?' she asked in confusion.

'Yeah. Sam gave me the Valium. Now she hasn't come into work. Wendy couldn't get hold of her. She's gone missing. Gary must have done something. I think… I think Sam's dead,' Aiden said feverishly.

Bec's heart pounded and her skin tingled with worry. She honestly couldn't believe a word her husband was saying. There couldn't possibly be any ghosts and Sam wouldn't have been killed for lending Aiden some medication. But Bec was worried about her husband. About his state of mind.

'Okay, uh, baby? I really need you to listen to me. Nothing bad is happening, alright? You know Sam. This isn't the first time she hasn't shown up for work. You said yourself she has been a no show after partying a couple of times already.' While she spoke, Bec felt her own rationalisations comfort her concerned mind. She shook her head slightly to banish the idea that Aiden might have even been convincing her something sinister had really been happening. It was ridiculous. Aiden just sat in silence, looking to his wife. He didn't argue but he didn't look convinced either.

'If… if Gary is real, I don't know what to do,' he whispered after a moment.

Bec stroked his face and lightly shook her head. 'He isn't real, honey. You just need to get some good sleep. I think you should try and rest as much as you can today. I'm going to give Lauren a call, okay? I'll make a new appointment for you to see her as early as possible. Alright? I'm sure Lauren can talk you through things better than I can.' She made sure to catch Aiden's eye as she spoke.

Thankfully, Aiden slowly nodded. It was as though he was giving in to the temptation of sleep. Bec was surprised that, after his erratic behaviour, his eyes began to droop.

'See, you're so tired! Come on, let's try and get you to sleep. Now, you'll be happy to see Lauren as soon as you can?' she said as she reached down and took Aiden's phone from his limp fingers. She set it on her bedside table, intent to taking it out of the room when she left. Her husband didn't need any distractions. With her guidance, Aiden shuffled down into the bed and rested his head on the pillow.

'Yes. I need to talk to Lauren. Need to tell her about Gary. She can help,' he said sluggishly as Bec took off his glasses.

'Good. I'll call her right away. Now try and rest, won't you?'

Aiden barely responded as he mumbled incoherently and began to drift into slumber. Bec gave him a quick kiss on the forehead before sliding off of the bed. She took up Aiden's phone; she would need it anyway to grab Lauren's private number. She hoped Lauren could do something. Maybe even prescribe something. The whole conversation had become so surreal. Aiden had shifted from erratic and babbling to drowsy so quickly that he might as well have been drugged.

As she watched her husband's chest slowly rise and fall in the sheets, she felt a curious sense of déjà vu. She had never experienced such a bizarre exchange with Aiden before, but Bec had tucked a young Hannah into bed in such a similar manner many times before. It frightened her to think how odd Aiden was acting. She quietly stepped out of the room and shut the door behind her. She wouldn't tell Hannah the details of her dad's ramblings, just that he was trying to catch up on his sleep. But before she would sit down with her daughter to enjoy some normality, Bec was going to call Lauren right away. Aiden clearly needed help as soon as possible.

CONNECTING

HANNAH

'We're here already. Meet you at the food court!' The text message from Abbi read.

'Be there in a minute.' Hannah quickly typed out the reply on her phone as she walked through the automatic doors of the Glen Marsh shopping hub.

The weather was as grey as yesterday and even a touch colder. Even so, Hannah merely unzipped her thick jacket after she had stepped indoors from the elements. Those sort of shopping centres had the air conditioning running for as long as the places were open, no matter the weather. As Hannah walked past the two-dollar shops and newsagents, she reminded herself to stay calm. She often came to the shopping centre, as did many people for an easy way to kill the time. Hannah and Abbi went window shopping, sometimes even buying something if they were lucky enough to have some money from their parents, birthdays or some other special occasion. Sometimes Brian would even tag along to waste some time or catch a movie. The Glen Marsh hub could almost be considered a home away from home for Hannah.

But this visit was going to be different. Not only was this one of the occasions when Brian would be joining them, but Abbi had told

Hannah on Friday night that she had managed to speak with Brian about his feelings. When Hannah had pressed Abbi for information, she learned that Brian might actually like her back! Abbi said that Brian was pretty evasive about the whole thing, pretty shy, which sounded an awful lot like Brian. But Hannah couldn't stop herself from feeling excited. At the very least, Brian hadn't just denied any interest at all. At least, that's what Abbi said.

Having been left to stew on her thoughts for two days, Hannah didn't really know what to think anymore. They had organised to all catch up, maybe see a movie or something today, and she had no idea what to expect. She was worried the whole thing would just be awkward. Even while she hung around at home with her mum all day yesterday, she couldn't help thinking about Brian. She hoped that Abbi's little chat with him hadn't revealed too much, that at least their friendship might still be intact. Though as time went on, Hannah couldn't help letting the niggling doubts in the back of her mind crawl their way to the surface. She wondered if Abbi had merely alluded to a more positive result. What if she had lied about how Brian had reacted? Maybe he really hadn't shown much interest at all? Maybe Abbi was mistaking Brian's general disinterest for quiet shyness? What if Abbi hadn't actually spoken to Brian at all?

But Hannah did her best to push such stupid thoughts out of her head. Abbi had always been her best friend and she was evidently excited for her when they last spoke over the laptop. At least, that's how Hannah thought she remembered it. That whole night had become a bit of a blur in her mind. She didn't even recall asking to sleep in her parents' room and was rather surprised when she woke on their floor. Her confused memory aside, what reason would Abbi possibly have had to lie about having spoken to Brian? No, Hannah knew that such doubts were just the manifestations of her own fear. She wanted something to happen with Brian. She wanted to be more than friends. But she was terrified that he might not feel the same way. That she might lose him completely.

'Ah, excuse me,' a middle-aged man with a large stomach mumbled as he shifted his step to avoid bumping into Hannah.

Snapping out of her daydreaming, she took a quick step back. 'Oh, sorry. My fault,' she said meekly with an apologetic smile. The place was pretty quiet considering it was a Sunday but there were still plenty of people wandering about.

'All good,' the man said as he continued on his way back up to the entryway Hannah had entered from.

Maybe don't run into everyone, idiot, her brain scolded her.

After turning left at the hairdresser, she could see the food court up ahead. The famous logos of the biggest fast-food companies glowed on the walls, almost completely overshadowing the lights and signs of the smaller food vendors. The sound of chattering people grew louder as Hannah approached and she saw many of the tables were occupied. She cast her eye over the crowd, looking past the mass of strangers. Families, couples, prams, teenagers and seniors were all scattered around the food court. Hannah slowed her pace and wandered with her hands slipped into the pockets of her jeans as she looked for the familiar faces of her friends.

'Hannah! Over here!'

Looking toward the source of the voice, Hannah found Abbi standing on the opposite side of a solid row of seats and tables. She was waving her hand in the air and wore a big smile on her face as she beckoned Hannah over. Abbi looked fantastic of course. Her golden blonde hair was hanging freely past her shoulders and she wore a cute, white halter top despite the cooler weather. Hannah returned her smile and quickly headed over. She was relieved that Abbi turned and sat back down. She always hated that awkward thirty seconds of silently walking towards a friend while they did the same, or just stood there dumbly waiting.

'Hey,' she greeted with a grin as she finally approached the table.

Abbi immediately jumped up and wrapped her arms around her as though they hadn't seen each other in months. Needless to say, they had only just been at school together two days ago. Brian was seated with his skinny crossed arms resting on the tabletop. He was hunched over and had to twist his neck at an odd angle to glance up at Hannah with a small smile. Hannah reciprocated before her eyes inadvertently looked over the white floor. An old French fry that had been trodden for God knows how long into the floor became immensely interesting to her for some reason.

'Hello? How are you, dimwit?' Abbi asked, evidently repeating her question as she sat back down.

Hannah shook her head to compose herself. How she hated this nervousness! 'Yeah, I'm good. How about you guys?' she said with more squeak to her voice than usual as she took a seat opposite Brian and next to Abbi.

'Doing great,' Abbi said with a sly smile on her lips, though Hannah didn't really focus on her. She glanced again to Brian and their eyes met for a second before darting elsewhere once more.

'I've been alright. Busy weekend. Homework. You know?' Brian mumbled.

Hannah was grateful to see she wasn't the only one who was nervous. She nodded to his words. 'Yeah. We just keep getting more of it, right?' she said. *Homework? What kind of small talk is homework?!* Looking to Abbi, Hannah saw her friend was wearing an incredulous expression as though she were begging the same question.

'Yeah, well, we're not at school today. What do you guys want to do before the movie? Shall we grab some lunch, seeing as we're here already?' Abbi suggested. Her tone was bouncy and light, but Hannah could tell she was trying to steer the conversation and she was grateful for the support.

'Sure. I mean, that makes sense. We've got, what, just over an hour before we have to be at the cinemas?' Hannah said as she absent-mindedly pulled out her phone to check the time. She had only just looked at it a few minutes ago.

'Yeah, sounds good.' Brian nodded.

'Hmm, what should we get?' Abbi said as she rose from her seat a little and looked around the food court. Just then, a shrill electronic tune wailed from Abbi's jeans' pocket.

'Who loves you then?' Hannah asked with curiosity to the phone call. Abbi did have a decent number of friends, not to mention she was pretty close with her older sisters, but usually people just texted her.

'Hang on, that's not my ringtone. It's the alarm,' Abbi said as she drew her phone out and fiddled with the touch screen.

Hannah wasn't sure if Brian was looking at her. She felt as though she could feel his gaze on her, but she was too immobile to check.

'Aww, man! How could I forget?' Abbi moaned after reading her phone.

Hannah squinted suspiciously at her friend.

'What?' she and Brian asked at the same time, their voices mingling together, both seeming to be of higher pitch than normal.

'I'm meant to be getting my hair done in like, ten minutes! I'll have to meet you guys at the movies,' Abbi said with a look of dismay on her face.

'Oh,' Brian managed to say.

Hannah couldn't hold back and audible gasp of disbelief. 'What do you mean? I thought you had your hair done last weekend?' she asked.

Abbi tilted her head and looked to Hannah as though she couldn't be any more wrong. 'Yeah, but do you know how much work has to go into keeping my hair this good?' she joked before standing up and slipping on her cardigan.

'But who sets an alarm for ten minutes before an appointment? What would have happened if you were at home?' Hannah persisted, the logical faults of Abbi's predicament hitting her brain like a hammer over and over.

'Maybe I'm just that forgetful that I have to set two alarms,' Abbi retorted. 'I'll catch up with you guys at the cinemas in an hour, okay?' she added with a coy smile.

Brian looked like a deer caught in headlights and Hannah could feel her face pleading for Abbi to stay with them as a buffer.

'Don't get anything too heavy. I'll totally need some popcorn later, seeing as I'm not getting any lunch,' Abbi said.

'Righto,' Brian said softly.

Hannah didn't know what to think of his mood. The boy looked practically glum. If she didn't know any better, Hannah might have thought Brian was upset Abbi was leaving. That he would much rather spend some alone time with her instead. But, as she caught another fleeting glance from his eyes, Hannah's heart skipped a beat. *He's nervous. Nervous to be alone. With me,* she thought excitedly.

'Oh, Hannah! Come here! I forgot to ask you something,' Abbi's voice called out.

When Hannah looked up, she was surprised to see her friend was already halfway across the food court. 'Yeah, okay,' she replied louder than she had intended. 'Sorry, I'll, uh, be right back,' she mumbled to Brian as she slipped out of her seat.

Brian smiled and might have even tried to say something, but if he did, Hannah couldn't make out any real words through his muttering lips. Hannah quickly made her way over to Abbi while the blonde waited with a hand on her hip.

'How are you feeling?' she asked softly when Hannah approached.

'Uh, I dunno. Kinda weird. It's never really been this awkward with Brian before,' Hannah replied while she glanced back to Brian with uncertainty.

Abbi reached up and gently took Hannah's shoulder, directing her friend to look her in the eyes. 'Hey, don't sweat it. You guys have been friends for ages. Just be yourself. You like him, so what? He likes you too. It's going to be great.'

'Yeah. Yeah, okay.' Hannah nodded with a smile. She tried to show Abbi that she was confident. In control. In truth, Hannah was just doing her best to keep the butterflies in her stomach from escaping.

'Trust me, a little time alone and you guys won't be able to keep your hands off each other.'

'Shut up!' Hannah retorted with no doubt in her mind that her cheeks were now resembling ripened apples.

'Well, what are you waiting for? Get back to your man,' Abbi said before her smile drooped, if ever so slightly. 'And, uh, if anything does go wrong, which it won't, but if it does, just text me and I'll come running. I'll just be wandering around the shops.'

Hannah raised an eyebrow. 'What, you mean you weren't really rushing off to an emergency hair appointment?' she asked sarcastically.

'Is it that obvious?'

'Uh, duh!' Hannah grinned. If anything, Abbi's poor attempt for an excuse encouraged her. Surely Brian wouldn't be gullible enough to believe Abbi had to rush off to the hairdressers like that. If he hadn't protested about her departure, maybe he was more interested to be alone with Hannah that she might have first suspected.

'Okay, enough. Move it, you! You don't want to keep lover-boy waiting,' Abbi said with a playful smooch in the air before she light heartedly pushed Hannah's shoulder and turned her back to Brian. Hannah could see Brian's eyes quickly drop away from watching them and he started swiping his phone with apparent interest. Hannah took a deep breath and started to walk back to him.

*

'You're kidding?' Hannah said as she struggled to take a sip of cola while she stifled her laughter.

'I dunno, anyone can get a recipe wrong, can't they? I mean, my mum asked me to cook so really, she brought it on herself, didn't she?' Brian said with a sheepish grin.

Hannah just snorted more as she desperately tried to keep her drink in her mouth. 'Yeah, I'm sure your mum wanted you to load the curry with enough spice to blow her head off,' she said after choking on the fizziness of the soft drink for a moment.

'Seriously, she went so red! She was making, like, I dunno, weird coughing noises. Sounded like a cat coughing up a furball. Dad and I thought she was gonna die.' Brian laughed.

'Okay. Remind me not to let you make me any dinner for a while,' Hannah suddenly felt embarrassed and looked away from Brian.

Don't be stupid! This is fine. We're having a great time, she thought, scolding her insecure mind. In a way, she felt encouraged by how embarrassed Brian looked too. The suggestion of him making Hannah dinner undoubtedly sounded very much like a date scenario to both of them. Brian loudly cleared his throat.

'So, uh, just buying you a burger now and then would be enough, huh?' Hannah had to concentrate to try and control her beaming grin. She was worried she looked as though she were insane with so much smiling.

'Yeah. That sounds fine. No way you can poison me if you're just buying, I suppose.'

'Cool.'

Is that it? Did he just ask me out? But we are out. Eating burgers. That couldn't have been it, right? God, how do I tell? Should I say something? Will he say something? What do I do?! Hannah's mind was running a mile a minute though she felt she was doing a pretty decent job not to show her anxiety on her face. A silence lingered between the two teenagers and it seemed that, every time their eyes met, they had to quickly avert their gaze or else the world would collapse around them. Hannah's heart pounded in her chest as she played absent-mindedly with the paper wrapper from her hamburger. Brian appeared to take a special interest in sipping his drink, apparently taking longer than anyone ever had to suck a mouthful up the straw.

'So, uh… Abbi, um, told me she spoke to you at school a few days ago?' Hannah finally said. Even though her voice quivered, it sounded to her ears as though she had screamed the words much louder than was necessary.

Brian choked on his drink and heaved a couple of coughs. 'Uh, yeah. She did,' he spluttered awkwardly.

Hannah pressed her tongue into her cheek, the excitement of finally having the conversation enveloping her. 'What about?' she found herself asking coquettishly without thinking. Of course, she knew what they had spoken about. But she wanted to hear what Brian had to say about it. She continued to twist and tear little strips of paper from the wrapper as she waited. Brian heaved a nervous sigh.

'Well, uh, she pretty much asked… if I like you. Like, like you, like you,' Brian's stuttering words indicated how little experience he had talking to a girl about his feelings towards her. In a way, Hannah just found it all the more endearing. After all, she had never spoken to a boy about such things either.

'Wow,' she said with feigned surprise, which she didn't doubt was all too obviously fake. 'And, uh, what did you say?'

As she asked the question, Hannah finally got the courage to look up. To her surprise, she found Brian had been looking at her rather than nervously glancing this way and that as had been normal of his behaviour for most of their meal. Hannah blushed when Brian didn't look away, but instead, his sweet lips curled into an excitable smile.

'Heh, I uh, I said I did. That I do, you know. Like you, like you.'

Hannah knew she was bright red. She dropped the torn pieces of burger wrapper as though they were no longer worth her time and instead played with her dark hair.

'Really?' she managed to ask as she felt her heart would burst with happiness.

'Yeah,' Brian responded and his smile fell a little. 'Um, what about you? Do you, maybe, uh, like me?'

Hannah's voice caught in her throat. She wanted to cry out and admit her crush to Brian. She opened her mouth a few times in silence before awkwardly clearing her throat.

'Yes. Yes, I like you too,' she said finally in a heavy, hoarse voice. *Oh god, why do I sound like a sick horse?!* she screamed in her head. But, to her relief, Brian just wore a wide, beaming smile.

'Really? That's… wow,' he said with apparent surprise and joy.

Hannah didn't know what to do, or what to say. She had just admitted her attraction to Brian. He had just done the same. If this were a Hollywood movie they would be making out or something. Hannah was nervous Brian might be expecting something like that. Suddenly, she was drawn out from her rapid thoughts as she felt a soft caress on her hand. She looked down and found that Brian had simply reached over and set his hand over hers. He gently stroked her skin with his fingers as he looked at her. Hannah's entire body was unbelievably warm and tingly. She couldn't help letting out a giggle of delight which, of course, made her feel all the more self-conscious.

'So, Hannah. Would you like to go out with me?' Brian asked as confidently as he could, though his voice still wavered a little bit. Hannah loved the feeling of his gentle hand on hers and she couldn't keep her smile down even if she wanted to. She became lost in Brian's soft, brown eyes and would be happy to stay sitting in the middle of the busy food court all day so long as she could stay with him.

'Yes. I'd like that,' she said, thankful that this moment was really happening and not just some wonderful dream.

THEY'RE EVERYWHERE!
AIDEN

Another cloudy day. Foggy even. Aiden could barely make out the buildings that lined the road as he drove. The sun was hidden behind a thick blanket of swollen, grey clouds creating an unsettling darkness. No light glowed from the streetlamps as it was actually past eight in the morning despite what the world of sheer grey would have anyone believe. Aiden knew he had plenty of time to get to his nine o'clock appointment with Lauren, which was just as well as he was forced to drive slower than the limit given his lack of vision. The steering wheel felt unfamiliar in his hands and the black dashboard had a strange shade of beige about it today. Aiden couldn't help feeling as though he had taken the wrong car. Had he driven off in Bec's car without realising it? Even so, Bec's little city 4WD had grey upholstery, not beige. And Aiden felt as though he was sitting far too low on the road to be driving the old family car. He contented himself in the knowledge that he was just feeling out of sorts from the trials of recent days. What with the lack of sleep, the constant studying of the supernatural, the frightful sounds in the night and missing co-workers visiting him as molesting corpses, Aiden figured the failure to recognise the intricate features of his car would just be expected of his weary brain.

'I probably shouldn't even be driving at all,' he muttered to himself with a forced chuckle as he turned carefully, almost painfully slowly around the corner. The red glow of the rear lights of a car ahead of him faded quickly into the distance. Apparently not everyone was keen to be as cautious a driver as Aiden despite the poor weather.

'Bec is right. Nothing insane is happening. Well, actually happening. Insane though? Maybe. It's all just in my head. Talking to Lauren is going to help. She has me all figured out. I mean, I've been seeing her for how many years now? Maybe I'll finally have a good, long sleep afterwards. After she clears my head a bit.' Aiden was thinking out loud. His own mumbling voice droned in his ear like the distant buzzing of a mosquito. The sort of sound you don't really pay attention to, but if the silence pervades long enough, it can become deafening. Aiden shook his head and quickly wiped his eyes. In the split second he had taken his eyes from the road, he began to veer to the right and he quickly adjusted himself.

'Jesus, get a grip, would you?! Thank God the roads aren't busy.' He scolded himself while banging his fist on the cushioned cover the steering wheel. It was strange, he never had a soft cover on his steering wheel before. Maybe that's why it seemed so unfamiliar to him. Usually, he would feel the thin leather in his clenched fingers, but the wheel was thick, soft and warm to touch.

'Bec must have thought they would be nice additions to the cars. Probably got one for herself too. Hell, she probably told me and I've just forgotten. Stupid arse brain.' Aiden smiled lightly as he continued to mumble away to himself. Things hadn't been going so well for him lately, he knew that. But how could he forget how lucky he was to have Bec in his life? That beautiful woman took such good care of him and how had he repaid her? By practically losing his mind and babbling about ghosts.

'I'm sorry, babe. You really don't need to deal with this shit. You're so right. I just need to get my act together. Talk to Lauren. Get this whole stupid shit sorted.' The droning of his voice was slowly becoming unbearable, but no matter what he did, he couldn't stop chatting away to himself.

Aiden reached up to the car stereo. He couldn't remember what CD he had left in there. After all, he usually just played music using the AUX cable and his phone these days. But he knew better than to start mucking around on his phone while he was on the road. He would just start the CD player and see what old, forgotten tunes were locked inside it. Some nice background music would help distract him from his thoughts and his own voice. Just as his finger set over the power button, the buzzing rang loudly in Aiden's ear. Specifically, his left ear. Something flicked over his ear lobe and he jumped with a start, taking his hand away from the stereo and up to his ear to see if something was there. He could feel nothing, but something had definitely been there. Aiden's fingers had gripped his ear just a moment too late so that the wasp barely missed his hand as it flew inches in front of his face.

'Shit!' he cried out in shock. How the hell had a wasp gotten into the car?

He leaned as far back into his chair as he could as he watched the angry streaks of yellow and black flitter back and forth in front of him. Aiden wasn't particularly scared of wasps, or any bugs at all for that matter. But being locked in a confined space with an arsehole of the insect world buzzing in your face is enough to send most people into a frightful panic. He glanced to the wasp intermittently as he tried to concentrate on the road. He slowed the car right down and carefully flicked on the indicator without trying to make any sudden moves that might really piss the wasp off. He pulled over while breathing lightly through his nose. The wasp buzzed dangerously close to his nose before retreating way from his face. Aiden's relief at the wasp's departure was short lived when the insect decided to land on one of his pale knuckles at the steering wheel. The feeling of the pointy little legs and hard abdomen sent a shiver up his spine. It was just a wasp. But that didn't mean Aiden wasn't scared of the burning pain it could so easily inflict if it so desired. Thankfully, he finally stopped the car on the side of the road. Only one other vehicle ran past him as, with his free right hand, Aiden pressed the button to lower the driver's window. The glass slowly slid down and the cold morning breeze nipped his tingly face. He sat with his eyes glued on the wasp as it agitatedly wandered along his index finger.

'Come on, you little bastard. Fuck off. Get out,' he hissed quietly. He wanted to just flick his hand to give the wasp the hint but his nerves were shot from his recent experiences.

He just sat and stared as the wasp turned back down his finger. Aiden got the feeling the evil little thing was staring back at him with its big, shiny black eyes, almost as though it were goading him into giving it a reason to bite and sting the crap out of his hand. Then, to his great relief, the wasp took flight from his skin. It hovered over the steering wheel, just looking at the broken man and he was suddenly worried it would dive at his face. But, after a few moments, the wasp seemed to realise the outside world was within reach and it took off, whipping out of the car window. Aiden heaved a sigh of relief when the wasp disappeared and he quickly raised the window again before it could have a chance to change its mind and come back. His whole body instinctively shivered away his adrenaline.

'Seriously, what the fuck? It isn't even the right time of year for wasps. Damnit.'

He took another minute to compose himself before getting back on the road. Sure, he knew he would be late, but he still didn't like to be waylaid by wasps in the car of all things. Though the fog made it difficult to see, Aiden knew he wasn't too far from the counsel offices where Laura worked. He was currently on Henderson Road, one of the main roads which led through Glen Marsh. It was only another couple of blocks before he would take a left onto Croydon Street where he would have to keep an eye out for a parking spot. The fact that he was on one of the main roads of the town just made it all the more bewildering that it was so quiet. Aiden would have thought something was seriously wrong had he not begun to notice a few more cars on the road. Even so, it was a very cruisy drive for a Monday morning. He squinted to the street signs to make sure of his bearings before he began to turn into Croydon Street. Just as he righted the car, something caught his eye. Had something moved in the lower right corner of the windscreen?

Come on, now what? He was convinced he had just imagined it when a large huntsman spider sprinted over the windshield. Aiden couldn't believe it. First the wasp and now this? He watched as the dark, hairy spider skittered over the glass, it's eight legs effortlessly gripping to the windshield.

'Seriously, what the hell is going on today?!' he cried out as he flicked on the wipers. He watched as the rubber blades swept over the windscreen. They knocked the spider back and it stumbled, wriggled and struggled as it was dragged over the windshield. After several screeches of the wiper blades, the spider finally became caught between the glass and the rubber. Splatters of brown fluid smeared of the windshield as the huntsman's abdomen burst and its ragged body broke apart under the wiper.

Aiden sneered in disgust and even a little pity for the arachnid as he switched on the wiper fluid to try and clean the liquid entrails from the windscreen. At that moment, something tickled over the right side of his neck. He instinctively raised his hand, smacking over his skin and he felt something moving under his fingers. Drawing his hand away, Aiden saw a long, dark millipede twisting and twirling between his digits. He let out a gasp of fright and threw the millipede to the other side of the car. Not only had the thing frightened him just as the other critters had, but he was becoming wholly unnerved at how many bugs he was seeing. He was just about to curse aloud when he heard a sudden, horribly familiar chuckle. The voice was low and menacing but there was something else to it. It sounded garbled, as though emitted from a mouthful of food. Years of driving experience had caused Aiden to look up to the rear-view mirror rather than turn around to see the source of the sound. He froze in his seat, unaware of his feet on the pedals or his hands on the wheel. Aiden couldn't move, couldn't breathe, couldn't think.

In the mirror, he saw a dark figure seated in the spot behind him. It could have been a silhouette, a shadow of a figure it was so dark. But Aiden knew it wasn't. He could tell by the way the very surface of the figure moved. How it trembled and writhed, how its very skin seemed to coil and shiver. The figure was made entirely out of insects. Long centipedes and millipedes, spiders, beetles, ants, worms and maggots crawled all over one another, forming the hideous humanoid shape. Even flies and wasps skittered amongst the thousands of insects, occasionally taking flight.

'Still looking for help?' the voice hissed and tutted its tongue to the tune of thousands of clicking insects.

Aiden felt an itchiness in his shoes, running up his legs. Something skittered through his hair and a sudden sharp pain burned on the back of his neck. A loud crunching, churning sound began to resonate from the dashboard of the car and he flinched in terror, barely conceiving what the car was doing on the road. The slats of the air vents shivered and trembled as shiny, dark cockroaches began to pour out from them. Aiden could only let out a stifled scream as more, tiny, clawed feet digging into his skin. More bites burned at his flesh and he flailed wildly at his own body. The stereo slipped from its holster and dangled by coloured wires. A thin, pointed leg like that of a black widow spider protruded from the new opening. But it couldn't be possible. The leg was longer than Aiden's fingers. Whatever monstrosity of a spider the leg belonged had to at least have been the size of an adult's face. But, before he could discover what creature was pushing its way out of the dashboard, he heard more laughter from behind. He looked with another terrified glance into the mirror. The figure was wearing that hideous smile, the locked, twisting teeth and burning red eyes barely perceivable beneath the blanket of insects.

'All for you... Aiden,' the voice sneered with cruel laughter.

At that instant, the figure of bugs swelled and churned before bursting forth. Aiden screamed as the last thing he saw out of the windshield was an oncoming wall. Then he was lost in darkness. Lost in a sea of spiders and bugs, the overwhelming pain of their bites and stings sent him into a blind terror. They were in his clothes, biting in his ears, stinging at his eyes, crawling into his mouth that he would surely choke. There was a sudden crash, everything shook and then, nothing but a black void.

*

Aiden fell to his knees, his sweaty palms splayed over the concrete wall as he retched and vomited. He groaned as his meagre breakfast of toast and orange juice lay splattered on the ground before him.

'Oh God... fucking... God,' he whimpered.

The morning sky was still dark and grey, but there was no fog. The sights and sounds of a normal Monday morning were all around. Rows of idling cars sat on the road, waiting for the traffic lights to change. People made their way along the footpaths, some hurrying on their way to work, others leisurely strolling with cups of coffee and chatting to friends and colleagues. No one came walking too close though. Aiden couldn't blame them. He hadn't had the energy to focus on how he looked before going out that morning. A man with a rough, stubbled chin and frazzled dark hair, wearing nothing more than an old t-shirt and tracksuit pants who was doubled over vomiting on the wall of the local counsellors' building would probably always keep decent people at bay. He sat back against the wall with his head turned away from the rancid pool he had just created on the concrete. He closed his eyes as he tried to gather his thoughts.

Whatever it was he was experiencing was getting worse. He could almost still feel his skin crawling with bugs and the stings of their relentless biting. But it had just been in his head. It had to be. He was already at Lauren's building. He could see his own car parked just down the road. It had all just been some terrible, waking dream. It was exactly what he needed to talk to Lauren about. He shivered as he realised that she would likely ask him to recall his visions as best he could for her. He wouldn't have to try very hard. He wished he could just forget. Forget being buried alive by the bugs in the car. Forget Sam's corpse taunting and molesting him in his bed. Forget about Bec carving her own eyes out to hand to him like hors-d'oeuvres. It was all because of Gary. Because of that messed up, fucking manifestation in Aiden's head. He needed to tell Lauren. He needed her to help.

Even if the only thing she can do is dig that fucker out of my head with a blunt spoon, she's gotta do it, he thought. He knew he wasn't being rational but the desperation was too strong now. Finally, after resting for some moments against the wall, he carefully rose to his feet. His feet were steady enough now and there was nothing left in his stomach to throw up. Aiden brushed down his shirt in a futile attempt to make himself look presentable. Just as he was about to turn for the front door to the building, a loud screech from the road drew his attention. He watched, noticing how a few other bystanders did the same, looking this way and that to seek out the source of the noise. They didn't have to search for long, however, as a silver sedan sped down the road. There was no way the driver was going the limit as the vehicle charged along the street. He scoffed at the hoon's antics before the car began to violently swerve back and forth across the road.

'What the hell?!'

'Slow down you bloody lunatic!'

The calls of several pedestrians voiced his own thoughts. The car made a sudden turn and drove recklessly across the lanes. Aiden's heart jumped into his throat when the car mounted the kerb only metres from where he stood. Instinctively, he jumped back, almost breaking into a run before stumbling to the ground. The car smashed into the wall of the counsellor's offices with a deafening crash. The plastic and steel of the bonnet crumpled against the concrete wall and shards of windshield fell like rain. Aiden sat, staring at the car in shock. He couldn't believe it. If the driver had swerved just a moment later, he would have been plastered to the wall as though the car was a stamp and he was the ink.

'Wha – how, uh… are you alright?' he called meekly as he tried to get a hold of his nerves. He was already shaken up enough with his own problems, let alone having to deal with this crazy person with a death wish. As he got to his feet, he tried to look in to see the driver. He was on the wrong side of the car but could just make out the grey business slacks of a woman beneath the remnants of the deflated airbag.

'Hello? Are you alright in there?'

He heard a low, pained moan from the woman and began to dash around to the driver's side. Aiden didn't know first aid, or at least, he could barely remember anything from the short course he had taken about ten years ago, but he knew he couldn't just walk away from an accident that literally occurred at his feet. In the corner of his eye, he could see some people rushing over. Most were holding mobile phones to their ears, no doubt calling the emergency services. He felt a curious surge of relief that he wouldn't have to try to take care of this injured woman alone at least. The window on the driver's side was still intact but Aiden couldn't see into the car for all the cracks and chips in the glass. He took the door handle and tugged at it with uncertainty. To his surprise, despite being a bit stiff, the door still worked as one would expect. He swung it open and leaned in to see if there was anything he could do for the driver. As soon as he did, Aiden froze. He stared with wide eyes of disbelief. The beige dashboard, the car stereo, the furry covering on the steering wheel. They were all identical to those he had seen in is waking nightmare. He didn't know what to think. Surely it was too bizarre a coincidence? As the reality of the situation came to the fore, Aiden shook his troubled head and focused on the driver.

'Hello? Are you alri – oh, fuck no...' His train of confused thought ran right off the rails when he realised that he recognised the driver's face.

Lauren sat in the driver's seat, barely conscious as she slowly shook her head back against the headrest.

'Lauren?! Lauren, can you hear me?' Aiden cried after he finally relocated his voice.

Lauren only gave a small groan in response, her eyes almost completely closed as she seemed to wearily wake up. Aiden saw the seatbelt had left its mark along Lauren's shoulder and neck. He instantly recalled the seemingly ancient teachings of his own driving lessons. The seat belt should have been lower, shouldn't it? It was important not to let the strap cross over the base of the neck, right? At least he knew that it was best to wait and let the paramedics move someone from a car accident, but that seatbelt was still tightly digging into Lauren's skin. Uncertain at what to do, Aiden reached over Lauren to unbuckle the seatbelt just to relieve some of the tension. He brushed aside the hanging airbag and heard a clattering sound as the car stereo dropped awkwardly from its brace. A shiver ran up his spine as he imagined that long, widow spider's leg sliding out from behind the stereo as it had done in his nightmare. No such creature revealed itself, however. But the stereo hung in the same haphazard manner. Aiden clicked the buckle open when Lauren suddenly let out a deep gasp of breath. It appeared relieving the pressure of the seatbelt had provided Lauren with some minor comfort before she screamed and began to tussle in her seat.

'Woah, calm down. Lauren, it's me! You've had an accident,' Aiden tried to console the woman before she started smacking him. Surprised by her violent outburst, he tried to draw back. Lauren tightly gripped his arm, her fingernails scratching painfully down his skin as she clawed and wrestled.

'Jesus, Lauren! Stop!' he protested but Lauren flailed wildly and tugged him back to her with surprising strength. Aiden hit his head on the roof of the car, but Lauren just dragged him in closer until their faces were mere inches apart. Her violent attack ceased as suddenly as it had started and now, Lauren stared at Aiden with wide, crazed eyes. She opened and closed her mouth a few times but no sound escaped her lips. Aiden's heart pounded relentlessly in his chest, but he knew Lauren must be in shock and she needed his help.

'Shhh, it's okay, Lauren,' he said as soothingly as he could despite the adrenaline pumping through him. Lauren just continued to tightly hold his sore forearm and stare at him.

'Uh, you've just had an accident. I... people are coming. They're calling for help. Just try and stay still and...'

'Gary,' Lauren said in a hoarse whisper.

Aiden froze. He looked at Lauren's face and, beneath the bruises which began to swell on her skin, he could see something more than the shock of an accident in her expression. Lauren's eyes were wide and unblinking. Her panting breath and twisted mouth exposed her fear.

'G-Gary?' He didn't know why, but he tried to act as though the name meant nothing to him. But he knew he couldn't hide it. Lauren trembled.

'He... said his name... was Gary. That they... were for you,' she whimpered.

Aiden was speechless. He didn't know what to think. What to do. 'That they? What? What was for me?' he asked dumbly.

Lauren closed her eyes and winced as she turned away. She shuddered and slapped her own shoulder. Then she cried out with sudden pain. Aiden watched as Lauren opened her eyes and looked down to her legs. She began to kick and scream. One of her shoes came off her foot as she manically stamped the floor of the car and slapped her legs as though trying to get something off of them.

'They're... they're everywhere! No! Please, no, get off! Get them off me!' Lauren began to scream and weep like a woman who had lost her mind. In her insanity, she let Aiden go and he almost fell back. He quickly looked around for help. The people who had been approaching were still on their way, but they had barely moved any closer to them since he last saw them.

'Help! For God's sake, help us, would you?!' Aiden screamed at them in panic. A few people were standing across the road, just watching while those who approached finally seemed to sprint as though they had somehow been running in slow motion before.

'Aiden! Aiden, please, help me! Help me! Get them off of me!' Lauren continued to scream. She tore at her clothes, scratched at her skin struggled to get up and out of the car.

'What? Wha – I don't know what to do! Lauren, what's going on? What's on you?' Aiden tried to take one of Lauren's flailing hands and calm her down.

'The bugs! Spiders! Everywhere! Gary said! Argh, get them off me! They're biting! No, no, get away! Aiden! Aiden, they're climbing in my …' Lauren wailed before she suddenly began to choke and gag. Sheer panic boiled up in Aiden's chest as Lauren started shaking and seizing. She stared into thin air, her face turning bright red as she continued to choke.

'Lauren! Lauren? What the fuck do I do? Lauren!' He instinctively reached around Lauren's shoulders and tugged her out of the car. He fell on the ground with her beside him.

'Oh my God! Is anyone a doctor? A nurse? Something?' a random man asked frantically as he stood over them.

'Um, I know first aid. Um, uh, quick, lie her on her side,' another woman said.

Aiden lifted himself up and helped the strangers roll Lauren over. Her veins were bulging and her face was dark purple as she fixed her gaze on Aiden's face with bloodshot eyes. Her convulsions became slower and weaker and the people who were now crowding around gasped and chattered with panic amongst themselves. He watched as Lauren stared at him, unable to speak with a bubbling foam of drool running from her lips as she finally stopped moving.

'Oh, Jesus,' someone murmured from behind as Aiden heard the sirens calling louder from the distance. He doubted the paramedics would be able to help. With her dark, vacant eyes staring up at him, Aiden knew that Lauren was dead.

*

The bedroom was dark as Aiden sat on the side of the bed. The blackout curtains did their job well, with only the smallest beams of daylight creeping in from the edges of the heavy material. The light globes were all cold, none having been switched on since last night. Aiden sat in silence, staring at his hands. He couldn't believe it was real. Lauren was declared dead once the ambulance had arrived. It hadn't been long before the police arrived too. The site of the accident was cordoned off, the people moved on. Save for Aiden and a couple of others who were deemed witnesses.

The police asked questions, took statements and were meticulous about the details given. It was a pretty open-and-shut case from the witnesses' perspective though. The car swerved off of the road and crashed into the wall. The driver, all suspected, had suffered from some sort of internal injuries, likely a blow to the head during the accident. Aiden had been the first on the scene but, with no medical training, had been unable to diagnose nor help the victim. The body was to be taken to the hospital for an autopsy to determine the exact cause of death, but none seemed to think it suspicious. There was nothing in the official reports of the victim raving about ghosts or being eaten alive and engulfed by imaginary bugs. The name Gary was absent from any of the statements. Aiden knew better than to tell the police about him. He knew no one would believe it. The police would hardly take his ghost stories seriously; rather, they might deem him unstable and insist he be taken in for psychological testing. As it was, the officer who took his statement had suggested a trauma councillor to him. He took the contact details and promised he would see them. He didn't intend on it.

Somehow, Gary knew he was going to Lauren for help. The thing didn't like that. A gaping hollow numbness enveloped his body as he made his way home. He hadn't meant Lauren any harm. He hadn't even hurt her. But, Aiden knew he was responsible for her death. It was Gary who had attacked Lauren, but Gary was only here because of him. Whoever Gary hurt, whoever he killed, was because of him.

When he arrived home, Aiden just absent-mindedly walked to the bedroom and sat down. He thought about calling Bec. To tell her what had happened. To get some help. But he was scared. What if Gary hurt her too? What if he hurt Hannah? It was one thing when this entity, this demon, was hurting him. But people in his life were dying. How long would it be before the thing came after his own family?

Aiden sat in silence for a long time. He thought long and hard, trying to work out a solution. In the end, if he was going to protect his wife, protect his daughter, he knew what he had to do. He thought he had been going crazy. But now, he knew better. This Gary was attached to him, latched to him like some evil parasite.

He didn't know how long he had sat in the darkness of the bedroom before he finally felt himself move. As though he wasn't really thinking about his actions, he raised his hand and reached for the bedside table. The corner of the small cardboard box was hard in his fingers. He opened the packet and slid the foil sheet of tablets into his palm. Only six of the twenty seals had been punctured. Aiden took a deep breath as he started opening the remaining fourteen tablets.

ENOUGH IS ENOUGH

REBECCA

The chime of the loudspeaker announcement rang like a melodic bell for what must have been the hundredth time. As the monotone voice called for staff to respond to a code blue, Bec filtered out the remainder of the droning message. She looked at her phone to see no new messages but found it was just after ten in the morning. Bec had known it was daytime at least, as the fluorescent light illuminated the white room to make up for the lack of any windows. Over the night, the light might have been off, but the thin curtain that blocked the rest of the hospital from her provided no defence against the sounds of the busy emergency ward. Beeping medical instruments, phones ringing off the hook, nurses and doctors discussing patients and the quiet conversations or moans of discomfort from the other patients all echoed with no end in sight.

Bec had become oblivious to all of the signs of hospital life as she realised, she had been sitting there for almost twenty hours. Sure, the time had been broken up by a few visits to the bathroom or the hospital cafeteria for some bland sandwich or coffee, but for the most part, Bec had remained in the uncomfortable chair by Aiden's bed. Her husband was hooked up to the monitors that beeped consistently with his breathing and heart rate. She still couldn't believe it. It was just lucky that Liz had wanted a few more hours of work that day and had swapped their shifts. Bec left the clinic early with such high hopes. Aiden would have visited Lauren that morning. Maybe he would have been feeling at least a little better, and an afternoon off from work was always welcome. Bec wasn't sure what she might have gotten up to. There was always housework to be done but to hell with that. For just one afternoon she might like to nestle down with a good book or maybe even watch a movie. If Aiden still wasn't feeling sociable, she hoped he would at least have been amicable to a nice, relaxing afternoon with her.

But Bec's hopes were dashed and in their place her worst fears came to fruition. The house was so quiet that if she hadn't of seen Aiden's car parked roughly in the carport when she got home, Bec would have thought he was still out. She didn't mind though. After switching on the kettle to make a cup of tea, she sent Aiden a text just to see where he might be. Then she made her way to the bedroom to get changed out of her work clothes. That's when she found him. Aiden was sprawled face down on the carpet. At first, Bec didn't know what to think. She had no idea what might have happened to him when she urgently rolled him over and tried to wake him. His lips were blue and he was barely breathing.

When she saw the opened and emptied packet of Valium on the bed, she couldn't help but assume what Aiden had done. A moment later she was on the phone to the emergency services and thank God the ambulance hadn't taken long to arrive. From the moment Aiden was admitted into the emergency ward, Bec hadn't left his side. She called her dad and, after giving him a brief explanation of what was happening, asked that that he and her mum could look after Hannah. She was grateful that her dad offered to call up the school to let Hannah know as well. At that point in time, her head was such a mess that she dreaded the thought of making yet another call, least of all to tell her daughter that her father had attempted suicide.

The doctors were quick to check on Aiden and they confirmed the suspicions that he had overdosed. Bec was almost happy her husband was unconscious while they pumped his stomach. She had never witnessed the procedure herself before but she, like many people, had heard how unpleasant it was for the patient. Even so, it was a very poor silver lining and Bec would certainly rather have never had the sorry situation develop at all. She had been lost in a turbulent whirlpool of emotions. A knot formed in her throat. The thought of losing Aiden, her love and anchor in life, pierced her heart like a cruel, icy blade. Though her eyes welled with tears, she couldn't allow them to fall. Not yet. In that sterile, fluorescent lit room, as Aiden lay unconscious and vulnerable, the fire of anger burned in her chest. It raged hot and fierce, threatening to consume her whole. The injustice of it all left a bitter taste in her mouth, making it hard to swallow.

She knew Aiden had been going through a bad time with depression and his sleep paralysis. But she thought he knew she was there for him. To support him and take care of him. He had grown distant, but nothing he had said indicated he was at this level of trouble. Bec needed to talk to him. To find out what he had been thinking. So, she sat and waited. Not only to make sure he would be alright, but also to finally get some answers. Aiden groaned softly and shifted his head on the pillow. The subtle sign of life seemed to shake the entire room. Bec, who had been feeling drowsy with exhaustion, was suddenly wide awake. She sat upright with the hairs on the back of her neck tingling as she watched Aiden intently, his pale face ragged beneath his rough, unshaven stubble and dark, sunken eyes. He had made similar motions every now and then over the hours but this time, it seemed more abrupt. Aiden shifted again and took a deep breath before his eyes groggily fluttered open.

'Hey, honey. Hey,' Bec said softly, unable to hold back her smile or the tears that welled in her eyes. The relief of Aiden's consciousness flowed through her like a warm glow of firelight. Aiden glanced back and forth and his bloodshot eyes blinked with uncertainty.

'What? Where?' he mumbled but Bec just leaned over him and stroked his hair.

'It's okay, don't panic. You're in hospital. You're okay,' she said reassuringly. Aiden looked to her in tired confusion before he slowly lifted himself up with a groan.

'Here you go. Don't try and move too much, baby.' Bec helped move the simple hospital pillow to support Aiden's slight change in posture. 'How are you feeling? Do you need a drink? Water?' she asked after Aiden had settled in a semi-reclined position. He loudly cleared his throat and nodded. Bec stood and turned to the water jug and empty plastic cups that were waiting on the small side table.

'Do you remember what happened?' she asked hesitantly as she passed Aiden a full cup.

Her husband took a sip before his body caught up realised how thirsty he was and he gulped down the drink. 'Uh, not really. I mean, sort of...' he said groggily, his eyes lowered.

Bec knew his memory might still have been fuzzy, but the way he avoided her gaze, she wondered if he wasn't feeling ashamed.

'Yeah. You gave me a real scare, you know that?' she said in a feeble attempt to stay in good spirits. She didn't doubt her rattled nerves wouldn't be so easily hidden by a little smile and faux happy tone.

Aiden was silent for a moment, nodding ever so slightly. He finally looked up, straight into the eyes of his wife. His own eyes were watery with tears. 'I... I'm so sorry, baby. I just... didn't know what else to do,' he said pitifully.

Bec felt as though her heart were breaking in her chest. She sniffled and wiped her eyes before leaning down and taking Aiden in her arms as best as she could so as not to tug at his monitor lines. 'It's okay. You're safe now. You're safe. Just please, please don't ever do something like that again! Please.' She sobbed as she lost the internal struggle for composure and finally broke down.

Aiden stroked and kissed her arm, the only part of her body he was able to reach in their awkward embrace. 'I know. I know, baby. I'm so sorry. It was just... he was hurting people. Oh God, he was killing them. I didn't want him to get you too. I thought... I dunno what I thought. I just wanted it to stop.'

Bec closed her eyes and couldn't help but let out an exasperated sigh. She just hoped that her husband could finally get the help he needed. But even though she didn't rightly know what was going on, she knew she would support him. She slowly drew back from the embrace and looked into Aiden's eyes. He looked panicked, distressed, but somehow more under control than in recent days.

'You mean… Gary?'

Aiden's eyes flicked nervously about at the mention of the name, his breathing growing faster. The beeping of the monitor was steadily climbing along with the numbers of his heart rate.

'Honey, please. It's okay.' Bec tried to console him, but when he finally looked back at her, he seemed deep in thought.

'What is it?' she asked nervously.

Aiden seemed to slowly be gaining control of himself again. His monitor became more stable. 'Gary… I haven't seen him. He hasn't said anything. I feel like, I don't know, a weight is off my shoulders. My chest.' Aiden spoke with increasing happiness in his voice.

Bec sat back, feeling a little alarmed.

Aiden looked at her with a curious smile growing on his lips. He laughed. 'Don't worry, baby, don't worry! This is good. This is so good. I think… I think Gary's gone!'

*

'Yes, Mum, I know.' Bec paced in the kitchen on her mobile.

It had taken her a long time in her youth to actually use a phone. It was a strange childhood phobia, really. She never seemed to like that she could make a mistake or somehow offend the person on the other end of the line. Maybe it was the fact she wasn't face to face with the person, the inability to read the body language. Something might get said that was meant one way but could be taken completely differently. Even so, as her dad had told her, what was the worst that could happen if she made a mistake when she would practice her phone etiquette by ordering the weekly pizza?

'You just apologise and clarify what you actually wanted. Nothing to it,' she remembered her father saying.

Thankfully, she had quickly grown accustomed to using the phone in a professional environment so it never became a problem at work. But to this day, in her private life, Bec couldn't help but pace awkwardly back and forth whenever she was on the phone. Especially when the phone call wasn't a pleasant one.

'Yes, I know you say you know, but I just want to make sure you are aware of the risks.' Her mum's s voice rang with authority through the speaker.

Bec frowned but her mother was off before she could interject.

'Aiden has very clearly been going through some new difficulties. Thank the Lord he wasn't taken from us but I can't help but still worry what this might mean for you, his family. You remember how he was all those years ago? Lying about, never doing anything for goodness knows how long.'

Bec knew her mother only cared about what was best for her family. But she had a terrible way of going about it. Her voice was calm and collected, dripping with wisdom and empathy. But beneath it all, Bec recognised the self-placed authority. The condescension towards actions that she neither understood nor cared for. It was the sort of voice that was well suited when telling a daughter off for sneaking out of the house. Giving warnings of what ill might have befallen her out at night. Painting dreaded pictures being attacked, drugged or, heaven forbid, made pregnant.

Well, that one didn't work out so well. So much the better, Bec thought with a smirk as she remembered breaking the news to her parents of her underage pregnancy with Hannah.

'I just want to make sure that Aiden will actually get all the help he needs in his time of crisis. Depression is not a foe to be set aside – it creeps up all the time, don't you know? Aiden must do everything he can to stay on top of it.' Pamela's apparently omnipotent voice dragged Bec back to reality.

'Yes, Mum, I know! Of course, I haven't forgotten last time. But if Aiden gets to that point again, we will just have to deal with it as it comes. Do you really think I'll just sit back and let him get worse? He has promised to work with me every step of the way. I already told you he regrets what he did so much,' she defended her husband while trying her best not to let her own fears take hold. Was she worried Aiden might sink into another pit of despair which he might not claw his way out of for years to come? Was she worried he might, in a daze of misery and confusion, attempt to take his life again? There was no doubt that she was. But Bec couldn't let those thoughts take control. She was in control and her husband needed her to be there for him. Not to fret and worry, but to support and care for him. She only wished her mother could be there to do the same for her. The trouble was Pamela undoubtedly thought that was exactly what she was doing.

'Yes, well, the less said about that the better. Though I wish you would tell me what brought all this about! I hadn't thought Aiden had felt bad enough to do something like that in, well, a very long time.'

Bec tried to quell the burning anger which was growing in her chest, fuelled by her mother's voice. 'No, Mum. You understand something like that is extremely personal? If you want to know, ask Aiden. He will probably say no too, as he should, but please don't expect me to talk about him behind his back,' she said with clenched teeth.

'Alright, alright, I know. You know I don't mean any harm by it. I just want to help,' Pamela replied with an impatient tone, as though her daughter refusing to tell her the intimate secrets of her husband was somehow offending her parental position. There was a silence on the phone though Bec could almost hear the disapproval in her mother's breathing.

'Anyway, he has been doing well now. He saw the emergency psych nurse and has already got himself booked with a new therapist. I mean, given what he was going through, what happened with Lauren couldn't possibly have helped,' Bec said after counting to five to quell her frustrations as best as she could.

She couldn't believe it. She had no idea what had happened to Aiden that morning until a good while after he had woken up in hospital. Bec hadn't even heard it first from her husband's own mouth, but from the psych nurse who had come to evaluate his condition. She confirmed her reports were correct with Aiden, during which it was revealed he had made witness statements to the police on the morning of his suicide attempt. Bec couldn't help but ask for all the details she could then and there. Her heart broke, not only for the fact that Lauren had passed away, but that Aiden's long-term therapist and friend had practically died in his arms. It had given Bec a far greater insight into Aiden's motives than she had first suspected. After all, when a man who is in the midst of struggling with a breakdown witnesses the death of maybe the one person he feels can help, what would go through his head? Bec tried to think that if she was in his shoes, what might she have done? Curiously, while the sleep paralysis was brought up, there was no mention of Gary in the consult with the psych nurse.

'Yes, that poor, poor woman. She will be in my prayers on Sunday. I'm glad to hear Aiden seems well. We just need to make sure he keeps that appointment, I suppose,' Pamela said.

No matter how long it had been, Bec was always amazed when her mother spoke in such a way. How could someone sound so sincere and sympathetic yet sceptical and judgemental all at once? Bec was curious how her mother might have acted if she had been privy to the information that Aiden had actually closely witnessed Lauren's death too.

'Don't worry, Mum. He'll keep the appointment. It's his last day in hospital today. He has been recovering well, sleeping and eating without problems and is pretty much ready to come home. I've taken a few days off work to make sure he settles in alright.'

'Yes, that's good to hear. And you're sure you want Hannah to stay too? You know she is always welcome to stay with us.'

'Uh, of course. Why wouldn't Hannah stay at home?' Bec asked, picking up her pacing along the kitchen bench again.

'Well, Aiden might just need his space. And I'm not sure if he will be in a good state for Hannah to be around?' Pamela said knowingly.

Bec set her palm firmly on the bench, grateful that her mother couldn't see the annoyance on her face. 'Thanks, Mum. But I think the best thing for us to do is just try to live our normal lives again. You know how much Hannah loves her dad. Maybe seeing each other a little more will actually help, don't you think?' she said as sweetly as possible.

'Hmm. I suppose,' Pamela said, quite obviously unconvinced.

*

Bec was nervous. She had read the last sentence in her book at least half a dozen times without really absorbing it. It was a cold night and she sat in bed with the covers over her lap. The sound of Aiden brushing his teeth in the bathroom echoed dully into the bedroom and Bec glanced at the door over and over.

Aiden had been doing so well since he got home. He seemed to have gotten a good deal of much needed sleep in the hospital. He was almost chipper; at least, chipper for someone who had been going through what he had. Bec had the next three days off work and had decided Hannah could have the week off school if she wanted. The whole family was home that day, and though a weight of tension hung in the air, it slowly lifted as the day went on. They didn't do much. Watched some movies, played some board and card games, really just remained by each other's side all day. No one brought up Aiden's hospital visit, save for when they first returned home and Hannah asked how her father was feeling. Aside from that, the conversations were surprisingly pleasant and happy. Aiden commented on how delicious the roast dinner Bec had made was as though he were a man more content with life than any other. And yet, now it was time for bed, Bec's dread came to the fore. She knew Aiden had slept well in hospital. But who knows what might happen, now that he was home, back in the same room, lying in the same bed that he had experienced so many terrors in his mind? Bec wondered if they might not dip into their savings and take a holiday. Maybe some time away would be just what Aiden needed to break out of his night terrors. But that couldn't help them tonight. Tonight, as he readied for bed, Bec wondered if Aiden was trembling with fear.

'How are you doing baby?' she found herself calling out before she realised what she was doing. She heard Aiden finish brushing his teeth and spit into the sink.

'Coming! Don't worry, honey. I'm almost done,' he replied, still with an apparent mouthful of foam.

Bec looked down at the book in her hands but didn't even bother to attempt to read it again as she heard her husband rinse and spit a few times. Finally, Aiden switched off the bathroom light and stepped into the bedroom. For a man who had been driven to such a sleep deprived and fearful state that he had attempted suicide only a few days ago, Aiden looked positively happy. Sure, he wasn't dancing and clicking his heels like some ridiculous cartoon; he wasn't even smiling. But something about the way he held himself, the way he moved, the way he had done a decent job shaving for once, made Bec realise how much she had missed her real husband. She had lost track of how long it had been that he had seemed hollow shell of himself. Thinking back, Bec realised Aiden had only been having his sleep paralysis troubles for maybe two weeks but that couldn't possibly be right. It had seemed like years.

'Can't get into the book tonight?' Aiden asked as he slipped into bed beside his wife.

Bec shook her head as she snapped out of her thoughts and returned to the room. She smiled self-consciously as she closed the book and set it on the side table. She imagined she must have looked rather odd sitting with an open book splayed in her hands as she stared into space.

'No, not really in the headspace tonight,' she finally said after she switched off her lamp, the only light in the room now dimly glowing from Aiden's side of the bed. She rolled over to find him leaning back with his pillows propping him up a little. Bec hooked an arm over him and snuggled into his chest. She felt a sudden warmth of happiness

– which she had long forgotten she had missed – spark inside when Aiden held her close.

'So, how are you feeling tonight? You doing okay?' she asked while she relished the loving hand of her husband aimlessly stroking her back. There was a silence but curiously, Bec didn't find it at all tense or ominous as she might have done in recent days. Something about the night just felt right now.

'Yeah. Yeah, I'm actually doing alright. I feel... good,' Aiden finally said.

Bec smiled and took a deep sigh of relief. She didn't know what to expect, for Aiden to start rambling about ghosts or demons again, for him to break down and cry after acting fine for the whole day. But he didn't. Aiden just continued to stroke her back and, with her head resting on his chest, Bec felt her husband's relaxed breath rise and fall.

'Good. I'm really happy you can finally get some rest.'

If she were honest, Bec wasn't only happy that Aiden seemed to be doing better, but with his problems seemingly under control, maybe her life could regain some order again too. As the thought of things falling back to how they were, maybe even to the time of Aiden's depression that her mother seemed too afraid of recurring, Bec's chest began to tighten.

'Just... let me know if you need anything though, won't you?' she asked as she raised her head and looked to Aiden's face.

He looked back to her and smiled. 'I will, honey. I promise,' he said before kissing her forehead. Aiden's smile faltered and he glanced away for just a moment but quickly looked back to Bec's eyes. 'I... I'm just really sorry. For everything,' he said sheepishly.

Bec shifted her body so that she lay on her stomach and rested her chin on her hands, her palms flat on Aiden's chest. 'It's okay,' she whispered and Aiden gave an encouraging nod.

'Oh, I know, I know. Don't worry. I just... it needs to be said. You... you've just always been there for me and... I mean, I really have no idea what was going on with me. It was all in my head just like you said, I know. And I know how bad I must have been to, I dunno, just be around.' Aiden looked aside with shame though Bec was encouraged that he didn't just turn away and block her out. He kept his hand on her back and she knew he wasn't going to leave her out of his head anymore.

'I'll be honest, things... got a bit tough,' Bec said hesitantly. She wanted to choose her words carefully but knew better than to lie about something so obvious. 'But you know you always have me, right?' she quickly added.

Aiden looked at her and smiled again. 'Yeah, I know, babe. I love you so much. I never want to lose you. Or Hannah. I just... I can't believe I was so stupid to –' he said but Bec shook her head.

'Don't think about it. What's done is done. Thankfully, things didn't turn out as bad as they could have. You just talk to me whenever you need, alright?' she said while fixing Aiden's eye with a stern look.

He nodded. 'Yeah. Enough is enough. It might be hard but... I'm through the other side of the worst now, honey. Thanks to you.'

Bec could hear the conviction in his voice, the determination not to allow himself to fall back into those pits of despair and she smiled.

'That's right. As long as we're together, everything will work out. I love you. Don't you dare forget that!'

Aiden's eyes widened and he quickly shook his head. 'No, ma'am,' he said.

Bec raised an eyebrow and stuck her tongue in her cheek. 'Oooh, I like the sound of that. Might be better if I could get a "yes, ma'am" instead...' she said in an alluring voice as she subtly twisted her body under the covers so that Aiden might feel the growing warmth she felt below. It didn't take long for Aiden to catch on but Bec wasn't surprised. The way she trapped his thigh between her legs, she would have given her husband maybe ten seconds tops to join the dots. She looked up to him and flashed her teeth in a coquettish smile which Aiden reciprocated.

'Yes, ma'am...' he said as he leaned in and took his wife tightly in his arms.

RECOVERY

HANNAH

Hannah stretched out her arms and slowly took a careful step forward along the old log fence. The cool breeze flowed beneath her arms, the mild current threatening to unbalance her if she lost concentration. It was the first time she had been out of the house since she had come home from staying at her grandparents' place three days ago. Even for a teenager, she had just about all she could take of staring at a TV screen, a computer screen, her phone screen. Hannah felt a sense of freedom in the fresh air and the open park around her just reinforced that sensation.

To her knowledge, it hadn't rained for a few days but even now on this Friday afternoon, the grass was damp with dew. The sky was cloudy, there hadn't been a truly clear day for at least a week now, but when the sun occasionally broke free of the grey ceiling, the wet ground sparkled as though diamonds had been scattered all over the park. The smell of wet earth enlivened Hannah's senses, waking her up from the dreamy state she had been in. The last week had certainly been as close to surreal as she could imagine. When her grandfather picked her up from school that Monday afternoon, she had no idea what had actually happened, only that her dad had some kind of accident and was in hospital.

She wanted to see him, to find out what was going on. But her grandfather told her it would be best to wait at their place, just for a little. Her mother would let them know when it might be a good time to visit. Hannah knew something was amiss, that it was more than just an accident. Her grandparents played dumb, claiming they only knew as much as she did but Hannah knew better. She could tell by the way they glanced to one another, the way her grandmother had said, 'No matter what, everything will be alright.' But most of all, Hannah could tell something serious was wrong because her instincts just told her so. She had a tight ball of fear wedged in her stomach from the moment she got the text message to say her grandfather was picking her up.

Hannah had tried in vain to get the truth from her grandparents. They were too cunning, or perhaps too loyal to her mum to let anything slip. She felt ashamed about it afterwards, but she lashed out. She couldn't help it. She was afraid for her dad and just wanted to know what was going on. To be fair, her outburst had actually gotten some minor results. Her grandfather had finally explained, much to his wife's annoyance, that something serious had happened but they all hoped for the best and they felt it wasn't their place to say any more. Hannah reluctantly agreed to wait to hear from her mum at that point.

When she had found out what had actually happened, she simply refused to believe it at first. There must have been some mistake. Her dad had been exhausted from whatever problems he had been going through. He must have just taken the wrong number of tablets in some desperate effort to get some sleep. It wasn't until her mum had taken her into the hospital for a visit, when Hannah had heard the honest truth from her father's own lips that she finally overcame her denial. Learning that her dad was okay, her worry and fear just turned into anger and hurt. How could he have done such a thing? Hannah knew her dad was going through a rough time but, how could he think to leave her like that? How could he do that to her mum? Naturally, her dad apologised profusely but to be honest, Hannah was happy when she finally got out of the hospital. She was happy he would be alright, but she needed to get away from him. She felt betrayed. Her mum tried to defend him. She explained what Hannah already knew about depression. You don't want the thoughts you have. You don't want to be in that dark place with no escape, but that's just it, sometimes there just is no escape.

Hannah knew this. She had heard it all before. But while she really did sympathise, she still couldn't understand the mindset her father must have been in. No matter how bad things were, he still had his daughter. He still had his wife. He would always have his family to support him. How could he turn his back on them like that? Hannah had quietly fumed at the thought right up until her dad returned home from hospital. She barely talked to him to start with. She couldn't bear to look him in the eye. But something curious happened that very day that he returned. Her dad seemed so much better. His stint in hospital had apparently had some great positive effect on him. He was smiling, sociable, happy and engaging. Something about his attitude was apparently contagious because that afternoon, Hannah managed to somehow let go of her anger and things almost seemed to be back to normal. As it turned out, maybe this last dramatic moment was necessary to get her dad on the road to recovery after all.

Yet, after sleeping soundly through the night, content in the knowledge that her dad was alive and well, Hannah woke feeling gloomy once more. She was pleased to see that her dad was still doing well and even her mum seemed happier than she had seen her for some time. Whether she was putting a brave face on it or not, Hannah couldn't tell, but her mum was smiling and laughing the whole time that she made pancakes for a big family breakfast. With none of the family having any need to leave the house for the day, they could leisurely enjoy each other's company and repair the damages of their relationship. It was generally a successful endeavour, but something was holding Hannah back. She had spoken honestly with her parents and they evidently understood her position. Her dad continued to apologise, condemned his actions and promised he would never do anything so stupid again. Hannah couldn't lie, she was relieved and encouraged by his words but she felt the need to vent. To let out all of her angst and frustration without hearing the humble apologies of the father who had, in his own painful way, betrayed her trust. The trust that he would always be there for his daughter. Hannah felt that she needed to speak to someone outside of the family, outside of the whole affair so she could try and gain the right perspective. So, after letting her parents know that she planned to go for a walk that afternoon, she now found herself balancing on the fence in the park as she waited.

After reaching the end of the log fence, turning and making it back to her original starting point, Hannah lightly leapt to the ground. She pulled her phone from her jacket pocket. It was about quarter to four; school had finished almost an hour ago. The Ibis Secondary college was only a few blocks away from the park and Hannah was beginning to get antsy with impatience. She just pulled up the message thread on her phone when in the corner of her eye, she saw someone in the school uniform walking into the park. It might have just been one of the roughly four hundred students from the school making their lonely walk home, but Hannah turned and looked to see if she recognised them. As he walked briskly out of the tree line that surrounded the park, Hannah could see the boy's head whipping this way and that as though looking for someone. She grinned as her chest burst with happiness that he had finally made it.

'Brian!' she called, waving a hand in the air. Her voice rang across the park, echoing as though the clouds above were the ceiling of an all-encompassing cave.

Brian's head snapped in the direction of the call and Hannah saw his white teeth bared in a nervously happy grin that must have mimicked her own. With his backpack hanging over one shoulder, Brian began to pace across the field towards Hannah. She wasn't idle and, with no idea what to do with her hands, she self-consciously stuffed them into her jacket pockets as she walked. Hannah didn't know if she should just keep looking at Brian and smile dumbly as she walked or if she should attempt to loudly make conversation while they slowly neared one another? She was irritated by the sound of her own breathing as they awkwardly walked to each other. For some reason time seemed to slow down and Hannah felt Brian was judging every step, every little movement, every blink of an eye that she made. Finally, the two teens stood before one another at a sociable distance.

'Hi,' Hannah said simply. She both loved and hated how she felt around Brian now. She enjoyed the warm, happiness which grew in her chest whenever she was with him, but she hated the butterflies that flittered wildly in her stomach and the uncertainty of what to do next. It was so much easier, comfortable one might say, when they were just friends.

'Hey. How are you doing?' Brian said, the same uncertainty seeming to plague his mind as well.

To Hannah's surprise, the shy guy actually reached forward and wrapped an arm around her in a quick hug of greeting. When she felt the warmth of his body beneath his high school jumper on her chest, Hannah's heart could have skipped a beat.

'Yeah, I'm alright. Been better, I suppose,' she said as she tried to work out if she was blushing or not. She wished Brian had held her a bit longer but how weird would it be if she just grabbed him for a longer embrace? Tempted though she was, Hannah held back.

'I'm sorry to hear about your dad. How's he going?' Brian asked, clearly searching for the best way to advance the conversation through the difficult subject.

To Hannah's knowledge, no one at the school really knew what had happened. Sure, her teachers had been notified that there was a family emergency and she wouldn't be at school for the next few days, but only Brian and Abbi knew anything more. Hannah had texted them the basic details of her dad's incident but had generally avoided the topic. It was only this morning when she decided she needed to talk about it more with one of them. Normally an issue of this magnitude would be reserved only for Abbi, the very best and closest of friends. But Hannah had a boyfriend now. And somehow, she felt more comfortable sharing her feelings with Brian first.

'He's not doing too bad really. It's weird. He seems to be way better than he was before... it. Does that even make sense?' she said and Brian shrugged with an uncertain expression on his face.

'I don't really know, sorry. I've never really known anyone who's, well, done anything like that before.'

'Yeah. I know, it's really messed up. Um, did you wanna maybe go for a walk or something? We must look super weird just standing in the middle of a park like this,' Hannah suggested with a light laugh.

Brian laughed with her. 'Yeah, that would be great.'

They began to slowly walk alongside one another.

'So, did you want to talk about it or?' Brian asked after a moment's silence in which the couple had found their bearings and began to meander to the gravel footpath which twisted and turned through the park.

'I guess. Maybe in a bit. How've you been? School just the same old, same old?' Hannah said after weighing her options. She didn't want to dive into the deep stuff right away and she was genuinely interested in Brian's life too, no matter how crazy her own had been lately.

'I've been okay. Just the usual, you know. School's fine. Kinda sucks without you there though.'

Hannah tried to hide her smile of appreciation that she was actually missed. 'Well, I'm coming back next week so things should start looking up for you then, huh?' she replied playfully.

Brian laughed. Hannah loved the sound so much.

'Thank God. You know I need someone whose actually smart to cheat off of, right?' he joked and now it was Hannah's turn to laugh.

'Yeah right. If anything, I'll be cheating off of you.'

'Well then I'll cheat off you, you cheat off me and we can fail together, how does that sound?'

'Yep, sounds like a plan. We've got this year's grades sorted.'

They were now making their way along the path. The park wasn't too big. It only took up little more than a block in the middle of a residential area and they were already almost halfway along the winding path.

'Anyway, what have you been up to out of school?' Hannah asked while she enjoyed the peaceful stroll.

'Hmm, you know, nothing special. Gaming mostly,' Brian said rather vaguely. 'Thinking about you,' he added much more softly.

Hannah looked over to see Brian sheepishly looking to his feet. She wanted to just hold him. To kiss him like they do in the movies. Her heart was pounding almost painfully in her chest and her pink face tingled with warmth despite the cold air. She didn't say a word; she wouldn't have known what to say anyway. But she reached over. A feeling of immense joy washed over her as her fingers entwined with Brian's and their palms clasped together. Brian looked at their enclosed hands with apparent surprise before smiling and looking at Hannah's eyes.

'I've been thinking about you too,' she said finally.

Brian looked at a loss for words and Hannah just giggled.

'Really?' Brian finally managed to utter. She just nodded happily.

They continued to walk, completely aimless as they enjoyed each other's company. To their left, Hannah could see the playground that resided in the small park. There wasn't much to it. An old wooden set up for kids to climb over. A blue plastic slide, some monkey bars, a see saw – pretty standard stuff for a playground. Hannah's eye fell on the swing set. Aside from the toddler swing with the little seat and a chain waist belt, there were two regular swings side by side. They each swayed lightly in the breeze and the black plastic looked damp, but not wholly saturated. Hannah caught Brian's gaze. She squeezed his hand, giggled and dashed away towards the swings.

'Wha?' Brian was evidently shocked by her random departure but when he saw where she was headed at an excited run, he quickly set after her.

Hannah wiped what little water there was from the seat of the swing with the sleeve of her jacket before sitting down and holding the cold chains. Brian's backpack dropped into the damp bark with a thud as he joined her and a moment later the two teens were swinging through the air. It was childish. It was silly. It was just what Hannah needed. She laughed as she felt the air rush past her ears, her dark hair flying about her as she swung back and forth.

'I forgot how fun this is! Do you know how long it's been since I've been in a swing?' Brian called to her as he joined her momentum.

'Please! Like you haven't been doing this every chance you get?' Hannah teased.

Brian gasped with shock. 'How did you know? That was supposed to be a secret.'

'I didn't know, but I do now!' Hannah laughed. 'Seriously though, they need to put some of these in the school! All us teenagers would be so less stressed if we just had a swing at lunchtime.'

'I agree a hundred per cent,' Brian said.

After some moments more of fun, Hannah and Brian finally slowed down and dragged their feet into the bark to stop. They sat side by side in the swings, and while Hannah was still over the moon to be hanging out with her boyfriend, she couldn't help but feel the sudden lack of motion had brought the mood down with it. Perhaps only hers. But Brian noticed.

'Everything okay?' he asked after a moment.

Hannah shrugged and looked up to the tree line around the park. 'Yeah, just thinking,' she said mindlessly.

Brian nodded. He locked his elbows around the chains of his swing and twisted slightly from side to side. 'So, what's been happening with your dad? I mean, you don't have to tell me if you don't want to, I just thought, I dunno,' he said in a soft, caring voice.

'Yeah, yeah, I do want to talk about it. It's just, uh, I dunno where to start. Um, well you know what he did, anyway,' Hannah said, trying to find the best way to explain her feelings.

Brian nodded but stayed quiet. Hannah knew he was ready to just listen to her if that was what she needed.

'I mean, I dunno, I've had some crap days before. I guess I can't really say I've been depressed at all. I mean, like, I've never been told I am by a doctor or anything. Even though they say like, everyone our age is these days or something. But I can't understand how bad things had to get for dad to do something like that, you know?' She didn't really think about what she was saying. She just let it all flow out of her and Brian, that sweet guy, just listened.

'I don't know. I guess things got really tough for him. Is that what it is? I mean, he has depression?' he asked.

Hannah sighed and nodded. 'Yeah, only like forever. When I was little, he really lost the plot. I barely remember, I was only five or something. But apparently, he didn't work, didn't leave the house, didn't talk to mum, nothing. That's what I don't get. He was pretty good up until a few weeks ago. Then things just, I dunno, went nuts. Even then he wasn't that bad. It was only the last couple of days before he did his thing that he went all quiet on us. Before that he was really just tired. Exhausted from not sleeping. Something about paralysis episodes or something.'

She was surprised that she wasn't crying. Or screaming. Or showing much of a sign of emotion at all. She did feel a little sad, like something was weighing her down inside but she would have thought she would be bawling thinking about this sort of stuff. That's what they did on TV anyway. But Hannah actually felt kind of distant from it.

Maybe it's some self-defence thing or something. My brain protecting myself, she thought, recalling some paragraph or another she read in one of her books for psychology class.

'What paralysis episodes?' Brian asked, bringing Hannah's attention back to him.

She looked at him and was surprised at just how interested he seemed. He was leaning forward in his swing, staring at her, but not really at her. Sort of through her, as though he was lost in thought.

'I dunno, I looked it up a bit. Something called sleep paralysis. It's kind of like, some sleep disorder thing.'

Brian made a small sound of mild amusement.

'What?' Hannah asked with an uncertain giggle.

Brian shook his head a little and looked at her properly again. 'Hmm? Oh, it's nothing. Just, I know what that is. I've had it before,' he said rather casually.

Hannah's jaw dropped. She wasn't even sure why, maybe just because of the curious connection she had discovered between her dad and her boyfriend. They do say something about you find your parents in the ones your attracted to or something don't they? Hannah shook her head. It sounded like a disgusting concept. Hopefully just psychological rubbish. 'You have?' she asked with interest.

Brian nodded. 'Yeah, I remember it started when I was twelve. I thought I was dying. I told my parents about it. They had no idea what it was either. So, they took me to the doctor where I found out I was fine. Still scary, though,' he explained while kicking his feet into the bark of the playground.

Hannah leaned closer. She couldn't deny she was really curious about whatever it was that had bothered her dad so much, especially to hear about it from someone who had experienced it themselves.

'So, what exactly is it then?' she asked, her curiosity getting the better of her. 'If it's okay to ask?' she quickly added, hoping that she wasn't stepping over some invisible line that could hurt her new relationship.

Thankfully, Brian just leaned back and looked pretty unfazed. 'Yeah, it's okay. So, it's pretty much like, you wake up in the wrong order. Your brain kicks in, you open your eyes, but your body hasn't really caught up yet so everything's still shut down.' He spoke slowly as he sifted through his memories.

'Sounds weird. Is it dangerous?' Hannah had already learned something similar from the net but was still intrigued to hear Brian's story.

'Not really, at least I don't think so. The trouble is because your body's still asleep, you can't really do anything. You have to just lie there and wait for it to catch up. But then, you can't really feel anything either. So, you don't even know if you're breathing or not. That's why I used to think I was dying,' he continued.

Hannah tried to imagine it. She imagined not being able to move or to even know if you were breathing. 'Freaky. Does it hurt?' she asked. She felt sorry that not only Brian, but her dad had to suffer through such a thing.

'Kind of. It didn't at first. Usually, it was just a quick thing for me. But sometimes it lasted longer. Then it kinda felt like suffocating, you know, that real uncomfortable feeling you get in your chest when you hold your breath for too long,' Brian said.

Hannah's eyes widened. 'Jeez, how much did this happen to you?'

Brian shrugged. 'On and off for a few years. Haven't had it in a while now though. They think it's brought on by stress, bad sleeping habits that sort of thing. But they don't really know yet.'

'That's so weird. I wonder if they'll ever work it out?' Hannah thought aloud.

'I dunno. But I still haven't told you the worst part yet,' Brian said with a sly grin. It was almost as though he was proud to be sharing his experiences.

'What, there's more? What else could there be?' Hannah asked, her interest piqued.

Brian leaned in close again so that from their swings, their faces were inches apart. 'Sometimes, it's like you're still dreaming. Like, not even all of your brain wakes up. Anyway, they say you hallucinate. Hear things. See things. I don't really know about hallucinations, but I can tell you it feels really damn real,' he said.

Hannah didn't know what to say. She was honestly feeling edgy just hearing about it.

Brian must have taken her silence for intrigue as he continued. 'Weird thing is it only seems to work with nightmare stuff. Something about it affecting the amygdala of the brain my doctor said. That's where fear comes from or something, you know. Anyway, I heard lots of things. Whispering. Footsteps moving around, always out of my sight. I just had this feeling something wanted to hurt me. It never did though.' Brian's face became more vacant the more he spoke. He didn't seem that troubled to Hannah but she suspected reminiscing about such a scary sounding experience couldn't be all that enjoyable.

'Well, that's good at least. We don't have to keep talking about it if you don't want,' she said, though she couldn't deny she was curious to hear more.

Brian looked at her with a smile. 'Nah, it's okay. It's weird, I kinda like talking about it. I mean, I can stop if you want?'

Hannah quickly shook her head. She abruptly stopped when she realised that she might have done so too quickly.

Brian just chuckled. 'Yeah, maybe because I haven't had it in a while it doesn't seem so bad anymore. But the more I think about it, the more I remember how scared I used to get. It really made me think like someone was in the house, in the room with me. Just watching me,' he said.

'Okay, that's just plain creepy,' Hannah said with a small, nervous laugh. She hoped she was covering up the shudder she felt as her imagination ran wild.

'Tell me about it,' Brian said. 'It got to a point where I could finally see something. It looked like a shadow, always hanging around the corner of my eye so I couldn't get a good look at it. I don't know why but I always got the feeling it was a man. Some stranger just standing there.'

Hannah twisted in her swing and shivered. She acted as casual as she could, as though it was just the cold. But she knew it was more than that.

'Don't worry, nothing else really happened with him. I'd just see him sometimes. He'd stand there, all scary and stuff. But as I got more of a hang of it, I just kept telling myself he wasn't there. That he wasn't real. Eventually I just called him Bob. Whenever he'd turn up, I'd just think, "Hey, Bob". He was never that scary after that,' Brian said with a laugh. His smile and the sound of his laughter was contagious.

Hannah felt that rising fear melting away as she joined in. 'Really? Bob? Guess it's as good a name as any,' she said lightly.

Brian nodded in agreement. Then, his laughter died down. Hannah watched as his beautiful smile faded too. Suddenly his face looked troubled.

'Brian?' She stood up and stepped over to him, wiping her wet hands together to warm them up. Brian was frozen in his spot, just looking at nothing.

'Hey, are you okay?' she repeated, reaching up and touching Brian's shoulder. He gasped as though caught by surprise before he looked up and his face became relaxed once more.

'Huh? Oh, yeah. I just... remembered something I must have forgotten.' He pulled himself out of his swing and stand by Hannah's side.

'What was it? Something else with the paralysis?' Hannah asked as she and Brian started to lazily walk around the old wooden play equipment. It was a little thing, but Hannah liked that they didn't need to talk about what they were doing. They just did it, as though their mutual instincts drove them to walk together. As they walked, Hannah took Brian's hand again. She loved the feeling as he clutched her hand.

'Yeah. To be honest I'm just surprised I forgot about it,' Brian said after quiet moment of thought.

'What was it?' Hannah asked curiously.

Brian looked hesitant. 'I dunno, this one was worse. I mean, I'm happy to tell you if you want, but, well, I don't have to,' he said.

Hannah nodded and looked at her feet for a moment. She wasn't sure what to do. She wanted to hear more, but she was already a bit shaken by 'Bob'. What else would Brian have to share? On the other hand, she was definitely curious about the subject and talking about it with Brian felt right somehow. He had experienced stuff that could help her understand her dad's problems a bit better. And, as he seemed happy to share such personal experiences, Hannah felt it only strengthened their growing relationship.

'Yeah, go on. I'd like to hear it.' She squeezed Brian's hand as though the physical connection would encourage him further.

'Alright,' Brian said with a nod. They were just walking circles around the small play fort and Brian ran his free hand along the wooden walls.

'So, Bob was one thing. He sort of became, like, the regular deal. I got used to him. But then, sometimes things were worse. I think it was, like, when I was super stressed or overtired or something. But something else came those times,' he explained.

Hannah was curious, but she could feel her apprehension growing. She wondered if Brian shouldn't look into learning about public speaking or something. For a shy guy, he was really able to tell a story. Hannah wondered why she never really noticed it before during their friendship. Maybe something about them being together helped Brian to open up a bit?

'What happened?'

'I remember I called her "The Screamer". I never saw her and I don't know why but I definitely felt like it was a she.'

Hannah said nothing but just listened with bated breath.

'I think she used to come a lot when I would be sleeping on my side. Just because, well, I remember always hearing her behind me. Footsteps. Like, slow thumping ones you hear just outside your bedroom door.'

As Brian continued, Hannah found her legs began to feel a bit like jelly. She felt so silly, being scared of some ghost story and she didn't say anything. Instead, Hannah just slipped into one of the many openings to the play fort and sat on the damp wood. She didn't care that her butt felt a bit wet. She just wanted to sit down.

'You okay?' Brian asked with evident care as he sat beside her with both of their backs facing the metal frame ladder which led to the top of the fort and the slide.

'Yeah, just wanted to sit again,' Hannah said simply with a smile. She didn't know why but she just didn't want to admit to Brian she was feeling uneasy. 'So, you were saying? The Screamer?' she added as though to emphasise the point that she was fine.

'Right. So, I'd hear her and I'd know what was coming. Well, except for the first few times, I guess. But knowing didn't help. You don't really think straight when you have the paralysis. Anyway, I could only lie there and listen. The footsteps would be slow. Distant. But getting closer. Like they were in the room now. Sometimes I heard like, a breathing too.'

Hannah listened intently and she felt her heart beating harder in her chest. Suddenly, a thump made her jump. To her surprise, Brian started beating his hand on the wood of the play fort. He beat it slow, making it sound just like footsteps. Hannah listened with every hit seemingly more impactful than the last.

'I don't know how long it would go on for but it was freaking scary. Then, eventually...' Brian's voice faded out and all Hannah could hear was his beating hand. In her mind's eye, Hannah imagined the sound of footsteps behind her, wandering back and forth. Suddenly, Brian used both hands and picked up speed. In her head, Hannah imagined the feet that had been stomping back and forth, suddenly turning in her direction and stampeding towards her. Brian rattled his hands fast and hard; Hannah almost forgot to breathe as she imagined whatever the thing was jumping on her.

'Then bang! She was on the bed right behind me, screaming in my ear. Screaming like some evil witch monster thing,' Brian announced and Hannah jumped out. She shook her hands and arms while making a face of distaste.

'Oh my God, that sounds so messed up! Crap, it's like a horror movie or something. Are you being serious? Really?' She was blurting her words out in quick succession and Brian stood up with his hands raised.

'Woah, calm down. Sorry, I didn't mean to scare you that much,' he said as he set his hands gently on Hannah's shoulders and rubbed them reassuringly. Hannah took a breath and looked at Brian's face. He looked mildly amused, but also caring.

'I wasn't *that* scared.' She pouted before smiling in embarrassment.

'Oh, I know. I just... wanted to make sure,' Brian said with a smile of his own.

Hannah glanced at his hand on her shoulder. She liked how this felt. Her new boyfriend's hands on her, his eyes focused on her face. Hannah could almost feel the apprehension and fear from the ghost story melting into something else. Something warm and far more enjoyable. She timidly lifted her hands and set them on Brian's hips.

He looked just as nervous as she felt, but Hannah didn't think that could be possible. She took a small step forward. Brian did the same. Their bodies were pressed ever so slightly together. Hannah looked into Brian's eyes and Brian looked into hers.

'Sorry I scared you,' he said quietly.

Hannah blushed. She didn't care about pretending to be brave anymore. 'I'm sorry that stuff happened to you,' she said in little more than a whisper. She didn't realise it happening, but she and Brian were getting closer and closer together.

'Yeah. I think I like this a lot better.'

'Oh yeah? What's that?' Hannah asked through quick, nervous breaths.

Brian opened his mouth to say something, but quickly closed it again.

Hannah couldn't take her eyes off of his. Was he leaning forward? Was she? In an instant, Hannah felt the warm, soft touch of Brian's lips on hers. She closed her eyes, wondering if Brian had done the same. She pulled away ever so slightly, her own lips feeling too dry. She quickly licked them and moved in again, bumping into Brian's chin. Hannah barely got out an apology before Brian was tenderly kissing her once more. Her knees went weak and Brian's arms closed around her, supporting her to keep standing as she flew through the ecstasy of her first kiss.

TIME TO SLEEP

AIDEN

Aiden had woken up early, rested and refreshed. He was amazed at how good he felt. Just from being able to get decent sleep again. Whenever he chanced to let himself remember what he had done two weeks ago, he felt a well of shame in his chest. How could he possibly have been so stupid? He barely even remembered why he had done it now. Of course, witnessing the death of Lauren was traumatic, but that alone shouldn't have given him cause to take his own life.

He tried to remember how he felt. How he was so convinced that the apparitions of his mind were real. That they wanted to hurt his family. Aiden scoffed when he thought about how he imagined himself doing his family a service, sacrificing himself to save them. It was so messed up. The only thing that committing suicide would have done would be to hurt his family, not save them. Aiden quickly realised his mistake. When he had woken up in hospital, when he saw the anguish Bec tried to hide in her exhausted face, he knew how much he had hurt her. And yet, his visit to hospital had been a blessing in disguise. Now, Aiden was better. He hadn't heard anything from his imaginary evils since the suicide attempt. He didn't have any episodes of paralysis, wasn't scared of shadows creeping in the night, wasn't afraid to close his eyes and lie down to sleep. He took it slowly at first. For the whole week since he returned from hospital, he tried to control himself. He felt so relieved from the burdens of his depression and paralysis that he just wanted to run along the street and scream how good he felt.

But Aiden knew it could all have just been a rush of pleasure from finally being able to relax. So, while he enjoyed his family's company, while he smiled and laughed with them as they played games and watched TV, in the back of his head, he never forgot it could all come crashing down again in an instant. No one could say he hadn't had experience with depression and he knew it never went away that easily. But as the days drew on and Aiden recovered, that niggling doubt in his mind grew quieter and fainter.

Hannah went back to school after the first weekend. She was such an amazing girl. In spite of everything, she was happy to get back to class as soon as she could. Or maybe it was because of everything? Hannah was getting to an age where she didn't exactly want to share everything with her dad anymore. Her mum was her confidant and it wasn't until the end of Hannah's week back at school that Aiden actually found out she had a boyfriend now. At first, he was terrified. Was his little girl really old enough to start dating already? Bec reminded him in private to try and take it easy and not to rile Hannah up with his objections or questions.

When he found out who Hannah was seeing, Aiden felt somehow more relaxed about the whole thing. He didn't know Brian well, but he had met him several times over the years. He knew that aside from Abbi, Brian was one of Hannah's best friends and he always seemed like a good upstanding kind of boy. Aiden was just grateful that his daughter hadn't gotten herself tangled up in some sordid romance with one of the bad sorts who smoked behind the bike shed at school. Shit, did kids even do that anymore? The way kids were growing up these days, Aiden was more concerned the early high schoolers weren't just smoking. It sounded like they were more likely having orgies, taking drugs and generally doing things that their parents had never even heard of. But Brian, at least on the face things, seemed a good kid. Aiden was surprised at how well he took to the idea of his daughter having her first boyfriend. Even so, he wanted to meet the young man properly and he hinted as such by suggesting Hannah invite him over sometime. She was evasive about the whole thing and merely said that maybe she might invite him in the next couple of weeks. Aiden and Bec shared some laughs about it that night, joking about how she was probably not ready to be embarrassed by her parents yet.

Now Bec. Without her, Aiden didn't know where he would be. His wife left no room for doubt where she stood on his suicide attempt. She was obviously worried about him and wanted to do anything she could to help him, but she was also determined not to let such a thing happen again. She had never gotten angry with him, at least not in an obvious way with shouting and threats of leaving him. But Aiden knew Bec was furious that he had done something so stupid. As he thought back on it, he didn't blame her in the slightest. What he did was so selfish, so insane that he was just grateful Bec cared about him enough to put on such a happy face.

He tried to imagine himself in her shoes. If he came home from work to find her unconscious next to an empty packet of tablets, well, he didn't know what he would do. The mere idea of it hurt him so much that he couldn't help but apologise to his wife and daughter at random times every day. Bec stayed home with Aiden for almost an entire week, just making sure he wasn't at risk of relapsing suddenly into a fit of despair. She was given a couple of days of compassionate leave but took a few extra with pay. She said it might eat into their next holiday a little but she would quickly make the hours back. Even so, Bec had to get back to work sooner than Aiden would have liked. He understood, of course, they had bills to pay and managers don't wait around forever for their employees. Still, Aiden couldn't deny he was nervous about spending the days alone. To his surprise though, the sun didn't fall out of the sky when he was left to his own devices. He still slept well and continued to wake renewed and energetic. Aiden took Leena for a long walk around the wetlands twice a day. He read books and caught up with his favourite shows and podcasts. Basically, he was enjoying life again.

Today, the second Monday since he had been taken to hospital, Aiden was ready to go back to work. He had called Wendy to give her the good news. Bec had already told her what had happened, at least the trimmed-down version, and Wendy had asked that Aiden take care of himself and just come back to work when he was ready. As it turned out, Aiden learned the café hadn't been doing so well, but even then, Wendy asked several times if he was sure he was ready to come back. He could tell that, despite her concern for him, she was grateful he was finally coming back. The winter season had begun in earnest, but even the cloudy skies and the chilly morning air couldn't dampen Aiden's spirits. He drove to work with a sense of excitement. After parking the car and stepping out into the crisp morning air, he took a deep, rejuvenating breath. He felt as though he had been locked in a cage and was finally free.

*

'Good morning!' Aiden said in a pleasant voice as he stepped into the Glen Marsh Grind for the first time in what felt like forever. He was greeted with several friendly but weary greetings from the kitchen staff. On the other hand, when Wendy saw him step behind the counter, her face lit up. She wiped her hands on her apron as she left Marcus and Eric to man the grills alone.

'You're finally back! What's it been, two weeks? Feels more like a month. How are you doing?' she cried as she enveloped Aiden in a big hug.

'Yeah, I don't know. It feels like forever to me. I'm sorry I've not been here to help lately,' Aiden replied a little sheepishly.

Wendy scoffed and smacked his chest with the back of her hand. 'Don't be stupid. It sounds to me like you've been having a much harder time than we have. Now, you're sure you are okay to be in already? You don't need a few more days?' she asked, following him to the espresso machine.

Aiden looked over the mess of dried coffee grinds and stains on the benchtop. One of the milk steamers wasn't properly cleaned and the packet of coffee beans hadn't been sealed and put away. It was only a small job at the cafe but Aiden felt needed and that just boosted his good mood.

'No, it's okay. Really. I just want to get back to work,' he said as he picked up and clipped the pack of coffee beans. 'Looks like you could use me here too,' he added with a playful grin.

Wendy pressed her tongue into her cheek and raised her dark, thin eyebrows with an unamused expression. She whipped Aiden with her handtowel. 'Yeah, yeah. We couldn't keep up without the coffee pro, I get it,' she said.

'I'm just saying,' Aiden continued to tease and Wendy rolled her eyes. It was all in good humour of course, but Aiden knew Wendy was relieved he was back at work.

'So, how have things been here? Really?' he asked as he began to set up properly for the day.

Wendy tilted her head from side to side and shrugged. 'Hmmm, so-so. We've been alright really. It's just been the family though. I mean, you needed some time off which is perfectly alright, don't get me wrong. But being down two people makes it a bit tough.'

Aiden felt a weight drop in his chest. How could he have forgotten?

'You mean Sam hasn't been back?' he asked with a feigned casual tone, which he wasn't sure was all that convincing.

Wendy sucked her teeth. 'Oh, that's right. Sorry, I didn't mention it over the phone. I've, uh, got some bad news about that,' she said as she lowered her gaze.

'What is it?' Aiden asked. He suspected he knew what Wendy was going to say and had to consciously check himself so as not to blurt out anything he might regret saying.

Wendy set a gentle hand on his shoulder. 'Well, Sam won't be coming back, Aiden. She, she had an accident around the time you left. A bit earlier, I guess. Anyway, I'm sorry but… she died,' Wendy said with delicate care. Aiden got the impression she was worried that giving him such tragic news might cause him to break down or something.

The weight in his chest grew heavier. He didn't know what to say. His mind spiralled back to that horrible encounter he had with Sam in his bedroom. He closed his eyes and shook the image of her torn lips, bubbling with black foam from his mind. *Shut up, fuck off. Don't think about it. It wasn't my fault. Wasn't my fault.*

'Are you okay? You sure you don't need another day or two?' Wendy asked, evidently troubled that Aiden didn't respond.

He gave a weak smile. 'Yeah, no, sorry. I'm all good. Just… wow, that's terrible. Do you know what happened?'

Wendy shook her head. 'Not much. We were just notified about it by her parents. They said it was an accident. That she tripped and fell down the stairs to her apartment. That's all I know of it really,' she explained.

Aiden nodded slowly. *See? Just an accident. A fucking awful thing. But an accident. No ghosts. No…* Aiden stopped short of thinking of the name. He tried to clear his head of the thought as best he could.

'Shit, that's… well, it's just awful. I'm sorry to hear it, Wendy.'

'Yeah. She was a good girl. Maybe she liked to party a lot but, well, she didn't deserve something like that. Her parents said we were all welcome to attend the service last week but, well, I didn't know if you were ready to hear about it,' Wendy said ashamedly.

'Yeah. Yeah, you were probably right,' Aiden conceded. He felt bad that he couldn't be there to say goodbye to Sam, even if he had only known her for about six months. But something about the idea of going to her funeral seemed wrong too. Like he would have been intruding. He didn't know her all that well after all. They stood in silence for what was growing into an awkward amount of time.

'Well, uh, thanks for telling me anyway. I hope her family will be alright. It'll be a really hard time for them, I suppose,' Aiden said finally.

Wendy sighed heavily and nodded. 'Yes. I do feel sorry for them. I guess we can only just keep on keeping on. Now you're sure you'll be okay?' she asked again.

Aiden suspected it wouldn't be the last time she asked that day either.

*

Aside from the bad news about Sam, Aiden had a surprisingly good day. He needed maybe an hour to get back into the swing of things but pretty soon he was running the espresso machine and selling meals as well as he ever did. He was reminded of the old saying, 'like riding a bike'.

He knew he had only been away from work for a couple of weeks but it encouraged him that he just seemed to know what to do and when to do it so quickly. When finishing time rolled around, Aiden felt like he was appreciated. That he was useful to someone again. Working at the café, he generally finished at three p.m. so he knew Bec was at least three hours away. Maybe he would enjoy some quality time with Hannah. He wanted to really establish the normality of his life with her too. Hannah had been pretty good at maintaining the status quo but Aiden could tell she was still upset with him under the surface. Maybe she would like to go out to a movie or they could enjoy a game of mini golf. They hadn't done something like that for a long time. But Aiden's hopes for a dad and daughter afternoon were dashed when he checked his mobile after work. The text message from Hannah read: 'Will be coming home with mum. Staying late to study in the library with friends.'

Aiden smirked as he suspected he knew exactly what 'friends' meant. No doubt Brian would be there. It wasn't new for Hannah to stay back and study in the library. She occasionally did that pretty much since she started high school. When either Aiden or Bec would pick Hannah up, they would always find her hanging out in library with the librarian and a handful of other kids who chose to buckle down and work hard too. But the boyfriend aspect was new. Aiden wondered how much work Hannah would actually get done from now on. He heard his wife's voice in his head, telling him to trust his daughter and let her live her life. Deep down he knew she wouldn't do anything stupid. Would she? In the end, he managed to type out his reply, 'See you tonight. Have fun', and drove home while telling himself that Hannah thought studying science and English was fun.

When he got home, Aiden realised he had a few hours of free time alone to kill. He called Bec at the clinic just to make sure he didn't have any errands to do or that he should pick up Hannah instead. He was happy to hear Bec confirm it just made more sense for her to do it as the school was on her way home anyway. They would get takeaway for dinner on the way too. Aiden knew that, while he called for legitimate reasons, he also figured Bec might have wanted some reassurance he was alright after his first day back at work. After hanging up the phone, he thought about what to do with his window of freedom. Spending that time shooting bad guys on his laptop sounded pretty inviting. He might have been over thirty but as the saying goes, 'inside every man there is a boy'. Aiden hunkered down on the sofa with his laptop, ready to escape reality for a few hours. As he started everything up and began to get into the zone, he saw the charge on his laptop only had ten or so minutes left.

'Ugh,' he grumbled as he shifted around on the sofa, reaching for the charger. He couldn't find it anywhere and let out a frustrated sigh when he recalled where it was. Bec was using the laptop the other night in bed. He remembered fishing the cable from its home in the living room to give her when she asked for it, oh so coquettishly.

Aiden put the laptop on the couch and slipped off his gaming headphones. He had pulled the coffee table up close to the sofa so he could easily reach his snacks and drink while he was gaming, but now pushed it aside with his foot. Walking out of the living room, he could see Leena curled up and dozing just outside the back sliding-door. The dog was nestled in the same position she had been when he first got home and Aiden paused a moment to make sure she was breathing.

Just lazy, he thought with a smile when he saw her back rise and fall as she slept. Through the glass door, Aiden's eye caught sight of the small shed at the end of the yard. He knew it was probably the perfect time to get out there and start cleaning it up a bit as Bec had been asking him to do for months. But he just shrugged. It could wait a little longer. He walked down the hall and into the bedroom where he saw the prized laptop charger on the floor beside Bec's side of the bed.

'Aha! Thought you would be here.' He knelt down to unplug it from the power board.

'Where else would I be?' a voice responded.

Aiden froze in place, one knee on the ground, one hand tightly gripping onto the charger. He recognised that voice. But it couldn't be. He was awake. Wide awake.

Nothing. That was nothing. Stupid imagination, that's all, Aiden thought as he remained still, listening for the slightest sound around him. Nothing happened. Aiden took a breath and looked up. The bedroom was empty. He chuckled awkwardly.

'Still telling yourself… that?' the voice whispered as though it were right next to Aiden's ear. This time, he dropped back with a yelp. He looked to the source of the voice and saw nothing.

'What… what the hell? You're not real,' he said pathetically. There was a hoarse laugh from the other side of the room. Aiden's head snapped to the sound. In the corner of the bedroom, he saw nothing but a small shadow. There were no windows on that side of the room but he knew that shadow shouldn't be there.

'No! Stay the fuck away from me!' He screamed, the dread of Gary's presence enveloping him all over again.

Aiden immediately remembered it all. The fear. The nausea and confusion. He quickly pulled himself to his feet and turned for the door. All he knew was that he needed to get away from that room. He ran out of the open door but stopped in his tracks. He couldn't breathe. He couldn't scream. A dark figure stood in the middle of the hallway. The daylight from behind obscured the silhouette's features, but Aiden recognised it. The figure took a step forward, shaking on thin, brittle legs. Its hands hung by its sides, the thin fingers emitting soft cracks of dried bone as they twitched.

'Where are you going, Aiden?' the figure said. But the voice wasn't Gary's. It was Sam's.

Aiden took a frightened step back. Sam stepped forward, her dried, rotting face grinning at him. Her head tilted to the side with a loud snapping sound as though her neck had given way to the weight of her skull. Aiden finally let out a whimper of fear. He glanced into the bedroom. The shadow in the corner was growing, somehow climbing along the walls and spreading out like a dark web of tangling branches.

'Coooome baaaaaack,' Gary's voice growled from the corner.

Aiden raised his hands to his face, tugging on his hair with fear and indecision. Sam was close, blocking his exit through the hallway but also in the way of the door to Hannah's room. Aiden couldn't stand his ground any longer. He dashed back into the bedroom, sticking to the far wall opposite the growing shadow. He stumbled towards the ensuite, hoping he might be able to make his escape by breaking out of the window in there.

He heard Sam's broken footfalls behind him and knew she was in the doorway of the bedroom. Just as Aiden clasped his hand on the open doorframe of the bathroom, a black wasp darted out in front of him. His eyes followed the evil-looking insect as it buzzed threateningly close to his face. He let out a scream when he felt something on his fingers. He tugged his hand from the doorframe as a large spider slowly climbed out of the bathroom and reared up angrily at him. Aiden stepped back against the wall. He knew Sam was behind him but dared not to look away from the bathroom door.

As the shadow grew in the room, Aiden saw a barefoot step out of the ensuite. It was red and swollen with insect bites running up the ankle, all weeping with pus and dark fluids. A hand slapped on the door frame almost exactly where Aiden's had just been and the spider ran over the flaking skin. The newcomer peeked out from the bathroom and Aiden's fears proved true. Lauren stared at him with weeping, bloodshot eyes. She entered the bedroom, dressed in that same outfit Aiden had seen her die in. She wore a broken shoe on her second foot which looked just as mangled and peeling as the first one. Her clothes hung over her body as though they had become several sizes too big. Aiden noticed with disgust that things seemed to be moving under the fabric too. A shiny black millipede with long red antennae skittered out of Lauren's blouse and ran up her neck. It was impossibly long, the rear of its hideous body just exiting Lauren's top as it began to disappear into her tangled hair. Lauren's pale, bitten face drooped as though she were disappointed.

'Aren't you... happy to see me... Aiden?' she asked and a dark fluid, similar to that in Sam's mouth ran down her chin. Lauren choked and gagged. She heaved a large cough and a cockroach, slimy with that black goo, dropped from her mouth and landed on the carpet where it flailed on its back and wiggled its spiny legs. Aiden felt as though he would throw up.

'No... no, no, no!' he cried as tried to back even further into the wall.

'You want both of us... don't you? You can have us, Aiden. You are the reason we're here after all,' Sam said in a hissing, garbled voice.

Aiden was so terrified by Lauren that he forgot about her and when he felt her sharp, bony hand on his arm he screamed. He launched himself forward, almost falling over the bedside table as he clamped back against the opposite wall. The black wall in the middle of the day.

'I wanted... to thank you... Aiden,' Gary's voice groaned as though he was everywhere at once.

A curious strong force was tugging on his body, as though the wall were sucking him back into it. He grunted and moaned as he tried to pull himself free to no avail. Sam and Lauren just smiled as they slowly hobbled closer.

'You... you brought me to that hospital,' Gary continued though Aiden just wished he would stop. 'Do you know... how many sweet... innocent... delicious souls are teetering on the edge of the abyss... in hospital?'

Aiden screamed with effort as he tried to get away from the shadowy wall. It felt as though his limbs were being held back by thousands of tiny claws. He watched as the shadow continued to creep along the walls, almost encompassing the whole bedroom now.

Lauren and Sam stared at him, dripping with dark ooze, writhing with insects and stinking of rotted flesh. They didn't come any closer.

'The old. *Strokes.* The brave. *Torn up bodies.* The stupid. *Broken bones.* The unlucky. *Chronic disease.* The innocent. *Childhood cancer.* You brought them all to me.' Gary cackled.

Aiden felt the weight of his heavy words. He envisioned the scared, innocent people who waited to die in hospital. Grandparents who were ready to say goodbye to their families. Young adults with hopes and dreams that would be torn away from them. Children, young and tragic who didn't understand and only wanted their parents to hold them. Aiden let out a cry of anguish. It couldn't be true. He couldn't be responsible for them all.

'You're lying! You're fucking lying!' he screamed through his physical and mental torments.

Gary's foul laughter echoed through the bedroom. Lauren and Sam's faces were twisted into grotesque smiles and they seemed to choke on the disgusting, thick goo that dripped from their blackened teeth.

'I never... lie, Aiden. Where have I been, you ask? Why have you been left in such peace? Because...' Gary's voice hissed, the sound moving across the tainted room until it suddenly came together at the opposite wall.

The black branches of the opposing walls pulsed and pulled outward. They twisted and melted together until a slimy, black human figure stood in the room. Two holes opened in its face like bright, burning red lights and that horrible web of tangled teeth stretched into an impossibly large grin. Aiden couldn't even fight the gripping wall anymore as he felt himself become paralysed with fear. It was as though he were having an episode of sleep paralysis, without the sleep.

'Because I was busy... feasting on the fear of those dying souls. Sucking the marrow of their life and sanity from their supple... broken bones,' Gary said as he stepped forward.

Lauren and Sam began to advance too and Aiden couldn't think, let alone try to run. He was frozen, unable to do anything but watch as the evil entities drew nearer. Sam moaned, in what might have been a sound of arousal, had her voice not been so garbled and shrill. Aiden felt her bony digits run up his leg and he became wholly aware of that terrible pain he felt when he last encountered her. Lauren stepped even closer and raised her face inches before Aiden's. She smiled before opening her mouth wide. Her breath smelt indescribably awful, as if it were a pit that was home to a thousand rotting corpses. Aiden would have retched and winced away if he could move.

Lauren leaned in closer still and dozens of tiny black shapes began to swarm out of her lips. Lauren let out her long, dark tongue and Aiden couldn't see what the little creatures were as she slinked up beside him but he didn't doubt they were spiders. He felt a horrid wet feeling on his face and imagined Lauren's foul, poisonous tongue on his cheek. Gary kept coming forward and Aiden felt a growing pain in his lower abdomen and crotch as Sam dipped down and out of his view. His eyes were uncontrollably fixed on the fire pits in the demon's face.

Gary chuckled. 'My gift… to you, Aiden. Time… to sleep,' he said as he raised a pitch-black hand with long, sharpened talon-like fingers.

Aiden felt the pain intensify and spread through his body as the leathery palm closed over his face. Everything seemed to spiral out of control and Aiden could do nothing to stop any of it as pain and nausea enveloped him. The world disappeared around him and the evil laughter of his tormenters became fuzzy to his ears. At last, like the only coherent sound in a night club throbbing with confusion, Aiden heard Gary's voice once more.

'Let's be together always.'

THE LAST PATIENT

REBECCA

'Okay, so I'm gonna head off alright?' Liz said as she pulled her handbag onto her shoulder and began to rummage through it for her keys.

Bec sat back in her office chair, finally taking her eyes from the computer screen that was still loaded with files to be completed. The last patient of the day was already in the office with Dr Pannu. Dr Winstead had left early for a meeting up in Melbourne. Bec didn't mind that. With an hour left in the working day and no Dr Winstead to interrupt her, Bec would likely get the last orders done to be able to leave on time for a change.

'All good. Anything nice planned for tonight?' she asked with a tinge of jealousy that Liz could leave already. Not that it mattered anyway. After getting some texts from Hannah during her lunch break it looked like Bec would be picking her daughter up from the school library after work, in which case it sounded like a good night for takeaway.

'Typical evening. Packet pasta for dinner, watch some TV, probably get in a fight with Tom, you know, the usual stuff,' Liz said while she kept hunting for her keys.

Bec raised her eyebrows. 'You guys are still actually happy right? I mean, I feel like it's been ages since you last told me Tom did anything nice for you?' she said before really thinking about it. She wasn't too embarrassed by blurting such a question out. She knew Liz long enough to know she wouldn't be fazed by the blunt approach.

As expected, Liz just laughed. 'Don't you ever sleep with Aiden after a fight? Tom makes up for his shortcomings. Well, most of them.' She grinned suggestively.

Bec pulled a face. 'Wow. More than I needed to know really. My fault, I know,' she said, turning back to the desk.

Liz laughed again. 'Aw, really? Why stop there? I could go into all sorts of details if you want,' she teased and Bec raised her hand in protest.

'Just stop. I'm good thanks, I won't ask again, I swear,' she said without looking up from her work. She heard the jingle of keys as Liz pulled them out from her bag.

'Shame, but I've gotta run now anyway,' she said as though she were sincerely disappointed. Bec felt her chair lean back a little as Liz rested on it and slid her face close to her ear.

'I'll fill you in on *all* the juicy details tomorrow,' she said playfully and Bec winced.

'Do it and you'll have to find another job.' She laughed back.

Liz clicked her tongue. 'Please, they won't get rid of me here for that! I'm just telling you some perfectly natural, sexual antics I enjoy with my husband,' she said.

Bec pretended to gag. 'Alright, I'll find another job! And nothing you get up to is natural.'

Liz finally let the chair go and gave an astonished gasp. 'Bitch! I was just going to tell you a few sordid details from tonight but now you're in for a few months of experience,' she said with a laugh.

Bec looked cautiously back and forth through the waiting room. As she thought, there was no one there, thank God. Liz could have kept the banter a little lower, couldn't she? Reassured that no one was in the room, Bec audibly shuddered as though she was truly grossed out.

'Can't wait...' she said in a monotone voice of revulsion. Suddenly, Liz's blonde hair blocked Bec's eyesight to her work and she felt her friend's lips on her head.

'Mwah! See you tomorrow, Bec. I really gotta run now,' she said.

Bec closed an eye and groaned with fake disapproval at the kiss. 'Bye. Have a... nice?... night,' she said with a feigned awkward wave as Liz walked around the reception bench.

'Oh, I will. You'll see. Bye!' Liz winked before she headed out of the clinic.

Bec took a deep breath and shrugged her shoulders while readjusting in her chair to get comfortable. 'Well, with that weirdness finally over with, back to... Mr Collins, you *are* over-due, aren't you?' She focused back on her work.

*

It was only maybe another ten minutes before the last patient came out of Dr Pannu's office. The elderly woman was sweet enough, the sort who liked to keep chatting a little longer than was necessary when processing a transaction. Bec normally wouldn't mind but she still had a lot to do and time was running out if she wasn't going to stay back late. Even so, she wore her usual, if not exhausted, smile and dealt as quickly as she could with the last patient's bill. A few minutes later, Bec heard another set of footsteps coming down the hallway.

'All done for the evening. How are you doing, Bec?' Adya asked as she stepped up to the desk, already wearing her coat.

Bec covered her sigh of exasperation with a cough. 'Almost done. Just one or two more cases to verify,' she said. It was more like nine or ten cases but she wanted to give the impression she was further ahead than she was. Possibly because it would have been as far along as she might have been if she didn't have to keep dealing with so many interruptions.

'Good, good,' Adya said while tapping the elevated portion of the bench with her fingers. 'Oh, I meant to ask, how's Aiden doing? You said he was going back into work today?'

Bec nodded. 'That's right. Uh, yeah, he's actually been doing remarkably well. I've not heard anything since he got home so I hope no news is good news?' A sudden pang of worry gnawed in her stomach.

Aiden's last phone call seemed pleasant enough. He sounded practically chipper as he said he had safely arrived home and confirmed Bec was picking Hannah up from school that evening. He said something about looking forward to just wasting some time and hardly sounded as though he had been having any problems that day.

'Let's hope, hey? I'm sure it's all fine. What does he have to worry about when he has you to take care of him?' Adya complimented with a smile, which Bec returned.

'True. What *does* he have to worry about?' she said with amusement. 'And how will you be spending your evening?' she added, half out of curiosity but also out of a desire to get the inevitable small talk over with.

'Journals to be read, articles to be studied. Must keep up to date. Maybe with a glass of red though,' Adya said with a wistful sigh.

Bec knew Adya had met someone not too long ago and no doubt she was fantasising about a much more interesting evening.

'How long before you see Mr Right again?' Bec asked with a sly grin as she attempted to multitask to get back to work.

Adya smiled with a blush. 'End of the week. I'm thinking we'll be going out for dinner and a movie.'

Bec smiled, feeling genuinely happy for the doctor. Adya was very dedicated to her career and hadn't left herself much time for a love life.

'Sounds like someone's recapturing her youth,' she commented suggestively.

Again, Adya blushed. 'Maybe. Maybe I'll let you know how it all goes if you like. But it stays between us?' she said. It was small, but it seemed to Bec as though Adya were extending her hand a little further to advance their friendship. Bec liked that. After years working together it was about time that they got a little closer than acquaintances.

'Yeah, that sounds nice. I'll promise not to let anyone know you're actually human in there, though,' Bec said jokingly.

Adya laughed. 'Well, good! I would hate for anyone to think their doctor is human. God forbid.'

Bec couldn't help but see a mental snapshot of the future. Aiden was doing so well now, maybe if this guy really was right for Adya they could actually meet him. Even have a double date. She couldn't remember how long it had been since she had done something like that. But Bec thought it better than to dive into that deep water and held her tongue.

'Anyway, will you be alright to lock up? If I leave now, I might beat the worst of the traffic home,' Adya said as she pulled her phone out of her coat pocket to check the time.

Bec waved her hand encouragingly. 'Yeah, of course. You know I lock up all the time. Get out of here while you still can. It all just starts again tomorrow anyway,' she said.

Adya put her phone back in her pocket and looked divided in her choice. 'Really? I don't have to leave you to do it all, you know?'

'Yes, really, I'll be fine. I've got… a bit still to do, anyway. Go, go, go.' She shepherded Adya to move along. Bec almost slipped and admitted she was further behind than she was, but she felt she kept it vague enough at least.

'Alright. Great, well, uh, I'll leave you to it then. See you tomorrow,' Adya said with a little doubt still on her face before she finally accepted Bec's reassurances and left the building.

Bec sighed as she sat back and fought the temptation to leave a little early herself. She knew she would be happier in the long run if she were up to date with her work and they would always need the money. So she took out her mobile, set it on the desk with a playlist of her favourite songs playing and got stuck back into her work.

*

The quiet music of Bec's phone echoed through the empty clinic as she finished up typing the last of her forms. The orders were done, invoices filed, appointment bookings up to date. She looked at the clock on the monitor before she shut the PC down.

Five past five. Not bad. Finally, I can get out of here. She was proud of the fact she had finished her backlog of work in just over half an hour since Adya had left and was simply happy she could finally call it a day. She looked over the reception booth to make sure everything was in order before she went to collect her handbag.

'Hello?'

Bec froze when she heard a faint voice call down the hallway to the doctors' offices. *Who the hell could that be?* she thought as she calmed her nerves from the sudden disturbance in what she had thought to be an empty clinic. She stood still with her ears perked for any further sounds, uncertain if it had just been her imagination.

'Doctor Winstead?' the voice called again. It sounded muffled, as if through a closed door but there was something familiar in the croakiness of it. Now convinced there was indeed someone in the building, someone who must have been missed by Dr Pannu before she left, Bec stepped out from the reception station and headed towards the offices.

'Hello? Is someone there? I'm sorry, everyone has left now,' she called out, hoping whoever might be in the clinic had a perfectly innocent explanation for their presence. Her mind raced as she thought about the possibility of a break in. But would an intruder really call for Dr Winstead of all people?

'Doc... Doctor Winstead?' the voice stuttered again.

As Bec approached, she heard the voice was indeed coming from Dr Winstead's office. The voice was frail, elderly and the stutter gave the voice's owner away.

'Mr Meadows? Is that you?' she asked in curious surprise as she approached the office door. It was possible Mr Meadows had come in earlier without her noticing; perhaps he checked in with Liz. But Bec didn't think he was due for an appointment for at least another week or two.

'He… h… help!' Mr Meadows cried with an unnerving desperation in his voice.

Bec's heart raced as she realised that he must have come in for something important and now, something had gone wrong. Any thoughts of why Mr Meadows had come to see Dr Winstead when he had been gone for most of the day, why he had waited so long in his office, why no one noticed he was in there, flew from her mind as she thought only to find out what was wrong.

'Mr Meadows? What's wrong? I'm coming!' she called as she rushed forward and burst the door open. Dr Winstead's office was just as it always was. His desk was neat and tidy, every form, every pen, every piece of medical equipment neatly set in its place. It appeared as though no one had been in the room since Dr Winstead had left, aside from the figure that lay on the examination bed. Bec quickly recognised the back of the brown cardigan that Mr Meadows almost always wore. He had said he had owned it for over thirty years and there was not a single piece of attire that could match its comfort, especially to keep out the chills. The old man was trembling on the mattress, his front turned to the wall as he lay in the foetal position.

'Mr Meadows! How long have you been here like this? What's wrong?' Bec asked as she raced over to check on the old man. When she set her hand on his shoulder, Mr Meadows screamed and flailed on the bed, knocking her hand away.

'It… it… hurts! Plea… please… help me!' he wailed as he jostled and kicked in evident agony.

Bec noticed a stain of dark red on the shoulder of his cardigan and it looked as though blood had been running from his ear.

'Oh God, alright, uh, okay. I'm going to call an ambulance.'

Mr Meadows screamed again, this time his head snapping back as he shifted and contorted painfully.

'Help! Ma… make it… st… sto… stop!' he screamed while Bec rushed to the phone. She had her back to him when she picked up the receiver.

Suddenly, Mr Meadows' screaming broke into chokes and gurgles. Bec didn't know what to do; the man was dying. Then there was a loud crack and everything went dead silent. A cruel, cold foreboding came over her, the suspicion that when she turned, she would see Mr Meadows had died. She slowly turned, still holding the receiver to her ear which beeped rhythmically. She hadn't had a chance to even start to dial. Bec was met with a ghastly sight. Mr Meadows now lay splayed on his back on the bed, his vacant face staring at her with glazed, frozen eyes. His arm hung lifelessly from the mattress, the palm open, as though he had tried in vain to reach for her before succumbing to his death.

Bec was numb, frozen in shock. She couldn't think what to do. She couldn't comprehend what had just happened. She tried to collect her thoughts. She still had to call for help. She was awoken from her dazed shock when another visceral sounding crack rang through the room. Bec screamed and dropped the phone as Mr Meadows' outstretched hand suddenly jolted. She was speechless as she watched the fingers curl and contort, snapping out of joint as they began to splay out. Mr Meadows' wide eyes were still glued on her face and now, they didn't seem so vacant. They were definitely staring at her. Bec didn't know if she should approach to help the man or give in to her instincts and back away from him.

Mr Meadows' jaw dropped open, his mouth a gaping dark cave and a horrible croaking sound came from deep in his throat. Suddenly, the man's entire body jolted upright until only his head and heels were in contact with the mattress as his spine audibly snapped. His arms bent backwards and blood began to stain through his clothes. Bec couldn't believe what she was seeing. She had never heard of a seizure like this; it couldn't be possible. Mr Meadows' knees dislocated, twisting the wrong way so that his legs seemed reversed. His trousers ripped and Bec felt sick as she saw splinters of sharp, bloody bone tear through his flesh.

'This… can't be…' she muttered before Mr Meadows screamed a terrible, inhuman scream. He spasmed again, this time so violently that his body fell to the floor.

Lacerations ripped through the visible skin of Mr Meadows' neck and his muscles tore through the fragile epidermal layers. Bec couldn't think yet she found herself stepping back to the door of the office. Mr Meadows twisted violently in her direction, staring at her as he lay in a broken, bloody mess on the floor. He barked at her, barked and snapped his teeth like a rabid dog. As he did so, he raised himself in a manner impossible for the human body. His torso faced upward while he stood on twisted, broken arms and legs, none of which looked as though they belonged to a human anymore. The webbing of his fingers ripped open, spreading his digits out grotesquely wide and each movement he made resulted in a disgusting cracking and squelching sound. His ribs were piercing their way through his chest like jagged spearpoints and Bec knew she needed to run.

Mr Meadows growled threateningly at her, as though he could read her mind and was ready to pounce. When his head suddenly snapped to the side and began to forcibly twist backwards, tearing the ligaments in his throat, Bec couldn't take anymore. She turned and bolted through the door, sprinting down the hallway in sheer terror. She heard a monstrous roar followed by the sound of something heavy smashing into the wall. She glanced back to see the disfigured body charging after her, splinters of bone and torrents of blood spraying over the floor and walls.

Bec didn't scream. She didn't cry. She could barely breathe as she sprinted, panic-stricken, into the waiting room. She skirted around the reception desk as fast as she could, listening to the chairs of the waiting room being smashed out of the monster's way with ease. Bec knew she had to pull open the damned glass door to the clinic. She prayed she had enough time. Approaching the door, she had to slow down to avoid ramming into the thick glass. A hoarse, primal yelp of fear emerged from deep in her chest when something swiped at her foot and she stumbled to her knees. As she tried to get up, she heard the thing behind her, growling in hideous, disfigured gurgles. It was practically on top of her.

Bec spun around, swinging her arm in a hook driven by her whole body. She couldn't see where she had made contact with the thing that had been Mr Meadows. She just heard the sound of cracking bones and spilling body fluids as the grotesque mass of flesh tumbled into the side of the reception desk. Without thinking, Bec took her chance. She forced herself up to her feet and opened the door. She didn't pause but dashed through the door and tugged it shut just in time. The loud smash of the monster vibrated against the heavy glass and Bec fell back on the cement path. She looked back to the fearsome, upturned face of Mr Meadows. He smeared his disgusting features across the glass, leaving streaks of red and dark brown. His eyes were wide, staring at her with a horrifying intensity. Bec backed away, crawling awkwardly along the ground as Mr Meadows' hand smacked the door over and over, trying to get through to her. White cracks were beginning to stretch along the glass.

Bec didn't know what to do. She couldn't get in her car or call for help. Her keys and phone were still on the desk in the clinic. She would have to just make a run for it, to get as far away from the thing as she could and find help. She couldn't help taking a final, terrified look at the twisted face of Mr Meadows. His mouth was gaping impossibly wide and the sinews and tendons of his cheeks were slowly splitting apart. Filled with disgust and dread, Bec finally found the will to turn away, though she feared as soon as she took her eyes off of him, Mr Meadows would break through the glass and do … God only knows what, to her. Yet, as she stood and turned, she hesitated. She couldn't believe it. The silence was so abrupt, so sudden. She looked back and found nothing there. Mr Meadows was gone. There were no cracks in the glass, no splatters of blood or viscera. Bec shook her head, but her heart continued to beat a million miles a minute in her chest. Her head was throbbing with pain and, somehow, she knew she hadn't just been imagining it.

'What... what the hell?' she managed to mumble as she held her aching head in her hands. She suddenly remembered it all. She could see Mr Meadows standing at the entry of the waiting room, staring at her with that inhumane smile while she worked. Bec felt nauseous as she remembered the whimpers of the girl who had tormented her in the shower before scurrying away like some diseased beetle. She remembered Hannah screaming in terror, rambling about something in her laptop that had tried to hurt her.

Aiden's voice resonated in her head. *Gary,* he said and she knew. Bec knew that *Gary* had something to do with it. She didn't understand, didn't know what to think. But deep down, Bec knew something was horribly wrong with her husband. She pushed through the searing pain in her skull and looked to the door of the clinic once more, still finding it as empty as would be expected on any other day. She needed to go back in to get her phone. Her keys. She wouldn't run anymore. Bec knew that she was in danger. But she knew her husband and daughter were too.

DISSECTION

HANNAH

Hannah stifled her giggles as she tried to focus back on her homework. The school library had always been the best place for her to get down to her studies. Sure, some kids thought people like her were just nerds, obsessed with good marks and being the teacher's pet. But Hannah honestly didn't think of it that way. The amount of work she and her fellow students were expected to keep up with was insane and no one would be able to keep on top of it all. English, history, geography, maths, science, commerce, psychology, literature, information technology, German, each subject with their own heavy loads of homework. It would be impossible for anyone to finish without going crazy. But Hannah liked learning. More specifically, she liked science, psychology and English. Those were the subjects she dedicated her time to. It might be at the expense of others, such as literature and commerce, but that was what Hannah had realised. Everyone was different, with different interests and potentials. It didn't matter how important each teacher insisted their particular subject was. Some people would just be strong in some subjects over others.

If Hannah got a D in commerce, she would shrug her shoulders, maybe dedicate a little more time to stay on top of the minimum standards, but it wouldn't affect her that much. Now if she got a C in science though? That would require immediate attention and focus to rectify and Hannah wouldn't feel comfortable until she got that A or at least a B. Yet grades were only one of the reasons why she decided to stay at the library that evening. With all the stressful things that had been happening at home, happening with her dad, she just wanted to hide away in the peace and quiet of the library with her laptop, her worksheets and Brian. Brian had joined her in the library from time to time through the years, but he had never proven to be such a distraction as he was now. For some reason, sitting at an empty table with, not just her friend, but her boyfriend made the whole idea of working the library seem much more fun. More inappropriate. Of course, they didn't get up to any real mischief. After all, there were always one of two other students hanging around somewhere and Mrs Cohen, the old librarian was careful to keep a close eye on her wards. Even so, Hannah found herself and Brian joking and talking a lot more than they normally would have. Maybe now that he was free to express his true feelings, Brian felt more inclined to waste time than work. To Hannah's annoyance, she actually liked this change herself.

'Okay, come on now. We really need to get this done. My mum will be here at six. That only gives us maybe an hour,' she said, trying her best to concentrate on the periodic table on her laptop.

'Yep, yep. You're right, I know. Sorry… baby,' Brian said before breaking into stifled chuckles again.

Hannah blushed and buried her face in her hand, her shoulders jumping up and down with her own muted laughter. She felt so embarrassed. Brian had asked her what sort of names she liked the sound of with couples. Hannah thought about the couples she knew, ones she had seen in movies and shows, read in books and just the general cultural norms she had grown up in. Without really thinking about it, she had told Brian she liked the sound of baby. Since then, a solid ten minutes ago, Brian had managed to reduce her to tears of laughter by trying his best to use the pet name. It was endearing, but it wasn't the right time and something in the way he said it just made them both hilariously giddy.

'Damn it, Brian, stop it,' Hannah wheezed through her smile.

Brian sat back, gasping for breath as he lightly waved his hand in defeat. 'Okay, okay, okay. Yep, I'm done. Maybe I need some practice,' he said and Hannah was off laughing again.

'Wha... wha... what do you mean? You're just going to stand in front of the mirror going, "Baby. Baaaby. Babyyy"?'

Brian laughed too. 'No. No, I don't mean that. I... I don't know what I meant.'

'Sure, sure. Just do me a favour and take a video of yourself doing it. I *need* to see that.'

They heard the sound of someone loudly clearing their throat. Hannah looked up to see the bony face of Mrs Cohen staring at them through her thin-rimmed glasses. That harsh stare washed over Hannah like a bucket of ice water and her smile, while not completely gone, faded.

'*Sorry*,' she mouthed while politely waving a hand to show she meant no harm.

Mrs Cohen continued to look at them with pursed lips for a moment longer before she turned back to her work.

'Yeesh. I never knew her to be so bad. What is she, like, one of those hundred and something year old crones that lurk the haunted libraries in movies or something?' Brian asked in a cool whisper.

Hannah smiled. 'My question is, with librarians always being so old in those sorts of movies, how do they all have bat-like hearing?' she responded and Brian snorted.

'Right. Ms Woods. Mr Zhang. As you will not be achieving anymore study for the moment, would one of you kindly assist me with something? I need some books taken to a classroom for tomorrow,' the harsh voice of Mrs Cohen rang out.

A sense of shame welled in Hannah's belly but she also fought down a new founded feeling of defiance. She didn't think Mrs Cohen really had a right to tell them off. After all, it was out of school hours now. But Hannah knew she had been misbehaving, even if only in some long out-dated sort of way. She glanced at Brian and he looked back at her with a nervous grin.

'I'll do it,' he said quietly but Hannah shook her head and tapped his laptop.

'No, that's okay, I can afford to move some books. Look how far behind you are, though,' she said.

Brian shrugged. 'I thought I could just get my girlfriend to do it for me?' He smiled cheekily.

Hannah looked taken aback. 'Right. You better have that whole worksheet done by the time I get back,' she teased like a strict parent before getting up and hurrying over to an increasingly agitated looking Mrs Cohen.

The librarian put the last of the textbooks she was sorting on a wheeled cart by her desk.

'Sorry about that, Mrs Cohen. So, um, what did you need me to do?' Hannah said a little sheepishly as she arrived.

Mrs Cohen looked at her carefully over the top of her glasses. 'Mr Novak asked to have these textbooks delivered to room S3 for tomorrow morning. Head over there and drop them off. And be quick about it, the rooms will be locked up shortly,' Mrs Cohen said sharply as she indicated the cartful of books.

Hannah nodded, relieved in some small way at least, that Mrs Cohen didn't seem keen on addressing her misbehaviour, despite her snappy attitude.

'Okay,' Hannah said, unable to meet Mrs Cohen's harsh gaze as she began to wheel the cart of books out of the library.

Though she knew Mrs Cohen had a reputation for being cold, Hannah had usually been on relatively good terms with her at least. She had never felt the piercing bite of the librarian's stare and she didn't like it one bit. *We're really going to need to try and rein it in a bit next time,* she thought as she wandered along the concrete path towards the S-section classrooms.

It was getting close to six o'clock now, and as it was mid-winter, it was already getting pretty dark outside. Thankfully the old, fluorescent lights that lined the classrooms were on, providing light and a curious sense of comfort against the dimming evening. After leaving the library, Hannah hadn't seen a soul. No doubt some teachers were still about, most likely in the office buildings, but most staff and students would be happy at home by now. The rolling grind of the plastic cart's wheels on the concrete mingled with the faint buzzing of the fluorescent lights, and aside from Hannah's own footsteps, everything else was silent. The S rooms were across the opposite side of the school's central courtyard and, rather than cutting through the thin paths which weaved through the garden beds of native shrubbery, Hannah kept to the main paths along the edge of the court. Finally, she found herself outside S3. As she pulled open the sliding door, she saw the class was mostly dark aside from one of the fluorescent ceiling lights by the teacher's desk. She wheeled the cart inside and walked past the rows of tables to the illuminated desk. She began to unload the books, piling them in neat stacks of five. Hopefully, Mr Novak might appreciate the general tidiness of his books. A curious sense of unease fell over her as she unpacked the books in the empty, dark classroom. There was a faint buzzing in her ears, as though her brain needed the silence to be broken by something to remain sane. Hannah set the last textbook down and turned the cart around, keen to get back to the library, and to Brian. She took a step forward when she paused in her place. At the far end of the class, down by the sinks along the wall which were used for science experiments, there was a dark figure. She hadn't noticed them when she walked in, but she hadn't heard a thing while she was unpacking the books and she had a terrible feeling the stranger had been there the whole time. Hannah got the uncomfortable impression that she had been watched ever since she entered the classroom and a shiver ran down her spine.

'Uh, hello?' she asked awkwardly as she took a nervous step forward, trying to get closer to the classroom door. The figure didn't respond and as Hannah's eyes adjusted to the shadows about them, she realised they were hunched over the bench with their back to her. Maybe she was just being paranoid. They hadn't been watching her. Maybe they were working at the bench when they fell asleep? As she got closer, Hannah could see the outline of a relatively familiar broad back and a cream business shirt.

'Mr Novak? Is that you?' she enquired again as she moved closer. There was a low groan but the figure said nothing. Hannah trembled.

He's just sleeping. It's okay. Just don't bother him. Get out and go. She stepped as quietly as she could, the low rumble of the rolling wheels of the cart grating her twitching nerves. She was about twice the cart's length away from the door, only a few more steps and she could manoeuvre her way out. But the stranger sitting at the sink was only a seat away from the door, so she would have to get even closer to them to leave. The figure straightened up, and Hannah made out a large head above the previously hunched shoulders. She saw the dark, thinning hair with faint hints of grey and knew at once her suspicions were correct. It was Mr Novak.

'A little late to be wandering around the school, isn't it?' he said in a low, monotone voice without turning. Hannah froze as soon as he had moved and his voice troubled her. He didn't sound as though he had just woken up. He spoke clear and concise, without any hint of weariness or emotion.

'Uh, yeah. It's just me, Mr Novak, Hannah Woods,' Hannah said nervously. 'I like to hang back and study in the library sometimes. Mrs Cohen sent me to drop off some books for you,' she explained to the now statuesque figure who sat before her.

'Ah, Hannah. My favourite student,' Mr Novak said slowly with a new warmth in his voice. It wasn't any more comforting than his previous robotic tone. 'Mrs Cohen sent you? She chose you specifically to come here, did she? She must know…'

Hannah didn't know what the teacher meant, but she didn't like the sound of it. 'Uh, no. She didn't choose me. Well, I mean, she kind of did, but I wasn't the only one she… asked,' Hannah said, her voice trailing off a little as her brain caught up with her words and she realised that she didn't understand why she was explaining herself, especially about something so trivial to Mr Novak.

The teacher gasped, but still didn't turn to face the girl. His shoulders shifted a little and there was a strange ruffling noise as though Mr Novak were playing with some fabric. Tearing it.

'Oh! Oh, but that's so much better. You chose to come? To come and see me? Then you know too,' he said with an excitable hiss.

Hannah nervously took another step forward, still pushing the trolley. She was growing desperate to just get out of there. 'Um, what do I know Mr Novak? I promise… I, uh, don't know what you mean,' she said awkwardly.

Mr Novak let out a strange groan and a took a deep breath of air. Hannah didn't know what she was hearing, but the strange crunching sounded eerily off putting.

'Oh… oh… but you… know, Hannah. You… know… you are my… favourite,' Mr Novak said between excited pants and the continuing crunches and cracks.

Hannah's whole body stiffened; her skin was tingling and her heart pounding. She was becoming nauseous as a bad smell teased her nostrils. It was too much, the darkness, the weird way Mr Novak was speaking without looking at her. Hannah couldn't care less about returning the trolley to Mrs Cohen now. The stupid librarian could just come back and get it in the morning. All Hannah cared about was getting back to Brian and the safety of the library.

'Well… I need to get going, Mr Novak. My mum is, uh, waiting for me.' She took a step forward. She didn't think about lying, it was just instinct. As though telling the teacher someone who really cared about her was waiting for her would give him some reason to let her go. Even though he hadn't technically been holding her back at all. Hannah's brain couldn't help recalling the rumours about the teacher and she became all the more unsettled.

'Leaving… so soon? I'm going to miss you, Hannah. Let me… give you something. For you to keep,' Mr Novak said and he suddenly hunched over again with a loud grunt.

Hannah stopped edging to the door, paralysed with apprehension. Her breath caught in her throat when she saw splatters of a dark liquid on the floor around Mr Novak's chair.

'Really, that's okay. I'll just see you tomorrow, Mr Novak,' she said weakly while the teacher remained still in his seat. The girl jumped when, in an instant, Mr Novak was on his feet. Slowly, he turned. Hannah couldn't move. She saw a glint of silver in his hand, silver tainted with blood. He held the scalpel tightly in his red fingers, but as the man turned, something else caught Hannah's eye.

In the shadows, she saw strange protrusions, one to two inches long, in the teacher's chest. Hannah found herself stepping back without thinking as she realised the sharp stems were the tips of snapped ribs. Mr Novak's shirt, shiny with dark blood, was ripped open at his chest and, impossible though it was, Hannah could see a large, gaping wound to the left side.

She would have retched in disgust if she were not paralysed with terror as the teacher took a step forward. He stared at Hannah with wide, unblinking eyes, his mouth twisted into an unsettling smile. Mr Novak raised his right hand, holding it out towards the girl as he stumbled forward. A hideous chunk of flesh and gore sat in his palm, the blood trickling down his forearm.

'Take it. Take it, Hannah. My heart... for you,' he said, his voice croaky as though he were choking up with emotion.

Hannah instinctively stepped back from the approaching man and she gasped as she felt her back bump into the classroom wall. Mr Novak was still some paces away from the trolley between them, but he was still all too close.

'I know. I know you've heard about the other girls. They... they meant nothing, Hannah. I swear. It's you. My heart belongs to you. Please... take it. Take it... and...' Mr Novak continued to approach, the blood dripping from the severed organ in his hand splattering onto the plastic surface of the library trolley. 'Give me yours,' he said, his lips peeling back to expose his teeth in a wide grin.

He raised his other hand as he spoke, pointing the sharp edge of the scalpel towards Hannah's own chest. Hannah's voice broke free of her tight throat. She screamed, but she didn't make the sort of sound she might have expected. The high-pitched wail of a damsel in distress. Her scream was hollow, deep and hoarse, a heavy groan releasing the sheer disbelief and fear that grew deep in her stomach. Without thinking, she jumped forward. The door was so close. She rammed her weight into the handle of the trolley that skidded across the laminated floor of the science room and crashed into Mr Novak. The teacher howled a grizzly, inhuman scream as he tumbled backwards and smashed into the bench. Hannah didn't stop, she couldn't think of anything except escape.

'NOOOOO!!! Hannah! You can't leave me!' Mr Novak wailed as Hannah quickly tugged the sliding door of the class open and dashed outside. 'Come back! Give me your heart… I neeeeed your heart!'

She heard Mr Novak screaming behind her. His voice cracked with misery but somehow growing more fierce and violent with every uttered syllable.

Hannah wasn't in control of her body as she fled in mindless terror. She ran too quick for her mind to catch up with her and, as she cut through one of the school's locker bays, she couldn't follow the corner in time. Hannah collided loudly into the sheet metal lockers and grunted with pain. She glanced back along the way she had come as she panted and turned to run again. Hannah gasped. The dark silhouette of Mr Novak was there, coming closer and closer. He ran on unsteady feet, like a drunken vagrant, his head lolling on his loose neck. The hand gripping the scalpel was swinging by his side as he continued to reach forward with his other hand.

'My heart for yours, Hannah! Take it. Eat it. Keep it inside you forever and I'll do the same!' The teacher roared, anger now swelling in his voice. The sort of roaring anger that jump starts a person's heart to hear so sudden and violent an outburst. Hannah yelped pitifully as she took flight once more, sprinting out of the locker bay and cutting through the courtyard. Her frightened tears burned in her eyes and she could hear the crazed teacher stomping and staggering behind her, his breath raspy and gurgling.

'BITCH!!! I… give you this. I give you me. You run away? Come back. Come back so I can cut your pretty face off. To keep with me forever. COME BACK!' Mr Novak roared.

Hannah tried to ignore his screams. She felt her legs becoming weaker, her muscles wearing down as though they wanted her to fall to the ground in despair and resign herself to her foul end. But she saw light ahead. The library. She fixed her sights on that fluorescent glow as though it were the shining light of heaven. She ran on, terrified that at any moment she would feel a vice like grip on her flying hair or the cold bite of that scalpel in her back. Mr Novak screamed, his voice less human than ever before, now roaring like an enraged beast. Hannah screamed too. She screamed out her fear and channelled it to force her onwards. The library door was there, closer, closer. She charged into the door with all her might. It still hadn't been latched and it swung open easily with the impact. Hannah lost her footing as her shoes suddenly met the thick carpet and she fell forwards, collapsing onto her arms, her head narrowly missing one of the tables as she went down. The library was filled with the sound of screams, the screams of a terrified girl.

'Hannah! Hannah!' Hands took hold of her arm and she flailed wildly, kicking and wailing.

'No! No! No, keep away! Don't touch me!' The hands let her go and she looked up, frightened to see Mr Novak's piercing, crazed stare. But as she blinked away the blurriness of her tears, Hannah saw Brian looking down at her, his face a picture of worry. Mrs Cohen was hovering behind him, looking deeply concerned herself.

'B… Brian?' she panted, her confusion and terror slowly drifting into a twisted sense of relief.

'Are you okay? What happened?' Brian asked nervously as he gently took her hand and supported her back, helping her to sit upright. Hannah's chest was aching as she heaved deep breaths, her lungs tight from the exertion of her sprint back to the library.

'I... it was... Mr... Novak,' she mumbled as she felt a sudden sharp pain in her head. She learned forward, cradling her forehead in her hands, her eyes closed tight against the pulsing throb.

'Oh, the girls in this school! Mr Novak left hours ago,' Mrs Cohen scoffed but Hannah wasn't paying attention to her. She gasped as the vivid memories of everything that happened over the last few weeks came rushing back like a wave of fresh horror. She remembered the bloody... thing in the school bathroom. She remembered almost drowning at the beach, the face of seaweed grinning at her as she struggled to break free for air. And she remembered the laptop. That dark, twisted hand reaching out for her.

'Hannah? Hannah! Hello? Can you hear me? What do we do? Do we call an ambulance?' Brian's panicked voice brought her back into the room. Her head was still pounding and she winced against the light when she opened her eyes to look at her boyfriend.

'No. I mean, I don't think so. I, um, I think I need to go home. Where's my phone?' she mumbled while she turned back to the desk she and Brian had been studying at. She rose to her wobbly legs and Brian helped her to walk over to their table.

'Are you sure you are alright, Hannah? I don't think Mrs Fletcher is still here but let me call sick bay and find out,' Mrs Cohen said, the evident concern growing in her voice as she carefully watched after the students.

'I just need to call Mum,' Hannah responded, barely registering that the librarian was already dialling the phone to reach the school nurse.

'Here, sit down. Careful. I'm really worried about you,' Brian said softly as he helped her to sit.

She gave him a weak, appreciative smile. 'I'll be okay. Promise,' she said, lying even to herself. Inside, Hannah had no idea what to do other than to run away and hide at home. She didn't know what was wrong with her, or who could help. She felt she was definitely going insane and had to shake the thoughts of being locked up in an institution wearing a straitjacket from her mind. She fumbled around in her backpack before she finally got hands on her mobile. She tried not to think about what had just happened, just as she tried not to worry about the future of being a patient in an asylum. All Hannah thought of was reaching her mum and getting her to pick her up. She just wanted to be held in her mother's arms and be allowed to cry her terror away. She unlocked her phone and gasped with surprise. There were four missed calls, all from her mum within the last ten minutes. Hannah looked further and found a collection of text messages.

'Answer your phone!'

'Hannah, where are you?'

'Get ready to go right away.'

'I'm coming now!'

'Please be safe.'

Hannah's sense of relief that her mother was already on her way to get her quickly faded away. The number of missed calls. The desperation between the lines of the text messages. Hannah knew something was wrong. And her mum knew it too.

THE NIGHTMARE

AIDEN

Aiden's head was throbbing as he fluttered into consciousness. He was weak, unable to move. Unable to even open his eyes as his senses began to return to him. He knew he was lying down. He could feel the sharp, jagged edges of a rough surface beneath his back, digging into his body. Aiden instinctively shivered as a bone piercing chill enveloped him. He tried to open his eyes again, finally parting the lids to reveal a blurry sight of darkness. Aiden blinked over and over, trying to clear his vision. His whole body began to ache and he let out a low grunt of discomfort as he struggled to sit upright. There was a faint echoing hum in his ears, as though he were in a cave deep underground. A foul smell teased his nostrils but Aiden couldn't place what it was. He lifted his hands to his face, his palms feeling damp against his cheeks. Aiden realised he wasn't wearing his glasses. He rubbed his eyes before trying to look out once more. He could make out faint shapes in the dark, but not much else.

Where the hell am I? he thought in sheer confusion. Suddenly, the memory of what had actually happened to him sprung into his mind. The pain of Sam and Lauren's treatment seared through him and he doubled over, clutching at his abdomen. He groaned through gritted teeth and tightly closed his eyes in an effort to forget the living corpses.

To forget Gary. He couldn't banish the image of Gary from his mind because Gary didn't really have an image to banish. He was darkness, far reaching, tangling webs of darkness with teeth and claws which ripped into your mind rather than your flesh.

'Ah fuck, what... is going on?' He growled, the pain finally easing enough for him to sit back up. He rubbed his hands down his legs in an attempt to soothe away the aching throbs. He could feel his skin, cold and wet and he realised he wasn't wearing any clothes. He trembled again, the cold of wherever he was seeping into his veins.

'Gary? What the fuck is going on?!' he repeated blindly into the darkness, his voice echoing in what must have been a giant chamber.

There was no response and Aiden hit his head with his palm, trying to wake himself up. He had to be dreaming. He was lost in a void of cold black and the only thing he could be sure of was the solid surface beneath him. He felt dizzy, the disorientation of the sheer darkness sending his brain into a frenzy of somersaults. Nausea quickly began to set in and he tried desperately hard to focus on the cold, hard surface he was sitting on. Without that, he might as well have been floating, falling in an abyss of emptiness. He clutched at his legs, curling himself into a ball of despair. He would have cried if he could keep himself focused enough from falling. He just wanted the dream to be over. Not just the dream – he wanted the whole sorry affair to be over. Why had Gary come to him? Why was he being haunted so mercilessly?

Aiden froze when he suddenly thought about his family. Rebecca. Hannah. Even the dog, Leena. The only thing he ever really cared about was his family and yet, he had been so worried about himself, so lost in the insanity of his own experiences that he had no idea what might have been happening with them. If Gary could do this to him, what was stopping him, it, from doing it to his wife and daughter? Aiden tried to steel himself against such thoughts. Gary was torturing him. Not them. It was his problem and he had to deal with it. Not his family. But, as he thought of Bec's beautiful smile, the way Hannah tucked herself under a blanket on the couch whenever they watched movies at night, a gentle glow ignited within him.

He focused on his family. He thought about how much they had shared over the years. When Hannah was born. When he and Bec finally got married. Just the day-to-day comfort of knowing that he had people who loved him and he loved with such strength that he couldn't comprehend life without them, Aiden felt reawakened. Empowered. He wasn't falling anymore. He knew he was sitting on the ground. He opened his eyes. To his surprise, he could see. He could only make out a few feet, but it was as though a light were above him, glowing down in a cone around him. He saw dark, shiny rock. Sharp and jagged stalagmites rose from the ground. Aiden managed to stand up and step over to the curious rock formations. He gasped as he approached and saw them more clearly. The stalagmites were the strangest sort of rock he had ever seen. In truth, they looked more like bones.

He leaned over and inspected one of the protrusions. It was jagged, as though the tip had been snapped away. At the top, it looked as though the stalagmite was hollow and a dark fluid was frothing from the end, running down the shaft in thick torrents. In the dim light about him, Aiden noticed how the dark goo had a tint of red to it. He reached up and pressed his fingers to it. The fluid was sticky and clung to his fingertips in wet patches. He took a step back in disbelief. He quickly looked all around him. The stalagmites were all over and the ground beneath his feet felt just a slick and shined in the light. Aiden suddenly realised what the putrid smell in the air was but he couldn't believe his own senses. It was just impossible. He was standing amongst a stalagmite forest of bones and blood. He clutched at his hair and cried out, wishing his broken mind would just let him out of his own nightmare.

'Not... comfortable?' a voice rang out from the darkness that surrounded him. The hideous voice was too familiar now. Aiden whimpered in frustration and despair.

'What do you want?!' he cried out, spinning around in a vain attempt to see Gary. He was not surprised to find nothing but the stalagmites around him. The following silence pounded in his ears.

'I already have you,' Gary finally responded in a gargled laugh.

Aiden shook his head. 'Wh – what do you mean? Please. Please just tell me what is happening to me,' he uttered, his mind broken by his torments. Gary's horrid laugh echoed around him.

'You need some... company,' the entity said and after another choke of distorted laughter, everything went quiet again.

Aiden's heart pounded as he tried to make sense of what Gary had said. He looked down at his hand, seeing the red tinge staining his fingers and palms. Suddenly, a terrible thought dawned on him. He looked up again. He didn't know where in the darkness to turn, but he began to struggle his way forward.

'No! No, you can't have them! Please! Please don't hurt them!' he screamed desperately as he twisted his way through the bloody stalagmites. Tears streamed down his cheeks. He had no idea what to do. How could he stop Gary form hurting his family? He didn't even know where he was or how he had gotten there. An ear-piercing scream cried out and Aiden froze in place. The scream had definitely been a woman.

'Hello?! Bec?! Hannah?!' he cried out, turning on the spot as he tried to work out where the scream had come from. He could hear a woman crying, her whimpers and gasps moving in the darkness. Aiden tried to focus on them. He heard the splatter of wet, pounding footsteps. Someone running.

'Oh God, I'm coming!' He tried to trace the steps, dashing forward into the dizzy maze of the void to find the other person.

'Gary! Gary, please leave her alone! Please! Leave them both alone!'

As expected, there was no response and instead, Aiden just tried to find the crying woman. He followed his ears, wincing in pain as his bare foot scratched over some sharp shard of rocky bone on the ground. The footsteps were growing louder, nearer. He turned this way and that, trying to keep the sound in front of him. Aiden let out a gasp of excitement when he saw a figure moving up ahead.

'Stop, I can see you!'

The figure slowed down and the crying seemed to calm slightly. Aiden ran forward, narrowly missing smashing into a particularly large stalagmite as he approached the figure. His light came over them and Aiden stopped, bent over and clutching his knees as he caught his breath and looked to the scared face before him.

'Is… Sam?' he asked, coughing away his exertions and tentatively taking a step forward.

Sam looked at him with wide, teary eyes. Her pale skin was dirty, but definitely living. At least much more so than the corpse visitor Aiden had seen more recently. Sam was panting with exhaustion and evidently the fear which consumed her. She was wearing clothes, but they were badly torn and shredded about her. They might have been a nice black outfit one might go to a party in, had they not been so mangled. Sam took a frightened step back as Aiden approached and she stared at him as though she didn't believe her eyes.

'Sam… Sam, it's me. Aiden…' he said cautiously. He didn't know what to expect. Was Sam really here or was she just another trick Gary was playing on him? Aiden was inclined to think the latter, but something about her shrivelled, frightened form made him doubt his suspicions.

'Aiden?' Sam asked in a hollow, dry voice. She carefully looked at his face, evidently trying to make sense of everything herself. She snapped her head back, looking into the darkness before struggling for breath. Sam jumped forward, clutching at Aiden's neck. He yelped, frightened she was going to try and strangle him, but soon realised she was grabbing for him out of sheer desperation.

'Aiden! Aiden, it's coming for me. Please. Please help me! Please, it wants you. It says it wants you. That you caused it. Please stop it! Please!' Sam raved manically.

Aiden tried to pry her clutching hands away from him. 'Sam… what… what are you talking about? Do you mean Gary? What's going on?' he tried to make sense of what the woman was saying but she was steadily becoming less and less coherent as she began to scream and wail.

'You bastard! You, fucking shit! Why? Oh God, run! Run!'

She let Aiden go and began to hastily run past him. A sudden fear froze his heart to ice. A fear that something would spring from the shadows and jump on him if he didn't follow. He quickly turned around and began to run after Sam as she started to fade into the dark.

'Sam! Wait! What's happening?' he called after her, but Sam kept running. Aiden couldn't hear anything except their own footfalls and panting. If something were chasing them, he had no idea what it could be.

'Sam, please listen to me! I don't know what's going on. What happened to you?'

In response, Sam yelped as she tumbled ahead of him. Aiden could barely see her in the edge of the dim light which seemed to enshroud him but he could hear Sam crying out and struggling. She seemed to have fallen into a sort of ditch.

'Sam? Sam!' he screamed helplessly as he got closer. He could just make out the hulking form of something else in the darkness. Something wrestling with Sam. The young woman screamed and struggled for breath in her exertions.

'No! No, help! God, please help me!' she wailed. Violent snarling and the panting of something like a rabid dog echoed in the empty darkness.

Aiden was too afraid to move, but as Sam desperately cried for help, he found his legs were forcing him forward anyway. Whatever was attacking her in the ditch was not much larger than a man and Aiden could just make out the unsettlingly long limbs flailing about. There was something sharp at the end of its long arm but it moved so fast in the dark that he couldn't be sure if it were holding a knife, or if the thing wielded some sort of claws. Aiden skirted to the side, trying to stay out of the attacker's line of sight, without really knowing how he could help Sam. He took a deep breath and without thinking, lunged forward to jump on the thing's back. Just as he moved, Sam's screams became blood-curdling gurgles. Aiden fell flat on his face, his torso smacking into the hard, bony ground. He quickly shifted himself upright, looking around for Sam and the thing. He was completely alone. Aiden felt a warmth on his face and chest and he looked down to find himself drenched in thick, fresh blood. He stared at his red hands in horror, unsure of his own sanity before he bent down and vomited.

'God. God, please... make it stop.' He tasted his own bile mixed with the metallic blood on his lips.

He lay in the foetal position on the cold, hard ground and clutched at his hair as he tried to think clearly. Had Sam even been there? He knew she was dead. She couldn't possibly have been there. What the hell attacked her? Where was it now? He actually wished that whatever it was would come back. That it would find him lying on the ground and drive whatever weapon it had into his heart. Suddenly, a low, hoarse chuckle pierced the air. Aiden clapped his hands over his ears and gritted his teeth.

'Just leave me the fuck alone!' he screamed in pitiful defiance. It sounded as though Gary were tutting his tongue. If whatever he was even had one.

'She had to meddle, didn't she? And you couldn't save her. No one can now. But maybe...'

Aiden did his best to ignore Gary's torments before the voice echoed out into silence once more. He didn't move. He couldn't think of anything else to do now but to lie down and wait for death. He only hoped he could do so without Gary toying with him anymore. He closed his eyes and tried to think of lying in his bed, snuggled up with Bec by his side and Hannah as a little girl cuddling between them. Despite being lost in wherever the hell he was, left to fend for himself against whatever horrors Gary had for him, Aiden couldn't resist his lips curving into the faintest smile.

'Aiden?' a hushed whisper of a voice brought Aiden back into the dark hole he was trapped in. He opened his eyes, that faint light about him still illuminating the few feet before him. He stared to the small, jagged rocks, like bleached bones coated in shiny gore. He closed and opened his eyes again, hoping this time he might see he was in his bedroom after all, but still the bony stones lay strewn about him. He had no idea how long he had been lying there, alone in the dark. Had he actually fallen asleep? That couldn't be possible. He was surely trapped in a dream and you couldn't sleep in your own dream, could you?

'Aiden, is that really you?' the voice asked again and a shadow crossed through the mysterious little source of light. Aiden arched his head back and looked to the source of the voice. He almost wasn't even surprised to see Lauren's face but, potentially expecting her still didn't make any of this make any more sense. He sat up and shuffled back a little.

'No. You're dead. I saw you die. You can't be here. Just like Sam wasn't really here. You're not you. Gary, I know you're doing this. You're just fucking with me,' he said, shaking his head suspiciously.

Lauren knelt down beside him. She looked frightened, but more than that, she was exhausted. Her eyes were sunken, and scratches crossed over her cheeks. Her hair was a wet, tangled mess and, like Sam, her clothes were ragged and torn. The dark blood of the void was all over her, just as much as it was over him.

'I... I don't know what's going on... but I swear to you... Aiden, I'm not him. I'm not... Gary,' Lauren said, her voice choking as she acknowledged Gary's existence, no matter how impossible it seemed.

Aiden stared at Lauren with squinting eyes. He was almost expecting her to transform, for her skin to melt away and reveal her corpse like visage once more. But Lauren just fell back with a grunt after squatting unsteadily for some moments. The sound of clattering bones echoed around them as she fell.

'What is this place?' Aiden asked in little more than a whisper, still not wholly convinced that Lauren wasn't just some new evil manifestation sent to terrorise him. Lauren shook her head and let out a small incredulous laugh.

'I have no idea. Hell? It might as well be.'

Aiden nervously looked around them. He shouldn't have been surprised to only see sheer walls of black shadow but his heart sank regardless.

'It must be… some sort of cave or something,' he said, though even he wasn't convinced by his poor attempt to rationalise it to himself.

'There's no way out. I've tried. I don't know how long I've run around this fucking place. Just to find some light. A way out. Even just some fucking water,' Lauren said before smacking her cracked, dry lips.

Aiden edged a little closer to her. He knew he shouldn't. He didn't doubt it was Gary playing some new trick on him. But somehow Lauren was convincing him enough that she was herself. Aiden just didn't know how.

'So… you died. Remember? The car?' he said slowly, trying to make sense of it all. Lauren shot him a piercing look.

'I remember the bugs. All over me. Inside me. Eating me. I remember them and the pain. The stings. The bites. I couldn't breathe. I was choking on them. The next thing I knew, I woke up here. Did I die? I don't know, maybe. But if I did, then you did too and this really is Hell,' she said darkly.

A terrible pain emerged in Aiden's gut as the idea of eternal torment in this darkness sunk in. He remembered Sam and Lauren. The corpses of them abusing him. Hurting him. He remembered the dark thing that was Gary, smothering his face. 'Shit… you think he killed me?' He gasped and his head started to spin again.

Lauren opened her mouth to speak, then closed it again. She shrugged. 'I don't know. All I know is that I'm not letting him get me.' She unsteadily rose to her feet. There was a determination in her voice now. But Aiden could see it wasn't one she wanted. It was forced upon her. He quickly stood up with her.

'What do you mean? Him? You mean Gary?'

Lauren turned around a few times, as though trying to decide which way to go before she finally looked back to him. 'That's what it calls itself anyway. You know it isn't a person, don't you? Obviously, you do. It's something bad. A ghost, a demon, who the fuck knows, but it's evil. We've been sitting around too long. I can't let it get me again,' Lauren said, her voice breaking from the pressure of the insane situation they had found themselves in.

'What do you mean? We just… run around in this place forever?'

Lauren massaged her temples with her finger and thumb. She looked as though she wanted to scream. 'I don't fucking know, Aiden. I just… we need to get out of here. Somehow. I don't know how, so we just move and pray. Right?'

Aiden opened his mouth to speak but quickly realised he no better suggestion. He just nodded. The eerie silence of the dark emptiness was broken by the sound of something small and hard, like a dropped stone clattering behind him. He and Lauren snapped their heads in the direction of the sound.

'What was that?' Aiden asked before Lauren cut him off by pressing her fingers to his lips.

'Shhhh. Don't make any noise. We need to move. Now,' she whispered almost too quietly to be heard.

He slowly turned with her, creeping between the grisly stalagmites and away from the fallen stone. Aiden didn't know what to expect. What might be out there. He desperately wanted to ask Lauren more, to see if she knew anything else. But the fear of being followed, being hunted, kept him mute. He and Lauren slowly moved forward, barely making a sound in the dark emptiness. Aiden wondered if this was to be his eternal afterlife. No singing angels, harps and clouds. No reunion with long lost loved ones or an eternity of bliss with his family. Not even a fiery, furnace of hellish fiends and torture. Just creeping in the eerie, bloody darkness of a cold cave without end. They continued on in silence for what felt like hours, but Aiden truly had no idea if it were minutes or days. The darkness was utterly disorientating and seemed to twist any sense of time.

'Lauren? How long do you think you've been here?' he risked asking in the smallest whisper.

Lauren didn't scold him, nor did she stop carefully manoeuvring her way forward. 'I honestly couldn't say,' she replied without turning back to him. 'I can remember my normal life as if it were yesterday. But this place just seems to be everything to me now.'

Aiden listened to her mournful words as he absently looked forward. Suddenly, he froze in place.

'Lauren, stop,' he hissed as he stared just past her. Lauren stood just before a particularly tall and thin stalagmite to her left. Aiden followed the length of it high above them. Something about it just looked off. While the others were jagged, sharpened bone and coated gore, this one looked sleek. Shiny without being wet. Jet black.

'What is it?' Lauren asked in a panicked whisper.

Before Aiden could respond, the stalagmite he stared at jolted. It dropped down swiftly but there was no crash. Instead of falling to the ground, the stalagmite bent and twisted downward, the sharp tip dropping on Lauren. Aiden watched on as the stalagmite drove several inches deep into her shoulder. She screamed in pain as blood began to run down her arm and she struggled to tug the black shaft out of her flesh. Aiden quickly moved up behind her and grabbed the stalagmite too. It felt curiously hard, like it was coated in some sort of plate. Lauren's screams turned into pitiful gasps of fear as something large shifted in front of them. Aiden froze, watching as the giant form scuttled forward. Another of the long legs they thought to have been the stalagmites dropped down just before them. Eight globes shined from the dark and Aiden realised the thing was a giant spider. She stepped elegantly forward despite her size, her giant legs barely making a sound as they delicately balanced on the rocks. A huge, black abdomen hurled into view and Lauren's terrified whimpers suddenly fell silent when large, stinging fangs broke through her collar bone. Aiden grabbed onto Laruen, trying to pull her free before the giant widow spider dashed backwards, dropping down into some descending ravine beyond Aiden's view. He tried in vain to keep Lauren on the surface with him before he fell with her, down into the spider's lair. He smacked through the spider's strong legs as it focused its attention on Lauren. He could barely hear his own scream as he fell past the behemoth and became lost in rushing wind. Aiden couldn't see the ground and had no idea when he might expect to the feel the sudden crash and agony as his body broke on the bones below. He grunted with pain as a thick, sticky substance caught him. He tangled in it, feeling himself wound up in ropes of adhesive material and thought of himself as a fly caught in a web. The spider's web broke away and clung to him but he continued to fall, albeit a little slower. Suddenly, Aiden's body collided with a hard surface and the wind was knocked out of him. He rolled along the descending rock and tumbled down further until he finally fell with a hard knock onto solid ground once more.

Aiden lay there, struggling to breathe, his body aching all over. He knew the giant spider was somewhere above him. Somewhere, doing horrendous things to Lauren. Was it eating her? Torturing her? Binding her up to drink her insides out later? Aiden knew he needed to get up. He needed to get away. He yelped in pain as he tried to shift his weight and his right leg felt as though it were on fire. His calf felt warm and for some reason, he thought about what limited medical knowledge he had. Didn't warmth indicate a broken bone? He shook his aching head. Injured or not, he had to get away.

He pulled himself across the ground, finally finding a solid surface to sit back on. Gasping in pain and fear, he finally opened his eyes. He couldn't believe it. Before him, he recognised the long, relatively clean wooden surface of the workbench in his shed. He could see the neatly stacked box sets of nails, screws and bolts in the corner. His tools, all in good condition as he rarely used them, were set on their hooks along the corrugated metal wall. Judging by the glow of the fluorescent light and the darkness of the small sheet window in the far corner of the shed, it was night-time. Aiden let out a gasp of relief. He was home. He had no idea what he was doing in the shed, but he was safe at home. But then, he realised he could still smell the foul smell of the blood. And he felt cold, the same cold he felt in the hellscape. He could feel the jagged, bony rocks pressing into his back. He tried to speak, tried to move, tried to turn away from the workbench and head for the shed door. But he remained still, staring at the wood surface. A strangely familiar pain began to swell within him.

'Welcome home,' Gary's voice hissed in his ear.

RUNNING HOME

REBECCA

'Hannah! Oh, thank God you're alright,' Bec cried as she tightly held her daughter in her arms. Hot tears ran down her cheeks before they dropped into her daughter's hair. Hannah had been stoic, silent and appeared as though she might have been sleepwalking when she approached the car. It wasn't until Bec had gotten out, run up to the school gates and taken her daughter into her arms that Hannah began to cry.

'Mum... Mum, what's wrong with me?' she sobbed pathetically as she tightly held onto her mother.

Bec absently stroked Hannah's hair, as she had always done to comfort the girl. From a grazed knee, for comfort when she was unwell, to the death of their first dog, Bec always stroked Hannah's hair in the same way. She felt it soothed them both through whatever difficult times they were going through.

'It's not you, honey. I don't know what it is, but I'm here now.'

Hannah wiped her eyes and looked up to her mum. 'You've seen things too?'

Bec's chest was heavy with worry and despair when she saw the fear in her daughter's eyes. She nodded slowly. 'Yes. Something bad is happening to us. We need to get your dad and, I don't know, go somewhere. Work out what to do next,' she said, thinking on her feet as she turned to the car, her arm still tightly held around Hannah's shoulders.

'Hannah! Mrs Woods, is Hannah alright?' a voice called out and, with her frayed nerves, Bec jumped at the sudden call. She turned back to see Brian running towards them from the school.

'Oh God. Mum, please, I can't talk to him right now,' Hannah said, her cheeks turning bright red as she nervously looked to her feet.

Bec knew something had happened, that her daughter was embarrassed. She only hoped it wasn't anything too serious. She could see Brian looked genuinely concerned for her daughter and, truthfully, she felt a little sorry for the boy.

'Hi, Brian. Don't worry, Hannah will be okay. She just isn't feeling very well,' she said when it was evident Hannah couldn't speak, even if she wanted to. The way she continued to cling to Bec's side reminded her of when she was a little girl, not the independent teenager she now was. Something had frightened her. Badly.

'Hannah. I'm sorry. I didn't mean to, I mean, it's okay,' Brian said, evidently at a loss for words.

Bec was curious if he knew what he had done wrong, if anything at all.

Hannah glanced at him with a faint smile. 'I'm okay, Brian. I just need to go home. To get some sleep,' she said meekly.

Brian might not have understood what was going on, but Bec could see how much he wanted to make sure Hannah was alright.

'Okay, um, I'll text you later maybe?' Brian said with uncertainty.

Hannah nodded slightly.

'That sounds nice. Don't worry. I'll take her home and help her to get some rest. She's just had… a bad episode. She'll be alright,' Bec said, taking the parental lead of the conversation.

She honestly didn't know what she and Hannah might do. Maybe all they really did need was to get some rest? But as Bec remembered the creature that had been Mr Meadows crashing into the screen door of the clinic, her heart pounded painfully in her chest. Whatever had attacked her had evidently sought to hurt Hannah too. A pang of guilt burned like acid inside her as she remembered Aiden and the fear that he also might be in danger grew.

'Alright, honey, let's get you to bed. Thank you for taking care of her, Brian,' she said as she led Hannah back to the car.

'I just, well, I'll see you soon, okay, Hannah?' Brian said, his voice broken with worry.

Bec opened the passenger door to the car and Hannah slipped into her seat.

'Thanks, Brian,' the girl said, finally meeting his eyes for the first time since he had arrived.

Despite the fear that welled insider her, Bec felt a warmth of comfort seeing the adoration in her daughter's weary eyes. Bec took her place behind the wheel, started the car and within moments they were driving out of the school car park. She could see Brian watching after them in the rear-view mirror. She took a few deep breaths to control her nerves. She glanced to Hannah with a forced smile.

'He has always been a sweet boy.' Her voice was strained as she attempted to distract her daughter with a topic of normality. If Bec was honest, she was hoping to distract herself just as much.

'Yeah,' Hannah said, her low voice barely discernible over the rumble of the car's tires over the road. The girl was curled awkwardly in the little space of the car's front passenger seat and she stared absently out of the window to the darkness of the evening. 'Mum. I'm scared,' she said after a long moment's silence in which Bec had merely been trying to gather her thoughts. She would have attempted to formulate some sort of plan but her brain was busy trying to merely decipher what the hell had been going on. The tremble of her daughter's voice broke her heart.

'I am too, honey,' she said, half concentrating on the road as her knuckles grew white over the steering wheel. She could hear Hannah shuffling in her seat and glanced over to see her daughter looking at her with wide, confused eyes.

'You said you've… seen things too?' Hannah asked in a hushed voice.

The image of the sick girl from the bathroom scuttled across Bec's mind, followed closely by the impossibly wide, upturned maw of Mr Meadows. She wanted to scream, to let out the fear and confusion in a momentary burst of adrenaline. But Bec quickly blinked back the hot tears that were welling in her eyes. She knew she needed to be strong. For her daughter. 'Yes. I've seen things,' she said simply with a small gasp, her lungs releasing a tight ball of tension that had been wedged deep in her chest as she admitted the insanity out loud to someone else.

'You saw Mr Novak?' Hannah asked after she had taken a moment to contemplate the situation.

No doubt she thought that she, herself, had been going insane. To know that someone else, even if it were just her mother, was experiencing the same thing just threw that theory out of the window. Bec knew how Hannah felt. She had lost count of the number of times she had questioned her own sanity in the past hour. But something deep inside kept telling her that she wasn't crazy. That what she had seen was somehow real, even though it wasn't. That same voice also convinced Bec that her daughter was experiencing the same thing. She hadn't needed to ask Hannah if she was suffering the same torments as herself. She just knew.

'Mr Novak? Your science teacher? No, I haven't seen anything to do with him. Not him, at least.' She might have had a strange intuition that her daughter was seeing things too, but the specifics were all but a mystery to her. 'What did you see with Mr Novak?' she pressed on, her curiosity and concern for her daughter reaching their limits.

Hannah sat quietly, playing with her fingers for some time like a younger girl might. 'Just… bad things,' she said finally. 'It wasn't just that though. Afterwards I… I remembered other things. Things from days ago, I dunno, weeks maybe? I mean, do you remember my laptop?' she added, evidently vocalising her own thought process.

As they drove past a speed sign marked sixty, Bec suddenly focused on the accelerator. She hadn't realised until now she was driving at least twenty kilometres over the limit.

'The laptop? I, yes, I remember it. Well, I do now. I can't really say, it was sort of blocked out of my head, you know what I mean? Later when I realised you had been sleeping in our room that night, I just thought you had a bad dream. It sounds silly but, I don't know, until today that thought just seemed so normal to me.' After the attack by Mr Meadows, it felt as though a thick fog had been lifted from her brain and she could finally remember things clearly for the first time in she didn't know how long. She took her eyes off the road for long enough to look to her daughter again. Hannah wore a shocked expression on her pale face. Their eyes met and Bec could see the glistening tears in her daughter's eyes.

'I know exactly what you mean. I mean, it doesn't make any sense. But it makes sense. I, I don't know what's going on, Mum.'

'Neither do I, honey. But I do know we need to get home. Get home and get out. We need to get –'

'Dad,' Hannah finished Bec's sentence for her. The mere mention of his familial title seemed to push Hannah into a panic.

'Dad! Mum, what about Dad? I, I haven't thought about him at all! Is this happening to dad too?' she cried feverishly.

'Hannah, it will be okay. Just try and breathe. I... I think all of this has something to do with your dad. I don't know, it's just a feeling. But, somehow, I think it has to do with his paralysis.' Bec would like to have said she had been putting the pieces together herself, joining the dots to make the picture from her own ingenuity. But she knew she hadn't come to suspect Aiden's paralysis was the source of their suffering herself. She just had a feeling that everything was somehow connected. And how could she forget how Aiden had, albeit manically, tried to explain things to her only a day before his suicide attempt.

'Dad's sleeping problem?' Hannah asked doubtfully before the apparent intuition of a connection seemed to dawn on her.

'Your dad said that he thought he was being haunted,' Bec said slowly, acknowledging the insanity of the claim but somehow feeling it was true.

'Haunted? By what? Mum, what are going to do? Can we, I dunno, call the police? Call someone? Anyone?' Hannah asked, her voice beginning to squeak with fear again.

'I don't know. I don't know who can help us. Let's just… take it a step at a time. We get home. Get your dad. Go… go to your grandma and grandpa's place. We'll work out what to do there. Okay?' Bec said. She felt what little confidence she had growing with the comfort of a plan to follow.

*

As she pulled the car into the driveway, Bec saw that the windows of their house were dark. She parked beside Aiden's car in the car port and switched off the engine, eyeing the house nervously.

'Maybe Dad's just sleeping again? You know, like he's been doing all the time,' Hannah spoke up with a slight quiver in her voice.

'Yeah, maybe.'

She knew that Hannah was trying to reassure herself as much as her mum as she attempted to rationally explain why the house was completely still and lifeless. She hoped that her daughter might be right, but something inside told her that likely wasn't the case.

'Alright. Do you want to wait in the car? I'll get your dad and a few things and be right out.' Bec wasn't sure what to expect in the house and above all else, she wanted to keep her daughter safe.

Hannah's face grew pale and she quickly shook her head in response to her mother's suggestion. 'No, no. I want to come in. I want to stay with you.'

Bec could see the apprehension in Hannah's face. She clearly didn't want to be left alone and, as she thought on it for a moment, Bec knew sticking together would probably be a better idea.

Come on, there's nothing to worry about now. Hannah's right, Aiden's just dozed off again. We'll go in, wake him, go to mum's place. Easy, she thought as she played with her keys in her hand.

'Okay. Let's go. We'll only need a change of clothes really. A few basics. We won't stay away for long.' Her voice sounded more confident than she felt.

She felt that trying to maintain a sense of normality was key in breaking the tension of the prospect of going inside. It was such a little thing. So normal. Going inside your own home. They did every day with barely a thought. If anything, Bec felt that everyone rather enjoyed finally closing the door to the world to relax in the comfort of their own home after a long day. This evening wasn't really any different, was it? They were just going to visit her parents for the night, that was all. Perfectly normal. Bec had gotten Hannah to message her mum during the drive home, just to say they fancied a visit and would it be a problem if they ended up staying the night. As such, they were expected guests now.

Bec tried to think about the lovely dinner her mum would surely be expanding for three extra mouths. She was a wonderful cook and was always happy to feed family. The thought of sitting around the old family table brought a warm comfort to her heart. To enjoy a delicious homecooked meal while they talked and joked about, just like normal. It wasn't until Hannah closed her car door, the loud bang echoing under the sheet metal roof of the car port, that Bec realised she was now standing outside in the cold, twilight air. She shook the fuzziness away from her head and gave Hannah a quick, encouraging smile as the teen stepped up closer to her than she might normally have done.

'Alright, let's get moving. Your grandparents will be expecting us soon,' Bec said as she walked up the path to the front door with Hannah mere inches behind her. She cringed as she realised how she sounded. She was speaking to her fifteen-year-old daughter as though she were still a little girl. Hannah hadn't objected though. The automatic sensor for the outdoor light was still broken and Bec clicked her tongue as she fiddled with her keys in the dark before she finally unlocked the door.

'Honey, we're home!' she called out of a sheer force of habit when she opened the door.

Where the house would usually be a light, warm, welcoming sight after a long day at work, tonight it was dark and there was a particularly grim chill in the air. It seemed more like the entrance to some vast underground cave system than their house. Bec could almost see the shapes of the stalagmites and stalactites in the shadowy living room. She flicked on the light and was actually surprised to see their normal, comfortable furnishings and decorations. Nothing looked out of place in the living room and the framed pictures along the wall, the worn but extra comfortable couch, even the small red light of the TV on stand-by helped to calm her frayed nerves.

'See? Nothing to worry about. Your dad's just catching up on his sleep. I'll go get him. Do you want to quickly pack a bag for grandma's place?' she said while she and Hannah entered the house. Rather than hang them on the hook by the front door, Bec slipped her car keys into her jacket pocket. With any luck, they would be back on the road in ten minutes anyway.

Hannah tentatively stepped forward and Bec noticed how her daughter still seemed apprehensive to step ahead of her mother. She took the lead and paced with apparent casualness through the living room to the small intersection in the middle of the house. From this point, one could veer left to the kitchen and dining room or take a hard right to follow the hallway to the bedrooms. Bec switched on the next light, illuminating the hall which, as she hoped, was empty.

'Right. I'll go get your dad up,' she narrated as they walked up the hallway.

'Okay. I'll be quick. Just keen to get to grandma's,' Hannah said, her voice louder than one might hear in normal conversation, as though higher volume would somehow bolster her confidence.

'Don't worry, we'll be off in a minute.'

Bec heard Hannah open her bedroom door before she reached her own. It was closed. That was a good sign. Their bedroom door was usually open unless someone was occupying it. She didn't knock.

She opened the door, switched on the light, and stood frozen in the doorway. The bedroom was empty.

'Shit,' she muttered under her breath. She had been hoping to see the lump of Aiden sleeping under the covers of the bed. She needed him to be there, safely tucked in bed. But he wasn't. The small light of hope in Bec's heart flickered out in an instant.

She stepped slowly into the bedroom. Everything looked normal, save that the bedside table on her side was slightly out of place as though it had been knocked. It was such a little thing, but it wasn't at all encouraging. She took a deep breath and walked across the room to the ensuite. She couldn't hear the fan humming from inside whenever the light was on in there but who knows, maybe Aiden just didn't care about peeing in the dark. Bec herself would stagger in the darkness to use the toilet in the middle of the night if she were tired enough. She opened the door and found nothing. The bathroom was just as vacant as the bedroom.

Panic grew in Bec's chest. Almost instinctively, she took her mobile out of her pocket. No messages from Aiden. She tapped his contact and held the phone up to her ear. She heard the dial tone and prayed Aiden would quickly answer. Then, she heard something else. Something faint from the bedroom. She turned and followed the sound before she was certain. With every chime of the dial tone in her ear, she could hear the buzzing of a vibrating mobile. Bec followed the sound, moving to the wardrobe in the far wall. The sliding door was partially open and the ceiling light cast shadows into the small space. She reached up and slid the door slightly further along the rail. At the front of the rack of coat hangers, she saw a pair of Aiden's black work pants. That wasn't where they would normally go and Bec didn't doubt they must have been the pair Aiden wore to work that day.

She stretched out her hand and set her fingers over the pants. She sighed, her suspicions confirmed when she felt the vibrating phone through the fabric. Hanging up her own phone, she fished her husband's one from his pants. Flicking over the touch screen, Bec found her own missed call and the text messages she had sent him over an hour ago.

After her experience at the clinic, she messaged Aiden right away to tell him she was getting Hannah and getting the hell home. She was hit by pang of shame that she had been so worried about Hannah that she hadn't realised he had never replied. Behind the pants, Bec noticed Aiden's work shirt neatly hanging on the next coat hanger.

He probably just got changed when he got home.

'And left his phone behind? Right,' she said aloud. There was no way her husband would do such a thing. Like most people these days, his mobile was basically an extension of his own body.

Something shifted in the deeper darkness of the wardrobe. Bec's blood ran cold as she heard the shuffling. She almost couldn't breathe as she instinctively took a step back. Glancing down, she saw the bulk of some form hidden partially under the hanging clothes. Bec fought the urge to turn and run. She thought about the sick girl who scuttled out of the bathroom. Was she back to torment her again? She let out a soft, pathetic gasp when she saw two small shining globes look at her from the wardrobe. What little light from the bedroom made it into that far corner of the wardrobe glistened off the eyes that stared at her. The eyes moved as the shape shifted forward.

Bec quickly reached up to grab the sliding door of the wardrobe and slam it shut before she ran out of the bedroom. But the thing was faster. In an instant, a dark form leapt from the wardrobe and pushed hard into her waist. Her scream was stifled as the wind was knocked out of her when she fell back, her butt bumping into the mattress behind her. She had lifted her arms up to defend herself in whatever way she could from the attacker. A heavy weight pressed against her, soft fur, a wet tongue. Leena whined and panted as she frantically tried to lick at Bec's face behind her arms. Relief flooded through her.

'God, Leena! What were you doing in there, you stupid dog? Hey, what's been going on?' she said as she took the Labrador's big head in her hands and massaged her fur. Leena dropped down, her tail wagging as she stared up to her and continued to lick at her hand.

'Come on. Let's get out of here,' Bec said as the chill of finding the (practically) empty bedroom came over her again. She quickly stepped out of the room and went to Hannah's with Leena right behind her. Hannah was just zipping up her backpack on the bed, no doubt having stuffed it with clothes, chargers and whatever else she might have needed. When Leena saw her, she dashed into the room and almost knocked Hannah over just as she had Bec.

'Leena! I'm sorry, I forgot all about you, girl! You're coming with us too, you know? Right, Mum? Is Dad up?'

The excitement of her dog's greeting, while initially shocking her, seemed to have lifted Hannah's spirits. Bec set a hand on the door frame and lightly shook her head. Hannah's brief smile immediately fell.

'He wasn't in bed. Why don't you get Leena in the car, hey?' Bec pulled out the keys and held them towards her daughter.

'Okaaay… what about Dad?' Hannah asked slowly as she took the keys.

'I'll find him. Don't worry. Just wait in the car a minute, alright?' The smile she wore on her face felt completely foreign to her. She didn't doubt that her attempts at implying everything was under control were pointless, that Hannah could see right through her. But Bec couldn't help it. Isn't that what parents do all their lives? Do their best to give their children the impression everything is fine, that they have all the answers and everything can be managed by Mum and Dad when in truth, they have no idea what they're doing half the time? Thankfully, despite the fragility of her act, Hannah seemed inclined to play along. Maybe she found the feigned sense of control as comforting as Bec did.

'Okay.' Hannah nodded before she turned and slipped her backpack over her shoulder. 'Come on, Leena.' She tapped her thigh to beckon the dog to follow.

Together, the three of them walked back down the hallway, but where Hannah and Leena now turned to the front door, Bec continued towards the kitchen. Her heart was heavy as she knew the chances were slim, but maybe she might find Aiden in the kitchen, the dining room or maybe even in the shed out the back. She heard Hannah opening the front door as she switched on the light. As expected, the kitchen was empty and the dining room was too, from what she could see. Bec slowly walked forward to look around the benchtop that separated the kitchen from the dining room. Guilt continued to torture her stressed mind as the idea of finding Aiden lying on the floor in the dining room crossed her mind. Maybe it might just be like last time. That he attempted suicide and she would call an ambulance to save him again. Bec found the idea more reassuring than any alternative. But, as she stepped around the bench, she found nobody. Then, something moved. With Leena accounted for, it could only be Aiden. Or something else entirely.

Bec's eyes were quickly drawn to the motion and she realised it was the long venetian blinds along the window and screen door at the back of the dining room. She imagined something jumping out at her from the blinds, this time to harm her rather than greet her as Leena did. But nothing came. The blinds waved slightly and as the chilly draught crossed her face, Bec realised the back door was wide open. The night-time breeze was wafting inside and swaying the blinds back and forth.

So, Aiden's gone outside after all? She stepped forward. As the blinds danced delicately in the breeze, she saw the distinct jagged lines of cracks in the glass of the door. Then, she glanced down again. The tiles by the open screen door were blotched with stains of red. Bec gasped as she saw the imprint of a bare foot leading outside, the shape of the foot formed out of dry blood.

'Fucking hell. God, Aiden, where are you?' she mumbled to herself. The smears of blood on the floor shook her to the core and she couldn't take anymore. She took out her phone again. It was time to call the police.

STAY AWAY

HANNAH

'Shhhh, it's okay, pup,' Hannah said as she petted the whining dog in the back car seat beside her. Leena was sitting as still as a statue, the dark hackles on her back standing upright. She was staring intently at the house, her brown eyes barely even blinking.

'It's okay. Another minute and Mum and Dad will come out, get in the car, and take us all to Grandma's.' She knew Leena couldn't understand her, but she needed to hear the reassurance out loud for her own sake. Her parents were going to come out any minute, weren't they? At least her mum would. The time dragged on and Hannah kept glancing at the bright light of her phone. One minute turned to two. Then four. Then six.

'Come on, Mum,' she said through clenched teeth. A cold grip of fear took a merciless hold of her when she noticed the whole car was moving, seeming to shudder as though the engine were on. She snapped her head back, almost expecting to see some new evil-looking thing sitting in the boot behind her. But there was nothing there. The car kept shuddering and as Hannah looked back around, she realised she had been doing it herself. Her right leg was twitching up and down without her knowing.

'God, just calm down. It's fine,' she breathed quietly as she gripped her knee to stop the nervous twitch. Another minute passed and Hannah let out a long, exasperated sigh. 'Where are they?'

Leena's tongue swept nervously over her wet nose in response and she kept her eyes on the house. She watched the front door, willing it to open but it stayed shut. Finally, she couldn't take it anymore.

'Okay, stay here, Leena. I'll be right back. With Mum.' She opened the door and slipped out of the car.

Leena shifted nervously on her front paws and tried to lick her hand. Hannah got the impression the dog was trying to convince her to stay in the car. But she couldn't just sit around waiting all night. What if something had happened? What if her mum needed her help? More to the point, she just wanted to get out of there and she needed her mum too. Hannah was worried about her dad, but if they didn't find him now, surely, they would find him a little later. She burned with guilt to think it, but she just wanted to be safe at her grandma's place.

Hannah made sure the car keys were in her pocket before she shut the door. The last thing they needed was to be locked out of the car when they tried to leave. She wandered slowly up the path to the front door, trying her best to just breathe and mentally assure herself that everything was fine. She opened the front door and stepped back into the house. The house she normally felt was like a fortress that could protect her and her family from anything the weird world might throw at them. Now, it felt like a dungeon. An old, creepy dungeon where ghosts were just waiting in the darkness to grab you. She quickly shook her head of the mental image of scary hands reaching from the shadows as she closed the door against the cold.

'Mum? Where are you?'

There was no reply and that just sent a shiver of dread down Hannah's spine. Her dad had already gone missing. She didn't know what to do if her mum had disappeared on her too.

'Mum? Come on, let's just go!' she called again as she slowly walked deeper into the house.

All of the lights her mum had switched on earlier were still on but the ability to see didn't really give Hannah any encouragement. She had never seemed to notice how the lights cast so many shadows in the corners of the rooms. The way the furniture, the appliances, held the light back to give whatever might enjoy the darkness some places of refuge. Inanimate things like dust the dirty build up that could go years being missed by the vacuum. Webs with spiders and the dried-up corpses of their prey. Something more sinister that Hannah couldn't even comprehend. She shuddered as she quickly paced through the living room, trying to stay within as much light as she could. Coming to the central intersection of the house, Hannah quickly looked up the hallway.

It was still empty. Her mum said her dad wasn't in bed. She must have checked the bathrooms and the laundry too, right? Yeah, there was no way she would miss them and what would her dad have been doing sitting around in the bathroom or the laundry in the dark? She nodded to herself as she rationalised there was no need to head down the hall. Something about the long corridor made her feel uneasy. Instead, Hannah turned and stepped into the kitchen. Her mum had obviously been this way as the lights were on here too.

'Mum?' She felt her voice falter as she tentatively moved forward. *Where is she?* Panic grew as she felt more and more alone. Hannah moved around the bench and into the dining room. She hesitated when she noticed the screen door was open and the darkness of the night loomed through the opening. Hannah was almost certain there was something there, something that hid in the shadows and watched her. Did her mum really go out there?

She took a step forward before her eyes fell to the ground and she paused. She saw splatters of blood on the tiles, the red stains tainting the hard, cream surface. Her breath failed her when she saw a footprint of blood leading to the backdoor. Whose was that? Her dad's? Her mum's? She needed to find out. She stepped forward again, her heart pounding painfully in her chest. Air was constantly catching in her tight throat, making it difficult to breathe. She could barely see anything beyond the grass of the yard that was illuminated by the lights in the house, but she could just see the shape of the shed. Was the light tricking her or was the door open? The cold breeze bit at her dry lips as she stood in the open doorway. She needed to go out there. To see what was going on. To see if she could find her parents. But something stopped her from taking that first step outside.

'Mum?' Hannah called out to the darkness. She stood there in silence, waiting with her ears perked. Did someone reply? She didn't know if she had really heard a voice echo from the night or if her mind was just playing tricks on her. At least she hoped it was just her mind.

Come on. Mum and Dad need you. Do it. Just go out and take a look, she thought, preparing herself to finally take that step outside. Then, the memories flashed across her mind again. She almost felt that cold hand gripping her shoulder like a vice. She saw the vacant, staring eyes of Mr Novak as he approached her, his chest carved open by his own hand. What horror might she find if she went out there? If she went to that small shed, what could be waiting inside? She couldn't do it.

Her legs felt like jelly and she just couldn't get them to move. It was as though her black school shoes were made of lead rather than leather. She looked away from the backyard, over her shoulder and to the intersection beyond the kitchen.

'Maybe I should just check out the other rooms... just to be safe,' she said aloud, as though her voice might give her confidence to move again. *You are such a coward,* the voice in her head chastised her. But Hannah pushed her self-criticism out of her mind.

She reached up and tugged the sliding door to the backyard shut. As the night was sealed away behind the glass, a feeling of relief washed over her. Hannah paused for a moment, her hand still gripping the handle of the door and her thumb was poised over the lock. *Should I lock it? I mean, no one will get in that way. But what if mum or dad really are out there?*

She hesitated as she debated what to do in her head. Finally, she let her hand drop slowly from the handle, the lock still open. Maybe it was the simple glass barrier against the night, or her hope that her parents would come back into the house, but she felt locking the door would be the wrong thing to do, even if she couldn't explain it. Her legs finally responded to her brain once more as she slowly backed away from the door. She felt the courage to turn her back on the backdoor. It was a good thing too, as she almost reversed straight into the opposite wall of the dining room.

'Right. Get a grip. They'll be here. Everything's okay,' she mumbled under her breath as she walked deeper into the house again. She was thankful the hallway was still illuminated as she slowly wandered along it. She stopped at the laundry, which was found next to the kitchen, and tentatively opened the door. Hannah poked her head in, opening the door wide to let the light from the hall flood into the little room. The washing machine, check. Dryer, check. Sink and laundry basket, ironing board against the wall, closet closed, check, check, check. She quickly closed the door before any shadows in the laundry might move for her. She exhaled her relief that everything seemed fine. She wasn't surprised. Why would anyone have been in the laundry?

Hannah moved along the hall to the next room, the bathroom. Sure, it was the main bathroom of the house but unless they had company, it was really her bathroom. Her parents just used the ensuite adjoining their bedroom all the time so there really wouldn't have been any need for them to be in there. Yet, somehow, Hannah felt more nervous about checking this room than the laundry. It didn't make any sense. She was more familiar with her own bathroom than the laundry which she only entered once or twice a week, and as her parents never used it, why should they be in there? Her head was spinning as she slowly took the doorknob in her hand. Maybe that's why she was so nervous. This was one of her rooms. A place where she might normally feel safest. For some reason, that seemed to make it all the more intimidating now. As though whatever was going on, whether they were indeed being haunted or if it were all just in Hannah's head, would somehow be more likely to strike somewhere she would normally feel comfortable. She held her breath, turned the knob and thrust the door open. She didn't know what to expect. Her dad lying in a pool of blood, her mum crying over him. The two of them fighting. Neither of her parents at all but some huge, grotesque monster that was intent on eating her as soon as she opened the door.

But Hannah stared into the bathroom and saw nothing amiss. Everything in the tiled room was as it always was. The bath and shower were empty, the curtain pulled as far open as it could be. The bottles of body wash, shampoo and conditioner were all in place on their shelf and the mirror and sink were as they always should be. She closed the door again. This time, while she still felt relieved, she was more troubled. Unless her mum had gone back to one of their bedrooms or was out in the shed, she had disappeared as well. Hannah was still petrified by the mere notion of going out to the backyard and she headed further along the hallway. Her bedroom door was still open and the light still on. She peered inside to find it just as she had left it not too long ago.

'That's it. One room left,' she said in a hushed voice. By the process of elimination, if her parents were in the house, they must have been in there. Her skin became numb as she stepped closer to the master bedroom. The door was shut. *Oh shit, did Mum shut that? Didn't she leave it open? I can't remember.*

Hannah stood in the middle of the hallway, clenching her fists over and over again as she took some deep breaths. It was horrible to admit to herself, but a part of her hoped she wouldn't find her parents in there. She reached for the doorknob. Just then, Hannah heard the heavy sliding sound of the backdoor opening. She instantly turned around to look back down the hallway. She wanted to call out, to see if it was one of her parents but her voice caught in her throat. She heard fast, unsteady footsteps. Panting. Whimpering. A woman.

'Mum!' Hannah finally screamed as she started to run down the hallway. A shadow crossed over the wall ahead and she prayed she hadn't started running headlong into some new evil thing. She stopped in her tracks when her mum leapt into the entryway from the dining room. She was panting for breath as though she had just finished a hundred-yard dash. Her flushed cheeks were shiny with tears and…

was that blood on her face? Hannah noticed her mum's fingers and palms were also red with blood.

'Mum?' she started before her mother began to run towards her, her face filled with a manic expression. Hannah was frozen, she didn't know if she should help her mum or if she needed to run away from her.

'Hannah! Oh, God, no! Hannah, you were supposed to be in the car! Go, go!' her mum screamed as she quickly approached.

Her shrill voice snapped Hannah from her frightened trance and now, she just felt sheer panic as her mum caught her in her arm and began to urge her back. Hannah heard glass smashing from the direction her mum had just run. Then, heavy footfalls and… low guttural breaths.

'Hannah, please run! Run, into our room! Now!' Bec pushed her daughter back.

Just as Hannah turned, she caught something in the corner of her eye. Another shadow crossed over the wall before something quickly followed it. But she couldn't possibly have seen it. It was her dad but she barely recognised him. He was completely naked but his skin was covered in scratches and carvings. Streaks of blood ran down his bare body and his face was barely recognisable beneath the red streams and the deep gashes. Her father was charging at them on his hands and knees. Crawling after them like a rabid dog. But he shuffled along the wall.

A high-pitched sound rang through the air and as Hannah sprinted with her mother right behind her, she realised it was her own terrified scream. She did as her mother said and bolted for the farthest room in the house, the master bedroom. She almost slammed into the wall of the hallway when she approached the room and stumbled, her glasses falling to the carpet. Hannah didn't stop to get them. She thrust herself into the bedroom with her mother right behind her. Her eyes were filled with tears as she turned to see her mum slam the door shut behind her.

'HELP ME!' Bec screamed in sheer terror of her own as she dashed to the bed and began to frantically tug the heavy queen-sized mattress from the base. Hannah didn't have time to think. She almost fell over as she bent to grab at one of the fabric-handles of the mattress and groaned with the exertion while she pulled the heavy load across the carpet. Her mother grunted with exertion as she pulled the mattress with all her might, trying to pitch it across the floor to block the door. A loud bang suddenly burst from the door and, despite losing her glasses, Hannah could see how the wood strained against the frame. She heard the most hideous, guttural scream from the other side of the door. It sounded as though her dad was gargling something as he roared with anger.

'PUSH IT! Just a little more!' Bec cried out.

Hannah pushed as hard as she could. The mattress caught on the carpet and dropped heavily to the floor. 'No!' she squealed.

The door banged again. Bec bent down and tried to tug the mattress once more before the doorframe splintered open from the repeated force against it. The door had only opened several inches as it caught on the fallen mattress and Bec dropped back and scrambled over to Hannah, quickly taking her tightly in her arms. Hannah immediately closed her arms around her mum, unable to think to do anything else. She shrieked as a blood covered hand and forearm reached in through the opening of the door and slammed against the wall. It was her dad's left hand and Hannah saw that his ring finger, along with his wedding ring, was gone. There was nothing more than a bloody stump. That horrible, gurgling breathing came again and the door slowly slid further, pushing the mattress along the carpet.

'NO! Keep away! Stay the fuck away from us, Aiden! PLEASE!' Bec screamed as she kicked at the mattress, trying to push it back along the floor.

The door pushed back a little and the heavy grunts of exertion became a vile scream as the arm became trapped in the door frame. The wooden door strained from the opposing forces before something smashed into it again. Hannah buried her face into her mum's shoulder when she saw something shiny emerge from the wood. Shiny and sharp. She heaved her panicked breath, her own tears and snot running down her face. Hannah wanted to be sick, her throat was closing tightly making it difficult to breathe. She couldn't even feel her body but she wouldn't have been surprised to learn if she had wet herself.

'MUM! Mum! What... what's he... what's he doing?!' she finally managed to cry out, her voice broken and shrill. She felt her mum's arm tighten around her.

'The window, Hannah, go for the window. Get out!'

Hannah felt her mum let her go and she clung back to her all the tighter. She couldn't leave her.

'Hannah, GO!' Bec screamed, actually pushing her away.

Hannah opened her eyes and struggled to her shaking feet. Even if she had her glasses, she wouldn't be able to see past the thick sheet of tears that coated her eyes. She turned to the head of the bed and slowly stumbled towards the window on her mum's side. As she stepped over her mum who sat with her back against the base of the bed, the door pushed forward again. Bec roared out as she used all her strength to try and kick the mattress back and Hannah's unsteady foot caught on her mother's leg. She fell awkwardly to the floor and Bec was pulled aside, if only a little. But it was too much. Having lost her momentum against the mattress, the door shoved forward and opened wider. Hannah pushed herself up to her knees, unable to speak of even to scream as she saw the blurry sight approach her. Her dad was crawling over to her, pulling himself on his forearms, his eyes burning with maddened rage as he stared at her. Blood and drool ran down his chin and as he exerted himself, he spit chunks of viscera into the carpet. In his right hand, Hannah made out the shape of an axe blade. It was her dad's hatchet that he had very rarely used for gardening work out the back. Hannah backed up as her blood covered, naked father clambered over to her and raised the hatchet up.

'NO! LEAVE HER ALONE!!' Bec screamed and Hannah saw her mother kick her father's upheld arm aside. She didn't stop there, kicking him again in the side before stomping on his back. Hannah just sat there and watched in terror, unable to move as she cried and watched her mother kicking her murderous father.

Aiden jostled and rolled on the floor from Bec's assault swinging his arms wildly around so that Bec had to drop back to avoid the blade of the hatchet. He scuttled back along the floor as though standing was somehow impossible for him. But then, Aiden shoved himself up to sit on his knees. Bec rushed to him again trying to kick at his face. Hannah's mum had never practiced any kind of marital arts in her life and she kicked wildly in a blind effort to protect herself and her daughter while keeping as far back from her husband as she could. Aiden roared as he took a blow in his side but as Bec tried to hit him again, he caught her leg and threw her back.

'MUM!' Hannah screamed as she watched her mother topple back to the floor. She tried to shuffle away again but Aiden was crawling over her in an instant, a sordid mass of flesh and blood that dropped over the terrified woman in an instant. Hannah tried to move, to help her mum but she couldn't feel her legs. She watched as her mum wildly flailed and smacked at her husband trying to fend him off. A shrill scream pierced the air and Hannah realised her dad had caught her mum's hand in his teeth and was ferociously biting down into her skin. Hannah struggled to move but she forced herself forward, her legs turning to jelly the instant she put weight on them. She couldn't stand but moved sort of hunched over and collapsed on her dad, bringing down her full weight as she drove her elbow into his back. Aiden screamed in anger and pain as he turned and the back of his bloody arm smacked powerfully into her face. She cried out in pain and dropped back, clutching at her cheek, the bone under her eye throbbing intensely. As she pulled herself up and looked on, she screamed with sheer denial of what she was witnessing. Her dad lifted himself up again and now raised the hatchet high above his head, clearly intent on bringing it down onto his struggling wife. He cried a gut-wrenching scream but then, Aiden's voice sort of petered out into almost complete silence.

Hannah sobbed as she watched the scene, her father ready to kill her mother in brutal cold blood but he sat there now as still as if he were posing for a painting. Bec was trembling violently beneath him, clutching at her bloody hand where he had bitten her and she stared up at him with wide, terrified eyes. The silence and stillness were so bizarre, Hannah absurdly felt as though she should laugh. But no sound, whether crying or insane cackles could escape her trembling lips.. She sat stuck in place, her eyes fixed on her parents, her heart pounding as she held her breath and waited for the axe to fall. Aiden still didn't move. It had definitely been some seconds now that he was just frozen. Hannah looked down at her mum and their eyes met, the terror and confusion evident in both their tear-drenched faces.

BREAKING THE DREAM

AIDEN

Aiden was helpless as he watched everything transpire before him. Not only was he an unwilling passenger, but he was also a reluctant participant in the terrible events that unfolded in his home. He was exhausted and broken in this, the brief moment of respite from his sufferings. He had lost all sense of time in the dark cave of bones and blood. He could do nothing but endure the tortures of his host and look on in morbid terror at the horrific acts his body was forced to commit. He couldn't tell how long he had been trapped in this prison and as he tried to think back to when he first saw the workbench in his shed, his head ached with the resounding pain it had then.

It had been a bizarre, nauseating feeling when Aiden opened his eyes to find himself back in his shed. He could feel two things at once and even before Gary had spoken, he knew he wasn't in control. He was consciously aware that he was completely naked as he stood frozen like a statue in the shed. The bitter cold air of the early winter night cascaded around his shivering skin. There was a distinct warmth over his forehead, slowly cascading down his face as though something was slowly pouring over him and he could smell the blood. It was as though his forehead had been bludgeoned by a hammer and a painful headache throbbed between his temples. Yet, as he experienced all of this physical suffering, as he knew he was standing there, Aiden also sensed his back was perched against the jagged bones of his nightmare. There was another layer of discomfort to his chilled body, as though he was being frozen in two separate places at once. The sensations of sitting and standing conflicted with one another, and the smell of blood was exacerbated by the mingling of his injuries and the lingering stench of the nightmare cave. Aiden tried desperately in vain to move in the shed. He willed his muscles to take a step, to clench his fists, to drop in a heap on the concrete floor, even just to blink. But he stood there, motionless and staring. The frighteningly familiar sensations of sleep paralysis were growing within him. He couldn't move and couldn't make a sound. He couldn't feel himself breathing and the fire of desperation for air began to burn relentlessly in his chest. That was when he heard the voice. When that sinister, hoarse whisper echoed over and over in his ear, 'Welcome home.'

The voice had broken Aiden from his trance, and he gasped for breath as though he had just sprung up from deep underwater. He lashed out, swinging his arms violently before him and he felt a sudden pain in his leg as he struggled to move. The sight of the bench in the shed slowly darkened away but it seemed to remain visible as though Aiden were looking at it through a sheet of sketching paper.

'What…?' he managed to utter as dark, jagged stalagmites seemed to rise from the wooden bench, puncturing through it as it retreated from view and Aiden became aware of the two separate realities. He couldn't understand it, but he was standing at that bench just as he now found himself sitting in the hellish cave. He realised that, as he moved, he shifted against the bones of the cave, yet the faded sight of the shed still remained. He was consciously able to manipulate himself within the cave, but he was just viewing the shed from behind his own eyes without really being there. The experience was debilitating and Aiden leant forward to retch in the cave. He closed his eyes in an attempt to gather his frazzled thoughts but, rather than the darkness of his own eyelids, he just saw the bench a little clearer.

'Ugh, what the fuck have you done to me?' he grumbled as he tasted the bile catching in his throat and opened his eyes again to see tendrils of his drool running down to the bloody ground of the cave.

'Is that any way to talk to your host? I invited you here, with me, and this is how you speak to me?' Gary's voice echoed out from the shadows.

Aiden rocked on all fours, trying to compose himself. The pain in his head and calf seemed to be pushing each other to new limits. 'Arrrrgh, fuck! Just kill me, you fucking...' he shouted as his confusion, frustration and pain overwhelmed him. He winced when he heard that dry laugh again as though it physically pained him to hear.

'Oh no! I couldn't do that. You are... mine now.'

'Why me? Why are you doing this to me? What do you want, goddamn it?' Aiden sobbed.

He felt as though every second that passed was breaking away at his sanity and he had to tense every fibre of his being to keep himself in one piece. Gary didn't say anything, leaving Aiden to hear his own pitiful moans and gasps echo about him. He could have been sitting there, tackling the growing insanity in his mind for seconds or hours, there was no way to tell. It was as though his mind, already seemingly split into two places, was being gnawed and pulled at from every direction imaginable. But slowly, ever so slowly, the struggle began to ease. He found that he could focus on his breathing again. Then he tried to move each of his fingers in turn and he could see them slowly twitch about as he directed them. The damned workbench was still in the back of his head, the frame of it visible like a shadow against the cave, but he was less nauseated by it now. Eventually, he managed to lean back and stretch out his body to take in a deep breath of air. It was putrid and heavy with bloody odours, but to Aiden it might as well have been the freshest clean air on the top of a mountain. He was utterly exhausted but taking a gasp of air enlivened his senses once more. It had taken him several attempts, but soon Aiden was standing on two feet again. He was in a world of pain, and he could barely put any pressure on his right side, but he felt more able than he had for longer than he could comprehend.

'Feeling better?' Gary finally spoke again, his taunt immediately sapping some of the will power Aiden had struggled for so long to regain. He didn't respond. He tried to ignore the evil entity that tormented him as he slowly hobbled forward. He had no idea where he was going, or what he could do. He was dimly aware of the spider that had taken Lauren and fear prickled down his neck. For all he knew, it was right on top of him, watching and waiting. Aiden felt more like a helpless fly that gets caught in a web and he did the only thing he could. He moved, hoping in vain that he might somehow escape this hell. Or that whatever death was in store for him might come quickly. He scoffed at the thought. Gary wouldn't let it be that easy for him.

'You want to know why?' Gary spoke again as though he and Aiden had been conversing without pause. 'You want to know why you have me now? It is simply because I found you.'

Though Aiden wanted nothing else than to ignore Gary and get out of the cave, he couldn't help but listen to the thing's words. He craved any explanation he could get for what had happened to him.

'You were a shining star. A light. A beacon. And like a moth to a flame, I came to you. It is you, Aiden. You are why I am here,' Gary said.

Aiden shook his head as he gave in to the pain in his leg and leaned back against another wall of sinew and bone. 'I never wanted you!' he shouted defiantly.

'Want has nothing to do with it!' Gary roared back, the loose stones and shards trembling with his ferocity. 'You neeeed me as I need you. You and I are bound together as Gary and I were,'

'What? I can't... I can't take this shit! You're a fucking dream. An hallucination, a fucking tumour, I don't care! You can't make any sense because you're not fucking real! Leave my head alone, let me die, just stop doing this!' Aiden ranted against the darkness.

'You can't get rid of me, Aiden. You know I'm more than a dream. More than a tumour. Much, much more. More than you could ever hope to be. You think you are special. You think everything must have a personal reason. A vendetta. A curse. You never considered that you are nothing. Nothing but prey. Rich or poor. Young or old. Good or bad. Did you do something to deserve me? Am I a divine punishment? No. Your crime is simply this. You exist,' Gary said in a cruel hiss of delight.

Aiden heard the echoing voice slowly converging to a singular point as it spoke. He looked ahead, staring intently into the pitch-black veil and he could still see the faint outline of the shed's bench.

'I... I don't know,' he said uneasily. Could it really be that there was nothing he could have done to avoid Gary? Was he really just an unlucky number amongst the billions of people on the planet? Was everyone vulnerable to this sheer evil? He didn't know what to think anymore. Then, he shuddered. Something was slowly emerging from the darkness.

Aiden could practically see the fiery eyes and the shining, twisted teeth already. He was expecting their frightful appearance. But as the figure stumbled into the dim light around him, Aiden saw something he could never have imagined. It was a teenager. A young man, maybe sixteen years old. At least he might have been. The teenager was practically falling to pieces as he shuffled forward. Aiden had thought he was wearing ripped and baggy clothes but realised he was naked, just like him. His grey skin looked as though it had been peeling from his muscles and bones for a long time and it hung about him in grotesque sheets. The boy's cheeks were hollow and what skin had remained on his face clung to his skull like a wet cloth. His eyes were sunken, the globes staring out from deep within their sockets. Aiden took a nervous step back as the teenager lifted a shrivelled arm and stretched his bony fingers out to him as though in greeting.

'Surprised?' the teenager said. His jaw cracked as he spoke and his teeth were stained with crusty, black muck. The sight was disturbing enough, but Aiden was more troubled by the voice. It didn't suit any teenage boy at all but hissed and gurgled just like the voice that had been torturing Aiden for so long.

'Gary?' he asked in disbelief that he had finally met the true embodiment of his tormenter.

'In the... flesh.' Gary laughed, the boy's lips stretching into a hideous grin. 'Do you see now... why *I* need *you?*' He stepped back and stretched out his ragged, bony arms.

Aiden couldn't think straight. He didn't rightly know what he was expected to say. The teen stood still and stared at him silently with his wide, lidless eyes.

'Youuuuur fleshhhhh...' he said finally, taking a step closer.

Aiden pushed away from the bony wall and backed up further. 'Wh – what?' he asked dumbly as the teenager kept stumbling forward. Mental images flew across what was left of his mind. He imagined this undead boy jumping forward and biting into his skull and tearing his body open with his teeth.

The boy laughed again. He shook his head and his neck cracked loudly. 'No. I'm not going to eat you. I've... plenty of that.' He cackled before turning to the side and waving his twisted arm. An unsettling shuffling sound whispered out of the dark and Aiden's eyes followed Gary's outstretched arm, looking to where his thin fingers pointed.

The darkness before them slowly crept away as a dim light, much like that which surrounded him, began to shine. There was no evident source for the light, but Aiden couldn't think to question how any of this worked. By rights, everything around him shouldn't exist at all. As his eyes adjusted to the newfound light, he saw tall, thin columns of bone and sinew stretching up into the black void above them. The columns lined side by side in a row and he realised with discomfort how much they reminded him of prison bars. He was almost not surprised when he saw the figure of someone behind them, clearly another prisoner at Gary's mercy. The person behind the horrid bars didn't move and their arms were held up by their sides as though they were crucified.

'Ai... Aiden?' a pitiful voice whimpered, and his legs grew weak. He supported his weight with a hand on the wall beside him, feeling the bumps of wet vertebrae beneath his open palm.

'Lauren? But... but you...' He could see the dirty torn clothes and recognised them as those Lauren had worn when he found her in the hellscape before. Her legs and arms were covered in dark wrappings from the wall behind her. She was bound and helpless, her limbs trapped by a sickening concoction of blood vessels, muscles and organs.

'She can't hear you, Aiden. I control everything here and now that Lauren has been reclaimed, she must give me what is due,' Gary sneered. He stood completely still beside Aiden, almost as if he were merely another part of the dead, gruesome environment.

'What... what do you mean?' Aiden managed to ask as he looked helplessly to Lauren in the cage. She was staring back at him, her eyes pleading for him to help her.

'Aiden! Aiden, please! Please help me!' she screamed as she tugged at her bindings.

Aiden lost his breath when he saw something moving on the wall Lauren was trapped upon. He couldn't quite make it out, but it was roughly the size of a cat or a small dog. It crept closer and closer to Lauren though the poor woman didn't seem to notice it. She was looking at the floor before her and started to scream frantically. The surface of the ground was shimmering and shuffling, coated in swarms of insects. The collection of worms, slugs, beetles, cockroaches, scorpions, spiders, wasps and God knows what else were edging closer to Lauren. They began to run up her legs as she struggled and screamed.

'No! Gary, stop it! Please!' Aiden begged as Lauren looked back at him, the confusion and fear evident on her face.

Gary's neck cracked as he tilted his skull in Aiden's direction. 'Stop? But it's time... to feeeeeed,' he growled menacingly.

Aiden clutched at his hair, feeling dangerously close to losing his mind. He had to do something. He took his eyes off of Lauren as she screamed with the insects climbing up her legs and that dark thing creeping closer and closer without her knowing. Aiden turned to Gary and swung his arm. He had no idea what he could do, but he had to try. His fist connected with Gary's skull and the hard bone crunched against his knuckles. The decomposed teenager stumbled back, his jaw dislocating from his skull and his tongue lolled without the support. Aiden heard Gary's laughter echoing amongst Lauren's screams. He jumped forward as best he could with his sore leg and hit Gary again.

'STOP!!' he screamed in what was left of the boy's face.

Gary just continued to look at him with those horrid, unblinking eyes. He raised his hand, pointing towards Lauren and Aiden couldn't help but look at her. The dark creature had just reached her. A long, thin spider-like leg slipped into Lauren's hair. She had suddenly become aware of its presence and turned her head. Lauren's scream of pain and fear from the insects biting her became a low, hoarse groan of sheer terror. The creature was some sort of gigantic bug with long thin legs and a bulbous dark abdomen. At first, Aiden thought it might be a spider but as he saw it more clearly, he thought it looked more like a giant tick. Lauren desperately tried to pull away from the tick as it stroked her face, seemingly finding its prey. When it was apparently content, the tick skittered forward quickly, climbing over Lauren's face.

'God, please, n –' Lauren tried to protest before her voice became muffled and Aiden saw the tick lunge forward. He couldn't make out the details too well from where he was, but the giant tick had evidently latched somewhere over Lauren's face. He could only see her right eye, wide and frightened behind the disturbing, pulsing abdomen that twitched and throbbed over her. Gary let out a low hissing gurgle from his broken jaw and it sounded to Aiden disturbingly similar to a moan of pleasure.

'You… what are you doing to her? Don't. Please.'

He stumbled towards the fleshy bars of Lauren's prison. He could see the tick feasting on Lauren as the mass of insects became a shimmering, black blanket over her torso. Just as Aiden reached for the bars, the light quickly dimmed out to empty blackness and Lauren's gagged, muffled screams echoed in his ears.

'NO!'

Lauren had seemed to all but disappear from before him yet, somehow, Aiden knew she had truly been there and was suffering the grotesque tortures he witnessed. He held onto the thin stalagmites as he fell to his knees in defeat. Just as he bent forward, he heard another cry. He looked up and saw a new light further on.

'No. No, no, no. What now?' he whimpered quietly to himself as the new figure came into view. This time, there seemed to be swarms of darkness around the restrained victim and he couldn't see them too well.

The person was lying on a slab, surrounded by the black figures, seemingly enveloped by them. Aiden suspected he knew who it would be and when he caught sight of the tell-tale blonde hair, he knew this was Sam. He pushed through the despair and pain and rose to his feet. He rushed forward, trying to catch Sam's prison before she might disappear too. He couldn't sit by and let her suffer if he could help it. He could hear Sam choking and gurgling but he couldn't see her face, save for a few peaks of hair and forehead. The rest of her features were obscured by one of the black masses. The things moved all over her and Aiden caught glimpses of pale, dirty skin. Was Sam naked under them?

'Sam! Sam!'

Despite Gary telling him that the victims wouldn't be able to hear him, he couldn't help but try to call for them. Sam didn't respond but continued to choke and gag. Aiden couldn't tell how many of the things were swarmed over her. They seemed to blend in together in the shadows. Sam let out a gut-wrenching yelp and Aiden swore he could see splashes of blood flying from the slab. He reached up for the new bars just as the sight faded as Lauren's had. He collapsed on the ground and screamed in rage and defeat. He panted from the exertion of pushing through the pain in his leg and slammed his bruised hand into the ground. Gary laughed.

'She was a fun one. A party girl. Drinks. Drugs. Sex. Such a carefree young woman. Just as she wanted you to see,' he said.

Aiden didn't get up but turned back to see the broken, dead teenager ambling slowly after him again. His jaw was still hanging by the sinews of one cheek, but his voice spoke clearly.

'Behind all the confidence, she was a terrified little girl. Never wanted to be alone. Always scared someone would hurt her. Well, now she has all the company she will ever need.'

'What are you doing to them? They're dead. They're fucking dead. You already killed them!'

Gary stood over him, staring at him with his tongue twitching by his throat. 'I killed their bodies. But their dreams. Their aspirations. Their souls. They are still alive. Alive and well for me to feed upon. The fear. The misery and suffering. It feeds me like fresh blood. I let them free. Give them hope. Trap them again. Sap their essence. Repeat until even their souls are reduced to empty shells. So, thank you Aiden. Thank you for feeding them to me. Them and...' Gary paused and suddenly the cave suddenly erupted into a frenzy of anguished screams.

Aiden clapped his hands over his ears and cried out miserably. He heard so many voices, men, women, elderly, children. Fucking crying babies. Aiden curled into a ball and cried as the suffering screams washed over him. Then, as suddenly as they started, the screams fell into a piercing silence.

'I told you the hospital was... nourishing.'

Aiden wept with pity and guilt burning in his chest. All of those people, innocent people who had been in the hospital. Gary used them while he slept so peacefully. He took them. Began to torture them. To eat everything that made them who they were.

'Now... your body, Aiden. I have different plans for your body. Gary is no longer useful to me. I'm sure you can see what I mean?' Gary said and Aiden opened his eyes enough to see the teenager reach up and tug on one of his own fingertips. The bone easily snapped away from the next joint. 'When you die, your body will do nicely. But first, first I will be sure to bring your wife and daughter here. I don't want you to think me ungiving.'

Aiden's body stiffened. Rebecca. Hannah. Here in this hell? Suffering the eternal torments of their deepest fears while Gary used Aiden like a puppet?

'NO!' He shoved himself up to his feet, staggered forward and shoved into Gary. Even if he had all of his muscle mass on him, the teenager was still much smaller than Aiden. He should have fallen from the sheer weight and force of the grown man dropping on him, but it was as though the ragged, skeletal teen was welded to the cave floor. Fresh, hot pain seared in Aiden's shoulder as he collapsed in a heap. He heard that sickening chuckle again.

'Time to show you who you belong to,' Gary said before everything in the cave began to fade and the shed came clearly into view.

*

Oh God, what's going on now? Aiden thought as he stood frozen in the shed. The burning sensation of his air starved lungs had returned and no matter how he tried, he couldn't move.

'You are mine now,' Gary's voice said from somewhere deep inside Aiden's head. He could do nothing but stare ahead but then, his own arm started moving. He wasn't controlling it but he watched as his right hand reached up to the workbench and haphazardly pulled open the drawers of nails, bolts, screws and other small tools.

'Hmmm, this will do,' Gary said. Aiden watched as he pulled a box cutter knife from the drawer and slipped out the blade. He tried with all his might to let go of the knife. He didn't know what Gary was doing but he knew it wouldn't be good. He watched as he slammed his own left hand on the wooden bench and splayed out his fingers. He slowly directed the box cutter down.

Please don't. Don't do it. Just stop, please! He begged in his mind while he strained to control his own body.

Gary didn't say a word or make any sound at all. Aiden felt wholly alone as he watched himself moving. The knife hovered over his hand until it suddenly dropped down. Aiden would have screamed if he could. Unimaginable pain raged as the sharp, thin blade carved into his skin. *Oh, fucking God. Shit, make it stop! Please. PLEASE!* Hot blood poured over the bench, soaking Aiden's fingers before the blade ground against bone. Inside, Aiden was writhing in agony though he was unable to pull away from the torturous pain. He watched as he began to saw at his own finger. Gary controlled him. He twisted the knife around, shifted the blade to dig under Aiden's wedding ring, pushing it a little further along his finger with his own blood acting as the lubricant.

'You won't be needing this anymore,' Gary said before he started hacking at the finger again.

You evil, sadistic fuck! God damnit! Just stop. No, arrggghh! Aiden lost track of his own thoughts as the intense pain of that blade severing the nerves and tendons in his finger overwhelmed him. As Gary forced him to saw across his digit, the blade of the knife shuddered in its casing. Such a knife isn't designed to hack through living tissues, and it ground down the bone into a blood-infused powder more than sliced through it. Aiden lost his mental capacity and his struggle to control his body. Even in his mind, he meekly babbled like a suffering animal as he was forced to dismember his own finger. He was helpless, unable to save himself from the torture, nor was he even capable of passing out from the agony. *Oh my fucking God... how... how can you... no. Please... no more... arrghh, aah... ah hahahaha!* He actually began to internally laugh with a twisted sense of relief when he heard the now dull blade of the box cutter thump into the wood of the table.

Aiden could see his ring finger sitting lifelessly in a dark pool of blood while the rest of his hand remained flat before it. He stood still, frozen helplessly in his position for some time and his internal laughter didn't last long as the sheer pain of his pulsing, severed stub sent waves of agony to his brain. *God no. No, no, no. What the fuck? I have to stop. Have to get out of this.* He struggled desperately to regain control of himself. Aiden tried to concentrate on moving. On just closing his eyes. For a brief moment, when he felt as though he was tensing every fibre of his being, he saw the hellscape come back into view. Maybe he could get back there and somehow avoid the tortures of his body?

The cave. That fucking hellhole. Get back there. The cave. The cave. He began to think solely of that one place he never wanted to be. He could see the bloody stalagmites a little more clearly. Could he still move in there? He attempted to raise his hand. In the shed, he remained still. In the cave, he faintly noticed his arm moving. He could see some figure standing over him. The shape of the teenager, Gary.

'Am I not keeping you entertained?' Gary's voice growled and Aiden froze as though he were a deer caught in headlights, forced to return to the cold shed. He didn't doubt that Gary could see what he was trying to do. He didn't sound impressed.

Why don't you want me to do that? Aiden thought rhetorically, convinced that Gary wouldn't give him an answer. The fact that Gary wanted to distract him just gave him the impression he might have finally found the right path to follow to his freedom.

'Because I own you now,' Gary snarled in response, much to Aiden's surprise.

As he heard the demon's words, his arm moved again. He anxiously watched as the knife in his hand drew closer. Though he remained still and silent in the shed, he struggled to keep his mind composed as the pain of the blade digging into his flesh reverberated through his being again. He carved the knife down his own cheek and hot blood ran down his skin to drip from his chin. Gary's low, gargling laughter echoed in his head.

'Nothing like feeling your own body pumping your life away, is there?' he said in an amused voice as Aiden tugged the knife from his face and suddenly dragged it down his chest, carving a deep diagonal gash before slicing his left nipple. Aiden became lost in a dark labyrinth of agony as he tried to overcome the torturous pain he couldn't escape from. Just as he felt his own torments, Aiden sensed Gary's enjoyment. It was as though he were performing his self-mutilation for a revolting voyeur who remained in the shadows.

Please, just stop. No more, Aiden thought as his body convulsed with pain and shock while the knife was dragged more and more across his flesh.

'No more? Oh, but there will be much, much more before the end,' Gary retorted sadistically. *The cave. The cave. Fucking, fuck. The cave!*

Aiden felt himself raise his arm high before he slammed the knife into his right thigh. The sudden, powerful blow dragged him in screaming agony from any thoughts of trying to get back to the hell cave. Just as Gary began to force him to tug the blood slathered knife down his muscles, a muffled voice called out from the distance, and everything froze. Aiden recognised the voice right away.

Bec! he thought with a guilty sense of relief as his torture was so abruptly interrupted. Bec was calling for him. She had gotten home. Aiden wanted her to find him. To help him. But then, he wanted her to leave. To get as far away from the house and himself as possible. He couldn't control himself. Gary could. What would he do?

'Looks like the real fun is home early. Shall we greet them?' Gary teased in Aiden's mind.

No! Leave them alone! They haven't done anything! Please, just leave them alone! The blade of the box cutter drew painfully from his leg and his blood-soaked hand hung lifelessly by his side once more. There was a silence in which Aiden's body remained still. Finally, he slid his other hand from the bench, leaving his severed finger and wedding ring in the pool of blood.

'Good idea. Why not let them come to us? I knew you would make things fun,' Gary hissed.

God. Please, please let this stop. Please just keep them safe. Don't let them be hurt. Please. Aiden prayed to a God he didn't wholly believe to exist. Then again, until a few weeks ago he was sure ghosts or demons or whatever the hell Gary was didn't exist either.

'God? I know you don't believe in Him. You know it too, Aiden. You're smarter than that. If you really need a god to worship… here I am,' Gary said with an amused, gurgled laugh.

Aiden continued to stand still in the shed, looking down at his severed finger as all of his fresh wounds throbbed with pain. Gary said nothing more and Aiden risked trying to focus on the cave again. He just wanted to be out of the shed. If he were in the cave, maybe

Gary couldn't use his body at least? He just started to envision the gruesome cave before he heard light footsteps in the grass outside. The vision faded once more.

No! No, don't come in here, Bec. Please! The footsteps grew louder. He could hear Gary's low, sadistic laughter in the back of his mind.

'Aiden? Are you in here?' Bec asked nervously.

Aiden wanted to turn. To see her. To shove her out of the shed and lock the door. He listened, praying the door to the shed was already closed and Bec wouldn't open it to check. But he heard her footfall on the hard cement of the entry.

'Oh my god, Aiden!' she cried out. Aiden heard her rush forward, her warm hands lightly touching his arm. Unable to turn to her, he watched her shadow in the fluorescent light as he heard her gasp in shock.

'What... what the fuck? What have you done? Aiden? Aiden!' Bec was shaking him, trying to get him to respond.

'Oh God, what did you do? Goddammit, where's a cloth? A rag? Something! Fuck.' She was rummaging frantically through the shed.

Soon, Aiden sensed her on his left side as she lifted his arm and in the corner of his eye, he saw her press an old paint cloth to the bloody stub of his ring finger. He winced internally with pain form the pressure. *Argh, shit, that hurts! Get away, Bec. Don't help me. Fucking get away!*

'Jesus, your finger! Shit, why did you do this? Talk to me, Aiden! Please, look at me! What's going on? It's this... this thing, isn't it? Gary?' Bec was pleading with her husband as she tried to help him. Aiden's heart broke and he wanted nothing more than to hold his wife and cry with her.

'Shall we help her, Aiden?' Gary's voice suddenly broke from the silence in his mind. He sounded amused. Aroused even.

Fuck you! No! No, don't! Aiden screamed in his head.

Without warning, his body swung around, waving his right arm quickly through the air. He was still holding the box cutter knife.

Bec yelped and fell back. Aiden saw her tumble into the boxes of old memorabilia they had stored for God knows how long.

'Aiden! What are you doing!?'

Aiden could see the confusion and fright in her watery eyes. He hoped the blade had missed and the blood smeared on his wife was his own. But he stepped forward with the knife raised. His feet and legs felt numb and it almost hurt to move them. He watched helplessly as he advanced on his wife.

'Oh, don't worry, Aiden. We'll cut her up nice and thoroughly before we let her die. I want to get the most of her fear before having her flesh,' Gary said.

Aiden couldn't even think of a reply. He couldn't think of anything else than imagining Bec in the hellish prison of Gary's creation. He couldn't let that happen to her. Or to Hannah. He raised his arm before slicing the knife through the air again. Bec held up her hand in defence and she let out a pained scream as the blade caught her palm. It might not have been a deep wound, Aiden prayed it wasn't, but he had still hurt Bec, and he was unable to help her.

'No! Aiden, no! Please stop.' She struggled to her feet.

Gary made Aiden swing the knife again. Bec stepped back, slamming her back into the aluminium wall of the shed with a loud metallic thud. She dodged the knife and, to Aiden's surprise, actually smacked it out of his hand. Gary must have been surprised too because Aiden's body froze for a moment. Bec didn't miss a beat and she sprinted past him and out of the shed. Gary's laughter echoed in Aiden's head.

'Oh, she is beautiful! I'm going to enjoy making you watch me defile her and tear her to pieces,' Gary said as he directed Aiden's body to turn around. 'Hmm, how about this?'

Aiden watched himself pick up the hatchet that hung from the tool rack on the wall. He couldn't let this happen. He couldn't let Gary murder Bec. He tried to concentrate on the cave again. He could hardly feel the wet grass under his bare feet as he ran across the yard. He could still hear Bec's panting as she desperately fled from him, and he couldn't focus. He felt the relative warmth of the house as his body was thrown indoors. The lights were on, and they blinded his senses, bringing him back from the cave. Aiden felt sick with fear as his body leapt effortlessly to the wall. Was he crawling over it? Gary could make his body do that? He heard a loud, garbled scream and terror twinged down his spine when he realised it was his own voice.

'Look at this! Hannah is here to play too. Her flesh has always looked… supple. And the fears your daughter has –' Gary taunted but Aiden cut him off.

Don't even say it, you sick fuck! You'll never hurt her! Aiden screamed defiantly even though he had no idea how he could stop him. His only hope was that sending his consciousness back to the cave would somehow help.

'Enough talk. Time to play with your girls' pretty insides!' Gary retorted and Aiden found himself charging headfirst into the bedroom door.

He felt the pain of the crash, but Gary didn't stop. He pounded and shoved against the wood before he started hacking at it with the hatchet. Aiden couldn't think as he watched the whole thing unfold, feeling the pain and the environment but unable to do anything about it. He watched himself force the door open. He saw Bec and Hannah, huddled and frightened for their lives in the bedroom. They had nowhere to run. Aiden had no more chances. He strained with all his might to focus on the cave. He needed to be there. Not in the house. He concentrated, trying his best to block out the screams and crying, to ignore the pain of his own fighting with his family. The stalagmites came clearer into view. The figure before him was becoming lighter from the darkness.

'What are you doing? You're going to miss it,' Gary said.

Aiden faltered for a moment but pushed harder. *Fuck you, you evil shit! I'm not letting you do this. Fucking bloody cave. The cave. Get back to the cave!* The bedroom suddenly faded from his sight.

He was in the cave. He could faintly hear Bec grunting as she fought him at home, but Aiden was back in the hellscape. He didn't have any time to lose. Gary was standing in front of him, the undead teenager staring at him with a hanging jaw and tongue. Aiden couldn't hurt him. He knew he couldn't kill him. There was only one thing he could think of to try and save his family. He struggled to move, but he sat up amongst the bloody bones, leaning on a stalagmite to support himself.

'Come back, Aiden. Let me show you how much fun you can really have with your wife and daughter,' Gary mocked.

The teenager stepped forward and raised a hand to grab at him. To force him back. Aiden pushed himself to his feet, leaning on the stalagmite. He shoved the jagged, bony shaft hard until the tip snapped off with a loud crack. Splinters of bone fell into the puddles of blood and he held up the sharpened stake.

Gary laughed. 'You know you can't kill me, Aiden. I am this whole place. I am you. I will feed on your family's flesh and fear, and you will be my vessel to hunt for more. More to feast upon,' he said.

Aiden faltered. He was afraid of what he knew he had to do. But he needed to do it. He needed to save Bec and Hannah. He raised the sharpened shard of bone to his own throat.

Gary froze. 'What are you doing?' he hissed.

For the first time since he had ever seen the demon, Aiden finally saw a shine of fear in Gary's eyes. He smiled. It was going to work.

'You might have Sam. Lauren. Kids from fucking hospital. You might have me. But you will NOT HAVE MY FAMILY!'

He dragged the bone across and felt the sharp edge carve into his own skin. Blood filled his throat as his muscles and sinews tore open. The desperate need to breathe sent him into fitful shudders and spasms as he began to choke and gurgle. He dropped to the ground in the cave. The collision with the rocky surface seemed to snap his reality back home again. He could see Bec whimpering under him. Had he been too late? He couldn't see any injuries on her, save for a bite mark in her bloody hand.

He was frozen over her, holding the hatchet above his head. Aiden knew he hadn't struck yet. He stopped Gary just in time. His real face faintly smiled. Then he fell to the side, collapsing on the floor and suddenly, he was back in the cave. The light was fading. The light of his life and hope that had been keeping him going. He was lost in the darkness where unseen monsters and horrors awaited him. Where nothing but Gary's low laugher could be heard.

AFTERMATH

REBECCA

Bec feared that every panicked breath she took might be her last. She held her arm out; her hand stretched open in an attempt to hold her husband back as he lay over her with the hatchet above his head. He hadn't moved for at least ten seconds, maybe even more. Had he finally gotten control of himself? Since she had found him in the shed where he had been mutilating himself, it was obvious that Aiden had lost his mind. But had he just gone insane or had whatever been haunting herself and Hannah gotten to him to? Had it done something to him to drive him mad? Bec didn't know nor did she really care. All she knew was that her husband, the man she loved and depended on, had been trying to murder herself and their daughter. But now he was frozen as though he hesitated to actually do the deed. Bec dared to hope he might have overcome some bout of temporary insanity but the way he sat over her, completely frozen, just made her all the more frightened. She didn't know when or if he was going to bring the blade down into her chest.

'Aiden… baby, please,' she managed to say, though her whispering voice was barely discernible through her heavy breathing.

Aiden stared down at her with maddened eyes. His face twitched and Bec was sure his lips had curved into the faintest of smiles. She painfully gulped in her dry throat, expecting Aiden to either say something or to feel the cold bite of the blade in her skin.

Then, Aiden slumped over and fell to the side. The hatchet tumbled uselessly to the floor before his body followed with a heavy thud. Bec lay still, trying to catch her breath before she let out an involuntary moan of shock and relief. Her throat tightened as she struggled to control her breathing and she brought her hands to her face, clasping them over her mouth as she fought back the tears.

'M-Mum?' Hannah asked nervously from the bedside.

Bec managed to look over to her. The girl was sitting back with her arms clenching around her legs so tight that her skin was ghostly white. Bec timidly shook her head, then nodded, then shook it again. She didn't know what she was trying to convey to her daughter. That she was alright. That it was over. That she had no idea what had happened. All of it. Hannah trembled as she very slowly leant forward and crawled over to her mother. Bec twitched at her gentle touch but then, overwhelmed by the sudden contact, she lunged forward and took Hannah tightly into her arms. Hannah buried her head into her shoulder and she tried her hardest not to cry out in hysteria.

'It… it's okay, Hannah. It's…' She couldn't think straight. She didn't know what to say. She just held Hannah even tighter in her arms and felt her hold her back.

Bec didn't know how long she and her daughter sat there in their mutually reassuring embrace for. It felt like a long time. Neither of them seemed to have the will or the desire to move. But finally, Hannah pulled her face from her shoulder and sat her cheek on her mother's chest, looking towards her father's motionless body.

'Is he dead?' she finally asked, her voice little more than a whisper

Bec looked at her husband too. He was a terrible sight to see. His naked body was bruised, carved and bloody. Who knew what he had done to himself in the shed before she had arrived? Did Aiden even know? Did he feel the pain he had inflicted on himself at all? His eyes were open, and they stared aimlessly into nothingness. Bec couldn't be certain, but she was sure she could still see that hint of a smile on his lips.

'I… I think so.' She took Hannah's head in her hand and directed her face back into her chest. 'Don't look, baby. It's okay. Don't look,' she said, the sudden urge to protect her daughter from the shocking sight of her dead father overwhelming her thoughts.

They sat there in silence and Bec tried to piece together what had happened. There could be no way to know. Everything that had happened to her. To Hannah. To Aiden. It didn't make any sense. Some sort of mass hysteria? Had they all been drugged? Some environmental hallucinogens? None of it seemed plausible. But then, did the alternative seem any more likely? Was it really possible Aiden had been haunted as he claimed? That whatever was tormenting him was reaching out to torture her and Hannah too? It couldn't be possible. There was no way that had been the case. But she still couldn't say she knew for sure. Her thoughts were broken when a faint sound began to grow in her ears. A foreign but familiar sound. One she had always heard in passing but never really taken much notice of. At least not as she did now. The sirens grew louder as the emergency services approached.

*

'Are you absolutely sure you want to do this? You know you can stay with us for as long as you need,' Pamela said as she carefully took the hot mug of tea her daughter offered her.

Bec circled around the table, setting her dad's cup of coffee before him as she moved to her own seat. The warmth of the sunlight resonated on her back as she sat by the large window of her parents' dining room. Summer was almost over but no matter how much heat they had endured over the past weeks, Bec felt there was still a chill deep inside that seemed never to be thawed.

'I know, Mum. But we can't keep living off of you two like this. I've got to get back to work. To feel useful again,' she said before she blew on her hot coffee.

Pamela clicked her tongue and glanced to Thomas who gave a slight shrug. Bec could read her parents like a book. She knew her mum wasn't keen on the idea, and she wanted her dad to speak up on their behalf. To discuss alternatives in a unified effort. Bec started to shake her head before Pamela spoke up again, having grown impatient with her husband's hesitancy.

'Well, of course, Rebecca, going back to work is a solid step forward. Why don't you get in touch with, uh, Dr Pannu? Didn't she tell you that you were always welcome back to the clinic when you were ready?'

An involuntary shiver ran down Bec's spine at the mention of the clinic. She had just about overcome the nightmares she had of that place but, hearing it mentioned again brought a light sensation of dread to her heart. She almost couldn't remember what the monster that Mr Meadows had become looked like anymore, but her imagination filled in the grotesque blanks for her. She shook her head and appeared to find her cup of coffee remarkably interesting.

'No. No, I won't be going back to the clinic here. I just can't, Mum.' She instantly noticed how her mother opened her mouth, ready to interject. 'I've got a good job lined up in Dandenong. Adya, Dr Pannu, put in a good word for me. She knows I won't be coming back. We've just got a handful of houses to look at and –'

'Are you sure you can afford a place right now? I know the old place is sold, but you only got a fraction of what you could for it,' Pamela said and Bec looked to her mother with stern eyes.

'After what happened there, do you really think we could have gotten more? No, Mum, we need to find a new place.'

'No, I understand, Bec. I'm just trying to say, maybe it would be wiser to stay here a bit longer? Go back to the clinic, save up a little, buy a proper place. There's no need to leave Glen Marsh for good.'

'Pam, we can't tell her what to do. Becky is an adult. She can make her own decisions. Even if we don't like them.' Thomas finally spoke up.

Pamela pursed her lips with annoyance that her husband wasn't backing her to the hilt. Bec appreciated her dad's honesty. His neutrality.

But she couldn't help picking up the sincere sadness in his voice as he spoke about his youngest daughter leaving their hometown.

'Well, what about Hannah? She doesn't want to go, does she? What about that nice boy she is with, Brian? Did you think about them?' Pamela renewed her efforts.

Bec knew her mother just didn't want them to leave. She wanted them to stay at home at Glen Marsh so she could look after them and make sure they were safe. Bec was grateful for her parents' support after Aiden had died. They didn't push in any way, rather they encouraged them to grieve however they needed. Bec didn't go back to work at all. She had let Adya know she was quitting over the phone before emailing through the formal notice. She knew it was unorthodox, but given the circumstances of what had happened, Adya didn't make a fuss. She said she would stay in touch as a friend, to check in on how she was doing and would continue to do so until she was ready to come back to work. When she had let Adya know she never intended to return, the good doctor encouraged her to do what was necessary.

Despite not returning to the Greenfield clinic, Bec was content in the knowledge that her friendship with Adya had actually strengthened. She stayed home with her parents but although she couldn't face the clinic anymore, she refused to wallow and waste away in her grief. She just busied herself with household chores, practically becoming a live-in maid for her parents. Hannah, on the other hand, continued to go to school. The principal had been made aware of what had happened and thankfully, the teachers kept a close eye on her. Her grade average had fallen, which was only to be expected, but Bec later found out that Hannah never attended any of her science classes nor would she visit the library anymore. When she asked her daughter about it, Hannah had been evasive in the reasons why, but she did reveal she spent her science periods trying to find the brightest, warmest spot outdoors to rest or study in.

Bec never pressed the issue. She could only assume the worst of Hannah's own experiences and she couldn't' bring herself to make her daughter live through them again. She just asked that the principal understand it was a necessary step in her daughter's grieving process. Hannah also spent a great amount of time with her boyfriend, Brian. Bec didn't pry about their relationship too much and she had no idea if Hannah had explained the details of her father's death to him or not. But, whenever she saw Brian, Bec perceived that he was always mindful and caring to Hannah. He seemed like just the support the girl needed at the time and she let them be.

'Mum, you know I wouldn't drag Hannah anywhere she doesn't want to go. Of course, I've talked to her about it, and she's talked to Brian. Dandenong is only about half an hour away from here. We're not flying across the world. Hannah said she will be okay so long as she can see Brian on weekends. And you know the sort of technology kids have these days. They can video chat anytime they want,' Bec explained. She was surprised at how well she managed to keep her cool with her mother. She couldn't deny she felt a sense of frustration and anger growing inside her, but she just reminded herself over and over that her mum was only worried about her.

Pamela pursed her lips again and said nothing.

'Well, it sounds like you've thought about this for a while, honey. You know that we'll support you, no matter what. I just want you to be absolutely sure before you do make the move?' Thomas said, his dark eyes fixing on his daughter's as he spoke. He wore a kind smile on his old face, but Bec could still see the concern in his eyes.

'Thanks, Dad. I know. I just think it's the right thing to do. Please, try and understand. It's not that I *want* to leave Glen Marsh. I just feel like we should. There's… too many things here to remind us about what happened.'

Pamela bowed her head, sipping her tea lightly in defeat.

Thomas nodded. 'We understand, Becky. No one could have seen the aneurism coming. And there is so much more to your lives than that house. It must be hard to see it all the time.'

Bec gave a light smile, hiding the pain she felt inside as her father spoke. It had been over six months now, but she still found it difficult to really talk about what had happened. The police who first responded to the call were amazing. They comforted Bec and Hannah as best they could while they waited for back up and the paramedics to arrive. But, as they spoke to them in trained, calm voices and used reassuring terms, Bec could still see the sheer horror in their eyes. It must have been a terrible scene to see. Blood trails through the dining room and down the hallway. The shambles of the bedroom. A hysterical mother and teenage daughter clutching one another beside the mutilated, naked dead body of their husband and father. The hatchet that lay at his fingertips. It wouldn't have taken a detective to piece together what had happened. At least what was going to happen before it abruptly stopped. That's where forensics came into the case.

It was determined that the cracked glass in the sliding door had been caused by Aiden's skull. It appeared as though he had repeatedly smacked his forehead into the door for a length of time before he wandered outside to the shed. His self-inflicted cuts, wounds and severed ring finger matched the blood covered box cutter knife that was found in the shed, further supporting Bec's testimony of how Aiden had attacked her with it. In the end, after the autopsy, Aiden's death had been declared to be the result of a bleed in his brain. As aneurysms in the brain are already rare, the attending pathologist was apparently astonished to report the bleed was even less likely than normal.

Given the witnesses' testimonies and the physical evidence, the pathologist suggested that Aiden had suffered an acute onset of psychosis, perhaps even schizophrenia before the aneurysm ruptured, resulting in his death. Everyone involved in the case that Bec spoke to agreed it was one of the most tragic and unpredictable scenarios they had the misfortune of working with. She heard the sorrow expressed by the law and medical professionals over and over and, while she appreciated their pity, at the time it had fallen on near deaf ears. She was in a state of shock for weeks after Aiden had died, so much so that she could hardly weep at her husband's funeral. Bec lightly shook the sad memories from her head and for a moment, she wondered how long she had been staring at the faint scar on her hand between her thumb and index finger, left there by her husband's teeth.

'Yeah, well, I guess that's all there is to it. You guys get it. We need to do it. It's happening. Once we have a place, Hannah and I are moving to Dandenong,' Bec said decisively. She knew it was the right thing to do. She and Hannah needed to move on. To try and restart their lives in a fresh place. She felt good about it. But, as she lifted her coffee to her lips, she doubted if moving would be enough of a change. If anything would ever be enough.

LEAVE THE LIGHTS ON

HANNAH

'Hey, you know I'll still call you tomorrow, right?' Brian said as Hannah held him tightly in her arms.

She was comforted by the feeling of his chest against her, the way her arms had to wrap around him while she gripped each wrist behind his back. She could feel his heart beating soothingly against her cheek and she just wanted to stay in his warm embrace forever. Hannah hated having to say goodbye. She wanted to be with Brian all the time.

It wasn't so bad in the middle of the week. Sure, she still missed him, but not having seen him in person for a few days somehow made it a little easier to cope. It was now, when he was leaving after they had been together for two days that it was hard. Hannah was grateful that both her mum and Brian's parents were okay with him staying over every Saturday night. He had to sleep on the couch of course, but her mum was always a little lenient in how much cuddle time they could have before they had to say goodnight. She loved those moments. She and Brian didn't even have to say anything. They would just lie in her bed together, holding each other close, basking in each other's warmth. They messed around sometimes too but they still had to be quiet. Hannah's mum was lenient, but she knew she wouldn't be impressed if she and Brian got themselves into trouble. She didn't want to ruin the good thing they had and was always conscious to keep that sort of fun to a minimum while her mum watched TV in the living room. Very rarely, they had the house to themselves though.

Hannah still wasn't ready for sex. She didn't think Brian was either, no matter how much he pined for it. But they still had other fun in their alone time, and it was always amazing. Now, as she held Brian at the open front door, she knew she would have to wait a whole week before she could hold him like this again.

'I know. It just isn't the same.' She sighed as she imagined seeing Brian's smiling face on the screen of her laptop or smartphone. Of course, it was nice to talk to him. To stay in touch. They talked so much online that in some ways it was almost like they lived together but just stayed in their own rooms. But Hannah knew she would miss the way Brian felt. The way he smelled.

'I know what you mean. I really don't want to go either,' Brian agreed. He squeezed her tighter to him as he spoke.

Hannah's small breasts pressed against his chest and, without thinking, that hormone fuelled desire grew in her lower belly. She sucked her teeth with frustration. Her mum was tidying up in the kitchen after their dinner and Brian's dad was just outside, waiting in the car. They would have to wait until next time to act on their desires again.

'Okay. I guess we need to let go. Do we have to?' Hannah moaned, playfully expressing the sadness she felt that her boyfriend was leaving again. They had been living in Dandenong for a few months now and had gotten a good routine going. It didn't make it any easier though.

'I mean, we don't really have to. You can just come with me to the car and, I dunno, accidentally ride back to my place.' Brian chuckled.

Hannah laughed, imagining herself clinging to Brian like a koala the whole way back to Glen Marsh. 'Totally. My mum won't notice I'm gone at all.'

'And my dad won't pick up on anything strange either. He always has random people in his car.' Brian joined in the jokes.

Hannah loved their banter. It could always cheer her up, at least for a few moments before the reality sunk in again.

A sudden sharp sound pierced the air. Brian's dad pressed lightly on the car horn. It was quick, just a reminder. If they took much longer it might become more insistent.

Brian sighed. 'Okay, I really got to go. I'll text you as soon as I'm home safe, alright?' he said as Hannah reluctantly pulled from their cuddle.

'You better! I don't want to be up all night worrying about you.' She grinned. It had been her idea. Brian had to let her know the minute he got home. He didn't complain, no doubt understanding that Hannah would be a little anxious since everything that had happened with her dad.

'I wouldn't dare. We'll talk soon, baby,' he said as he picked up his backpack and slipped the strap over his shoulder. His warm, brown eyes fixed on Hannah's, and she knew what was coming. Her heart fluttered every time she saw that sensual expression on his face.

She lifted herself to her tiptoes and closed her eyes. She felt Brian's lips gently meet hers and the bliss of the kiss spread through her body. The desire in her abdomen screamed to be satisfied and she let out a pleasant yet anguished sigh.

'I love you,' Brian said in little more than a whisper.

Hannah's cheeks blushed as red as apples and she smiled coyly. They had only been saying it for a few weeks now and it felt so wonderful to hear. 'I love you too.'

Brian smiled and kissed her cheek. Hannah could see the internal struggle on Brian's face, his desire to throw his bag down and slam the door to stay with her. He growled with frustration, smiled and turned on his heel, ripping the hypothetical band aid and walking away. Hannah watched him reach his father's car. Brian turned back to her when he opened the door and tossed his bag in. She waved to him and admired his bright smile before he slipped into the car and closed the door. The car pulled out of the drive and was soon halfway down the street. Hannah leant her head on the door frame for a moment, letting the evening air cool her desires before she finally closed the door.

'Brian's left okay?' her mum called from the small kitchen as she walked deeper into the house.

'Yeah,' she responded miserably as she stepped into the kitchen to find her mum loading their plates and glasses into the dishwasher.

Bec paused in her chores and looked up to her daughter with a cheeky smile on her face. 'So, did you say it?' she asked teasingly.

The redness in Hannh's cheeks quickly returned. 'Muuum,' she whined.

Her mum raised her hands innocently. 'Okay, okay! I just think it's cute, that's all. I still can't believe you said "I love you" to each other for the first time weeks ago and I only heard about it this weekend?'

Hannah shot her a playful, accusative glance. 'Oh yeah, you act like you want to know everything as soon as it happens, but I could tell you some things,' she joked.

Her mum backed up and pressed her fingers to her ears. 'Alright, I get it! What you do is your business, no more nosing around,' she said as though she were begging for mercy.

Hannah laughed. 'Yeah, don't you forget it, Mum. Anyway, thanks for dinner. I think I might just head to bed, okay?' she said before letting out a yawn and stretching her arms.

'Good idea. School night, remember? Oh, damn it, that means it's a work night too, right?' her mum joked as she resumed stacking the dishes in the machine.

'Yep. If I gotta get up early, you do too! Night, Mum. Love you.' She turned to wander down the hallway to her bedroom.

'Night, honey. Oh, and just make sure you use protection, okay?' her mum called after her.

Hannah cringed. 'Muuum!' she shouted over her mother's echoing laughter from the kitchen.

Hannah's new bedroom was smaller than at the old place. In a way, she didn't mind though. The snug feeling was somehow comforting to her and with less room to dump her clothes, she managed to keep it tidier too. As she began to change into her pyjamas, she couldn't help but think about the warm embrace and the sweet kiss she had enjoyed with Brian. Her mum's jokes didn't help either. Hannah's mind wandered to the possibilities of the future. The enjoyment that might be had.

'Maybe I won't go to sleep straight away,' she mumbled to herself as she felt the now-familiar tingling sensation in her body. She bent down and switched on the nightlight by her bed. She would have been devastated if anyone found out about her nightlight. A teenager who still needed a baby light to sleep? Maybe if they knew what she had been through they might understand. But Hannah wasn't about to tell everyone at her new school about the terrifying experiences she already had in her young life. Even Abbi didn't know about the nightlight. Since leaving Glen Marsh, they had grown a little distant, though they still considered each other best friends. It was just harder to catch up these days. On the other hand, Hannah knew she could trust Brian and no one but him, her mum and Hannah herself knew about her nightlight.

*

Hannah opened her eyes. The dim glow of her nightlight illuminated the small bedroom and shadows cascaded along the walls. She wasn't sure what time it was but there was no daylight shining from the break in her curtains, so it was definitely still night-time. She was very groggy, her heavy eyelids slightly falling and opening a few times. She needed to roll over to get comfortable again, but as her mind became more alert, she wondered if she might as well grab a glass of water. Hannah got up. Or she tried to. She was sure she moved upwards, hadn't she? Yet she didn't move and continued to lie stationary on her back. A sense of panic sparked inside her. She tried to shift in her bed but found she remained still. Could she even feel herself lying down? Was she in her bed? She couldn't even turn her head to see where she was. Then she realised she wasn't even breathing.

Oh God, what's going on? Just breathe. Breathe! she thought frantically. She couldn't feel her lungs fill with air. They began to burn, aching in her chest. She tried to scream. She wanted to shout, to cry out for her mum to help, but she couldn't make a sound.

God, am I dying? What's going on? God, help me. Please, move. Just move! Her mind was racing as she struggled to twitch a finger, to wiggle a toe, to jump upright and gasp for air. Her eyes swung back and forth, looking as much as she could around her room. She desperately tried to turn her head and her panic grew more and more as the moments painfully passed. She looked to the shadows on the wall, the outline of her own bed in the glow of the nightlight. Were they moving? The memories of all her terrifying visions sprang back to her mind. She would have screamed, helplessly cried out, if only she could.

Please no. Not again, she begged as she couldn't help but watch the shifting shadows on the wall. The darkness twisted slowly, floating around like a sinister cloud. It formed into the rough outline of a person. Hannah managed to close her eyes tight, to block away the sight of the visitor. She just wanted to get up and run from the room. To be with her mum. Then, she heard it. A soft, menacing voice that hissed across her ears. Beneath the frightful gargle, she heard something familiar. Something impossible. Her father's voice.

'Hello, Hannah.'

Shawline Publishing Group Pty Ltd
www.shawlinepublishing.com.au

SLP
SHAWLINE
PUBLISHING
GROUP